THE BROKEN AFTERLIFE

Tyler Tullis

Cover layout, typography and interior layout
by Miyeko Takeshita

ISBN-13: 978-0615700687 (The Broken Afterlife)
ISBN-10: 0615700683

THE

BROKEN

AFTERLIFE

a novel

TYLER TULLIS

one

I think most people would be surprised at how many reporters hate the First Amendment. There has never been a greater double-edged sword. It's our all access pass to the truth, sure, but it's also a megaphone for the crazy, and worse, the irrelevant. So when the insane and insignificant get ahold of that megaphone, I'm forced to write up their bullshit in the name of serendipity and editorial balance, aka headlines that sell.

I'd been pondering the phenomena for the better part of my interview with Jerrod Owens. My sense of propriety, what little I started with, had drained with each question I asked and each pretentious answer Owens provided. I knew my zinger was eventually going to roll out ahead of a question if I didn't do something.

Which is probably why I didn't do something.

Don't get me wrong, I didn't go around looking for fights anymore, but people like Jerrod Owens needed to be taken down a peg or two. Everyone knows the type—the Christian who misses the entirety of Christianity and lays down judgment every opportunity he gets. His inflection alone tells you he's better than you—you immoral, misbegotten, sinner—and he knows it.

Owens was somewhere between Pat Robertson and Tim Tebow in the frequency with which he uttered the word "God." Scarce was the sentence that didn't mention the Almighty and how a life without the man upstairs was empty and futile across the board. This guy would have had the pope rolling his eyes.

At this point, with God's goodness firmly lodged in my throat by an interviewee who had already decided I was the bad guy just for trying not to choke on it, I prepared to go off script. I'd tactfully convey my own opinion on the matter through a loaded final question. One that would bring the interview to a screeching halt. I relished the act as would a comedian unleashing the final punch line at the end of a show, not for how good it would feel, but because Owens had it coming. Then I spoke, but it wasn't my clever question that came out.

"Your God is a prick."

I'm still not sure why I said it. Strike that—I know exactly *why*, just not *how*. True enough, when most people get angry they tend to bypass the clever line or logical argument, if they have one, to heatedly blurt out the thing that's really pissing them off.

I was not one of those people.

I made a living guarding my opinions and emotions, strategically planting factual barbs instead. I'd been doing this long enough to have a library of one-liners in reserve, each equipped to let Owens know how full of shit he was and leave him thinking about it for months. I was in the business of cutting through spin and talking points. I had built a career systematically dismantling people like Jerrod Owens.

So why didn't I?

In the moments following my outburst, I tried to trace the situation back to what caused the uncharacteristic—and uncharacteristic is putting it mildly, I'm a pro—lapse of poise. My first thought was that morning when Harris gave me the assignment.

"Get down to Arlington Heights, there's a community church group painting over graffiti with hipster art or something. Lots of high school kids. Here." Harris handed me a shoddy press release one of the aforementioned kids probably threw together.

"They couldn't come up with anything more original than Good Samaritans?" I asked, skimming the paper.

"I don't care about their name, Perry, I need—you need—a human interest piece. You haven't turned in anything but doom and gloom for months."

"You'll have to excuse my penchant for chasing real stories, or at least ones that won't go straight to a blog," I said, folding the release in half. Harris scoffed.

"I'm not in the mood to be bullshitted. You haven't chased anything but a paycheck since you've been here, you're lucky I have a blog to fill. I thought I hired a pit-bull, not a—"

"I'm a freelancer, you can publish what I write or not."

"Well I won't be publishing anything of yours if you don't go rundown our little Samaritans. The rest of my staff—what damn few are left—are all on the earthquake or the mayoral scandal." I bit my tongue (illustrating my previous point about self-control) and turned to leave. "And don't ask them about the gang arsons," Harris shouted as I made my way from his office. "This is a sunshine and sprinkles story about religious hipster kids, not gangs."

Harris is loud enough that I couldn't pretend I didn't hear him, but I'm sure he didn't pretend I wouldn't ask about the fires. Rumor was some new Crip set was behind a string of arsons across South Central—that they were marking buildings to hit with blue and purple graffiti.

Harris knew the game, though. The mayor (embattled in scandal though he was) was running his re-election campaign based on how much he had cleaned up the streets. And as my current employer, the LA Times, was endorsing said mayor, we couldn't run too much heat about gangs until after the election.

So I was off to interview hipster kids.

A shit assignment, but it wasn't like I had much leverage with Harris. Or any editor for that matter. My quality of work over the last five years hadn't exactly matched up with my reputation from before.

I hadn't been in a very reflective mood lately, but now that I was, I recognized my outburst wasn't the result of one lousy assignment. Every once in a while you do something that shows you what you are, and what you aren't. This was one of those moments.

I knew full well most of the stuff I'd written lately was pointless or straight garbage. I hadn't done any sort of combative interview either. But in all that time I always figured I still could. I could still chase down the big story and make it sing at the drop of a dime if I wanted to. I could still handle any interviewee with a little wit and the right facts.

Suddenly I wasn't so sure.

Getting rusty shouldn't have been a surprise given that I hadn't worked on anything of consequence in half a decade, but like I said, I avoided self-reflection at all costs. This hit me harder than I thought it might, and it all happened in the seconds between my outburst and Jerrod Owens' response.

I'm sure the look I received from him after my quip about God was akin to my calling his great-grandmother a slut to her face. In one boiling motion his chest puffed out, face tightened, cheeks turned red. When I saw his fists clench, for a moment I thought he was going to throw the game and hit me.

He'd grown increasingly hostile throughout the interview once he realized I wasn't going to bite on what he was angling. I had asked a few token questions about his blandly named group and why they were out here painting away on a Saturday, but my questions quickly zeroed in on what Harris warned me to avoid. Owens wasn't any more enthusiastic about gang arsons than I had been in his verbal crusade.

He didn't throw a punch, but I didn't care either way at that point. All my pent up aggression from listening to Owens' rhetoric deserted me. Owens' ire, on the other hand, was finally coming to bear, though I was too lost in thought to focus on much of his tirade.

"How dare you blaspheme the Lord God and His good works?! And in the presence of these hardworking kids donating their weekend to brightening a suffering community with a little creativity and love!" Few to none of those hardworking kids would have noticed what I'd said had Owens not begun screaming. They had gone back to painting after their ring-leader usurped the interview, but now all brushes ceased moving.

The parents and volunteers turned to watch the pious eruption. "It's people like you from the secular liberal media in this country hell-bent on attacking family values with your war on religion... Your agenda only encourages the culture of poverty and crime that these brave youth have gathered here today to wash away with God's love! You may not have the heart for faith, but you have no right to persecute..."

You get the idea. He went on like that until after I got in my car and drove past the shaking heads and middle fingers of the Good Samaritans. I could hear them cheering Owens as I pulled away. I'm sure he, lamenting that he didn't have a pulpit in some Texas mega-church, had been waiting for an opportunity to launch an assault on God's behalf long before ever meeting me.

I'd certainly handed him his opportunity. It would have given me plenty of ammo for an editorial on religious hypocrisy had I been in the mood. But given my epiphany during Jerrod Owens' storm of condemnation, I didn't give a damn about an editorial, much less the story Harris assigned me. Just finding a drink.

My lapse of patience with Owens turned out to be quite the catalyst for a morning of introspective self-loathing, the likes of which I hadn't allowed myself since the move. Five years is a long time not to look in the mirror. When I finally did, the can of worms I opened made up for all the lost time.

I wasn't the person Harris and all the others thought they were hiring. I moved out here because I was trying to forget that person. I was even planning to forego the annual visit home this year. It would be the first time. I thought maybe breaking tradition, staying away, would help me let go. But here I was, years later, and the pain still felt as sharp as the day it happened.

"You okay, buddy?" It took me a moment to register that it was the bartender and that he was talking to me. I lifted my head off the bar. A drop of tequila dripped down my forehead, stinging my eye. I tried to play it off like the alcohol had caused the tears. I gave him a wave, fearing to reply and risk my voice cracking. He nodded and set a glass of water beside the empty shot glasses.

"Bad day?" he asked.

"Bad life," I returned.

"Sorry to hear that."

"No you're not. My misery is good for your business." He paused and shot me a look.

"I find people buy more when they're having a good time."

"I wasn't always a cynic, you know," I managed without missing a beat. He did.

"I never said you were."

"You're an optimist. You can't help but spot cynics."

"What makes you think I'm an optimist?" he asked, increasingly annoyed his small talk was leading to conversation. I pointed to the wall above the bar where a small crucifix hung.

"You aren't a man of faith?" he asked. I couldn't help but laugh as I buried my head in my arms. "What's funny?"

"He's pulling me into this twice in one day," I returned. I decided to accept the challenge. I had nothing better to do. "Do you want me to answer your question?"

"Sure," he said, probably meaning no.

"Then yes. If I believe in anything, it's the existence of God. I just don't believe he's the person people say he is." I never capitalized pronouns for God, by the way. Small victories.

"So you're one of those guys who loves God but hates religion."

"No and no. Religion is great for a man so long as he treats it like his penis—be proud to have it but don't wave it around in public. My beef is just with God. If he was Mr. Benevolence as he's billed, I wouldn't be here in Los Angeles. I wouldn't be alone. I wouldn't be in a mid-life crisis. And I sure as hell wouldn't be nursing shots of tequila at a bar at 11:45a.m. while a pair of hookers shuffle money behind me in a darkened booth."

The bartender stared at me, not sure if he wanted to ask what happened to me or not. I wouldn't have told him either way. I sipped on my water.

"Yeah, God's up there all right. And he's still got me directly in his crosshairs."

"I don't think you understand the whole faith thing, brother," the bartender offered. I chuckled dryly.

"I understand it better than you, friend." His expression hardened. He put both hands on the bar and stared at me.

"Why don't you explain it to me?" I knew I was walking into trouble, possibly another Owens all over again, but that didn't stop me.

"Okay. It starts like diapers—forced onto you as a baby. Depending on the church, you either get a drop of water on your head or dunked. On Sunday mornings you sit in a class and listen to fairy tales about a cosmic evolutionary cycle taking place in six days and 50 million species in a confined space on a pleasure cruise. There are pictures of it right there in your junior illustrated bible—what's there to doubt?

"To most kids this is about as fun as actual school, but you suck it up 51 weeks a year because that other week is Christmas, and no kid in their right mind is going to risk losing that. So you memorize a few ancient hymns or b-string pop songs written by people who can't make it writing hits for Katy Perry, and you grow up with something of a moral compass because there's a good message behind all the fairy tales.

"Then you get older and gain the cognitive capacity to question the world around you. At one point you probably decide to truly commit to faith, and for that one moment in junior high school you feel invincible. Like some pious crusader for good.

"A few years later you realize you haven't felt like that in a long time. Maybe ever, despite what your hormone-ridden junior high self thought at the time. Church, bedtime prayers, the effort it takes to keep convincing yourself that you believe—it all becomes a chore.

"Before long God is your new Santa—it'd sure be something if he was real, but you know better. You probably don't want to stop believing, but you can't help it. You're terrified at first. The very thought of doubt seems enough to send you straight to hell on the spot. But eventually you get over it. Because if you can't bring yourself to believe in God, that means you don't believe in hell either.

"Life goes on without God. You may or may not tell anyone how you feel—you might not even be completely honest with yourself—but you know. You get married, have kids, and you basically just pretend. It's not worth upsetting the relatives or all your friends thinking you've become purposeless and empty.

"Eventually you're back into the same routine as when you were a kid. You've got a good example to set for your kids, and if nothing else, it can't hurt to go through the motions. Maybe you even tell yourself you believe again—who really knows for sure? Maybe you'll get points for trying.

"Then you die, but just before you do, you throw the proverbial Hail Mary and reach out to God on the off-chance it was true all along. You ask for forgiveness, point out a life lived the best it could be, and pray that even if you don't end up in heaven, that you don't end up in hell. And that's it."

The bartender's expression was a mix of intolerance and pity, the latter of which was probably for himself for having asked. I kept going anyway.

"Having told you this, you're only going to react one of three ways, meaning there are three types of people. At least as they concern me. One small group agrees with me. Most of them would probably like to have faith, but they have thoughts. And to them, thoughts really torpedo the whole faith thing.

"The second group will infer that something terrible happened to me that left me such a bitter fuck. Those people are always curious to learn what the terrible something could be, either so they can pity me or avoid a similar fate. Some of them have the nerve to ask me what the terrible something was so they can console or debate me. The ones who don't ask me stay curious and ponder over their inference for hours, days, years, sometimes their entire lives.

"The last group of people, and by far the most common, is the group that doesn't give a shit what happened to me what I have to say about it. They know I'm just another asshole and tell me to fuck off either straight-up or with an impatient eye-roll. To them I'm a lost cause, a waste of their time. To them, all I am, all I ever was, and all I'll ever be, is a drag on humanity."

The bartender and I stared each other down for a moment, both of us waiting.

"So which type of person are you?" I asked eventually. He let out a dry huff and shook his head, reaching for a glass to dry.

"I'm not really sure, brother. But I am sure almost everyone could agree on one thing."

"What's that?"

"That you are about the biggest pessimist who has ever walked the earth." I thought about reminding him I wasn't always that way, but what did I care.

"Sounds about right."

I sat at the bar for another few minutes but kept quiet, remembering my earlier wish about a world where people kept their beliefs to themselves. The bartender probably hated me more than I hated Owens. When I finally looked at my watch I thought it was broken, but the clock behind the bar confirmed it was almost 3:30 that afternoon.

Time passes fast feeling sorry for yourself.

My back ached from having passed out on a stool and my head

from the hangover. Things were still pretty blurry but I gradually grabbed my jacket and pulled it on, then reached for my wallet. I might have ordered something for the road had I not spent everything on hard liquor.

I was still wearing a shirt and tie from the interview that morning—hardly dressed up but enough to stick out amid the sordid company that had filtered into the bar since I passed out. It was the bartender who tried to warn me.

"I'd take your time finishing that water," he said. When I looked at him he flicked his eyes to the door and the table of four rough looking teenagers in blue. They stared at me the way lions identify the slowest, fattest zebra in the herd. Served me right for pulling into the first dive I could find—the mayor's gang cleanup campaign hadn't reached much of the Watts neighborhood yet. I let out a huff and took a quick swig from the glass, chewing on an ice cube.

"Way to check for ID," I said, to which the bartender frowned. He turned to fill a pitcher, obviously less inclined to help me. I straightened my jacket out and trudged for the door, keeping my eyes ahead. The teens rose as I passed, followed me out, and were around me when I reached for the keys in my pocket.

And here I was having such a nice day.

The biggest one—still probably no more than 18—stood between me and the car, his arms folded. I raised my bloodshot eyes to his with a loud breath.

"Do you mind?" I asked.

"You mind emptying those fuckin' pockets?" In the spirit of the apathy that had come to define me of late, I left my hands in my pockets and held his gaze.

"Yeah, I do." The kid's eyes flickered with uncertainty for a moment, exchanging quick glances with his crew. This was probably an initiation—their first or second time out. Still, they had plenty of muscle to do the job. The broad daylight wouldn't deter them either. The parking lot was wedged between two buildings obscuring view to the street.

I felt the kid's punch across my jaw before I saw it. It wouldn't have been enough to floor me without my lingering buzz, but I was on the cement tasting blood when the blur subsided. My alcohol/misery induced indifference gave way a bit when another one pulled a knife instead of a gun.

Still, it was a gunshot that sounded from behind me. I was so startled I barely heard the teens running off or the voice shouting after them. Something about them knowing better than to come so far past some street.

When I turned the bartender was tucking a hammerless pistol back into his pocket and leaning to help me up. "You got a death wish, brother?" he asked, shaking his head as he lifted. I didn't say anything, just gave him a nod of thanks while I dabbed the blood on my lip.

"And here I thought I had pissed you off," I said eventually. He shrugged, patting my arm before he turned to head back inside.

"You tip good."

I pulled into the parking slot of my duplex about 20 minutes later. I'd lived in Brentwood for almost two years. Moved from the condo in Santa Monica when I couldn't pay the rent anymore. I'd burned through most of my savings in recent years. Booze when I felt shitty, more potent substances when I felt really shitty. Never touched Pita's college fund though. It had a sanctity about it that I didn't want to violate until I had to. Hopefully by then I wouldn't be around to need it.

I didn't enjoy the daily grind, obviously, but I didn't have a death wish, to answer my new friend's question. I wouldn't commit suicide, tempted as I had been on several occasions, today included. Gabby wouldn't have wanted me to. You're better than that—there is still good left undone in you, Jonathan. As much as I disagreed, I could hear her saying it.

I tried not to think about it, feeling emotion rising up my throat as her image flashed by. I turned off the car and climbed out. I never bothered to lock it. There was nothing in there but a rancid smell.

A flurry of barks muffled behind glass sounded from the other half of the duplex. I rolled my eyes and tossed my keys to and fro as I walked to the back door.

"You don't have to remind me, you know I'm not gonna forget about you," I said, walking to my neighbor's sliding glass door. I allowed a smile upon seeing Doggy's little paws frantically sliding over the glass. He leapt out at me when the door was open enough for his escape.

As always, the mutt spent a solid 30 seconds circling my feet at hyperspeed while I waited for him to run out of steam, then I leaned over and scooped him up under his front legs.

"You sure smell bad, yes you do." I'm sure he thought it was praise since I gave him the customary rubbing of his head against mine. "Sorry I haven't been by yet, I've been working." I used to tell him I was out bringing home the bacon, but he had figured out what that word meant after enough leftovers from the diner.

Doggy wasn't his real name, of course, just the one I gave him since I was such a creative rascal. His actual owner didn't have a collar or personalized doggie dish that I could find. I suspected Doggy heard his improvised name a lot more than whatever his real name was, though.

The owner was rarely at home. Only a few nights a week, if that. Given the place's cleanliness and decor along with the time of day the owner was actually around, I pegged it for a mistress den. Some guy from a gated community in Santa Monica or Hollywood who was clever, deceitful and rich enough to keep up an actual pad where he could bring his not-wife a few nights a week.

Fine with me, made for a quiet neighbor. Until the first time I heard barking about five months ago, that is. Either the guy thought a little Boston terrier would make for a nice addition to his den of iniquity (which is pretty perverted if you ask me), or one of his bimbos straight up left Doggy there and our boy was pussy-whipped enough to take care of him. Either way, every few nights the playboy would swing by with or without his girl to drop a load of chow.

I dropped in every day to make sure the apartment's regular occupant had enough food and to get him outside to stretch his legs. (The owner hid his emergency key under a statuette, I saw it used plenty.) Doggy usually spent the evenings with me watching TV or writing, and the afternoons playing with Meredith, the 14-year-old living in an apartment across the street who I assigned as primary fun provider. I told her I needed help watching Doggy for my neighbor, gave her five bucks a week.

I loved the little guy—he never judged me—but I wasn't up for fulltime adoption.

I let Doggy scamper around the meager yard, go number one and two (disposal being another of Meredith's duties) then sealed him back up. I wasn't in the mood for his energy at the moment. The buzz had faded but the hangover hadn't.

When I reached for my own back door I caught a glimpse of something move inside my house. I froze, making sure I wasn't still drunk, then shrank away from the window while I sharpened my gaze inside. I regretted never cleaning the windows—too much grime to see anything more than one of my chairs moving, its back to me.

A burglar probably wouldn't take a rest in my recliner or leave my laptop, about the only thing of value in there. I could see its blue glow on the desk through the window. Still, the Boston terrier next door was about the only friend I had, nobody I knew would just drop in. The in-laws didn't know where I lived anymore.

I hurriedly tiptoed to the front yard. I had a gun but it was inside, hidden on a closet shelf, so I went for a junior slugger bat that Meredith's brother left near my mailbox. I always left my front blinds closed so I couldn't get a view of the intruder. The front door was shut but not locked. I turned the knob at the speed of a slug to make sure I wouldn't tip him off.

Then the thought occurred to me that whoever was in there knew I was outside. He had to have heard my car pull up and Doggy running around. I put two and two together when my eyes caught the sign I had yet to remove from my door.

"Jon Perry, Private Investigator," I read in a murmur. My anxious frame loosened while my eyes rolled back into my head. An elongated expletive came out with a sharp breath. I pushed the door open and walked into my living room.

I successfully masked my irritation for not having removed the sign, but not my surprise when she rose from my La-Z-Boy. First of all, she was a she. Second, she was a young and beautiful she. Blonde. Slender. Natural. That last one dashed any hope she was a hooker who had stumbled into the wrong half of the duplex. This girl didn't have the look. She was too beautiful—unspoiled.

My entrancement wore away quickly once she spoke.

"You're Jon Perry?" she asked, shifting her weight and raising her eyebrows. I probably looked too young to be credible (though too old to be of any interest to her) and too Hispanic for my name to be real (it wasn't). "Where have you been? Your sign said—"

"Monday through Friday, eight to five, I know," I returned. "I've been meaning to update it." I've been meaning to take it down, is what I meant. I hadn't been doing the Dick Tracy thing for over a year. "How long have you been in here?"

"The sign said wait inside and the door was unlocked," she reminded me, as if I was accusing her of breaking and entering. I tried to keep my expression limited to surprise and away from incredulity.

"Yeah I know, it's just, that's usually for clients with appointments when I'm running late." From the attitude in her stare I could tell there would never be a situation in which this girl would hold herself at fault. If he didn't want me in here, his sign should have been specific then, she was thinking.

"I tried to schedule an appointment but you don't have an email address. Or an answering machine." There were a number of things I could have said but I decided to push them aside. If she had the balls to barge into this cesspool and wait, she clearly had some business. I figured I'd at least hear her out. Because she was gorgeous, I guess.

"You'll have to excuse the mess," I offered, forcing myself to look away as I strolled through the waiting/living room to my office/kitchen. She noticed the bat I was still carrying in one hand and eyed me peculiarly. I set it down. "Sorry. Thought you were a Crip or a Good Samaritan here for revenge." She made a show of her distaste for my unconventional file storage receptacle—the floor—and the stacks of dishes extending into all corners of the room.

"Sorry if you were expecting more," I said, pouring myself a glass of water from the sink.

"It's not much of an office," she replied. I wasn't talking about my office. "Do you live alone?" When I turned she was pointing at the picture I kept on the desk of Gabby and Pita.

"Yes." She waited for more. When I didn't volunteer any she made a visible gesture of trying to shake off her annoyance in her experience so far. She folded her arms and followed me into the kitchen.

"So you're a P.I., huh?" No, but when I moved to LA I figured the deductive skills of an investigative journalist might be worth more uncovering marriage infidelities for jealous Hollywood wives.

If that's what this girl indeed was, she would have been the first one who ever looked me up. I never had the energy to really pursue clients so I basically gave it up when none of them (with money, at least) ever called. I didn't tell her any of this, of course.

"Sure am," was my answer as I moseyed around my desk and sat. I swept my forearm across the desktop to remove the crumbs of that morning's pizza. I pulled my laptop closer to at least try looking professional. "What about you?" She tilted her head and summoned defiant pride to her face.

"I'm a hair stylist," she said, already defensive. I tried not to deflate in front of her. So much for the rich Hollywood wife. Again.

"Do you have a name, Miss Stylist?" I asked, already hearing a drop of enthusiasm in my voice by several degrees.

"Cora Avery," she said.

"And what use would you have for a P.I., Miss Avery?" I asked, already knowing the answer. She didn't reply right away, taking a seat in the cushioned folding chair. She set her hands in her lap after placing a lock of her long hair behind her ear.

"Mrs. Avery," she answered. "At least for now. I think my husband might be cheating on me." I had one last shred of hope for a payday.

"I see. And what does your husband do?"

"He's a cop."

Great. Well, I'm sure not going to collect a paycheck from Harris this month so I might as well hear her out and give her a quote, I thought. She wouldn't have been there if she wasn't willing to pay something.

"And what exactly would you like me to do, Mrs. Avery?" She seemed surprised by the question, as if the answer should be obvious. Part of my haggling strategy. If I gave her pause that this wasn't something I usually did, it could go one of two ways. Either she'd think marriage infidelities were beneath me and my usual caseload, meaning I was expensive, or that I didn't know what I was doing, meaning she'd leave. I tried to project the former but the state of my office projected the latter. I figured it could go either way depending on how bright she was.

"I want you to catch him in the act," she said eventually, finding the passion that brought her there.

"That sounds a bit more definitive than 'might be cheating,' Mrs. Avery." She raised her shoulders, beginning to seethe.

"I started wondering when he took graveyard shift full time. Always excuses for why he's back late. Always acting strange—shifty. He won't even look me in the eyes. And when he does it's like he's someone else. He never wants me anymore."

She said that last bit as if it was inconceivable—I mean look at me, how could you not want this? She was vain, of course, but with that body she wasn't wrong.

"When you say catch him in the act, are you—"

"I want hard proof I can shove in his face along with my ring. I want everyone to know this was his fault. I want him to know he never had a clue how lucky he was—that he threw away the only thing that ever made him matter, the only reason people ever said his name at all."

Like I said, I never actually landed a case like this before, but I didn't have to strain too hard to see the forces at work. Sitting before me was a former queen of high school whose only real assets, the ones she had depended on to land her a movie director or plastic surgeon husband, were pertly on display in her low-cut shirt.

Unfortunately she'd made a terrible miscalculation right after graduating, settling for the star quarterback who didn't have enough ambition or intelligence to power an RC racecar. He would not only keep her on the wrong side of the gated community and the life of luxury she thought she deserved, but keep her glued to whatever rundown LA neighborhood she had been desperate to escape her entire life.

She had probably been waiting for an excuse to lose Officer Avery for the year or two they'd been together so she could try again. His apparent affair was both a godsend and the ultimate insult. Cora here was once the master of all that lay before her, and therefore entitled to the same attention and yearning for the rest of her days. How dare he presume to cheat on her?

Call me a cynic if you want (you wouldn't be wrong), but I saw the way she moved, heard the honest-to-God offense in her tone. She stopped short of cupping her tits to emphasize the implications of jeopardizing a marriage with her.

I cleared my throat, deciding to make an overt push toward the notion this was hardly worthy of my attention. "Mrs. Avery, I sympathize, but you should know I don't usually take on this sort of case. Most of my work is usually to supplement an investigative report I'm putting together for a major publication. I don't often work on private cases of a personal nature, and when I do—"

"I know about what you do, Mr. Perry," she said, silencing me instantly. She reached into her purse and pulled out a few folded papers. She read aloud. "Jon Perry, freelance writer for the Los Angeles Times, the Union-Tribune, policiesmatter.org, and other notable Southern California publications."

She read off the headlines of a few things I'd written over the last year, all pointless drivel. "It looks like you haven't written very much at all lately. Definitely not anything investigative." She looked around the office. "And it doesn't look you've done much work as P.I. lately either, so—"

"You know how to Google a name. That doesn't mean you know anything about me or my work." She fumbled a little when I didn't blink, but she wasn't about to back down yet.

"Why don't you tell me about your work, then?"

She wasn't as dumb I pegged her for. Had she actually read a few more articles, she would have eventually found my real name and learned a lot more. I had changed my name, sure, but not much. There was no point. Any editor who read the newspaper he published would know my face when I showed up looking for work. The change was just to help wash the taste of who I was from my mouth.

"I investigate and then I write about those investigations. If you don't think I know what I'm doing, why show up?"

"I didn't say I don't think you know what you're doing." She reached into her purse for one more piece of paper. She didn't read this one, just turned it around for me to see. My heart skipped a beat. "I'm here because I think you're this guy too."

Kids today. Their idea of research is randomly stumbling across pictures in articles they don't read. Sure enough, it was the front page (of my former employer) with my mug shot and the headline about my exoneration from the evidence planting charges. The subhead mentioned I had been terminated due to lingering suspicions and questions of ethicality.

I made a show of looking unaffected, because I was. What did I care if Cora Avery knew about my life from before? She probably hadn't even read down to the part that mattered.

"Well I am," I stated flatly. "So what?"

"So I know you're good at this. Pulitzer Prize good. There are half a dozen other P.I. wannabies in the Yellow Pages I could have called, but I wanted you. I want to tell people I hired you. And I know it's not exactly a big case, but I still think it looks like you need the work. Can you do it or not?"

I liked this girl despite the fact that I didn't. She continued to surprise. That was probably why I caved.

"I think the question is, can you afford me, Mrs. Avery?" I asked, still playing hardball while I grabbed a handful of loose papers and stacked them on the desk. "I haven't even quoted you a price for this sort of thing yet."

"I'm not worried about that."

"No offense, Mrs. Avery, but considering the pedigree of the publications and award you just mentioned, a hair stylist and soon-to-be-divorcé might want to be." She looked at me for a moment, searching for something. When she found it, she rose from her chair, set her purse down and sauntered up to the desk.

"Well I think there's something you haven't considered."

"And what's that?" She put her hands on the edge of the desk and leaned down, watching my eyes shift as predicted.

"If you take the case, I probably won't be married anymore, will I?" I realized she hadn't worn that shirt and those short shorts in the middle of winter for no reason. My gut reaction was to find her eyes and give her a look that said it would take a little more than that, but at the moment, it didn't. So I let her inch closer, searching for what I knew would be the tantalizing scent of her skin lost somewhere in all the product. "You can call me Cora."

She knew she had me and offered an overt smile that let me know just that. I took a final deep breath of her and then leaned back, folding my hands and nodding.

"Tell me about his routine lately. Where does he go and when. All the habits." When she finished and I knew it would come down to a stakeout or two, I estimated I could have what she wanted in about three days, a week max.

After Cora left I sat staring at the picture of Gabby and Pita she had pointed out. I put it in the bottom drawer of my desk face down.

two

My earlier characterization of Cora Avery's marriage to her husband being a miscalculation turned out to be quite the understatement. Whatever she once saw in him other than his broad shoulders and angular jawline escaped me.

Brett Avery had the energy and gusto of a reanimated corpse. After four and a half days of tailing him, never once had I seen him smile, laugh, or... emote. He rarely found reason to speak, even to his patrol partner or his wife. And on the rare occasion I came within range of his voice when he found use for it, it never deviated from the pitiful monotone of a fast food cashier.

Nothing seemed to surprise him. His life appeared carefully scripted, objective oriented. He applied only the effort necessary to complete the task at hand. From routine reports over his squad car's radio to cleaning out the gutter over his garage, there was never an activity that called for any sort of zeal. It didn't take me long to surmise that his predictable routine existed in an effort (however fruitless) to distract his wife from the fact something was amiss.

Obviously his marriage had deteriorated, but surely Cora couldn't have been *that* bad. Even if his trophy wife's shine had worn off quickly, I can't imagine him not looking forward to getting home every night (or morning in his case) and jumping straight into bed with her. I was sure as hell looking forward to it.

Still, there was nothing that seemed to give Avery any joy. He didn't sleep much, usually getting to bed around 6:20a.m. when he returned from graveyard shift. He rose four to five hours later, spending a little time watching the news and poking about on an antiquated desktop computer, then working out. Weights and pull up bars were in the backyard, and he usually jogged around the block for about half an hour. His physique was about the only thing he seemed to put excessive energy toward (excessive to me anyway—I hadn't worked out at all in years).

Cora got home from the salon around 2:00p.m. most afternoons. She returned for evening shifts or to take care of her niece at her sister's house a few nights a week. She noticed my car on the block the first day, carefully glanced around for me, but never spotted me.

This wasn't my first rodeo.

A Fed I used to cover during the Quito case told me there's a math behind this sort of thing. 10% distance, 10% disguise, 10% lip reading, 10% peripheral vision, 10% hiding (9% of which is in plain sight), 10% distraction, 10% lying, 10% tools (simple stuff—you don't need a utility belt), 10% patience and timing, 10% *active* observation, and another 100% improvisation.

Always keep your face at an oblique angle. Never draw attention by doing too much or too little—blend. Always leave yourself an immediate out. And above all else, never make eye contact with your subject. That's an instant KO. Stick to all that while never losing your cool and James Bond won't have anything on you but looks and charm.

Having said that, Avery was a slightly harder mark than I anticipated. I had to be particularly careful following him when on patrol with his partner, for one thing. He was nothing if not alert, even off-duty. He constantly looked over his shoulder, dedicating an extra moment to scanning his environment or locking himself inside when he checked his cell phone.

The man was paranoid.

It was a stretch to imagine Avery suspected his wife of skipping work to spy on him. Or that she was getting reports of his activity from their neighbors, with whom they barely had any relationship. Was he worried someone else would observe him constantly checking his cell phone and report out to Cora? No, the only mystery here was why Avery was so concerned about being watched in broad daylight when he was just out for a run or raking leaves. Particularly when his distance toward his wife had so obviously betrayed his secret already.

Unless there was another secret.

Yes, something else had this man on edge, and I found myself curious to discover what.

I saw it Wednesday night while Avery was on patrol with Garcia, his partner. He pulled into a gas station to fill up and let Garcia take a piss. After his partner was gone and he spent the longest moment yet looking around to make sure no one was watching—again missing me in my darkened car—Avery pulled out a smart phone from his pants pocket. I hadn't seen it before.

He kept it well concealed in his palm and the flap of his jacket, but with a few inconspicuous keystrokes of his thumb he responded to what must have been a text message, then hid the device back in his pocket. The fact that this was the first time I had seen a separate phone after four days watching him told me it wouldn't be easy to get my hands on it, but I knew I had to.

I was waiting at the salon when Cora arrived for her shift the following morning. I told her about Avery's secret phone and instructed her to sneak it out of his pocket while he was taking a shower that afternoon. I warned her not to confront him about it if she wanted me to catch him in the act of whatever he was doing (I kept my theories to myself for now). I asked her to bring me a list of any and all text messages she could find on the phone that night once Avery was out on patrol.

She showed up that night, but only to tell me she couldn't find the phone. From the way he guarded it, I assumed Avery kept it on his person at all times. Still, it was worth checking the precinct for it. I sent Cora there to gain access to his locker under the pretense of leaving her husband a gift. She persuaded an officer to open the locker (likely with the same cleavage exposed as the day she came to me) but uncovered nothing.

We finally found the phone when I told her to search every last electrical socket in their house while he was sleeping. It had to be charged at some point. It took her an hour searching but she finally found it plugged into a socket in the garage hidden on a shelf behind an old cooler.

The first thing we noticed was the name written in marker on the back. Jack Malone. The name didn't mean anything to Cora but I made a note to check it out.

Next was his call history. There was only one contact in the list, a blocked number, but it called him every afternoon around 1:00. I had never seen him take the call since he kept himself locked inside, but I gave Cora a voice recorder and told her to hide it somewhere in the middle of the house before she left for work. I think she was having fun by this point.

There were no text message conversations recorded but after spending a few minutes sorting through the apps he had installed, I found an address programmed into his map program.

225 W. Birch.

The address belonged to the Orange Forest Motel, a cheap little 12-

bedroom complex just west of Beeks Place on the fringe of Anaheim, about an hour away. I arrived the next morning and pulled into the gravel parking lot. Heavy overcast, even a little fog.

Beeks Place was far from forested, but plenty greener than Brentwood. Made for good hiking for residents of Corona or city dwellers in need of a little outdoor excursion. Trails wound through the hilly expanse for miles. About as close to nature as you got without leaving the mega-city, excluding the ocean.

Pretty far out of the way to meet a mistress.

I let Doggy out of the car to stretch his legs. The little bastard didn't get to take many trips so I figured this would have to do. He sprinted as far as he could before nearly choking himself on his leash. His lips were probably numb from putting his head out the window most of the drive.

I had called for the information I needed, but the owner, an obstinate old woman, wouldn't divulge anything about former guests on the phone. I'd have to try another approach. Plus I wanted to check the place out for myself. If it turned out there was nothing immediately apparent that linked Avery to the motel, as I suspected would be the case, I'd need to do a more in-depth scan in person.

After I let Doggy sniff around for a minute, I put him in the back seat and wandered into the motel office. I pulled off my sunglasses to get a better look at a woman reading a magazine behind the counter. Not quite elderly but certainly past her prime, if she'd ever had one. Looked like the only excitement she ever had came from flipping through those pages. Definitely the one who'd refused me on the phone.

"Morning," she said without looking up at me, giving herself a moment to finish her paragraph.

"Morning," I returned, infusing my voice with a chipper tone I hoped would conceal the one she'd heard over the phone.

"Just a room for yourself or do you have others?" she asked, marking her page and scooting her chair closer to the counter.

"Neither, actually," I returned, casually opening the flap of my jacket to reveal a fake police badge I'd used for years. I had my gun holstered along my belt for effect. "Detective Larry Burns. I'm investigating an internal matter about possible officer misconduct and I'm hoping you can help. Has an Officer Brett Avery checked in here recently?"

The woman let out a huff. "What would this have to do with me?"

"I have reason to believe he stayed here, ma'am. All I can tell you is the officer is under investigation."

"Do you have a warrant or something?" All the motel owners in the world and I had to run into this one. The heavy handed approach wasn't going to work with her, so I let my smile turn boyish. I felt as though I had aged 20 years in the last five but despite the lines I still had the face that first took Gabby's notice. The eyes, at least.

"I'm sure you can save us both the time and effort of my having to go get one and come back out here. I'm just looking for a yes or no." She was immune to the boyish charm, but despite another huff I suppose she thought I looked trustworthy enough.

"How do you spell that?"

I told her. It was too much to hope she would recognize it. If he were a regular he wouldn't need directions on his GPS, after all. "Not seeing anything." I figured Avery was probably smart enough not to use his real name.

"Please check his partner's name, Jack Malone." She tried again but still nothing. "Do you remember seeing a squad car on any of your security tapes?"

"No, before you there hasn't been a cop here that I can remember in years," she said.

"I wonder if either of those names have anything booked here in the future."

"Listen, honey, I didn't check a cop in here recently and—"

"Please, ma'am, just this last search and I'll be out of your hair." With anyone else I could have detailed consequences of obstructing an investigation but I knew that wouldn't get me anywhere with her. Sure enough, she searched again, this time placing a finger on the screen and squinting.

"Malone, Jack. Reserved 112 for Friday, February 4th." She glanced at me. "Happy?"

"Does it say how many he—"

"Family of four, likely," she interrupted. My smile glitched.

"He said that?"

"112 is the double room, four beds." I nodded and asked for a copy of the reservation I could use as evidence in my farce police investigation. Once I had it I climbed back in the car, staring at room 112. I let Doggy out for another bathroom break while I pondered why Avery would book a room for four people, two weeks out, an hour from his home.

Doggy's whines interrupted my thoughts. I turned and found him being petted by a little boy in an orange t-shirt, all by himself. The boy wasn't squeezing him or anything, but the dog clearly wasn't happy. I called Doggy's name but he didn't rush back until the boy lifted his hand. He smiled at me then ran away.

It took Cora three days of moving the voice recorder around the house before she hid it close enough to pick up Avery's 1:00p.m. conversation. He spoke softly and the recorder's battery almost died by the time he took the call, but we got it.

All one word of it.

"No," he said after taking the call, then hanging up.

Both Cora and I were sufficiently confused, but we decided to keep recording while we waited for February 4th.

Two weeks waiting took the wind right out of Cora's sails. She was ready to call off the stakeout and confront her husband on the calls and the room reservation, but I persuaded her to wait. Avery adhered to his routine every moment I followed him, never once sneaking off to some mistress. His tardiness home on certain nights persisted, but a valid excuse always presented itself.

Or so I assumed. I had given up following him after the first week. No sex was worth the price of my gas, and by then I was convinced Avery wasn't up to anything during his nights. Everything checked out except for his upcoming rendezvous at the Orange Forest. He continued receiving his bizarre afternoon calls, always one word long, always the same word.

Truth be told, I didn't much care about Cora or getting her into bed at this point. I wanted to figure out what the hell this guy was up to. His booking a room for four was what had my mind bent. Brett Avery was not my duplex neighbor—he had good looks, yes, but not an ounce of charm or charisma to go with them. There was no way this guy was throwing some orgy in a cheap motel next to Beeks Place, and that sort of thing certainly wasn't planned weeks in advance.

I had broken into room 112 before I left the Orange Forest the week before (upon closer inspection, the curmudgeon owner only had one security camera angled at the office and the first few rooms). I got in through a back window with ease.

Sure enough, there were four beds, two to each divide of the room, but that was about all I found after an hour of searching. I checked inside every drawer. Felt every pillow and mattress. Opened every vent. Peered down every nook and cranny. There was nothing sinister or salacious in the room.

I couldn't tell you what I was looking for—drugs, guns, money—but my gut told me this was more than a guy going to extreme circumstances just for a little pussy. He could have got that anywhere within 10 minutes of his house.

The surprise came the afternoon of February 4th. I was filling up my gas tank for the eventual drive back to the Orange Forest that night when I got a call from Cora.

"It was different today," she told me in a whisper, breathing heavily with excitement. "He was actually talking to someone." Avery should have been on his run by now but I asked her if she was alone. "Yes he's gone, but listen." She put the voice recorder up to the phone. I could barely make it out.

"There was an incident today," Avery had said. A pause. "No, she called me. Someone barged in and saw her." Another pause. "Yes. I may be late." He hung up.

"Is that all?" I asked.

"Yes. What do you think it means? Was that her? It sounds like he was talking about her to someone else. I—"

"Calm down, I'm on my way over to pick up his trail. Don't give anything away. We knew something was going to happen today." I just had no idea what.

I pulled along the end of the street where the Averys lived half an hour later, waiting for him to make his move. I'd brought a coffee thermos and stopped for a cheeseburger. Even for winter, it had been unusually cold for LA this year.

It had been raining all day so I wore my long coat. It was beginning to taper off, but the sound of drops pattering on the roof lulled me into a peaceful trance. Well, as close to peaceful as I got.

I had developed a fondness for rain since the move. I'd even considered picking up my three remaining possessions and setting up shop in Seattle. Doggy was about the only thing deterring me. An overcast sky felt safer, as if it stilted the view of whoever was up there looking down. I didn't like the idea of anyone watching me, God included. Maybe it was because I did so much watching myself.

The rain kept people indoors, inactive, which suited me fine. I couldn't stand most people anymore. Being around them, at least.

Don't get me wrong, for as full of vitriol as I was for the Almighty and his bullshit master plan, I never ceased being an optimist when it came to humanity. I routinely marveled reading about people rising to overthrow oppressive governments. Of our discovering new phenomena in space or genetic codes that slowly advanced our knowledge of the universe. I even puffed out my chest when the president cited some inspirational American in his State of the Union every year. Made me... I dunno, proud of us, I guess.

But pride and joy are two different things.

I found some measure of solace to be taken when the world's mood matched my own—dreary and subdued. Bright skies filled with merrily chirping birds only reminded me what had once been and would never be again in the life of Jon Perry. As pessimistic and pathetic as it sounded, joy—observing it, certainly feeling it—sharpened the pain. Refreshed the guilt.

So I sank further into my uncomfortable seat as rays of warm evening light pierced the gray ceiling overhead. The sky over LA was certainly unlike any other at evening. A smooth mélange of oranges and pinks recolored the cityscape, painting the ocean into a massive mango cocktail. Beautiful. Just like Gabby.

I reminded myself it was just smog.

I waited for Avery until he left the house at dusk. He was in uniform. I didn't think he was on duty that night but I followed him to the precinct to pick up his squad car. It was the first time I'd seen him drive it without Garcia.

Whatever he was up to, this was it.

I made sure to keep my distance following him. Now was hardly the time to get made, and even if I lost him I'd know where to pick him up. That's why I was surprised when he missed the turnoff that led east to Beeks Place and the Orange Forest. Instead he kept on further south into Mar Vista. It was part of his usual patrol, but he and Garcia usually didn't make it there until much later in the night. Darkness had only just fallen.

Still on his usual route, Avery pulled up on the side of a street and shut off the engine. I circled around a backstreet and did the same once I had an inconspicuous view. I glanced for a street sign but couldn't find one in the darkness. I popped a map from the glove box. Palms Boulevard. I'd followed him here several times, but he'd never stopped before.

I wondered if I was missing something after the first 15 minutes. I was pretty far back but I didn't see any glow from the car's laptop or either of his cell phones. He didn't look to be moving at all. Just staring out the window toward an apartment complex. The Colonial Building, it was called.

He had to have been waiting for something—someone. My curiosity made the minutes pass slowly. At one point I noticed the wall of the building next to me, smothered in a cross and rays of light from hipster brushes. "Long way from Arlington Heights, Owens," I murmured with a grimace beyond hope of stifling.

My mind played with Avery's latest call that Cora had passed along. *There was an incident today*, he had said. Certainly didn't sound like part of a plan, especially one premeditated weeks in advance. I now knew there were at least three parties involved in Avery's secret—himself, whoever called him every day, and the "her" he had referenced on the call. *Someone barged in and saw her.* Was he hiding this woman? From Cora? From someone else?

By now I had convinced myself this wasn't a mere extramarital affair. Brett Avery was wrapped up in something else. Something that had fundamentally altered his personality from the confident jock Cora had married to the paranoid zombie sitting down the road from me. Something that had prematurely tainted a bright-eyed policeman still devoted to his ideals into something so shadowed I had yet to find a trace of it.

I hadn't originally given him much credit for being good at deception. On the surface, he didn't even bother trying to hide the change in his personality from his wife, and his paranoia was painfully obvious. But he *had* managed to completely fool Cora into thinking he was a dense grunt since they had had been married, possibly before. Whatever he'd been wrapped up in, he couldn't have gotten there without cunning and guile he had somehow kept hidden from her over the years.

I still couldn't tell if he was meta-intelligent or just sharper than he let on and lucky, but there was no doubt in my mind this man was a key player in something big.

That's why what happened next was so disappointing.

After nearly an hour waiting I noticed Avery sitting forward. My imagination wilted when I caught sight of the only movement around the apartment complex—a woman exiting her door and locking up. No mystery man in a suit and sunglasses at night, no high ranking city official with a briefcase, not even a few Crips with bags slung over their shoulders. Just an average looking, stocky woman in her mid-to-late-thirties.

I dared to hope Avery was looking at something else concealed from my line of sight, but when the woman slid into her aging station wagon and pulled out of the complex onto the street, Avery started up the engine and followed after her. I swallowed my pride.

I found myself angry as I drove. After all the covert dealings, all the misdirection, Cora had been right all along? Could this really just be an affair? I grimaced. Avery had a trophy wife who could have landed an A-List actor waiting for him to get home every night, and he was after *this*?

I shook my head and writhed my palms over the steering wheel. No, there had to be something else at work here. All I had to do was keep following them and I'd find out what.

My suspicions were restored when Avery kept far enough back to suggest he was trailing her the same as I trailed him. This couldn't be "her" from the call today. It had to be a fourth party. Possibly the "someone" who had barged in on her.

That thought made me uneasy. If this woman had indeed been responsible for creating the "incident," for upsetting weeks of carefully laid plans, chances were Avery wasn't following her to politely admonish her for it. No, now I'm the one sounding paranoid, I thought. He's an on-duty cop fully uniformed in his squad car. They can track where he goes. And as much credit as I had begun giving him for deception, the man didn't strike me as a murderer.

Still, I reached into the crevice between the middle and passenger seat for the glock I'd stored there. It was the first time I'd loaded it since the move, but if any of my wilder suspicions ended up being true, I figured it wouldn't hurt to have it along that night.

No sooner than I reached for the gun, Avery sped up. For a moment I wondered if he had made me, that he was trying to burn me, but then red and blue lights pierced the night. I dropped back some, my brow furrowing as I watched him pull behind the woman's station wagon and follow her to the curb.

"...the hell?" I heard myself ask as I parked a block back. I leaned closer over the wheel, squinting to make out Avery as he stepped out of his car. I figured he would have turned his flashing lights off if he was planning anything sinister, but the squad car remained lit up like Vegas. Besides, there were witnesses looking out of windows all along the block.

I'm sure my expression in that moment made it look as though I was witnessing a CIA agent's defection. Maybe it was because I hadn't chased a real mystery in so long, but I had never felt more curious. Avery tapped the glass with his flashlight and asked for ID, which she seemed happy to provide, honestly caught off-guard.

I could see her confusion when he made her step out of the car and perform a sobriety test, then her horror when he leaned her over the side of his hood and put her in handcuffs. She wasn't making much of a scene other than constantly rolling her eyes and giving him an "are you kidding me?" look, so it looked as though the arrest was legitimate. I wasn't sure if he had been waiting for her to speed or whatever had given him his excuse to stop her, but after 10 minutes he was driving away with the woman in the back seat.

I followed Avery's car back to the precinct until he surprised me with a turnoff into South Central. I wasn't exactly sure where we were when he finally pulled to a stop in a darkened parking lot beside a vacant building and a pair of dumpsters. There were hardly any other cars nearby and no one on the street, so I had to keep my distance, headlights off.

Avery parked and got out of the car. He left the engine running but turned off all the lights. The moon and a flickering backlight from the adjacent alleyway provided only enough illumination to make out Avery leaning into the back seat. I froze when he emerged with the woman in his arms.

Her head hung limply, her hair dragging on the ground.

I forced myself to take the gun and the flashlight from the glove box, keeping my eyes out the windshield while I groped through the darkness. My racing heart skipped a beat when Avery got to one of the dumpsters.

He threw her in.

It took a moment to register. But sure enough, Avery turned with empty arms, casually walked back to his car, and closed the door. Didn't even brush off his hands—like she had only been the weekly trash bag from the kitchen. He looked around like always but displayed no tension in his movements that I could make out.

I was so shocked I didn't start running until Avery put the car into gear and rolled out of the parking lot. Had I been closer and 100% sure of what I saw, I would have raised the gun and shouted for him to stop, maybe even fired off a warning shot or two, but by then it was too late for it to have done any good. Also not a good idea to open fire in the darkness of a South Central neighborhood I didn't know.

When I got to the dumpster Avery had already disappeared around the block. I wasn't sure if I was panting from how out of shape I was, the shock of what I'd seen sinking in, or both. Avery hadn't even shut the dumpster lid or bothered to conceal the body. Flipping on my flashlight, I leaned over the side.

She was white, 5'7", 140 pounds or so. Certainly double Avery's age, not very attractive, but innocent looking enough. She wasn't moving—wasn't breathing—but within the first seconds I found myself whispering at her. "Ma'am, are you alright?" I wasn't sure why I whispered. There was no one around, and if she was somehow still alive a shout probably would have been more appropriate.

But she wasn't still alive.

I checked her over with the light without climbing in and contaminating the scene. There was no visible injury or wound. No blood. No bruises. No scrapes. He'd taken off the handcuffs. There weren't even stress marks along her wrists. Suddenly unsure, I leaned in to check her pulse. Nothing.

I replayed the brief seconds of Avery leaning into the back seat and tossing her into the dumpster. I had seen the woman moving normally though the back windshield the entire drive here—what could Avery have done in the seconds of taking her from the back seat to kill her without leaving a mark?

I leaned away, staring at the woman before my eyes drifted into the darkness of the pavement at my feet. I considered a call to 911, but hesitated reaching for my phone. She was already gone, but Avery's business couldn't be over tonight. I'd lost him but I knew where he was going. Selfish though it was, I wanted this for myself. I ran from the dumpster back to my car.

I approached the Orange Forest Motel on foot once I was nearby Beeks Place. Both the gun and flashlight were tight in my sweaty palms. I hadn't felt the rush of excitement in what felt like forever. My mental stamina was as out of shape as my physical stamina. I felt the buzz making movements sloppy, diluting my situational analysis.

I forced myself to halt my jog along the darkened road to the motel, crouching in the brush. I wiped a sleeve along my sweaty forehead. There weren't likely to be guards posted along the perimeter of whatever deal was going down, but I knew full well this was a game that would hurt if played wrong.

I continued on in a roadie run as quietly as I could manage until I came to the lit parking lot of the motel. I paused behind a tree trunk, scoping it out. There were seven cars, four of which were parked together at the end of the lot nearest to 112. Out of the one functioning camera's range. Avery's squad car was among them.

112 was the only room with lights on. I checked my phone for the time. Almost 11:00. The blinds were tightly shut but I observed the occasional shadow of someone moving inside.

There was no movement outside. I could make out the crotchety owner in the lobby, still awake. She flipped through a magazine like last time but she was facing the window and occasionally glanced out toward 112. I wondered if she knew something or if she was in on it, but decided that even in the extremely unlikely event that she was, it would do me no good at the moment.

Recalling what I had learned from my sweep through the room two weeks prior, I ducked through the underbrush of the trees beside the lot, then emerged from the darkness once out of sight from the lobby. The diminutive bathroom window didn't quite shut all the way and I had worked a little wedge of bark further into the grooves to make sure it couldn't be locked.

When I leaned against the wall and caught my breath, I pressed closer toward the window. Every once in a rare while I heard the occasional murmur of a voice, but specific words or how many voices spoke them was indistinguishable. They were too far away.

I looked around for the best spot to wait out whatever was going to happen. I'd need to be in a position for snapping pictures of Avery and his nefarious crew along with any evidence they might shuffle between them when they emerged—there wasn't enough light from the sparse trees and foliage. Tracing the best sources of light, I spotted the closest tree overhanging the roof of the building.

I silently groaned, reflecting on the comparatively little physicality required from most stakeouts I'd been on before this night. Tucking the gun and flashlight into my coat pockets, I began the arduous process of climbing the pine trunk, reaching with everything I had for the first branch. From there I inched my way out over the closest branch to the roof, praying it wouldn't snap.

He'd better be smuggling nuclear launch codes for this, I thought as I awkwardly heaved my way onto the roof. I made myself as comfortable as possible on the back slope with my head popped over the peak. It was a perfect view toward the back of the cars, angled right into the trunks if they were opened.

Quite pleased with myself for my ingenuity and not falling to alert Avery or break my neck, I waited them out. For hours. The excitement left me promptly as I lay there while the rain started. Not a downpour, but enough to leave me waterlogged by one in the morning, by which time my spirit had all but deserted me. I felt as stiff as the shingles I was draped over.

Just before I considered lifting up for a moment to sit and stretch, my heavy eyelids lightened at the sound of a door opening and footsteps emerging into the night. I ducked as low as possible past the roof's apex, switching to my phone's camera with one hand and clutching my gun in the other.

There were four men that I could see—men who couldn't have looked less likely to have anything in common. The first to enter my line of sight was Avery, still dressed in full uniform. Behind him was a tall black man with dreadlocks down to his shoulder blades. I didn't get a good look at his face (he was wearing sunglasses for whatever reason) but something about him was familiar.

The third man walked into the parking lot with a gray suit jacket slung over his shoulder. His head was balding and his skin beginning to wrinkle, but I could see the gleam off his cufflinks and tie clip. He too looked familiar, but I couldn't place him. The darkness and distance kept me from analyzing his face, but even from the roof I could discern a fierce hostility.

The final man walked beside the one with the suit as if to showcase the contrast between them. This one looked as ragged and filthy as any panhandler I'd ever seen. He scratched his unkempt brown and grey beard with one gnarled hand while the other pulled his dilapidated plaid jacket tighter around his gaunt frame.

I took a few pictures of them together, getting as many shots of faces as possible, but they separated quickly for their respective cars. Nothing was exchanged, no one carried a bag or briefcase. There was nothing suspicious other than the composition of the group and the fact they'd been together in a hotel room for over two hours.

Avery and the man with dreadlocks had already started their cars when I caught sight of the Orange Forest's owner darting their way from the office. A smile lit up her face. All four of them caught sight of her as she approached the man in the suit's car, calling out as he prepared to shut the door.

"Senator Connor!" she called, giving a little wave. "I thought that was you when you arrived!" The name registered quickly—Bruce Connor, California State Senator in the headlines for speculation that he would join the GOP vice presidential ticket later in the year once the nominee was locked down. I could barely believe it myself, but there he was.

Connor didn't seem to react for a moment, but eventually let out a breath and rose from the car to shake the woman's hand with a tired smile. Avery rose from his car as well, striding past the other cars for Connor. "I don't want to take any of your time so late, but when I recognized you I had to come over to say hello and that I voted for..."

She trailed off when she saw Avery reaching out for her, probably assuming it was his security detail. About to apologize, she flinched when Avery gently laid his palm against her left cheek.

She collapsed in a heap where she stood, leaving Avery's hand suspended where her head had been.

When she fell her temple impacted the gravel at an angle, drawing blood. At first I thought maybe she had been shot, but there had been no sound, even from a suppressor, and Avery had only barely grazed her with an empty hand.

But she was dead.

The second after she collapsed I nearly fell off the roof from shock.

I managed to dig my toes in to prevent sliding back but I lost grip of my cell phone while clutching at the roof. It slid across the opposite side, catching in the gutter with a loud smack.

I was already sliding down the back side before Avery and the others turned my way. I was blown. I'd only have a few seconds lead on them to escape into the darkness. My heart beat against my ribs, probably more from the jump off the roof than the prospect of gunshots soon to be coming my way. It was about a 12 foot drop into dirt and foliage. I cut my hand on some bark and probably sprained something in my left leg, but I was too scared to notice specifics.

I was off and running full bore the moment I staggered to my feet. I tripped in the first few seconds from the disorientation of the fall along with the rush of blood and adrenaline, but picked myself back up. There were no shouts or gunshots behind me, but it wasn't long before I heard footsteps tearing through the gravel parking lot, then disappear as they penetrated into the foliage.

I still had my gun clutched tightly in hand but I was in no hurry to use it. Even if I found a good position in the next few seconds, a one-on-four shootout in the dark held little appeal. I was maybe 15 seconds ahead. My only chance at survival was stumbling upon a hiding place. Any strategy involving the gun was tantamount to facing a firing squad.

My problems went from bad to worse when I emerged from the already sparse treeline to the wide open expanse of Beeks Place. There were about as many trees from here to Corona as in downtown Los Angeles. Just miles of grassy hills in every direction. Every step into the darkness was blind and threatened to bring me down.

I'd only have a few seconds to keep running before Avery and the others tore out from the treeline as well. I debated taking my chances making a run for it, letting them see me. Clouds had blotted the sky during my stay on the roof so it was nearly pitch black. They'd never be able to get a clear shot off and eventually I'd find either a solid position to take a stand or...

No, I was kidding myself. I was already out of breath and there was nothing for miles that would be of any help. No vehicle, no one to call out to, no fortress to barricade myself in. There was a slope just discernible a few dozen feet to the left I could have slid down to at least escape their line of sight, but they'd hear me sliding and pinpoint me.

With only seconds left, I decided my only shot was dropping. The grass was long, reaching past my knees. That and the darkness would have to save me. I dove forward and turned over on my back, the gun in both hands pointed between my legs toward the trees.

Three, two, one...

I could barely hear them but they were out in the open with me. I was shaking, cursing myself for breathing so hard. I had to gasp through clenched teeth for air. If any of them came within a few feet they'd certainly hear me.

My ears might have been playing tricks on me, but after lying as still as possible, just listening, it only sounded like one set of footsteps slowly passing through the grass behind me. Had they spread out farther along the edge of the trees to comb for me? Would they have only sent one pursuer on foot? Unlikely, but if they had it was surely Avery. He was nothing if not fit. He'd have run me down in moments if he'd seen me.

The others may have split—one taking a car on a dirt road through Beeks Place, one removing the owner's body, one checking to make sure no other occupants had seen anything. That was more likely, but I had to assume all four of them were back there parting through the grass.

As I lay waiting for Avery to notice the indentation in the grass or my painfully loud breath, I wondered if I didn't want him to find me. I'd been waiting for death for five years now. I knew it was coming according to whatever twisted timetable of "justice" God had in store for me. Here it was bearing down on me—why didn't I stand up and face it?

Because...

Something felt wrong about this. Avery wasn't supposed to kill me. At least not yet. I had uncovered something here. I didn't know what it was, but in that moment with death breathing down my neck, I felt a connection to something—an understanding. I couldn't tell you if it was God, Gabby, fate, or something else, but in that moment, if only for that moment, I was at the forefront of something. I was needed. I had to survive this.

Somehow when I should have been at my sharpest, my senses blurred and time trickled by. Then gushed by. It had to have been ten minutes before I realized my breath was the only sound on the air. The flow of time restored, I waited for another few minutes before I had the courage to shuffle my position a little. Avery or the others might have been crouched in the grass the same as me, waiting for me to get up and expose myself.

My newfound instinct for survival kept me down for another hour before I was satisfied enough to lift my upper body to the grass line. It was still too dark to see anything, but no shot came. No movement was heard. Swallowing hard, I began crawling through the grass toward the decline I'd noticed that would take me to the dirt road and out of Beeks Place.

three

"Brett Avery, badge number 3742," I repeated from a folding chair in the police station nearest Brentwood. Grogginess masked my impatience, but not very well. Not that I had the luxury for impatience with a story like this.

The exchange of uncomfortable glances between the officers in the room had become predictable with each mention of Avery's name. As much as they didn't believe me, I'm sure it was unsettling for them to hear. This was his precinct after all.

It was a risk to come here, the lion's den, as it were, but I wanted him to know I wasn't going to be another faceless "incident" he could toss into a dumpster. After a two-week stakeout, two murders witnessed, and a night crawling through grass and darkness while frantically looking for a cab or someone to hitchhike with, I was, I thought, justifiably pissed. I wanted to rub his nose in it.

So far that was easier said than done.

I ended up taking a bus back into the city and running through back alleys the rest of the way to the station, constantly feeling a bullet or a hand about to snatch the life from me. I made it in one piece but didn't exactly receive a hero's welcome. I don't know what I was expecting. *Hey, your buddy Brett is a soulless murderer who may or may not know some sort of krav maga/jujitsu, instant kill move.* Imagine their skepticism.

I'd given my statement to two officers and a detective, but word had spread fast. Most of the station was milling about by five in the morning. The accusations earned Avery suspicion and me contempt. He seemed well liked by his cohort. I could tell by passing expressions that no one bought the idea of Avery as a murderer, much less one in cahoots with a US Senator doing who-knew-what.

My credibility didn't benefit from informing them I was a P.I. who'd been tasked to follow Avery on suspicion of an extramarital affair. A few of them recognized my name from the paper, but I'm sure the more curious ones dug deeper with a full background check. Whatever they found wouldn't do me any favors in building trust.

Still, they were obliged to give me a styrofoam cup of black coffee and hear me out, asinine though my story sounded. The detective who'd been questioning me for the past half hour let out an exasperated breath and turned, gesturing with his head to a nearby officer. I'm sure he was waiting for a lieutenant or captain to show up and take over now that word was out, maybe internal affairs if I was lucky.

"Mr. Perry, maybe it would help if we picked this up from the beginning," he suggested, probably to kill time waiting to pass me off. My lack of sleep and sprained ankle soured my inclination to go through the motions again.

"We could do that," I said, setting my coffee on the table and leaning forward. "Or hey, maybe instead we could go to that dumpster on Juniper and 97th and try finding a scrap of evidence to back up my story. Provided there's any left now that Avery's merry band has had the whole morning to move the body and clean the thing out while we've been sitting here bullshitting."

"Mr. Perry, please," the detective said with a gesture of his hand more impatient than diffusive. His name was McGregor. A mustache covered his lip like runny tar. "These are very serious allegations against a Los Angeles police officer with a sterling record. We need to ensure—"

"Then ensure," I interrupted, leaning back with my ripped jacket in my folded arms. "Get whoever you need to get to make this official, then get some guys over to that parking lot and to the Orange Forest Motel to search that room and the surrounding area. They had to have left something."

"We've already dispatched officers to the dumpster in question," he returned, "but before we authorize any larger investigation I need something to corroborate this story. Now you said you had a camera?"

"Camera phone, and the key word there is *had*. If I hadn't dropped it I wouldn't have been chased off a roof and you'd already have Avery and his pals in cuffs. Look, try to find the woman from Colonial Building or the owner of the Orange Forest. You won't."

"That's not evidence against Brett Avery on its own, Mr. Perry."

"Then get his wife over here. Cora has the recordings of Avery taking his calls every day. While you're at it, look into Avery's cell phone—the one listed under Jack Malone he's been keeping secret for the calls. That's the name he booked the hotel room under."

"Cora." He stated it as if everything I'd said after her name hadn't mattered. I held his stare, waiting for him to say it. "Sounds pretty familiar for a client, Mr. Perry."

"Tell you what, McGregor, why don't you start by investigating the accused and then you can investigate the accuser. 'Cause right now you've got a stone cold murderer walking around, possibly at home alone with the only person left holding evidence against him."

"Cora, you mean," McGregor repeated, still holding my gaze. Again he waited. "Certainly is a beautiful woman, isn't she?"

"A hell of a lot more so than any you've ever had, I imagine." I was past the point of caring how deep into the shit my credibility sank. McGregor grit his teeth but held his tongue as an officer tapped his shoulder. McGregor's smoldering eyes veered off me as he rose. He instructed me to wait.

"Get the cell records," I shouted as they walked away.

I waited for nearly an hour, moving back and forth between rooms while a few black and whites scrambled for whatever scraps of evidence may have been left. As hollow and one-dimensional as Cora was, I couldn't help fearing her corpse would be the evidence that would vindicate me.

I was accustomed to no-win scenarios, but I knew another innocent on my head would push me over the edge for good.

I felt like hammered shit. Looked and smelled like it too, I'm sure. My right leg required a limp for movement. Every muscle ached from the shingles and rocks. My feet still burned from all the walking. My hair was greasy and my face grimy, even after splashing water in the bathroom. My breath was a combination of sleep and stale coffee.

I spent most of my time playing back the scene from the motel parking lot. I still wasn't sure what happened, but I knew what I saw. The woman just collapsed. She was dead. Instantly. How? I thought there had been enough light for me to be sure but... No, there had to have been a knife in Avery's hand. I was tired and waterlogged—I must have missed it.

Another 40 minutes went by while I compared everything I'd seen in both parking lots, trying to find the common links, before McGregor and his lieutenant walked into the interrogation room. I couldn't read anything on the lieutenant's face, but I could tell from the smirk on McGregor's they hadn't found anything.

I released a loud huff and folded my arms. "You at least had to have confirmed the cell and the mystery calls."

"We haven't been able to trace any phone or service to Officer Avery under his name or the name of Jack Malone," the lieutenant answered, not bothering to introduce herself. "Mrs. Avery was anything but calm when we let her know about your story. We'll need to bring her in for questioning about these recordings once she's willing to settle down some."

"But you didn't find a body," I said, looking off to the side.

"Nor any blood, tissue or hair."

"Or signs the dumpster had been cleaned out," McGregor chimed in.

"Nothing off about 112?" I probed, still addressing the lieutenant. "Not even a record of the reservation?"

"Nothing. Amanda Pallance, the Orange Forest's owner, is indeed missing, along with Jessica Stillwater from the Colonial Building. But until such time as they are found or further evidence is collected linking Officer Avery to either of their disappearances—"

"You won't be doing a damn thing," I finished. The lieutenant exhaled sharply and folded her hands.

"These are very disturbing charges, Mr. Perry. With or without evidence to validate them, I don't like them. But given the exemplary record of Officer Avery against, shall we say, a wild allegation involving—"

"Maybe I was wrong about Connor. He looked familiar, sure, but it didn't even cross my mind until the old lady said his name. Don't let my credibility hinge on someone who looked like the Senator being there—I know it's unlikely."

"Because why wouldn't a US Senator meet a beat cop and two homeless schmucks in a hotel at the ass end of nowhere?" McGregor asked. "Everybody's a little gay, right?" The lieutenant stepped between us before I could fire off an expletive.

"An investigation is proceeding, Mr. Perry. During that time Officer Avery will remain on duty. Also during that time I suggest you return home and avoid any further detective work of your own. If there is evidence to be found, *we'll* find it. That's the best I can do."

I stewed for a moment longer than I should have, searching for anything else I could offer. When I saw their eyes I gave up. I'd escaped from Avery last night, but he'd won this round. Gathering my dirtied coat in my arms, I rose and trudged past them for the corridor leading to the lobby. I absorbed my fair share of dirty looks on the way out, most from the assumption this had all been a ruse to frame a good man for his lecherous wife.

When I exited the building a familiar squad car pulled into its usual slot. Avery made a show of not noticing me until I walked by. With nothing else to do, I gave him the look I'd been saving since first deciding he was a piece of shit, but it was wasted on him. There was a dead look in his eyes. I wasn't sure if it meant he wasn't worried in the least or if he'd be seeing me soon.

Probably both.

I'd been doing a lot of waiting over the past few weeks, but it's an entirely different experience when you're waiting on someone to kill you.

Trust me—this wasn't my first time grappling with the scenario.

I knew he'd come eventually. It wouldn't say much about his innocence if either Cora or I wound up face down in a ditch the day after filing my statement, but if this really was a secret worth protecting, that might not have mattered.

And did I want to know what that secret was.

The word 'obsession' had fallen from my vocabulary since the move, but the rest of the day found me wearing tracks in the carpet from pacing. Thinking. I hadn't worked my mind any harder than my body in a long time. It hurt.

I racked hours sorting through every detail. Categorizing them. Assembling them into motives, plans, and outcomes. Ripping them down and putting them back together again in new ways. Cross referencing them with every headline and rumor of crime and corruption in the LAPD, the US Senate, and the Crips.

I looked into that last one because I finally realized where I'd seen the man with dreadlocks a few hours into my research. Ran into him again in a lovely mug shot—Rince aka Delroy Rizwan. Territorial kingpin of the South Central Crips, including the new purple set supposedly behind the arsons Owens was so devoted to cleaning up. His name hadn't seen a headline yet, but I'd been trying to convince Harris to let me make one out of him after the rumors I'd picked up on the street.

After spending the afternoon inches from the laptop screen scouring for any connection between the men or their respective institutions of power, I was still no closer to a sensible conclusion than my first moment seeing them together. Unless I had stumbled onto the makings of some Junior Illuminati trio looking to make a power play for Los Angeles, nothing added up.

I still couldn't believe how thoroughly some fencepost IQ jock like Avery had hidden his tracks. After two weeks on his trail he'd never betrayed anything into the actual operation he was into. And picking up the trail for new evidence wouldn't be the walk in the park it had been so far.

This obviously went higher than Avery in the LAPD, but I'd never be able to trail him again. He'd be watching for me now, ten times beyond his usual paranoia (I still hated calling it that—he was way too calm to label it paranoia, but I couldn't call it situational awareness either. If he had the latter I would have been made after the first few nights.) Avery would completely change the game if he was left in play, unlikely though it was. He'd probably be replaced by another dirty cop, possibly left in a dumpster himself for bringing attention to the operation.

Either way, there wouldn't be any more phone calls or hotel meetings.

Picking up the trail with Senator Connor or Rince was even more of a non-option, of course. They both had security (their own very distinct brands) that would have been near impossible to penetrate before, but now I'd have to be Jason Bourne to learn anything.

I wasn't Jason Bourne.

Not that much of this mattered. If this was half as big as I was trying to make it out to be, I'd probably be in the aforementioned ditch before things cooled off enough for me to pick them back up. A week.

A year. Eventually I'd be hearing from one of the three parties, if not all.

I blinked and forced myself alert again, if only for a few moments. I kept forgetting the fourth guy from the Orange Forest Motel. The gaunt man seemed more out of place than any. A wrinkled old panhandler, he was the only one who didn't appear to represent anything larger than himself. I spent a sizeable portion of the day trying to peg him to something or someone like the awkward piece of the puzzle that didn't seem to fit anywhere.

Which likely meant he was a key element.

Finding myself circling back on the same questions I'd been branching from all afternoon, I sent my right arm soaring across the table. A glass of water and cheap brandy flew across the room into the kitchen as a result. Doggy jumped when it shattered, rising from his half sleep on a pillow. He wandered into the kitchen, watching. He tilted his head as I leaned over with mine in my hands.

I couldn't take anymore. Even having lost my edge, which the events of the past night—hell, the past two weeks—had thrown into sharp relief, I had never been good enough to assemble a jigsaw with only half the pieces. This mystery would remain just that unless I picked up a new lead.

True, all leads available would likely end with me in a dumpster, but when had I ever cared about the risk?

I breathed a sigh of relief that I wasn't in my duplex. Had I been, that question would have immediately drawn my eyes to the bottom drawer of my desk where I'd last put the picture of Gabby and Pita. I cringed at the sensation of tears welling in my eyes. I reached up to brush the water before it could stream down my cheeks. That would have opened the floodgates.

All the mental gymnastics of the last two weeks had kept my mind off the past more than just about any other event in the last five years, but I suddenly felt very lonely. So much so that I almost abandoned common sense and called Avery's wife. Aside from little Meredith or Harris, Cora was the only person I'd spoken to regularly in what felt like forever.

"You don't count," I said with a sniffle, opening my arms to the oversized Boston Terrier across the room. He immediately took the invitation, as if offended at the notion he couldn't be counted as a meaningful person in my life. He was too big to fit in my lap anymore, but jumped up my legs and rested his mug on a knee. I pet him and tried to force my mind as blank as it had been before ever meeting Cora Avery.

I mentioned I wasn't in my duplex. To clarify, I spent the afternoon in my neighbor's side of the duplex while I researched. I figured if anyone was on their way to kill me, this would give me a heads up. The walls were pretty thin—if anyone managed to slip in on my side I'd hear it.

I had the gun with me. I'd hidden it in a bush outside a bus stop near the police station before I went inside. Doubted I'd get it back since I didn't exactly have a permit for it.

Doggy wasn't much help in dispelling my loneliness. Meredith must have taken him for a long walk or something that morning—he fell back asleep almost instantly after our brief exchange. The loneliness quickly eroded into hopelessness, magnified by my failure to solve the riddle of Brett Avery.

I'd hit rock bottom long before this, but the combination of a fresh lack of purpose and the last of what little alcohol my neighbor kept hidden around the house brought me back to that spot. Closer than I'd been since the move, anyway. I forgot what day it was after polishing off the brandy and wondered if my neighbor would walk in at any moment.

And this is how big a shit I give if he does, I thought as I spread my arms wide for no one to see.

I drifted between laughter and tears for about an hour while the buzz wore off. It was late into the night. I considered taking Doggy out for a walk. Or going to find more booze. Or getting the picture of the girls from my desk. Maybe I should just go over to Avery's, put the gun to his head and see what comes out, I thought.

I just sat there.

Then I put the gun to my head.

I spent a while trying to discern any action I could take at that moment that would matter. I tried to recall the feeling from the voice in my ear when I lay out in Beeks Place—that I had to stay alive. Somehow I still mattered, and I was the only one who could do whatever I still had the capacity to do.

I laughed at how pathetic it sounded.

Anything I did—solving the Avery case or walking up the street to buy a forty at the gas station—would end with me coming back to this chair, sitting down and waiting.

To die.

Whatever purpose my life once held, whatever reason I was there, ended that day five years ago. I'd done nothing of consequence, nothing to contribute to humanity in any real way, since then. And short of taking care of an abandoned dog, I never would again. As much as Gabby would have wanted me to, it wasn't going to happen.

I'd come to this conclusion hundreds, maybe thousands of times before, but this time the shame of disappointing her finally gave way to reality. I had already resigned myself to disappoint her with whatever time I had left. I was just sitting there. I could either keep sitting there for another 30 years, maybe more, or not waste the world's time.

I breathed deeply and wiped the tear stains from my cheeks. There was nothing I hated more than those lines of sticky saltwater on my face. Sure enough, they had opened the floodgates. Always did.

I put the gun in my mouth and leaned my head back. My eyes caught Doggy lying peacefully asleep on his pillow. Meredith would take care of him. Or not. Either way I couldn't do it anymore. Still, I didn't want the little bastard to see. Or have him tracking blood and brains all over the neighbor's kitchen. I may have been an intolerable cynic, and I never shared any love for my neighbor, but I wasn't that big of a dick.

Slowly rising so as not to wake Doggy, I tiptoed across the kitchen to the sliding glass door that led into the backyard. When I pushed the blinds to one side to reach for the handle, I saw a man standing outside. His back was to the house. It was dark but the heavy orange of the streetlight reached far enough back to illuminate a stream of urine spraying from the man into the yard.

I shook my head and let out a sharp breath. Just the thing you want to see before you blow your head off.

"Hey guy," I said after sliding the door open a bit. He turned his head unhurriedly, still going on with his business. "It may look like a toilet, but my backyard is not..." I trailed off when I realized I'd seen him before. The bony face covered in dirt and a graying adventure beard.

My missing link in the mystery of the meeting at room 112.

My heart racing, I prepared to push the gun through the doorway at him. A body charging through from the other side interrupted me. I made out two of them in addition to the homeless man, one grasping for the door while the other hit me with a flying tackle.

I was dazed as I squirmed on the floor. I didn't realize I'd gotten a shot off until the concurrent realization that I no longer held the gun. Probably knocked out of my hands during the hit. From the shout of a young man still outside I guessed I'd hit him.

I quickly found my focus while desperately holding back the other young male roughly twice my weight. He lay on top of me with hands rapidly overpowering mine for a grip on my neck. Looked like the boys who'd tried to hold me up at the bar a few weeks back, probably Crips.

I would have been dead in another few seconds had my only friend not scrambled to my rescue. The kid screamed and wheeled back when Doggy sank his teeth into an arm. I never thought the little guy had it in him.

I remained dazed while oxygen rushed back into my lungs, but I was already reaching for the table. The first thing I grabbed was the leg of a chair, which I weakly cast toward my attacker. I wasn't strong enough to lift the chair over my head and do any real damage while prone.

The kid slammed a fist downward to Doggy's skull like a sledgehammer. There was a sharp yip but nothing followed as the mutt was tossed across the kitchen like a stuffed animal. It probably gave me the angry adrenaline I needed.

When the kid turned back for me with a hand over his bleeding arm, one of the empty beer bottles from the table was there to meet him. It shattered across his forehead and he stumbled back. I rushed him. It was far short of a tackle but I sent him back outside the way he'd come.

Before I could turn for Doggy I heard another shower of broken glass, this time from the gunshots coming through the sliding door. The other kid stumbled over the first with my pistol in hand after what must have been a frantic search through the darkness for it. I dove away further into the kitchen but he got my lower thigh.

Stung like a sonofabitch but it barely nicked me.

I shouted some terrible curse and hobbled toward the bedroom door. I caught sight of Doggy just as I slammed it shut to barricade myself in. He wasn't moving.

The gunfire stopped but I heard the kid rushing after me. I'd lost count of the shots fired, but unless he had another piece—unlikely since the first thing to hit me would have been a bullet rather than a flying tackle—he couldn't have had more than two or three more rounds.

I'm sure he was equally cognizant of this since he decided to kick at the locked door as opposed to shooting through it. I bolted for the opposite door that led to a hallway and the front of the duplex.

A lamp was the only sizeable weapon I had time to pick up in the dash to escape. The other kid was probably winded but not down. There was a look of madness I'd never seen in the eyes of both of them. I'd never known even the staunchest of these little gangbanger shits to take a bullet or a bottle over the head and keep coming. And the mystery man was still out there as well.

When I tore into the front room my luck seemed to improve. The kid behind me was stumbling through the darkness of the foreign house and the other two were nowhere to be seen. I reached for my keys on the way to the front door, preparing to either rush for my car that I'd recently recovered from Beeks Place, or Meredith's apartment building for help. I couldn't remember which would be closer.

Instead I came to a sharp halt when I opened the door.

Brett Avery stood in the walkway.

Just stood there. No sense of urgency or stress evident, just the usual poise as if waiting for his 1:00 call in the bedroom. He'd left his uniform at home. I didn't even see his gun on him.

My heart pounded as he started toward me in his nonchalant manner, raising his arm as I'd watched him do when approaching the owner of the motel the night prior. I considered diving back into the house, but I could hear the kid in the hallway and at least one other moving through the kitchen. I'd have to charge Avery the same as the kid and hope his wrist blade or whatever he had hidden in his hands couldn't catch me in time.

This all happened fast, but the next part barely even registered until it was over.

The heavy orange of the streetlight washed out as headlights poured onto the walkway. The rev of an engine stopped both Avery and me in our tracks. Standing in shock, I watched a car leap over the curb at 40 plus miles per hour. It nailed Avery dead center.

The car screeched to a halt just before it smashed into my side of the duplex, ripping what little grass that grew in the yard to hell. Avery didn't quite make it through the wall, though he had to have come close from the dent he left. It looked like he'd just fallen from the top of a skyscraper. He was pulp.

I probably would have just stood there in lingering shock had the car's driver not opened the door and screamed for me to get in after the sound of another gunshot behind me. Cora sat behind the wheel, sweaty and panicked but steely eyed in a way I would have never imagined her capable.

Especially not after ramming a car into her husband at 40 miles per hour.

The kid with my gun must have fired the last shot and missed because no more came. All I felt as I hobbled across my yard for the car was a hand grasping at my leg. At first I thought it was another bullet from how cold it felt, but when I turned to kick the assailant away I found the homeless man grasping at me from where he crawled. A streak of blood from a wound in his gut marked his path around the house. My errant first shot must have hit him, not the other kid.

I tore away from him and bolted for the car, which I now recognized as Avery's. There were more gunshots, these coming from directly beside me. Cora had her late husband's nine millimeter in hand, spurting covering fire to keep the other kid inside the house. I stared at her as if looking at another person while she emptied the clip. She reached across the seat to pull me in with purposeful strength.

She had the car in gear and peeling out before either of us closed our doors, certainly before the kid could catch up with us.

"Get inside!" she bellowed when she caught my right leg still dangling out the side. I realized it wasn't responding. I managed to pull myself all the way into the seat and shut the door as we swerved down the street.

Erratic behind the wheel, Cora nervously pumped the breaks and gas while fumbling over turn signals and windshield wipers. I prepared to ask her if she was alright but decided to say something else when she nearly drove us into another house with a wild turn.

"Watch out!" I blasted, reaching for the wheel. I assumed she'd been shot from the way she handled the car, but when I asked her she told me to shut up and hold on. Taking her eyes from the road (which I strongly protested against) to look me over, she caught sight of my wound and fresh panic set into her eyes.

"Don't touch your leg," she ordered as we accelerated. Somehow as sarcastic in that moment as ever, I considered telling her she never learned much about gunshot wounds from her husband. I prepared to apply pressure but she swatted my hands away, her eyes ferocious. "I said don't touch it!"

I suddenly worried that maybe Cora hadn't come to save me. I started to ask her how she knew to come, but cold began settling in over my leg. I realized the entire limb was numb up to my thigh.

Cora nearly slammed us into another car. I didn't know what was wrong with her but I knew she was going to get us killed. "Give me the wheel," I managed despite my voice weakening. The other headlights and streetlights began to blur. Cora's expression softened with genuine concern when she saw me sinking further into the seat.

"Just hold on, Jon," she told me before I lost consciousness. "I'm here to help you."

four

You know that feeling like you're about to fall that stops you from getting to sleep? Usually lasts for, what, a split second? I'm still not certain that I ever passed out in the hours between our escape and waking up in the back seat of the Averys' car, but that sensation was over me almost the entire time. Felt like my body was liquid, drifting apart in sloshing globs.

I startled Cora when I woke. It was dark in the car, still night. No light coming in from the windows, no sound of other cars. But I was pretty sure I heard running water nearby. I remained dazed but pushed myself upright when she popped her head over the seat from the front. Her expression was caught between anxiety and relief. She gripped the back of the seat with both hands, as if bracing for something.

My right leg was propped up on the edge of the window ledge across from me. Doors and windows were closed and the heater in the car was on, but I was freezing. Cora had laid my jacket and hers over me. I pushed them aside and prepared to move my leg, then realized I couldn't feel it. She stopped me from grabbing it with a clenched hand around mine.

"Don't," she instructed. "You need to stay still and rest a good while longer." Her cheeks were stained black from running eyeliner.

Understandable, given what she'd just done.

I was soaked in sweat despite the cold. I ran a hand down my shirt to find it damp, then noticed it was only my undershirt. My white button down was in shreds, wrapped around my right leg from thigh to foot. It was literally dripping around putrid red and yellow stains. I didn't think the gunshot was that bad but I must have been hit on the lawn when the limb first went cold.

"Where are we?" was the first thing I thought to ask, meaning to point out that it should have been the hospital. I hadn't heard that much fear in my voice in a long time.

Cora took her hand off mine and readjusted her stance on the front seat. She had to have been on her knees. "You passed out," she offered as if to prep me for more. "I've... never been here before. I wasn't sure where to go." I wasn't sure how she'd managed to get lost in the heart of LA being a lifelong native, but between the darkness and her panic I let it go.

"Well I'm glad you showed up when you did, but seeing that I can't feel my leg I think you'd better get me to a—"

"We cannot go to a hospital. They will be looking for us there. We cannot go anywhere right now." A swell of impatience immediately overwhelmed my gratefulness for the rescue.

"They?" I bit harder than I should have given her state. "You knew what was really going on here since the moment you stepped into my house, didn't you? You knew Brett wasn't out with some hooker, he was out killing people."

"I—"

"Why the hell did you pull me into this? You knew what you'd be sending me into. You lied to me about him, about everything!" Frustrations I'd kept bottled in for years, completely unrelated to Avery, broiled my temper on. It was the first time I'd had an avenue to unload it. Cora just happened to be the easy target.

"That isn't—"

"Now my dog's dead, it feels like I'll never walk the same again, if at all, and 'they' are out looking for me to finish the job. Just what in the fuck is going on here, Cora?!"

When I finally gave her a moment to get out a thought she didn't take it, swallowing hard while a tear streamed down her cheek. Guilt settled in over my anger, but it gave way to surprise when she took a breath and answered.

"I'm not Cora." I stared at her a moment, making sure my eyes weren't playing tricks on me in the darkness.

"What?" She took a moment to wipe her eyes and collect herself, armed with the same uncharacteristic expression of strength as when she unloaded a clip from her husband's gun.

"What I am about to tell you is going to frighten and confuse you, but you have to listen. You are part of this now whether you like it or not." I wasn't in the mood to hear that but this time she cut me off with her eyes alone. "My name is Adelaide Martin." She paused, looking away to find a suitable starting point for what she was hyping to be a long story.

"When the police came to the house to tell Cora that her husband was under investigation because of your allegations, I knew she wouldn't live to see the next morning. Neither would you. Not without my help.

"Brett Avery came home after darkness fell. Cora had been in the bedroom with the lights off, waiting. I'd been trying to warn her to get out, or at least prepare her, but I wasn't sure if I was getting through. Her emotions were a storm, I could barely navigate them.

"When he came in, she could tell by the look on his face I was right. She knew she was going to die, and there was nothing she could do to stop it." I was staring at her, utterly lost, but whatever her delusions, they stemmed from sincerity. The guilt and fear in her eyes told me that much.

"In that moment I reached through. I offered to save her. She only had a few seconds to decide and she knew what it would cost, but she let me in to do what she couldn't. I pushed her up and drove her to the gun Brett kept in the closet. It didn't stop him but the bullet slowed him down enough for me to get away.

"I knew he would have to go for you at once so I went to your house and waited. By the time I heard the commotion Brett had pulled up and made it to your front door. I... stopped him." I couldn't take my eyes off her. I wasn't sure if she had skipped over a critical detail or if she needed a hospital as badly as I did.

"You're telling me Cora Avery was some kind of cover for you?" My skepticism was bladed. She shook her head.

"Cora Avery is sitting right here with you. She is the woman you met in your home a few weeks ago. But I am Adelaide Martin."

"And who is Adelaide Martin?" She awkwardly pushed a lock of hair obscuring her view behind her shoulder as if she'd never done it before.

"She was the daughter of an Australian cattle baron. She died in the war in 1944." When I opened my mouth to ask her what she was talking about, her eyes found mine again. "I am an angel, Jon. My body died a very long time ago but my soul endured into heaven. Until a few hours ago when it took possession of Cora Avery's body to save her. And you."

I could scarcely believe how far I'd fallen from the days when I could pick apart a personality and mine truth from it like second nature. Not only had I misjudged Brett Avery as a deflated high school jock whose glory days were behind him, I'd picked up zero trace of the dementia in his wife. I wasn't sure if I had just been lazy or if the pair of them were master actors, but either way I was embarrassed.

I decided the safest option at this point was to humor her while I looked for a way out of the car given my leg. "And an angel would be looking to help Cora and me because...?"

"Because Cora's husband was possessed first," was her reply, again halting my train of thought.

"By an angel." She shook her head.

"By what you might call a Horseman," she answered. "One of four. Death. I came here to help Cora escape him and figure out why he was taken. That is how I knew about you. When I passed into her I could see her mind, her heart, even her soul, so much as angels can see them.

I knew where to find you, what you had told her, and that you were in the same danger."

"A Horseman," I repeated while my hand slid closer to the handle of the door. She nodded. "Of the Apocalypse." Another silent nod. "And a Horseman of the Apocalypse possessed Brett Avery because...?"

"I told you. That is what I am here to find out." My hand reached the door but I knew I wouldn't be able to outrun her if she decided to give chase, so I continued the attempt to disarm her, which, given her apparent mental state, didn't seem too dissimilar from disarming a bomb.

"Well no offense, Adelaide Martin, but even if I believed in the Four Horsemen, I'd have a hard time believing that God would care enough to send an angel to protect me."

"God did not send me," she recoiled immediately. "But I gather you are asking for proof." I asked if she had any. "I don't. No feathers or halo or golden glow. When angels reenter the mortal realm we are bound to the same laws that bind all those here. I can do nothing more in this world as an angel than I could when I was alive in my own body. That is a... rule."

She studied me for a moment with what looked like embarrassment. She took a deep breath and sank back on her knees, dropping her shoulders in defeat.

"Fine. Take a moment to relax as best you can, then pull back the bandages from your leg." I held her gaze for a moment but again she encouraged me to look. I wondered if I was to receive a healing touch. I didn't want to give her the opportunity then watch her fly off the handle with the realization she couldn't do it, but I did need to assess the damage to my limb.

Leaning up as best I could, I reached down for the ends of my shirt wrapped around my thigh. It was slimy, and the odious smell that escaped when I pushed the first sticky strip away told me I was in serious trouble.

"Calm down, Jon," Cora told me as I hurried to roll back more of the bandages. My heart rate quickened. I ignored her when I caught sight of a misshapen growth over my inner thigh. Desperate for a better view in the darkness, I reached up and punched the dome light.

I barely stopped myself from throwing up when I got the full view.

My leg looked like it had been blown apart from the inside. Flesh was reduced to molten or rotting ooze dripping with blood while brown and green veins protruded. Splotches of hardened scales spotted a few areas that looked more like a mummified corpse than living tissue. It grew worse to the spot where the homeless man grabbed me, which was essentially just a crater where flesh had once been.

I shouted something and pushed my way out of the car on my back after forcing the door open. Cora tried to stop me but I pushed her away once she was outside. I crawled over rock and dirt, looking through the darkness while she pled for me to wait and breathe. When I pulled myself halfway up I began hyperventilating and everything went black again.

"You were touched by Pestilence," she said a few hours later when my eyes opened. Dawn was approaching. Streaks of murky orange dipped in between the thick trees of wherever we were. I was still sweaty but considerably warmer. I'd hoped the night had all been a bad dream (as I'd hoped about much of my life) but I still couldn't feel my leg. She'd pulled me back in the car and bandaged the decaying limb with paper towels and her coat.

I reached for my eyes to wipe away the sleep, then sat up. The door across from me was open. She sat on the ground outside, leaning against the door frame. I could only see the back of her head, but I could tell she was huddled with her arms around her legs, probably cold.

"What?" I asked. She didn't turn as she continued.

"Pestilence. Another Horsemen. He possessed the homeless man who attacked you. He doesn't have the capacity to kill anything directly, but anything he touches becomes diseased and decayed. Just as

Death kills instantly with a touch. Pestilence only grazed you and didn't make contact with your skin so I believe you will heal after a short while, but you will always carry a terrible scar."

"Who are you?" was my question when she finished. "Really?" She turned and stared at me for a moment. There was enough light for me to get a good look at her face. It was Cora Avery alright, but... her eyes. They stared at me as if coming from another place, stronger and weaker at the same time.

She pointed to the floorboard beside me. "I found some water from a fountain nearby. Drink, you'll need it." I grabbed a thermos and instantly downed its contents, finding myself parched. She was standing when I set it down, her arms folded and covered with goosebumps. I couldn't offer her coat back after being wrapped around...

I think I actually whimpered at the prospect of all this.

She knelt outside the open door, looking away. "I... One moment I was here, alive, and the next, I was somewhere else. Heaven." She smiled, but it was sad. "I don't know how to describe it for you other than to call it abstract. It's full and empty all at once. You exist as will and memories instead of flesh and blood.

"There's a veil between the worlds, but angels can see through it to look back. There are a different set of senses once you move beyond your body. You can't 'see' anything specific in the beyond, much less the world you came from. Instead you can feel certain things. Emotions, mainly. Time is a little more fluid there than here, but I spent most of my time looking back. Feeling. That's how I noticed something was wrong."

She stopped when she looked at me and saw my remaining suspicion. "You still do not believe me?"

"What would you believe if you were me?" She glanced down the length of my leg again.

"Take another look." I told her I'd seen all I wanted to. "Trust me." Taking a nervous breath, I lifted her coat up. The smell persisted, but again I was surprised at what I found. Where the limb had looked all but destroyed a few hours prior, it was mostly reassembled. The craters filled in, the swollen veins beneath flesh where they belonged. The skin looked like skin, if still a little putrid.

Her relief seemed to match my own. "I told you it would only last a while. If Pestilence had touched your bare flesh or gotten a better grip, there would likely be nothing left by now, but it was only a graze. You'll be walking again before the day's end."

I shifted my befuddled eyes back to her. "You... really are..." She just nodded, not proud or warm as I thought she might be. Just tired. "So... you're here because of the Horsemen?" She shifted her position outside, sitting on the edge of the floorboards. She moved somewhat clumsily, as if not used to moving. At least in that form.

"They were—are—on the move. I could feel them using their power. At first I thought it was the end—that they had been sent to do what they were made for. But something felt wrong about it. They were barely doing anything, certainly not initiating Armageddon. I wanted to know what.

"So I focused on the emotions around them. That's how I found Cora. She seemed to be closest to Death."

"So you possessed her," I said. She looked at me, waiting for me to say more. "I just didn't think it worked liked that."

"That angels and demons are people who have died? That they can come back by taking control of a living body and displacing the owner's soul?" She looked away. "Neither did I.

"But it doesn't quite work like that, and it certainly isn't commonplace. When angels or demons focus hard enough on a living soul in this world, they can eventually whisper to that person. Plant subtle thoughts in a mind. That's how I warned Cora. I'd been whispering to her since I realized Death was hovering around her. Since before she met you."

"So Cora is..."

"Still inside. She can hear us, on some level. Her soul lives on, but her mind and body are mine to direct now. I will live on inside her now until the body dies, and we both move beyond." She looked guilt-ridden. "The rest of Cora's life will be spent passive, trapped in her own body, but that was the price she knew she would have to pay. I'm not proud of what I've done, but she wanted to stay alive, and I needed a vessel to investigate the Horsemen."

"So anybody I run into could really be an angel or a... demon? Or a Horseman?"

"Yes, but I highly doubt you've ever encountered a possessed before the Averys. As I said, it doesn't happen very often. Angels don't do it barring extremely rare situations and demons are wary of it."

"Why?"

"There are rules once you die. God's rules, I suppose. They're unspoken for the most part, but once you exist in a world where they do, you just know about them. Sort of like gravity—no one has to tell you about it for you to be aware of it, but you never really think about it.

"It basically works like this. There are four types of living beings. Mortal creatures, mortal creatures with sentience, what we become after death—angels and demons—and what I guess you'd call constructs. Beings with a specific function to perform. Each plane of existence has its own laws, its own science. By comparison to heaven and hell, this plane is incredibly structured. Part of that structure is that angels and demons cannot interact until the end of days when the final confrontation commences. Whenever—whatever—that is.

"What we *can* do is whisper our will into the ears of humans. We can't directly influence them or use any, well, supernatural power in the mortal realm, but we can put ideas in their heads."

"And there's nothing supernatural about possession?" She frowned at me.

"A poor choice of words, but these aren't *my* rules. I don't decide what is and what is not supernatural. And like I said, it doesn't regularly happen. Angels have little need for it—there isn't exactly a line of us clamoring to leave heaven. And to answer your earlier question, demons are wary of it because it draws undue attention."

"What does that mean?"

"At one point there was a concerted effort by demons to possess all of humanity and escape hell. There are only so many host bodies and it would only be a temporary solution, but when one is in hell I imagine escape of any kind sounds very appealing. Remember the bible story about the Flood?"

"I could never get past the part where Noah crams 50 million species onto a boat."

"Well biblical hyperbole aside, the Flood was real. It wasn't quite the scale of the bible's version, but it was enough to send a clear message. There are certainly a handful of demon possessors in this world at any given time, but they'll never risk so many as to draw that kind of attention again."

"But how? How does this work? Or why? You said Cora had to agree to let you in—you convinced her. Why would anyone let a demon take control of their body for the rest of their life?"

"Whispering is sort of like singing," Adelaide replied. "Anyone can do it, but it takes some talent to be good at it. To move people. Talented demons listen for emotions they themselves are familiar with, that they know how to exploit. They whisper false encouragement or add to pain, usually with carefully planned manipulations that prey on flaws and faults.

"Then, once they're burrowed deep enough in, they make an offer. An end to heartache. Strength to replace weakness. A deal. 'Let me take over and I'll make things right for you.' It's the oldest story in the book, but it's usually the pitch that works.

"Still, it's extremely difficult to pull off. To most people whispers are just stray thoughts, fantasies or déjà vu. They never register as another actual voice. The offer is always a gamble because if the mortal rejects, that mortal will never again be able to hear whispers from that whisperer. Beyond that, both sides are always whispering into every ear, cancelling each other out. It always comes down to which whisperer is more persuasive. Demons tend to be better at it, but it takes a truly insightful mind to work someone down for possession."

"Like you." I couldn't help but say it. When she didn't say anything back, I asked something else. "So how do you know all this? About demons I mean."

"I can feel it. Feel them. Heaven and hell may be two different realms, but they're much closer than you'd think. It's like having a view into your next door neighbor's house through an open window. Angels and demons can feel each other and our intent far clearer than anything we can discern in this world."

There was a long silence when she finished. I fought to digest everything I'd heard, attempting to sort through the 'rules' to account for the incongruence I'd been mulling over.

"So angels and demons are human, or were, at least, but that means the Horsemen aren't." She looked at me, surprised.

"What makes you say that?"

"You said angels and demons can't use any supernatural power in this world." I lifted up her coat from my leg, letting a waft of the aroma free. "That doesn't smell too natural." She nodded.

"You're right. The Horsemen are constructs. Semi-sentient creations that flow between worlds to enact a specific purpose—the will of God, I suppose."

"But you think these ones have gone rogue." I could tell from the look on her face she knew it sounded absurd, but I think she failed to realize it was talk of Horsemen, not them going rogue, that made it absurd. She buried her head in her hands.

"I do not know what I think."

"Only that something is wrong," I said, coaching her for more.

"I... think so." She let out another deep breath. If any part of me still wasn't convinced that I was talking to a woman other than Cora Avery, the distress on her face told me otherwise. As insane as I felt buying into this, I knew right then I was doing so. Adelaide Martin or not, Cora was gone.

"So what's the function of the Horsemen, then?" I asked, just to make sure.

"Pretty much what it says in the bible, from what I can tell. The end of the world. War, Famine, Pestilence and Death. There are variations, but that's what they boil down to. The latter two you've met, the others I think you've seen."

"Senator Connor and Rince," I said more to myself. I almost smirked at the notion that a Horseman of the Apocalypse possessing a US Senator didn't seem that outlandish to me. "So what do you think they're doing if not setting the stage for doomsday?"

"I have no idea."

"Well what are you planning to do about it?" Her silence told me the same answer. "I don't get it—why come down here if you had no plan? Why should you even have to? If these guys are messengers of God or whatever, wouldn't he have his eye on them? How could they possibly go rogue if they're just tools? I thought they weren't even sentient? Why would—"

"I do not know!" she nearly shouted. I saw her eyes moistening so I fell silent. She certainly wasn't my picture of an angel. Adelaide Martin was just a person—strong, but scared. Alone. For as much as she knew, she didn't seem to have much more of clue of what was really going on than I did.

She sank further into the seat. "I do not know what they are doing, I just thought... something was out of place, and I seemed to be the only person who cared."

"What about God?" She let out a sharp huff.

"Who knows about him."

"I thought you were an angel. You know the ins and outs of heaven and hell but nothing about the guy who created them?"

"I hate to dampen your hope or ruin the surprise, but death doesn't bring you any closer to God. For as long as I've been in heaven, as long as anyone has been there, he's been silent. Sometimes I think I just don't know how to listen for him, that I'm still too focused on the world I came from. But as far as I know he's turned a blind eye to the Horsemen. To everything. To me."

Her voice took a tone of disdain I recognized all too well with regard to the Almighty. Suddenly I thought I may have had more in common with the angel than I'd first thought.

"So God didn't send you."

"Hardly. I did this on my own. I'm not even sure he's watching."

"Oh he's watching," was my reply. Her eyes found mine, and I'm sure she realized my assertion came from something other than pious devotion. I didn't offer anything else to that end, though.

When she didn't seem to have anything else to say, lost in doubt as her face drooped, I took a long breath and sat up. My leg felt more asleep than numb now, and a little sensation signaled in my thigh at last. I sat up straight and waited for her to look at me.

"One more question," I said. "That night in the field at Beeks Place. An angel was whispering to me, right?" She stared at me for an uncomfortable moment.

"There are as many angels whispering as living people talking every day. More. I could never be aware of each instance."

"That's a guarded way to say absolutely nothing." Again she stared at me. Either from Cora's previous knowledge of me or from dealing with other people like me in her life, Adelaide didn't seem put-off by the way I was, but I don't think she was pleased.

"Yes," she said at last. "I think an angel was whispering to you that night." I nodded. I considered asking her where one had been for the past five years but decided against it. She was probably sick of me already, no need to make it worse.

"Well, Adelaide Martin, I think we're both crazy, because I think we both believe all this. That's why I'm going to help you." Her head tilted a bit to one side, but she just looked at me, searching.

"Why?" was her question, in lieu of how.

"Aside from being crazy, because I'm curious. If I've got a streak of anything, it's curiosity. Even now. Especially now. I'm an investigative journalist. I live for conspiracy stories, and now I may be smack in the middle of a divine one. How could I pass that up?"

"You do realize this is not some game," she told me, detecting my flippancy. "These are the Horsemen. We may have pushed Death from

Brett Avery and Pestilence from the other, but they are likely to have found new hosts already. Constructs can take possession with little difficulty—they are made to do so. That enough should frighten you, but if this is indeed some manner of conspiracy, there could be more at risk than your life if you get any more involved."

"Wouldn't worry about that. My soul is already done for. But it sounds like I don't have much of a choice if I want to live out the week. If these boys are gunnin' for me I doubt they're going to let up now. And if you really are from the 1940s, I think you're going to need some help getting around. God knows your driving needs some work."

She didn't laugh. Didn't emote at all. But eventually she nodded, what looked like a glimmer of relief somewhere in her eyes. "Thank you."

I returned her nod. The silence hung for another minute or so before we both heard my stomach growl. I sniffed and scratched at the stubble on my chin. "You hungry?"

five

Looking back on it, I think the foremost reason I had trouble accepting that Adelaide Martin was who she said she was (past the absurdity that angels existed), was her lack of... I dunno, angel-ness.

I'm not sure what I was expecting—who's anticipating a run in with an angel—but this wasn't it.

If Adelaide had really been a resident of heaven, she certainly bucked the stereotype of the gently smiling, near omnipotent guardian with wings. She exuded no confident warmth, no sense of cosmic knowledge, no aura of holiness—not even one of spirituality.

She was just a person. And like most people forced to interact with me, she didn't much care for me. She didn't seem to hold my skepticism of her story against me, but it was clear from her personality we were primed to butt heads from the start.

Despite her tenuous emotional state after commandeering a body, given the implications, Adelaide was a woman on a mission. She had no time for patience and no stomach for advice that wasn't solicited. From the way she quickly arrived at decisions without a full context to work from, I guessed she was either used to being in command or that she operated from some black and white code. If it was the latter I had no idea what code it could be, given her earlier comments about the Almighty.

Whatever the case, this wasn't the angel from your mother's storybook.

She remained tense while we drove back into the city that morning, visibly uncomfortable in the passenger's seat and in her new skin. I thought about asking her what it was like occupying another body, if it felt natural or not, but thought better of it given her mood. Her eyes were somewhere between anxious and fearful as they took in the cityscape through the window. She sat low in the seat, hands balled into fists.

She had told me she could "feel" the world she left behind since passing into the next, but she couldn't see it. I supposed I'd have been more than a bit overwhelmed taking in modern LA if the last thing I'd seen was 1940s Australia.

I didn't have much time to consider her feelings before she began feeding me instructions. "Be sure you avoid any police or anyone who could stop us. Avoid anyplace you know. Do not speed or do anything that could draw attention, but get us where we need to go as quickly as possible."

"Yeah, I can handle it. It's not much farther."

"We cannot afford to be found by anyone, Jon. We must get rid of this car as soon as possible. Are there no less populated roads we can take to this place? There are people everywhere."

"I know this is all new to you, but this isn't rural Australia. These *are* the back roads."

"You do not know where I lived," she said without looking my way. She was silent for another 30 seconds before she started again. "Surely there is a safer route. Everyone can see us."

"Yeah, well, there's been this thing called population density since the '40s." She shot me a quick glare that reminded me of the look in Cora's eyes when she thought about her husband cheating on her.

"Are you sure we will be safe at this house?"

"Yes."

"And you are sure you can get us in?"

"I'm sure."

"And there is no one you know who would think to look for you there?" This time I gave her a look, silent. She didn't back down, her expression justified. "Have you any idea how important this is?"

"I don't know how many ways I can say it—this is the safest place I know of. If you have another place we could go, I'm all ears." She tried to hold my stare, angry, but eventually turned. When she raised a hand to her face I guessed it was to wipe welling tears away. I exhaled from the guilt of stepping over the line. "You'll be safe. I promise."

"You think I'm doing this for me?" My next breath was sharper but I forced myself to stay quiet. I kept driving.

Not many enjoy the company of a pessimist, to be sure, but Ms. Martin seemed to resent that I was the one she was stuck with for her divine investigation. I couldn't blame her.

Adelaide had driven us to Topanga State Park that night, probably the first empty place she came to outside the dense city. With my duplex compromised, I didn't have many options for places to hide out. The Horsemen would be looking for us, but so would the cops after finding three dead bodies at my duplex, one of them being Brett Avery. It was risky enough driving Cora's car, but we didn't have another choice.

My only thought came to me after we started driving and I saw the turnoff to Hollywood. I didn't tell Adelaide where we were going other than to say it was safe. She was in a contradictory mood. As desperate as she was to remain off the radar (an analogy wasted on her), her desire to pick up the trail of my investigation was equally paramount.

She was convinced there wasn't much time to uncover whatever the Horsemen were up to. Let's figure out why Death possessed Brett by putting the screws to his acquaintances, she suggested. Not in so many words, but there was a ruthlessness in the way she laid out her ideas that I found disturbing.

Seeing as most of the Averys' friends were cops or surrounded by cops now that Cora was missing, I reminded her we couldn't get anywhere near them. The last thing she wanted to do was nothing, but I convinced her laying low was our only option for the moment. We'd have to pick up the trail elsewhere.

We were both filthy and hungry, and since she wouldn't even let me pull into a drive-thru for a breakfast burrito, I took her straight to my improvised safe house. Adelaide was surprised when we pulled into the driveway of the illustrious three-story house in West Hollywood. I hurried her out of the car and around the house to a back door, promising her I'd hide the car once we got inside.

She eyed me suspiciously as I groped a lamp affixed to the back porch for a hidden key. "I take it this is not your house."

"What gave it away?" I asked as I slipped the key through a hole.

"So whose is it?"

"Stevie Walker. Small time movie producer." The look Adelaide gave me told me she may never have seen a movie.

"Is she your friend?"

"You might say that," I offered, opening the back door. "I interviewed her once. I don't usually write features but she knew who I was, asked for me. She gave me a tour of the house that day, I saw where she kept the hide-a-key. I read she's out on a movie shoot in South America or something. We'll be fine."

I stepped into the house, waiting for her to do the same. "So you are breaking in?"

"No, I'm letting myself in." Adelaide didn't budge, staring at me disapprovingly. "Look, the only place I had in the world was my shitty duplex, now crawling with cops. You were the one who wanted a place no one would ever look for us. This is it." She held my gaze for a moment before exhaling sharply and striding past me into the house.

I remember thinking the place was gaudy the last time I'd been there. Movie posters and props littered the walls while rows of disorganized souvenirs from around the world adorned every stray shelf or table. Still, compared to my place it might as well have been the Ritz penthouse.

Adelaide moved through a garden room into the kitchen at an uncertain pace, taking in all the décor with wide eyes. I told her to stay put for a moment while I hid the car. I checked for any witnesses before opening the garage door and pulling the car into a vacant space. It was a fairly secluded property, bordered by fencing and tall bushes around the perimeter.

Adelaide stood aimlessly in the middle of the kitchen, scanning an open cabinet stuffed with food. Deciding we were safe for the moment, I let out a deep breath and leaned against the kitchen doorframe. "Why don't you go take a shower and I'll get some breakfast ready." She raised an eyebrow my way.

"It is not bad enough that we are hiding here? You want to steal from the owner as well?" I raised a hand to massage my eye, fighting impatience.

"You can't stop Death on an empty stomach, I'm sure." Her expression didn't change. "Look, you requisitioned a body. I'm requisitioning us some food. Fugitives can't always be white knights." She fought to hold back whatever she would have liked to say back, instead folding her arms and looking around.

"Does she keep a gun in the house?" she asked.

"Uh... I doubt it," I replied, wondering why that was her first thought. "Hollywood liberal, and all." She nodded.

"Check, please. Where is the washroom?" I pointed her down the closest hallway, not knowing if a shower was down there or not but trusting her to find one. When she closed (and locked) the door at the end of the hall, I lazily collapsed into one of the large cushioned chairs adjacent to the kitchen. I needed a shower more than her. I still reeked of BO and lingering gangrene.

A squeak in the pipes signaled the flow of water.

I slid a hand down what remained of my right pant leg, feeling the hardened skin below. It felt almost natural by now—most of the feeling had returned. The oversized chair was a godsend after the night in the uncomfortable back seat, and my moment of rest turned into sleep.

It only felt like a few moments rest, but when I roused from the chair I glanced at my watch to see almost 45 minutes had passed. Remembering I'd promised my new partner breakfast, I looked around for her but saw nothing. I heard the water still running down the hall. I squinted, wondering if she was alright. I wouldn't have expected her to take so long when she clearly didn't feel comfortable in the house.

I pushed myself up and tiptoed down the hall. The door remained closed. I waited for about ten minutes, wandering around the kitchen looking for something easy to make. Still the water flowed. I walked to the bathroom door. I thought about asking if she was alright when I heard her. It may have been my imagination, but I think she was crying.

I stood there for another minute, considering what to do. "Adelaide, are you alright in there?" I decided to ask. She fell silent before asking me to leave her be. More than a little uncomfortable, I did as she asked.

Turned out Stevie did keep a gun around. Found it while looking for an extra towel for my own shower. It was high but poorly hidden in a linen closet. Just a little .325 hammerless pistol, much like the one I'd left behind at the duplex. I set it on the kitchen counter while I worked on breakfast. Ended up making eggs. There was a carton just ready to expire in the fridge—thought I'd do Stevie a favor and use them before they went bad.

Adelaide emerged from the hallway almost an hour and a half after she'd locked herself in the bathroom, dressed in the outfit I'd laid out for her. A casual shirt and slacks from Stevie's room. A towel draped her shoulders to keep the shirt dry. She looked a bit uncomfortable wearing it.

The shower had washed away her makeup and the stains on her cheeks but she—Cora, I suppose—was still every bit as beautiful as before. Adelaide tended to look down as if to contain Cora's naturally emotive face. I wondered if that particular body made her uncomfortable more than the act of possessing it. Perhaps Adelaide wasn't used to being beautiful.

I left her to the first batch of eggs and some toast while I went to take a shower. Before I left I turned on the TV in the living room for her. She stared, jaw agape, not touching her food. Her reaction to the screen lighting up reminded me how out of place she must have felt. Waking up in a different world couldn't have been easy.

I stayed with her for a moment, observing while she watched a news anchor reporting updates from the latest Middle Eastern conflict. She never asked a question, just stared incredulously. When a report came in about a repair being made to the international space station with footage from space, she raised both hands to her mouth.

Again she tried to stifle her tears. One escaped her control, sliding down her cheek. She knew I saw and tried to shake it off, rhythmically breathing. "I just... can't believe how much has changed..." she offered, seemingly annoyed at her cracking voice.

"Yeah," was all I thought to say at first. "So when you say you know everything Cora knew..."

"I never knew this," she whispered, leaning closer to the screen as the camera panned out to an astronaut floating above North America. I supposed her 'knowledge' of Cora was more limited that she'd let on, probably exclusive to the most prominent thoughts and feelings of her host.

I encouraged her to eat and left for the bathroom, not sure what else I could say. When I finished my considerably shorter shower and dressed in a gray suit Stevie had hanging on the wall from some movie (the only men's clothes in the damn house) I ambled back into the kitchen, glancing into the living room. The TV was still on but Adelaide had backed away from it. She hadn't eaten much. She sat on a couch inspecting the gun I'd found.

I considered asking for it but figured she wouldn't respond well to that. It appeared as though she knew how to handle it better than me from the way she unloaded Avery's piece into the duplex.

Turned out I was wrong.

Halfway into my own plate of eggs and toast I nearly fell off my stool when a gunshot fired off. I tore into the living room to find Adelaide holding the weapon, a smoking hole in the carpet beside her. She looked up with her face flush red, fumbling for words.

"The safety," she started. "It..." I cut her off when I marched at her, intent on ripping it from her hands and going into a tirade about blowing our cover. When I tried for the gun she tensed and reeled away.

"Give it to me," I ordered, again reaching for it. I got my hand on it but she violently grabbed my wrist and seized the weapon back in a nimble move I'd never seen. Suddenly the gun was pointed at my head. I froze, looking past the barrel to a look of disdain in her eyes.

"Never," she started, again holding back emotion, "come at me like that again." I slowly raised my hands defensively.

"Alright," I replied as calmly as I could. She swallowed hard before lowering the gun.

"I am not a child, Jon." I nodded.

"I get that. And I'm sorry. But just calm down, okay? I know you're in a new place and this is all a lot to take in all at once but—"

"Don't!" she nearly shouted this time. She was still red in the face, chewing over what she wanted to say. "You don't know anything about me. Do you understand that? You don't know what I have seen or done, and you don't know what it took to get here. I came here of my own free will. I don't want your sympathy and I don't want anyone to hold my hand."

I wanted to say something to appease her, but the look in her eyes brought out another question. "What do you want?"

"I want... I need you to trust me," she said.

"Okay. I trust you." She shook her head a little.

"And I want you to be honest with me." It was like she could see clear through me with those eyes.

"Fine. But you have to earn trust." She was quiet for a moment, then turned to set the pistol on the couch.

"I agree." She took her plate and walked back for the kitchen.

"Do you trust me?" I asked before she disappeared from view. I expected her to repeat a variation of my answer, but instead she said,

"I wouldn't be here if I didn't." If she'd said it any other way I would have asked for the same honesty she demanded of me, but somehow I could tell she meant it. I didn't know why. Whatever she thought she knew about me from Cora, she didn't really know anything more about Jon Perry than I knew about her.

She told me she was tired and needed a few hours' sleep. I pointed her to a bedroom then found one for myself. I still wasn't sure if all this was a dream or not.

Wondering about Adelaide's past brought out memories of my own. Which cued the nightmare. I knew it was coming before I fell asleep, but I was too tired to fend it off by staying awake.

It was always more or less the same. I could see the girls across the terminal. Pita spun around in her little pink dress, her birthday tiara already strapped on. As with everything, she'd decorated it with plastic jewels and glitter.

Gabby sat beside her on an uncomfortable bench, watching with a tired smile. Her hair was tied back into a loose ponytail. Our luggage was collected around her, ready to go. She never saw me coming, but Pita caught sight of me with the ice cream in my hands. The worst part was watching her face light up, knowing what was coming.

I've heard it said you can't dream sound, but if nothing else I felt the pulse of the explosion. Everything darkened and Pita's smile faded. Fire converged on her and she disappeared inside.

She was there again when I woke. Adelaide. Refreshed, fully alert. At first I was afraid she'd heard me screaming or groaning from the nightmare and rushed in to check on me. I hadn't woke to sweat or a racing heart so I doubted I'd made a scene this time. Turned out she'd just been waiting.

"Not for long," she said when I asked. "But I think we should get moving. I can feel the Horsemen."

"What do you mean?" I asked, pushing myself up from the guest bed I'd landed on hours prior. I swept a hand through my hair. "Do you know where they are?"

"No. I can only feel them when they are using their power, and even then I only have a brief sense of their general location. But I believe the Horsemen we displaced, possibly the other two as well, have possessed new bodies. I felt... flickers while I slept."

"Flickers, huh," I managed with what likely came across as annoyance. It wasn't much to go on, but her expression remained resolute.

"I know they are out there, likely killing more people. And there is something else. What I sensed was far away, at great distance to this city. They may have moved on. We've rested enough. We need to get out there and—"

"And what? Go gallivanting after them? I appreciate your determination, Ms. Martin, but if we're serious about doing this we're going to need a plan. Even if any of the Horsemen are still in the bodies we know about, we won't be able to get close to them. And they wouldn't just leave us at large. If a few of them have gone long distance they probably left at least one here waiting for us to resurface. We..."

I realized she was giving me a look meant to reiterate her point from that morning. Seeing as I'd accosted her, I leaned up and put my feet on the ground. "Sorry. Did you have an idea?"

"Yes, if you'd care to let me finish my thought," she stated with a passive aggressive finesse. I made a gesture giving her the floor. "Surely we can investigate the original hosts without being in their physical presence. We must discover why those particular bodies were chosen, what they have in common."

"You're sure they didn't just pick four random bodies?" I asked.

"Do you think that?"

"No. But I'm not sure that divine, semi-sentient constructs operate along the same lines of reason that I do."

"There must at least be a reason why they were all together in this city. We must find out everything we can about the men they possessed and what they stand to offer the Horsemen." I kept to myself that I'd already spent an exhaustive afternoon delving into the backgrounds of Avery, Connor and Rince without coming up with anything. Looking at them again with all this in mind may indeed turn up something new, I hoped.

I offered an alternate plan. "Alright, but we've got a hotter lead to check out before it goes cold."

"What lead?"

"Jessica Stillwater," I said, catching her by surprise. "That's the name of Avery's—Death's—first victim the night of February 4th. The one he staked out at the Colonial Building and threw into a dumpster. She has to be the 'incident' he reported to the others that afternoon on the phone. She saw something, what sounds like someone, to be precise, the Horsemen didn't want her to."

"Why would the Horsemen be protecting a person?" Adelaide asked, looking to the side.

"You're asking the wrong guy. But if we find out more about Stillwater, maybe we'll find out."

"But as long as we're alive, Stillwater, even dead, is a loose end," she observed. "So you think they'll be expecting us to go to this Colonial Building."

"You don't?"

"I don't believe they see us as important compared to their larger plans. If they did, they'd still be here in this city. There could be one left behind as you suggested, but I don't think so. In all the time I was watching them from the beyond, they were never separated across much distance."

"So you think we should risk it," I summarized.

"I think we should *plan* it. Carefully." As she asked me questions about the Colonial Building's layout and the likelihood of police being there, I found myself increasingly curious about this woman's past. She was out of place in this window of time, but she was a tactician. Interesting for the daughter of a cattle baron.

"As of yesterday, the police still haven't found her body," I answered at the end of her questions. "They'll be looking for us more than her, but I'm not worried about cops so much as I am Horsemen of the Apocalypse."

"That part we will have to risk." She reached around her waist to pull out the pistol I'd found. "To a certain degree."

"Are you alright?" she asked as we drove into South Central that afternoon. We'd borrowed one of Stevie's cars from the garage. I snapped out of my thoughts and glanced her way. She was staring at me.

"Do I look that out of it?"

"No, but... you look uncomfortable most of the time. Like you are someplace else." I wasn't sure what to say so I just shrugged. She pressed on. "Were you having a nightmare before you woke last?" This time I held her stare, but put on my sunglasses.

"I'm just hungry, is all."

"No you are not." It wasn't a guess or an assumption, she stated it like fact. I raised an eyebrow her way, to which she turned to look out the windshield. "I should tell you now before it gets you in trouble—I can always tell a lie from the truth."

"Wait, you mean like you have a talent for it? Or like it's an... angel thing?"

"It is part of who I am now, something common to angels and demons alike. Whether word is spoken, written, or otherwise expressed in any manner of art, we see through to the truth it was intended to convey or to hide."

"That's handy. Did God just think that would be a neat perk after you die?" Again I sounded more callous than I intended. It had been a long time since I'd carried on regular conversation with someone.

"I already told you—sensory perception is different in the next realm. I can only see emotions there, but I see them laid bare to the source that created them. If I could not, I could never have whispered to Cora. I was not expecting the ability to translate into this world when I took her body, but I've noticed I can always tell when you are lying."

I let out a bland sigh and rested my head against my fist propped on the window edge. "How comforting. Sounds an awful lot like a supernatural ability for someone who claims you have to conform to the rules of this world."

"I don't claim to understand it any more than you," she returned defensively. "I suppose certain traits of myself from the beyond are internalized to the point where they can carry over. That doesn't mean I can fly or make flowers grow by standing in the dirt. Being an angel doesn't make me a sorceress, or whatever you seem to think."

Again I sighed, rolling my eyes behind my glasses as we pulled onto Palms Boulevard in Mar Vista. "So do you have any other 'loop-hole' tricks up your sleeve you haven't told me about?" She folded her arms and told me there were none that she was aware of.

After a long moment she relaxed a bit. There was something on the tip of her tongue she was deciding whether or not to let out.

"What else?" I pressed. She frowned but decided to come clean.

"Before I fell asleep this morning I let my mind slip a little. I think I can still see back into heaven when I'm like that. To some degree, at least." I was silent for a moment, considering the implications while we pulled up to a spot within a few blocks of the Colonial Building. I parked in a similar location to the night I was staking out Avery.

"Really," I said, putting the car in park. "Can you show me?" Again she frowned.

"Why would I do that?"

"So you can?"

"No. I mean, I don't think so."

"Could you try?"

"Why?"

"Call it a final measure of proof." She looked at me hard, searching.

"I told you I can tell when you are lying. You want this for something else."

"What does it matter why? I just want to."

"I'm sorry, but no."

"You won't even try?"

"Even if I could, which I almost certainly cannot, it is not my place to show you something like that."

"Suddenly you're a strict conformist to the rules?" Her glare had some bite to it this time.

"This is not about a rule. No one should have sight into something like that before their time."

"You're assuming I'll ever see heaven at all."

"Still. And you do not have the senses necessary to perceive something like heaven. How many times must I say it—sight and sound don't exist there."

"If you can still perceive it the way you are now in 'earthly form,' what makes you think I couldn't?"

"Enough of this, you sound like a child. Even if you could perceive it, which you can't, I couldn't simply reach out and touch you to give you a window to another plane of existence. And even if I could do that, I wouldn't."

"You really don't like me, do you, Ms. Martin?" She prepared to say something but cut herself short, looking out her window away from me.

"Stop calling me that."

I learned about another angel ability shortly after.

We spent a few minutes in the car scanning the street, the complex and the surrounding area for anything unusual. The street was clear of cops or any potential Horsemen conspicuously standing around, so we got out of the car to conduct a further sweep on foot closer to the building.

I was considering climbing a fire escape to get a better view into the walled apartment complex from the third or fourth story when I heard Adelaide gasp. When I turned she was tensely pressed against a wall in the alley, staring with wide eyes around the corner. She grabbed my arm and pulled me after her before I could say anything.

"Across the street," she said in a needless whisper. I peered in the direction she stared, expecting to find Avery reanimated from her alarm. There was nothing immediately apparent. No cops, no one familiar. I almost asked her what I was supposed to see before I caught sight of a car parked in another alleyway, at least two men inside.

"The car?" I asked.

"Those men are possessed," Adelaide said.

"Horsemen?" She shook her head.

"Demons." My gaze shifted to her, incredulous.

"What? How do you know?"

"I know."

"So you can feel them? I thought you could only sense Horsemen when they're using their power."

"Yes, but I can also tell those men belong to demons. They are hiding in those bodies, Jon. I can see it."

"So is this another loop-hole or is it part of your truth detector power?" She completely tucked her head back and glared at me impatiently. "So they can tell you're an angel?" I continued.

"Only if they see me, I think."

"Did they?"

"If they did we would be running for our lives right now."

"They'll just attack angels on sight?"

"Think, Jon. They have to be working for the Horsemen."

"How is that even... Why? I thought the constructs were neutral. Why would demons be helping them?"

"I am not sure, but why else would they be just sitting there? And the two men who attacked you with Pestilence at your home were possessed by demons as well. I saw them."

"You're just telling me this now?"

"I did not think to before, I'm sorry." I made a show of sighing and risked another look across the street. They were likely Crips, judging from the blue dash cover. Like the ones from my house.

"Demons are possessing kids in gangs? Why?"

"Angry youth looking for dominance are more easily taken. It is not surprising."

"So what do we do? No way we're getting to the front of the Colonial without them seeing you." When I looked at her she only returned my gaze. I sighed and leaned against the wall, thinking.

The cops showed up about ten minutes after I made the call. Adelaide wasn't enthusiastic about the idea, but the enemy-of-my-enemy-is-my-friend approach was all I could come up with. I could get us around cops. I wasn't so sure about demons.

"There are two guys with guns on Veteran Ave and Palm Boulevard," I'd said into a nearby payphone with as much panic as I could drum up. "I think they were selling something out of their car, maybe drugs, I don't know. They're sitting in the car in an alley, but they look like they're about to... Oh my God, they're getting out! I have to—"

I hung up, slamming the phone to the hook. I'm sure I looked proud of myself afterwards, but my celestial compatriot looked at me disapprovingly, her arms folded. I ignored her and dashed back to the corner where she'd spotted them.

The bust couldn't have gone much better. The pair of possessors pulled away down the alley in a rush the moment they spotted the cops, who proceeded to give chase. When the demons knew they were caught in the alley they tore out of the car and ran, cops hot after them.

"Clear?" I asked Adelaide. She took a long moment sweeping her eyes along the road, through windows in nearby buildings, all the nooks and crannies.

"It looks that way, but there could be more anywhere. I don't like this."

"Just keep your hat low, this is the best shot we'll have."

"A hat will not hide me from demons." I told her to stay behind me.

We walked from the alley as casually as possible to the Colonial, hats and sunglasses hiding our faces as best they could. I'd wanted to change Adelaide's hair color that morning since it was fairly unmistakable to anyone who knew her, but she didn't want to take the time or make any changes to Cora's form. From her reaction I guessed she wanted to preserve the body as she'd found it, probably out of some misplaced guilt.

I was breathing heavily as we made the turn into the Colonial's parking lot, as anxious as Adelaide that a demon or Horsemen was waiting with a gun or a touch of death. No killing blow came as we made our way to the staircase up to the third floor where I'd seen Jessica Stillwater that night. The door was shut and locked but there was no police tape or any indication any party had been here since her death.

I knocked a few times, hoping she'd have a spouse or someone we could get information from, but there was no answer. I considered knocking on the doors of her neighbors to ask them a few questions when I spotted a security camera down the hallway. I led Adelaide back to the first level and the main office. There was no one at the desk but I heard someone moving in a back room so and poked my head around a corner.

"Hello?" I said just short of a shout.

"Yup, one second," a man's voice came from the back. I put my hands in my pockets and waited alongside Adelaide. She tapped her heel impatiently, still looking through windows for another threat. Eventually a portly man in a UCLA hoodie appeared, a hand towel thrown over his shoulder. "What can I do for you?"

"Hi. I'm hoping you could help us with something. My name's Jake Stillwater. This is my wife, Addie." I offered my hand but didn't take off my glasses. Enough daylight streamed through the window that I didn't think it would be rude—I didn't want him getting a good look at my face. Adelaide twitched at the introduction but offered her hand as well.

"Tony Reeves," he returned. "My family owns the Colonial. You wouldn't be related to Jessica, would you?"

"Distant cousin, actually," I lied. "We were coming by to see her yesterday but I've heard she's been reported as missing. We've been asking around but we're hoping you'd be able to tell us something." Tony let out a disturbed breath and shook his head.

"I'm sorry. Yeah Jess works for me and my dad, she's maintenance for the Colonial and another two buildings up the street. The police were by asking about her yesterday morning, they told me she's missing. Haven't seen her in two days now."

"Do you know if she'd been in any sort of trouble with anyone?" Adelaide asked. I tried not to look annoyed, wishing she'd let me handle the questions.

"No, nothing like that," Tony answered, surprised at the very notion. "Why, had she said something to you?"

"We're just worried, trying to get a sense for anything that may have happened," I interjected quickly to preclude another question from Addie Stillwater. "I noticed her car isn't here."

"So did I. I went back through security tape yesterday and she left with it the night before last. It hasn't come back."

"Did the police say if they'd found it when they were here?"

"No, but that was before I looked at the tape. I reported when she left once I saw it but they haven't contacted me about finding the car."

"I wonder if we could take a look at your tapes." Tony didn't answer right away, rubbing his whiskered chin.

"Well it's against policy unless you're a resident. I didn't see anything unusual though."

"Please," Adelaide said. I winced when she took off her sunglasses, showing Tony her eyes. They were remarkably sincere, a look I'm not sure Cora would have been capable of. "This may be the last time she was seen—I'd like to see for myself." Whether it was Addie's earnestness or Cora's beauty that convinced him, Tony nodded and told us to follow him into the back. We did, waiting while he sorted through a drawer of DVDs and pulled out one labeled *January 30 - February 4*.

He pulled up footage from two different cameras, one from the third floor and another in the parking lot that captured her pulling away for the last time. Like the night I'd seen her in person from a distance, I didn't notice anything unusual. I asked Tony if he knew where she was going but he had no idea, saying she often met friends a few nights a week for dinner or a movie.

I was taking down the names of some of her friends when Adelaide caught my attention. "Jake," she said, her voice tense. I looked up to find her staring at another screen playing a shot from the second floor camera. A man walked up the staircase then made his way down the hall. I wasn't sure how she made out his face so early but my eyes went wide with realization once he stopped in front of a door and let himself into an apartment.

"Can you freeze that image?" I said in a rush to Tony. He seemed confused, reminding me that the screen with Stillwater was the one above, but I insisted. The screen froze just before the man disappeared behind the door to an apartment.

"Do you know him?" Tony asked. I nodded, trying to not to grimace.

"His name is Brett Avery," I replied. "We know him. I'm not sure what he'd be doing here though, he lives in Brentwood. Do you know him?" Tony spun his chair, creaking under his weight.

"I thought his name was Kohler. But yeah, I see him on occasion. He's usually here about once a month to check in on his parents."

"His parents?" I shot Adelaide a glance. She subtly shook her head—she must have known from Cora that Brett's parents didn't live here. "Did he tell you that?"

"No, his folks did. The Kohlers. They've lived in that apartment for about two years now. Nice enough but they don't get out much. Their son is about their only visitor. But wait—what does this have to do with Jess?"

"Oh, nothing I'm sure, he just knows Jess as well." It might not have been a lie. "Did he ever visit Jess before?"

"I don't think so, I wasn't aware they knew each other. But I didn't even know she had a cousin, and we're fairly close."

"Maybe they met through the Kohlers," Adelaide offered. "I wonder if we could talk to them—maybe they'd know something about where Jess is." Tony shrugged, releasing a frustrated huff.

"You could try but I wouldn't get your hopes up. The Kohlers are nice enough if you talk to them but it practically takes a police warrant to make that happen. I spent the last week trying to get them to open up so Jess could get in there and fix their pipes. They've been dripping into the unit beneath them on the first floor."

"So Jess got in recently," I said.

"Yeah, the complaints from the tenant beneath them got so bad that Jess let herself in the day before last to see if she could just make the fix. They're contractually obligated to let us make repairs in their unit if a problem is affecting other units."

"The day before last," I repeated. "February 4th." Tony nodded.

"The day she disappeared. But you don't think—"

"No, but it would be great if we could talk to the Kohlers. They may have been the last people to see her in person, so they might have something to tell us that could help."

"Well, like I said, you can try knocking or even calling but don't expect much."

"Thanks for the heads up. We appreciate all the help, Tony. We'll let you know if we hear anything about Jess."

"Thanks, I'll do the same if I hear anything." He wouldn't, of course. Before Adelaide and I walked out of the office, giving him fake contact info, she turned back.

"Tony, have you actually seen the Kohlers?" she asked. "Been in their physical presence, I mean." Tony looked confused at the question but paused and thought about it, staring at the ceiling.

"Well, I'm sure my dad or someone else has, but... I don't think I've actually ever seen them. I've spoken to them through the door and on the phone a few times but that's about it."

There was no response when I knocked on the Kohlers' door. I tried saying we were with building management to follow up on the pipe repair, then had Adelaide try a line about their "son" as his wife to elicit a response. Nothing. I couldn't hear a sound from inside. I'd seen windows on the reverse side of the building during the drive in, but even at night someone would see if I tried to climb.

I'd had enough climbing lately anyway.

Instead I sent Adelaide back to the office to steal a key. As usual she didn't respond well to the immorality of my plan, but marched off to her objective nonetheless. I got the sense she had a fairly rigid moral code but one that she had often comprised for a greater good.

She was back with the key in 15 minutes, stolen straight off a master key ring while Tony was in the video room. I told her to ask for a copy of the security footage we'd looked at as well. He never would have surrendered it to me, but few men, myself included, could say no to Cora Avery's curves, whether Adelaide knew how to work them or not.

We waited by a car, pretending to make calls to the Stillwater family on my cell phone until Tony left the office and we were sure there was no one else inside. Once he was gone we hustled up to the second story and threw my hat over the camera lens.

I let Adelaide have the gun while I opened the door to the Kohlers' apartment. Figured she'd be quicker on the trigger if nothing else. We didn't say it but neither of us was sure what we'd find inside. If Stillwater had indeed been killed for having seen the mysterious Kohlers, they were likely as dangerous as the Horsemen. Possibly constructs or demons themselves.

Heart racing, I pushed the door open with my foot and ducked away. Adelaide swung inside to a corner with the gun extended. From her stance I could tell she'd done it before. There was no reaction, no sound. She pushed along a wall to the next room. I stayed farther behind her than would have been considered brave or even responsible. Eventually she came back into the apartment's main hallway, her frame relaxed and the gun pointed down.

"It's empty," she said. I shut the apartment door and leaned against it, letting out a long breath. I didn't say anything but ambled inside, carefully scanning over the living room. It couldn't have looked more typical. From the drape patterns and wooden frames bordering dated artwork on the sparse walls, it looked like the Kohlers were an older couple, if not elderly.

It was nothing if not tidy. A shawl on the back of the worn couch was perfectly folded and the dining room tabletop was wiped clean. I could smell cleaning spray on the air. "They were here recently," I noted.

"I thought they almost never left," Adelaide returned, gun still in both hands. I wandered into the single bedroom. The closet was open, but most of the hangers held no clothes. I checked the drawers. Empty but for a few stray socks and undershirts.

"They took off in a hurry. Probably to whatever distant place you felt the Horsemen at."

"Why would the Horsemen be protecting..." She trailed off, knowing I wouldn't have the answer.

"Just keep looking." It wasn't promising. No obvious clues around the apartment. Most of the couple's few possessions had been left behind, but there was nothing that betrayed anything about their identity. No mail. No files of any kind. No computer. No...

"No pictures," I observed aloud as I ran a finger along a windowsill. Not one of them, not one of family, not one of anyone.

"Maybe the Kohlers were a cover for the other Horsemen. Maybe they were living here, and now they've moved on after all this."

"Death said it was a 'she' who called him to tell him about Stillwater walking in. The Horsemen were all men."

"Well I can't believe they would be protecting anyone. Human or otherwise. It makes no sense."

"Maybe they aren't protecting. Maybe they're holding hostage." I heard Adelaide release a huff. She didn't buy it. We scoured over every inch of the little apartment for half an hour, keeping an eye out the front window for any sign of Tony or a neighbor suspicious of the blocked camera.

Adelaide plopped herself on the floor in front of their book cabinet, reading over the spines of a few novels in the meager collection. I went through cabinets in the kitchen, beginning to believe there was nothing to turn up. Frustrated, I opened the fridge and took out a half gallon of milk. I went to the living room and sat on the couch. Adelaide frowned as I took a gulp from the carton.

"Nothing?" she asked.

"Not unless there's a clue at the bottom of this carton." She sighed and turned her attention back to the books. She plucked one she'd had her finger on for a while, a green hardcover missing its dust jacket. She looked intent.

"What is it?" She rose, both book and gun in hand.

"Nothing. It looks as though we missed whoever was really here. Do you think they may come back?"

"No. Whether the Kohlers are dignitaries, hostages or made up, if they're important the Horsemen will have cleared them out for good." Again she sighed. She turned for the hallway to the bedroom.

"Put the milk back. I want to check one last time." I rolled my eyes and lumbered back to the kitchen. I knew she wouldn't find anything, but seeing as we came up short on a lead I didn't see the rush in leaving.

I went to the window to check the office again. I thought about going down to see if anything was in the Kohlers' mailbox when I noticed something outside. The doormat was turned upside down. Opening the front door, I turned it over, hoping to find a key or something.

Instead I found my address.

It was written at the top of a letter marked to "The Loyal" on the reverse side, typewritten and folded in half under the rug. "Addie!" I yelled as I walked back into the apartment. She rushed into the room with the gun raised. "We need to go."

six

2301 Estercott Road, #2
Los Angeles, CA 90049

February 5

Dear Loyal Friends,

We have decided to move to a safer neighborhood. We will
send word when we are settled. We hope you will continue
to do your part in making your neighborhood safer for future
residents by taking a stand against dangerous individuals
as you have capacity to do so. Please watch over our
former home here while we are away for any intruders, and
share this letter for any other of our friends curious to know.

Sincerely,
The Kohlers

I showed Adelaide the hit letter once we were back in the car. She was still picking it apart after we arrived at Stevie's house.

"It means they are not as well organized as we first believed, at least," she concluded in the living room after another long silence studying every word.

"Because they have to hide the specifics?" I asked from the kitchen. I was frying up frozen potatoes and vegetables in a skillet. I didn't feel guilty for breaking into Stevie's food, but I did about the Jack Daniels I'd been nursing since we got back.

Sorry, Stevie. I need it more than you.

"They printed your address, Jon. I'd say it's pretty specific. I'm talking about the delivery system. Leaving one note under a rug is hardly targeted."

"You were expecting a bunch of demon possessors to have a phone tree set up?" I could tell by her grunt the reference was lost on her. She appeared around the corner, letter in hand.

"We have agreed this undertaking of the Horsemen's is not some random excursion into the mortal realm, have we not?"

"Sure," I said, stirring the pan as I added more oil.

"Whatever is going on here has to be coordinated. Brett Avery maintained a daily schedule reporting on the Kohlers to the other three Horsemen—he checked on them in person at least monthly. The Horsemen were conducting secret meetings. They obviously had a contingency for safeguarding their secret in the event they were discovered or they would not be on the other side of the country. They—"

"You don't have to sell me, Addie. I get that it's coordinated." I'd been calling her by her abbreviated name since our trip to the Colonial. I'm not sure she enjoyed it, but it was easier to get out and she hadn't told me to stop yet.

"Then if they've put this much structure into whatever they are doing, why are they leaving notes under doormats to their confederates? The technology they have access to in this time is staggering. With a few buttons on their computer phones they could reach anyone. It means as organized as the Horsemen are, for some reason they are not in regard to the demons involved in this."

"To think, demons wouldn't be good team players," I said. Addie shifted her weight between feet.

"I could use your deductive skills far more than your flippancy. This is a serious matter. Perhaps the most serious matter of all time, and you're standing there *drinking*." The disgust she placed on that last word reminded me how different a time and culture she'd come from.

I bit my tongue and set my glass down until she left the room. "Sorry. Why?"

"Why what?"

"Why do you think there's such shitty communication between the Horsemen and demons working for them?" Again she shook her head, continuously aggravated with my manners, I'm sure.

"I can't say. Perhaps the Kohlers wrote that letter and they were coordinating with demons without the knowledge of the Horsemen, but I find that unlikely. It's more likely the Horsemen couldn't talk to the demons helping them because they didn't know who they were."

"How would that work?"

"It could be there is a high rate of turnover, to put it indelicately. Whoever these demons are taking orders from, they seem to be regularly placed in dangerous situations. You and I killed at least one at your home, the others from today may have been detained by the police. They are likely expendable in the larger picture."

"So other demons are possessing more people to fill the vacancies?"

"More likely what demons remain to serve the Horsemen are recruiting others possessing bodies into service. I'm not sure, but I find it strange that this lot seems to be so disorganized."

"Well it was sure as hell organized enough," I commented as I dumped some of the stir-fry onto a plate. "There was at least one car of demons waiting for us. Who knows how many more saw the letter before we took it. They could be waiting at my house for us to come back. I'm still just wondering why demons would be helping the

Horsemen."

"We'll have to figure out what the Horsemen are actually doing before we can answer that," Addie said. She seemed surprised when I put the plate in front of her then went back for my own. She sniffed it. "Thank you."

"So what do we do now?" I continued. "We know the Horsemen are safeguarding someone or something that may or may not be an elderly couple, and they've shipped them somewhere far away from Los Angeles. Do we wait for them to use their power again so you can get a lead on their location?"

"I am not a human compass," she said, "and even if I were, we cannot afford to just sit here waiting for them to make another move. We are not safe here, and the world—not just this one—is not safe while the Horsemen are free to enact whatever they have set in motion."

"Well unless you found another clue at the apartment you haven't told me about, we're about fresh out of leads," I reminded her. "I'll keep looking for links between the people the Horsemen possessed and see if I can dig up anything else about the Kohlers, but if they've never even been *seen* by their landlord, I doubt the Horsemen will have left much of a paper trail on them. Their first names weren't even listed on their lease for christsake."

I'd stepped back into the office of the Colonial Building before we left, looking for anything at all on the Kohlers. Found nothing. Addie clearly wasn't satisfied with my defeatist attitude, but she kept silent. She was as fresh out of ideas as I was.

After dinner I tried to set up Stevie's computer to conduct some new research into the Horsemen and the Kohlers. I'm sure she had a laptop with her but all I could find was an old desktop. I got it running fairly quickly but syncing the damn thing to the wireless network was beyond me.

Outside her domain of expertise, Addie just sat there as frustrated as I'd seen her. Not with me (I don't think) but at our current lack of options. I supposed I'd be pissed too if I'd died and made it to heaven, then been forced to possess someone to stop an apocalyptic plot nobody else, God included, seemed to give a shit about. It wouldn't help my mood to be cooped up watching some asshole I didn't trust fiddling with technology beyond anything I'd ever thought possible.

She'd taken a short walk in the backyard to avoid cabin fever. Even in the dark she didn't want to risk walking around on the street. The darkness wouldn't hide her from another possessor. She settled onto a couch on the other side of the living room with a book. She'd taken it from the Kohlers' apartment.

She eyed the TV before sitting down but obviously decided against turning it on. Curious though she'd been taking in all the new developments in the world since she'd left it, I don't think she cared to learn about much more. My guess was she felt as uncomfortable being here, in this time, as she did being stuck inside a body not her own.

It was the way she moved. Always tense, guarded, but mindful of the way in which she directed her physical form to do anything. She was defensive and careful with the body the way a normal person would be careful driving a friend's car with both hands on the wheel. I could read the guilt in her eyes for what she'd done to Cora Avery.

I found my eyes on her more than the computer screen after a while, still trying to account for the fact I was sitting in a room with an angel. Imagining the world she'd come from, questions from our earlier conversation fought their way back to the tip of my tongue.

"How do angels... interact with each other?" I asked. "In heaven, I mean." She looked up from the couch, confused.

"What do you mean?"

"I get that heaven is too abstract for me to wrap my mind around, but just generally speaking, how does it work from a relationship standpoint? Are loved ones still together or do your connections from this world not matter up there?" Addie closed her book and set it in her lap.

"I'm not sure how to answer that. For most in the beyond, relationships from this world are the most important thing they have. Loved ones find each other immediately there, but... well, you're thinking about it in a way that doesn't apply.

"Souls are together, yes, but not in a physical sense where they can embrace or talk. They... cluster, you might say. Meld against each other. They spend most of their time reminiscing over memories from their corporeal lives. It's easier with another soul to reflect with. Heaven is a great deal of thinking. Remembering. It is nice, but not very productive."

"I wouldn't think many people who have died would be concerned with productivity," I observed. She didn't say anything, for a moment, waiting to see if I'd add to my inquiry.

"You have loved ones there, then?" I took a drink of the Jack Daniels in the glass I'd been hiding behind the computer tower.

"Yes."

"And that is why you want me to show you."

"I need you to try." Her sigh wasn't born from frustration this time, only regret.

"Jon, I am sorry I put the idea in your head, but it is not possible."

"You're saying you won't, not that you can't."

"Both are true."

"How do you know unless you try? You don't know for sure that you can't, do you?" She leaned forward, fumbling for words.

"I'm not even sure what I can still see in this form, and for you... Expecting you could comprehend a view into heaven in any way is like expecting an infant to understand algebra. You don't possess the capacity."

"I need you to try."

"And how should I do that, Jon? Do I have a special psychic power because I'm an angel? If I do you clearly know more about it than I do."

"I saw your eyes in the car. You thought it might be possible. If only just for a second. *I need you to try.*"

"I understand you want to see a loved one, Jon, but—"

"Don't tell me you understand. You don't." I was unnecessarily bitter, but she snapped right back.

"And neither do you! You are asking me to do something *I don't want to do*. Not because God said so, not because I am some biddy who enjoys seeing you suffer, but because doing so is wrong in a way you can't comprehend. Knowing that your loved one is safe and in a better place is what faith is for."

"Just because I know heaven is up there doesn't mean I have faith in it," I barked. "Spare me the pious bullshit, you don't buy it any more than I do. I need to see it—feel it—for myself. I need you to show me. Otherwise you can..." When I trailed off her expression turned fiery.

"What? I can find my own damn Horsemen?" I looked away and took another drink. She shook her head in disgust and rose, stomping across the room. She paused when she came to the table, her eyes locked onto mine.

"Let's get something straight," she growled. "I didn't pass through death and back, when all the rest of heaven wouldn't lift a finger, to come here and have some alcoholic misanthropist whose life I saved dangle his help over my head. If you want to help me, fine. If not, I'll get my things."

"You're the only one holding something over someone's head, Miss Angel, and I've already risked my life plenty for your little crusade, thank you. I may not have much to live for but I need this shit like a hole in the head, so I'll ask you not to take it out on me that you couldn't enjoy heaven enough to stay there instead of stepping back into this dump."

Like my interview with Jerrod Owens, I didn't realize my filter had slipped until after I'd said something I regretted. Addie tried to maintain her anger but I saw I'd touched a nerve to an emotion far more painful. She swallowed hard and leaned back.

"Fuck you, Jon." When she started for the front door I stood but I wasn't sure what to say.

"Addie, wait," I tried. She didn't slow down. "Look I'm sorry, okay? I didn't..." She opened the door and marched outside into the night. Cursing myself, I shot after her. "Will you please wait? Where do you think you're go–" When I put my hand on her shoulder she took hold of my arm and pulled me over her, literally off my feet. I was on my back in the grass before I knew what hit me.

"Away from you," she said, her voice taut with emotion, then continued away. I was slow to lean up, my back killing me and the breath knocked from my chest. She was almost to the front gate before I found my voice.

"I just want to know that my daughter's okay." I wasn't even sure she'd heard me, but her footsteps halted. She turned back for me. I could barely make out her face in the darkness but her expression remained hard.

"What happened to her?" she asked. I took a long breath and sat up.

"She was taken from me. And my wife." Addie stayed silent, her expression conflicted. While she decided whether or not to keep walking I tried a final plea. "Don't go, Addie. I know I'm an asshole, but... I'm the only asshole you've got. I owe you, and I *want* to help you. Either way."

Still she stared, unmoving. "Am I telling the truth?" I asked.

She looked away for a moment, but eventually came back to me and extended a hand. "Yes. You are an asshole."

She sat me on the couch and pulled a chair in front of it for herself. We both spent an awkward minute or two "clearing our minds." I was probably more anxious afterwards, but it did wonders for her. It was the first time I'd seen her truly relaxed.

With eyes closed and a deep breath, she reached out with her eyes closed and put her hands on my shoulders. She told me that touching me probably wouldn't do anything, but it couldn't hurt. She told me to calm down. At first I wondered if she could sense my mind aflutter, then I realized she could just feel my heart beat.

I waited for a few minutes, just concentrating on breathing like she instructed. I snuck a peek at her at one point. She looked peaceful, almost asleep. It ended with a sharp breath and a shake of her head. "I think I can still feel some sort of connection with heaven, but I have no idea how I could transfer it to you. I'm sorry." I swallowed hard. I'd be lying to say I hadn't gotten my hopes up, but I was used to disappointment.

"Thanks for trying. I mean that." She nodded, put her hands back on her lap and looked off into space. "Do you... have any way to tell if they're there? If they're at peace?" She spent a moment searching for words.

"If I was there, and I knew who I was searching for, I suppose I could find them. But like this? I'd be lying if I said yes."

"With however many billion souls are there I guess it's a tall order," I said, lazily leaning back into the couch.

"Not really. For as many as there are, I know all of them. Not by name or even in a context of identity, but I know them. I just don't have a way to discern which of them are the ones you're looking for. Not from this world, anyway."

I nodded again, lost in thought. Addie scooted her chair away and took a seat on the other side of the couch. She reached for her book on the nightstand and rested it on her leg. She liked holding it. I think it meant something that she had something familiar to her time to call her own.

"Can I ask how you lost them?" she asked, gently.

"I..."

"It's alright, you do not need to tell me."

"It's not that I don't want you to know, I just... don't like talking about it." I looked down to see I'd made fists. She had noticed. "But... they were taken from me. I know why and I know who took them, I just don't know why he decided to punish the innocent to get to the guilty."

"Because his justice isn't justice. At least not to the people who get caught in its crossfire."

"Of all the surprises you've given me about the afterlife, the one that still has me most confused is how an angel gets to resent God."

"What's confusing? I had to live in this world before I made it to the next." She smiled a sad smile. "Cheer up, Jon. Of all the angels in heaven, you met the one who's as much a doubter as you." As curious as I was to ask who she had been, I wasn't in a position to ask for anything after I'd clammed up about Gabby and Pita. Still, I watched her eyes glaze over as her memories came to bear. I guess she decided to trust me.

"I was born on a ranch in the Northern Territory. Dry Downs. My father had worked it up from nothing after coming from England as a lad. Reginald Martin. He wanted to be known for quality, not quantity, so he invested in the best drovers and the best cattle and stayed independent. It made for good sales at the docks in Darwin.

"Reginald was a great businessman, just not a great father. I don't really blame him. He needed a son, not a daughter, but mother died of the typhus when I was a baby before she could give him one. He didn't know much about children, certainly nothing about girls. I tried my best at being a boy when I grew up. I could ride faster than most of the drovers by the time I was ten. I was light. I loved it.

"By my adolescence Dry Downs had made enough of a profit that my father could entrust the operation at the ranch to his men. He set up offices in Darwin to handle new sales, deals with the larger ranches through his land, picks of the stock. He brought me with him, thinking a lady should be in the city attending parties and wearing dresses instead of getting dusty on horseback through the bush.

"I'd loved the life I had. I didn't know how to fit in at the events father dragged me to any more than most of the drovers who'd raised me. I tried to run away when he arranged for me to marry the son of a rival rancher. It was a business decision first and foremost, but I'm sure he thought it would make me happy.

"I hated him—my husband—almost as much as I hated the city. Clarence Fletcher. His cows had more gusto than him. He brought me out when he needed me on his arm at events and expected me to stay at the estate the rest of the time. Father never minded me riding but Clarence found it... unbefitting.

"Eventually the Fletchers betrayed my father and bought out Dry Downs from under him once they controlled all the surrounding land. I thought about killing Clarence and running back to the bush forever, but my life turned upside down again when the war touched us for the first time.

"As caught up as I'd been in my own life, I was shocked when the Japanese dropped the first bombs on Darwin. They killed Clarence before I could. I think my father survived since he was out of the city seeing to the sale of Dry Downs, but I never saw him again.

"I spent 1942 tending to victims, mainly the children. Many of them were aboriginal—they had no one. I'd been teaching them to ride to keep their minds off things when the raids got worse. I was going to lead them further inland but the Japanese came ashore after a raid one night. I tried to get us out on a boat but..."

She paused for a moment, looking away and raising a hand to her mouth.

"With the children gone I didn't have anything left. Faith least of all. I died bitter and angry in the Philippines a few months later, riding messages between rebel leadership. I always knew how to take care of myself, but even with military training I was no spy. I was caught my third time out with a letter. It was an inglorious end. I don't remember much of it, but then I was in heaven."

Her contempt was palpable. She smiled darkly. "The funny part is, I died not believing in God. Having cursed him with everything I had that night on the beach in Darwin with a lifeless 40 pound body in my arms. But somehow, here I am, an angel." She shook her head, still smiling as she looked at me for the first time since she'd started. "Does that make any sense to you?"

I wasn't sure what I could possibly say. My mouth was dry.

"I guess he figured you earned it anyway," I offered. She nodded and ran her finger over the spine of her book.

"God works in mysterious ways. Mysterious ways..." Mysterious here having the meaning of unjustifiable. She couldn't have been more clear if she'd said it that way. While I searched for words in the silence, she finally rose, stretching her legs. "I am very tired. I think I will go to bed."

"Okay." She nodded and started for the hallway. "Addie," I said before she turned the corner. She turned back, waiting. As vulnerable as I'd seen her. Whatever I thought had been a good idea to say deserted me. "Good night."

"Good night." When I heard the bedroom door close I took a long breath and got up to keep working on the wireless network.

I was waiting for her in the kitchen the next morning. She walked in fully clothed with a blanket around her shoulders, surprised to see me milling about at the pace I was. She probably heard the coffee brewing or smelled the bacon. (Thank you, Stevie.)

Her cheeks were red when our eyes met but I tried to keep moving to avoid what I'd correctly assumed would be an awkward encounter after the previous night. "Hey," I called while pouring us coffee. "Rustled some grub, or whatever a cowgirl-drover would say." I'd been working on that line most of the morning, but as predicted it fell flat.

"Thank you," she said, clearing her throat. "Good morning." I beckoned her to the table where I'd left her food and asked how she liked her coffee. She asked for a little sugar and watched in silence while I poured it. Her frown returned when I tilted the contents of my flask into my mug.

I tried to smile. "I *am* an alcoholic, actually. I'll start cutting back, but I'm afraid if I stop all at once the cumulative hangover would kill me." She stared at me blankly for a moment.

"Is that a joke?"

"Yes. Just trying to add some levity. How am I doing?" She remained still for another moment but told me I needed practice. I'm pretty sure I caught the beginning of a smile on the corner of her lips as she turned to her plate, though.

I joined her at the table and lay the stack of papers I'd printed in front of her. I could have just showed her on the computer but I figured she'd be more comfortable reading from the page. "What is this?" she asked.

"I got the computer working after you went to bed, thought you'd like to see this. You were right as rain about the Horsemen taking care to cover their tracks." I pointed to the headline on the first page but read from the lead I'd memorized. "California Senator and GOP Vice Presidential hopeful Bruce Connor was found dead in his home the morning of February 5. The cause of death was not immediately apparent."

I took a bite of my toast with one hand and flipped to the second page in Addie's stack with my opposite hand. "LA gang kingpin Delroy "Rince" Rizwan found shot dead in South Central after apparent gang execution."

"They've moved to new bodies," Addie said, ignoring her food to read the details. I encouraged her to eat while her eggs were hot.

"I don't suppose you caught any 'flickers' off that," I asked.

"I... do not think so. I do not expect I can sense possessions. There are likely several every day."

"It wasn't Death who iced them though, huh? You'd have felt that."

"Probably, but I am not even certain Death could kill a body inhabited by a Horseman." She sank in her chair, a dejected expression on her face. "So now all of them are in new bodies somewhere else."

"Looks that way. I spent the night trying to match the original four to each other some way. I have pieces of half-baked theories, but nothing that makes any real sense."

"Pieces?" she asked. I shrugged.

"This is going way out on a limb, but all four of our boys have a different power, so to speak, right? What if those four hosts were in the best position to execute a particular power? Avery would have allowed Death access to plenty of places normal folks couldn't go. Pestilence is breathing disease, so I'm sure it would look less strange for a panhandler to be surrounded by grime and decay than some suit.

"Speaking of which, Connor was a member of the Senate Foreign Relations Committee. I'm not sure what power War would have, but that seems like the place to exert it. Famine, or whoever that last one is, would probably have some beneficial correlation to Rince. It's thin, but it's about all I've got."

Addie chewed on my theory along with her eggs for a moment before pointing her fork at me. "You do your best work in the morning, don't you?" I smiled, which may have been the first time I'd done that from genuine contentment in a long time.

"I am a journalist, after all." Addie spent another few moments reviewing the details of the articles before pushing them aside and asking me what we should do now. "Well, given that we have no idea where or who the Horsemen are after yesterday's change of the guard—and the Kohlers might as well be ghosts from how little I could find on them—I'd say we're going to have to make our own lead. I think I found it, though."

She stared at me, waiting, but I gestured at her plate with my fork. "Finish eating first, no one likes cold eggs." She blinked, clearly surprised. Again she tried hiding her smile, but it broke through after she took another bite.

seven

"P-p... pahleee..." Wells' grip was too tight around Christopher Lamont's neck for him to get the word out. Lamont's initial shock, then the fury, from the attack had long since passed as he fought for breath. Now there was only terror. Certainty, as he collapsed to his knees on the thin carpet.

He was going to die.

And his superior, a colleague of 20 years and dear friend, was going to kill him.

Both men had been with the Bureau most of their lives. They survived Iraq together as youth, "retired" to the Bureau shortly after, worked God knew how many cases over the decades. Wells had been appointed Director a few weeks ago by the President at the advice of several senators, among them old war buddies Carl Obregon and Bruce Connor.

When Wells stopped in at Sacramento a few nights after his confirmation to pay a visit to Lamont, still Deputy Director of investigations along the West Coast, Lamont hadn't anticipated it would end like this. One moment Wells was pouring the scotch, the next his hand was around Lamont's neck like a vice.

Lamont's grip failed after another moment. His neck was numb under Wells' grip. Saliva dripped from his lower lip while his sight darkened. Even in Iraq when they'd been pinned along the ridge, he'd never been this afraid.

In what would have been his final moments, Lamont heard it again.

"*I can save you,*" the voice sounded from someplace deep and away. They weren't those exact words, but Lamont knew what they meant. He'd been disturbed by hallucinations of something following him, always on his shoulder, for days now. In his dreams, in the morning briefings, hugging his wife, everywhere. Every moment of complacency.

Urges came and went, most of which he hadn't experienced since war or before. Violent. Sexual. Furious. Lamont had never been a patient man. He assumed it was what prompted Obregon and Connor to recommend Wells for the Director's job instead of him. It hadn't bothered him in the least at the time, but now as his life slipped away, it was infuriating.

Everything was an injustice. Suddenly it was clear. Wells had always been there, one step ahead, outdoing him, taking the glory for both of their accomplishments. Now here he was, taking what little Lamont had left. "*I can make him pay,*" the voice continued, ebbing in his mind like a gentle lapping wave.

Filled with violence, driven not only to survive but to take his vengeance, Lamont agreed. He felt the burning power behind the voice's words and reached out for it, grasping it with shaking fists. He was suddenly more. Reinvigorated. Focused.

Preparing to rise with his newfound strength and crush his attacker, Lamont felt himself falling. Within himself, as control of the power shifted. Like all of them, he realized he'd been deceived too late, and Christopher Lamont faded into the depths of his own body while another took control.

Seeing the shift take place from the pulses of Lamont's body, Wells released his iron grip and stepped back. Lamont took a long breath, running a finger along his collar. He rose immediately, readjusting his tie. "I am sorry, Christopher, but this takes priority," he murmured, shifting focus from the vengeful thoughts erupting from the back of their shared mind.

"Carnegie," said Wells. The man that had been Lamont narrowed his eyes.

"War," Carnegie observed. "Appropriate. Where are they now?"

"The hopeful or the troublemakers?" War asked.

"Both."

"The hopeful are safe in a new city. Death is with them. The troublemakers have eluded us for the moment." Carnegie gritted his teeth but took a long breath, finding his poise.

"That's why we took these particular bodies. Do you have the information?" War pointed to the table they'd been pouring the scotch from. Carnegie flipped open a folder to the first picture. He spent a moment studying it, then the sheet it was clipped to. "Jonathan Perez."

Carnegie raised a hand without looking back. "Return to your work. I will see to this." Without any acknowledgement, the Horseman turned for the door and walked into the hallway. Wells' security detail tensed as they grouped with him into the elevator. They'd been easily agitated recently.

Carnegie spent 20 minutes reviewing the file and both the individuals within, then reached for the phone on his desk. "This is Deputy Director Lamont. Assemble the taskforce, we have a new priority."

Addie was decidedly less pleased when I got around to telling her my idea. We debated it after breakfast but eventually she folded and climbed in the car with me for our road trip. I offered to let her drive but she politely declined, saying she'd like to watch me do it and get a better feel for the modern technology.

"This is hardly a Darwin street buggy," she'd said of Stevie's BMW when I opened it up on the freeway. I didn't suppose a lifelong cowgirl would have an affinity for driving, but she agreed that she should learn in case the need arose. I think she just liked that I asked her.

She sat silently in the passenger seat for a while, her legs tucked up on the seat with her shoes off. Apparently over her guilt of taking from Stevie, she'd selected another outfit at the house to her liking: a striped long sleeve shirt and formfitting black jeans with a crème leather jacket and a charcoal scarf.

I'd caught her flipping through a magazine after breakfast—I'm sure she cobbled it together based on something she'd seen in there since she asked me if she blended in. Between the shimmering blonde tresses, her curves and that Hollywood face, it didn't matter much what she wore—she would never blend with that body.

I gave her the answer she wanted but immediately regretted it, recalling from the look she gave me her ability to discern lies from truth. "Well it looks good either way," was my follow up, hoping the truth in that statement would make up for the previous one.

I think she was somewhere between embarrassed and fascinated with suddenly being so pretty. She constantly did double takes into any reflective surface, often blushing when she did. She never told me her own body hadn't been attractive, but I could tell being *this* attractive was a new experience for her.

In the end I don't think she much cared how she looked, focused on her task at hand. She must have read over the new material I'd printed for her a dozen times in the car. Her doubts about my plan persisted the more she read into it.

"This man sounds more mentally disturbed than insightful," she said with another shake of her head.

"Well if you'd told me a few days ago that I'd be working with an angel to track down the Horsemen of the Apocalypse—"

"There is nothing here at all to substantiate his claims."

"That's probably because he's claiming he's passed notes back and forth between angels in this world and heaven. Doubt we're going to dig up much in the way of proof on that."

"And yet you remain set on driving hours to see this man? A disgraced, excommunicated Vatican priest who writes his delusions in a..."

"Blog," I finished for her. "It's like a journal you put on the internet." She understood the basic concept of the net from Cora, but I still wasn't sure she grasped the difference between it and TV. "And delusional though he may be, his name is known around occult circles. He's only a few hours away in San Jose. Maybe he's on to something. Sounds right up our alley, at least."

"The occult," Addie repeated with a disgruntled huff. She tossed the printouts to the middle seat and folded her arms. "You are likely the only living person who knows the truth about the afterlife—that it's random at best. Anyone knowledgeable about the 'occult' knows exactly nothing about angels and demons. About God. All the little rites, the superstitions, are a waste of time. Mythology, nothing more."

"This guy was a Catholic priest most of his life," I pointed out.

"Priests are no different. Worse, even. Pretending to understand the will of God. Making up rules about how to worship, how people can get into heaven by saying the right prayers however many times, moving their hands in a pattern over their chest and eating a cracker with a sip of wine. I spat at those things in my last years and here I am. But what about all the people I knew who did all those things? Who honestly believed them with all their hearts, and weren't allowed in?"

She had worked herself up again, shaking on the seat. Her focused stare into space told me there was something else on her mind.

"If you're looking for someone to blame, I think you're going after the wrong person." She was silent for a moment, turning for her window to watch the desert as we sped by.

"I'm just saying it's a waste of time worrying about some pointless ritual. Some people get in, and some people don't. It's a broken system. The fact that I was there, in heaven, and am now back here at the cost of Cora Avery's freedom is proof of that. No one, living or dead, understands the will of God."

I kept my eyes on the road but I caught her reaching to her face from the corner of my eye. I assumed the emotion was around her own circumstance before she said it.

"They were innocent, Jon," she said. "So many of them who died that night. The children were innocent." She turned to me, already aware I'd seen her tears. "They weren't there. Why... why would he let me in but not them?"

I could scarcely believe that. I knew better than most how full of shit the Almighty and his little plan was, but I couldn't imagine children being denied entrance to heaven. I tried to think of some logical alternative, even an illogical one. A separate afterlife for the young. Maybe they had been there and Addie just hadn't encountered them. No, that was all impossible from what she'd told me.

"I don't know," was all I managed. She looked away slowly, fiddling with the frills of the scarf around her neck. I couldn't remember feeling that depressed about the state of existence before. It's never reassuring to believe in an all-powerful God at the helm just throwing the chips and letting them fall where they may.

Still, I knew dwelling on it would only get us angrier, more depressed, so I tried to focus. "So are you on board for this or not?" I asked, reaching for the paper she'd left between us. She took a heavy breath but accepted the stack when I offered it to her.

"I'm not sure where else we would go," she returned. "I'm sorry, Jon. I didn't intend to be so negative. I know you are just trying to help."

"I'm as skeptical as you. But if nothing else I'm curious. Crazy or not, maybe this will mean something to our guy." I tapped the top of the stack of papers where I'd left the letter. The reverse side where someone had written out "The Loyal" was showing. Addie just nodded.

"Maybe."

We ate at a greasy roadhouse burger joint along the freeway that afternoon. We hadn't talked much in a few hours. I was curious to ask her questions about her past in both worlds, but I felt guilty and cut myself off before I opened my mouth.

As strong willed as Addie was, it was understandable when emotions came up after all she'd been through. I wasn't sure how one emoted in heaven (another question I had lined up) but I imagined this might have been the first time she'd ever confided her past in someone. It wasn't easy sorting through so much pain, so much injustice, that she was powerless to correct.

I knew from firsthand experience.

Still, my questions about the afterlife built up over the hours on the road to the point where I couldn't contain them anymore. It was selfish, but I had to know. "Were you ever happy there?" Addie was in the middle of a bite in her cheeseburger. She looked at me but kept chewing. She didn't answer right away, leaning down to take another sip from her straw.

"Up there?" she asked almost facetiously. I nodded. She shrugged, looking out the window of the diner to the dusty road. "I don't really know. It's certainly nice enough. It must sound listless from the way I've described it, just existing intangibly with thoughts and memories. It's more than that, I just don't have the words to describe it properly. It seems to be enough for most people who have souls to share their thoughts with."

"But not enough for you."

"Maybe it was because I did not have anyone to share things with the way most do. I don't know."

"I'm sorry for asking." She looked back at me.

"Do not be. You are just wondering about your family." I didn't do anything for a moment, but eventually went back to my burger. She kept her gaze on me while I dunked some fries in ketchup. "I wouldn't worry about them, Jon. Everyone else makes it work. I think something is just wrong with me."

"Or something is wrong with the place. How could it be heaven if you weren't happy there?" She probably knew I was hoping for more despite my guilt of pressing her.

"To me heaven is like a vacation I never asked for when I would have rather been at home working. At first I was surprised at the way it was. Everybody is. But most people settle in quickly. I took longer, angry about how many people weren't there who should have been.

"I spent a lot of time trying to make sense of it all. It only frustrated me, isolated me, more from the others. So I did more and more watching of the world I left behind. Listening. Whispering. That was how I found Cora."

"Were you looking for a way out before Cora?" She leaned back in her seat, setting the few remaining bites of her burger aside.

"I thought about it." The guilt was heavy on her words. "Of leaving just to leave. I told myself it would be for the greater good—to help someone when they needed it like Cora—but most of the time I just wanted out. Even if only for a short while. I thought I could be happy in heaven if I tried, but... sometimes I wonder if I will ever be happy anywhere."

She looked back out the window, her sad smile returned. "Some angel I turned out to be." Again I wasn't sure what to say, and I regretted opening my mouth to begin with.

We pulled into San Jose late in the afternoon. I made Addie drive the rest of the way to put her mind on something productive. A half-assed way to atone for making her feel like shit in the first place, but it was all I could come up with.

The ex-priest's name was Carmine Romano. I came across his name somewhere between researching Revelations for more information about the Horsemen and conspiracy websites about angel sightings. Links to his webpage were caked on most of the latter.

Apparently he talked to angels about demons.

He'd been something of a renaissance man at the Vatican—a

devout priest but a famed painter and poet as well. From what I'd read from excerpts of books he'd published after his excommunication, he'd become increasingly reclusive as he moved into his twilight years, eventually getting the boot from the church after claiming angels were using him as a conduit to quell the work of demonic activity.

His deportation was apparently quite the embarrassment for the church. He'd literally fought to stay in the Vatican, wildly charging into St. Peter's to warn of a demon infiltrator before being taken to a mental ward for two years, then discharged to his native Tuscany.

"How did he end up here, then?" Addie asked as we rolled up to his house in the hills outside the city. It was a single-story home nestled into a sunken ridge to shield it against the wind. No one lived nearby.

"Dunno. I know he moved to the US about a decade ago but nothing beyond that. There wasn't much of his book posted online and his site is full of nonsense about the dichotomy between good and evil." Addie let out another disgruntled huff, convinced we were wasting our time. "What if somebody *was* whispering to him? Using him for something, like he says?"

"We've been through this," she practically groaned. "It doesn't work like that. It's possible he's possessed by one side or the other, but he's claiming to receive commands. Whispers appear as thoughts—accentuated emotions. They would never be loud or strong enough for him to make the connection that it was an angel speaking to him."

"But he believes what he's saying, at least."

"How do you know? What if this is just some pathetic old man starved for attention?"

"Because he passed the Adelaide Martin test," I said, to which she tilted her head. "You can tell the difference between lie and truth even written, right? Well you read excerpts from the book that he wrote—was he lying?"

"We don't know that he actually wrote any of that," she rebuffed. "And even if he did, it is likely he is just believes his own delusions."

"Well we've come this far," I said, exasperated with her pessimism (the irony of which was not lost on me). "Let's at least talk to him."

Addie brought us to a lurching halt at the end of the gravel road leading to the house. I'd found Romano's address on his website. From what I could tell he was something of a P.I. himself, asking for reports of celestial or demonic activity. I'd tried calling to set up a meeting but he didn't answer the phone and there was no voicemail.

The Santa Ana winds seemed to follow us from Los Angeles. Addie's arms were tightly folded even with her jacket. I was still in the gray suit I'd found at Stevie's. I'd grabbed a t-shirt from the diner that afternoon but I was too lazy to change.

I knocked a few times. We waited. I tried again while Addie went to take a look through a window. They were all sealed. I thought about walking round the back to see if there was any sign of activity when Addie starting knocking on the door with the butt of her fist.

"Father Romano!" she called just short of a yell. "We need to speak with you!" I rolled my eyes and started for the back. Before I made it around the corner of the house I heard the front door unlock. It opened a little, tied to a chain on the wall. I couldn't make out the figure through the narrow slit, but a withered voice sounded through.

"Patience is a virtue," I made out. "Who are you?"

"My name is Adelaide Martin. This is my colleague Jon Perry." She pointed at me while I found my way back to the steps. "We're hoping you can assist us with a case we're working on."

"Are you police?" the man asked.

"Journalists," I answered. "But we're working on a story that we think would hold particular interest to you. You are Father Carmine Romano, yes?"

"No," he said. "Mister Carmine Romano. And I'm not interested in being heckled by media, Mr. Perry. I've had more than my fill of that. I'm retired."

"I think you'd come out of retirement for this, Mr. Romano. What if I told you I've recently had a similar experience to yours in dealing with angels?"

"I'd say I'm retired. Sorry, young man. I could barely find the strength to get out of my chair and unchain the lock just now. I don't have the stamina for another disappointment."

"I am an angel." She just said it. Neither Romano or I said anything for a moment, just staring at her.

"Prove it," he said eventually.

"I can't," Addie returned.

"Yes you can. I am wearing a purple sweater right now." I squinted, wondering if his delusions had mixed with dementia, but to my surprise Addie responded right after.

"No you are not."

"But I am holding a brush," Romano continued.

"You are," Addie agreed.

"Because I've been painting."

"Yes."

"Just started before you knocked."

"No." Romano fell quiet, staring through the slit in the door. After a moment he wordlessly slipped away, leaving us staring there for almost a minute solid. I was encouraged by the fact he knew about Addie's interesting ability but I found myself as skeptical as she had been in the car. After another minute Romano returned, slipping an eight-and-a-half by eleven canvas through the door.

"It's still a bit wet," he said. Addie accepted the canvas. I raised an eyebrow, watching her study the image. It was a mess of sharp red and black blotches strewn in random, angular tangents from a fiery center. I wasn't sure if it was complete or not. "Was this born of anger or avarice?" Romano asked after giving her a moment. Addie kept her eyes on the image, running a thumb over the edge while her face fell passive.

"Love," she stated. She looked back up, offering the canvas to its owner. Romano's eyes had shifted as well, wider and gentler despite their shock. I listened as he unfastened the lock and opened the door wide.

"Please come in."

Carmine, as he insisted we call him, was smaller than I'd guessed. He looked 80 at least, bald and wrinkled, always hunched. His voice was full and exultant despite its raspy wear and tear. The accent was thicker than I'd heard through the door—Italian with traces of something else Mediterranean.

He hadn't released his smile since he opened the door. His eyes held a glimmer uncommon in any but those of a child on the first day of school. I obviously couldn't call him animated, but the man was as enthused as I imagine he'd been in some time.

Carmine had been a Jesuit, he told us as he poured us tea. He told us a *lot*. I got the sense he hadn't done much talking in a long while. The way he fumbled for words but continued their rapid flow seemed more out of nervousness than Alzheimer's, but he was joyous to be doing it. I'm sure I looked more annoyed than taken aback, but Addie ignored me, pleasantly surprised. She looked at Carmine affectionately right away, patiently nodding as he spoke.

The pace of his tangential anecdotes alone was tiring him. Addie and I could both hear it in the laborious breaths between sentences. His voice barely carried from the kitchen to the living room. Addie tried to help him carry a fresh tray of tea but he insisted she sit and let him attempt to be a decent host.

Carmine was a fighter, or had been at one point. He didn't like relying on any crutch, literal or figurative. He could have benefited from a cane, probably from an oxygen tank as well. When Addie asked about his back from his show of pain he told us he refused to take medicine, then quickly shifted the conversation back to us.

"It's been so long since I've had guests," he managed as he set Addie's cup in front of her. He offered her crackers and handed her a folded napkin before ever looking at me. It wasn't that he was rude, just enamored with Addie. Not so much her beauty or her equally antiquated manners, just the fact he was serving tea to an angel.

I continued eyeing the house while they chatted over the tea flavor and temperature. It hadn't looked like much from outside, but the place was like a baroque museum. Ornate, in an old world fashion. The living room was cluttered but immaculate, its curtains, candles, book shelves and crucifixes all arranged by design.

To say nothing of the art.

Paintings, sculptures, bowls—you name it. Most of the décor looked handcrafted, though I wasn't sure how much of it had actually been done by Carmine. When I heard him tell Addie he'd crafted the tea cups by hand, I guessed most of it.

"Years ago," he managed as he set a cup before me, "I taught pottery and literature at university. Not much of it survived the trip to the states, I'm afraid."

"Do you still sculpt?" Addie asked.

"Oh no, I don't have the equipment for it here," he returned, slowly backing himself into the chair across from the couch where he'd seated us. His hand shook as he reached for his own cup and settled back into the chair. "No, these days I just have my paints."

"Did you paint all of these?" she asked, sweeping her gaze over the walls and mantles. Carmine nodded as he took a sip of his tea.

"What do you make of them?" he asked with a tickled smile. Addie's expression was a mixture of genuine and feigned amazement.

"They are incredible. You should be very proud of your talent."

"You know that is not what I meant, blessed." He'd taken to calling her that. I'm sure Addie didn't care for it but she let him continue even after she let him know her name would suffice. Addie tried a meek smile and gave the images around the room another look, probably uncomfortable to be put on the spot.

I thought about jumping in to change the subject but she answered before I could. "You are... a very earnest man, Carmine," she began, staring between two paintings on the wall across from her. "Mournful and disappointed, but still very hopeful. Still resolute." Carmine held his smile, shaking his head while glancing at me.

"Magnifico," he murmured.

"How did you know?" I asked. "About her... gift."

"I assume you know about my claims if you've come to see me," Carmine said.

"So you've met an angel before?" I pressed. Carmine shook his head.

"Never. Miss Adelaide is the first." Addie and I exchanged glances. "Can you tell me how you were given that name, blessed?" So he knew about her ability to sift through lies and truth, but not the truth about the afterlife.

"All angels have names," was all she said, obviously deciding that was all he needed to know about it. "But if you've never met an angel before, how do you know so much about us? How have you communicated with us?"

Carmine looked confused, probably wondering how she could be an angel and not know. Addie saw it and told him angels are not God— they can't all see and know everything. "I see," Carmine said, struggling to account for it. "Well, I never spoke to an angel, I only relayed messages from the heaves to those here on earth." He reached for a brush laying on a table beside him. "I am merely a tool for them to use as this is a tool for me."

"The paintings," I said. "You made them for angels to read messages through?"

"Not read, I'm sure," Carmine said. "At least not with their eyes. And not just paintings. Poetry, sculpture. I was an artist in my youth. I had some skill but never much passion for it. I ended up finding my passion was for God, the church. Shortly after I became a priest I found new inspiration for the arts. I would dream such vivid dreams. Feel such moments of clarity. It was as if my heart had been opened anew.

"I was never sure where the inspiration came from, but the more I painted or wrote, the more I began to see the messages, the emotions, behind the work, speaking to me. There were themes, ideas, some incredibly specific, in everything I did. Sometimes I did not realize the meaning of my work until after it was complete. Some of it was bright, holy, but much was of darkness. Of terrible feelings and acts I could not account for.

"Then I realized the themes of my work were unfolding in the world around me. I would write a story of a killer primed to slay a young woman, and the next day I would hear of the arrest of a man who had abducted a girl. The characters in my stories, in my paintings, would even fit those I heard about in the news."

Carmine beamed again after taking a sip of his tea.

"My inspiration came from you, blessed," he said to Addie. "Or your blessed brethren, at least. I knew it. God was speaking through my brush, my pen. Sending knowledge for his chosen in this world so they might stop acts of evil. I wasn't sure how they knew of my work since most of it was never viewed by anyone, but some of it must have been. I knew someone could see the truth in my art. The truth in all things."

Carmine looked to Addie, eyes literally watering with hope. "It is true, isn't it? I was right all these years?" Addie tried her best to smile genuinely, offering a single nod while she set her hands in her lap.

"I believe so," she told him. "Angels could certainly whisper you inspiration. You must be a very pure spirit to listen so clearly and block out, well, negative influences."

"And there are more of you here," he pressed. "In this world among us. Acting on messages from the heavens. That is why you are here?"

"In part, yes," Addie answered, still trying her best to be both warm and honest.

"But the church didn't share your faith in all this?" I posed as a question. Carmine shrugged, his smile weakening.

"I told them the truth as I knew it. That heaven was passing knowledge through my hand. That someone was listening and acting in the name of good. They tried to keep me quiet for a while, but I only grew louder the more they pushed me into obscurance.

"One day I drew out a scene of a terrible tragedy on a sinking boat. I recognized the vessel I'd painted and went to see it, eager to witness its salvation for my own eyes. When disaster was narrowly averted I made quite the scene about it to all those there, media included. The church decided enough was enough. They called my art blasphemous and my ideas heresy. I was excommunicated and sent away."

"I am sorry," Addie said as if on behalf of all heaven. Still Carmine smiled.

"I was saddened, yes, but I knew what I knew. I was afraid the visions would stop. They have lessened in recent years, but still they remain."

"Why did you move all the way here from Italy?" Addie asked.

"I've been in California for over a decade now. I found the most activity here."

"What does that mean?" I asked.

"The struggle," he answered. "Between both sides. Once I was forced to leave the church, I decided it was my duty to show them the truth. While I was passive with my visions before, I since began investigating them for myself. It was rare that I arrived to a place in time to witness anything at all, much less a miracle, but I began looking more into the presence of angels. And demons.

"Most lore was simply that. Most sightings or reports were rumor only. But as I began to investigate the pattern of all my work over the years, I could see a profile type of those who set out to do evil and those who would stop it. After enough backgrounds investigated, I uncovered common links. Beliefs they held. Mental and physical conditions. Places many had been."

Carmine stopped to spread his arms wide over the arms of his chair. "That is what led me here. To this very city."

"You're saying angels congregate here?" I asked. "In San Jose?" Carmine's smile faded for the first time since he opened his door.

"Not angels," he said. Addie glanced at me worriedly. "The largest common denominator in the background of most criminals or dark events I detailed through my art was a place in this city. It was thin evidence at best, but I came out here to look around. By the time I found what I was looking for I was too old to do anything about it.

"Other than write about it, of course. I published books based on my research and my experiences, but none of them were ever taken seriously. I have become a fascination in occult circles, but nothing more. These days I simply write my thoughts on the computer blog, but I have few readers. For as much good as I like to think the Lord has used me over my life, I'm afraid my knowledge is likely to die with me."

"What was it you found in the city?" I asked. Addie shot me an unhappy look criticizing me for my impatience after hearing Carmine empty his heart, but I had to know. Carmine took a long breath and then another drink of tea. He was tired after having spoken at such length, but forced himself on.

"There is a bar," he said. "A place where evil congregates. I have spoken of it in my writings, but no divine force has ever acted against it that I know of. I settled here because it was the end of my trail. I found it but didn't know what to do." Again he smiled, looking at Addie. "Until now. Surely God has left me here to tell you this. To help you confront the evil of this place."

I'm sure Addie didn't have the heart to tell him we weren't here on God's order. "It may be what we are looking for," she said after a moment. "Can you tell us more about it?"

"Only a bit," he answered. "I have never set foot inside. As bold as I like to imagine I am, I would not have the courage to enter there. The bar is downtown. A placed called Ode to Joy." I let out a huff without realizing it. Hardly the name for a devil bar, I thought. "Dark ones come and go from there. I have watched it from afar, but I knew they were watching me as well. I don't know much more about it."

I was watching for Addie's reaction. Didn't look like she knew anything more about it than Carmine. A demon bar. Sounds ridiculous, I know, but if it was true, certainly worth checking out. I reached into my pocket and laid out the paper on the table.

"This is why we're here," I said at last. "Does this mean anything to you?" Carmine slowly reached over to pick up the letter I'd found under the rug at the Kohler apartment. He read it over a few times before looking between Addie and I.

"You think this may be a message like my art?" he asked.

"Though slightly less subtle," I offered. "And written to the other side. We're investigating a case involving demons—we're the intruders mentioned in the letter. That's my home address at the top. We think this was a message to have us killed." Carmine read the letter again then crossed himself, setting the paper back on the table.

"May I ask what you are investigating?" he asked. I wasn't sure how much we should say but he had apparently earned Addie's trust, as she gave him a brief recap of the Horsemen and why she had come.

"And if the Horsemen are indeed in league with these demons," she finished, "this entire world could be at risk. We came to see you in hopes you would be able to tell us something about this note or something more. We had no idea you had been exposed to so much from the beyond already. You have already been very helpful, Carmine."

"Dear God," Carmine breathed, visibly pained. Again he picked up the note, looking for anything else that might help.

"Does 'The Loyal' mean anything to you?" I asked him. Carmine shook his head regretfully.

"I have heard demons refer to themselves as many things, but never that," he confessed. "I..." he trailed off, breathing so heavily he couldn't speak. We'd clearly upset him. Addie rose first, asking if he was all right. He nodded but gestured her away. Eventually he said he would be fine, but he'd like a moment to rest after hearing so much.

He allowed Addie to help him to his bedroom. I tried to tell her we didn't have time to wait around but she ignored me. I sat back down on the couch and waited.

Darkness had fallen by the time Carmine woke from his brief rest. It was nearly 8:00 that night. Addie and I spent the time talking in the living room about his story and the bar. I was predictably skeptical of it all but she defended him, saying everything he said was the truth, or at least what he believed to be.

She had never heard of angels in heaven passing messages to those possessing bodies in the mortal world as he described, but she confirmed it was certainly possible. Surely there had to be others like her who cared, she believed. She didn't say it, but I could tell.

We were discussing the likelihood of the bar being a worthwhile lead when Carmine hobbled back into the living room. I fell quiet while Addie rose to ask if he was all right. He smiled and walked back to his chair. "Feeling a little refreshed, thank you. My apologies for making you wait further. I'm actually surprised you're still here. I thought you would have already gathered what you needed from this old man and left."

I'd suggested just that but Addie, usually the one to drive us forward, insisted we stay until we could say a proper thank you to the former priest.

"Of course not," she told him. "I want you to know how much we appreciate your help, Carmine. You may have given us exactly what we need to discover more about the Horsemen."

"You intend to go down to the bar then?" he asked us. Addie nodded.

"Is there anything else you can tell us about it before we do?" I asked. "Any immediate security you saw we'd need to get around? Would Adelaide be in danger there?" He looked somewhat lost.

"I'm not sure they would just let anyone in," he answered at last. "I do not know what to tell you about your safety, blessed. If harm is indeed something that can come to you, it is likely you would find it there. Many of those who have come to that place committed or were set to commit terrible acts. I cannot imagine an angel would be greeted warmly by a house of demons."

"Jon and I will need to find out," Addie told him, "but we will be careful. I know how to take care of myself." I noticed she left me out of that statement.

"Perhaps I could help you," Carmine said, leaning forward. "I have been waiting here in this house without purpose for years. Surely your finding me is my call to act once more. I could come with you." Addie responded right away to cut me off.

"I believe it was providence that we found you, Carmine," she told him, reaching out to put a hand on his, "but ours is a journey that belongs to Jon and me alone. You have played a great part in this already. I could not guarantee your safety outside these walls."

"Your safety weighs greater on me than my own, blessed," he said. "Surely there is some use I can yet be."

"There is," Addie said, to my surprise. "You have been entrusted with a unique responsibility by those in heaven, Carmine. You must remain here to continue on with your work. Perhaps a message will come for me. If it does, we will need you in a safe place to send it."

"How will I contact you?" he asked.

"We can read your journal on the internet anywhere. If you have news, write it there and we will see." She smiled and leaned closer to him. "You are a good man, Carmine. And brave. Brave to have faced so much doubt but continued to believe. I am glad to have met you."

"I am blessed to have met you, Miss Adelaide," he said, dipping his head. "I..." He was struggling for breath again, looking for his words. "Through all the years, I prayed there was a reason I had survived this long. I had all but given up on ever discovering why this had been my fate."

A grin lit up his withered face. "The Lord works in mysterious ways." Addie blinked, her face passive. She said nothing. Neither did I.

eight

Carnegie climbed out of the SUV and marched with purpose through the night. He'd been in Los Angeles most of the day personally combing over Perry's duplex. The LAPD had done a fantastic job making a mess of the place in their misplaced priority of investigating the murders.

Carnegie grimaced as he walked, reminding himself to make sure the amateur assassins paid for their failure for as close to eternity as his plan allowed. It wouldn't be long, but an example had to be made. Mistakes couldn't be tolerated this close to the end.

He had uncovered next to nothing at the duplex, Perry's office, or his impounded car. The man had no friends or colleagues, no one he could turn to. His only family was an estranged mother and father in-law he hadn't seen in years. Men were on the way to interrogate them. Carnegie would have to wait to use them more forcefully until Perry resurfaced, but he would leave the assets in place.

They were on the search for Cora Avery's car when the cyberteam in Sacramento made the hit. A computer in West Hollywood that had been used to log into a research database profile belonging to Perry. The house of a movie producer. They found the car along with traces of Perry's blood.

An arrest warrant was immediately sent out for Stevie Walker but she was apparently in South America. In the meantime Carnegie ordered a search for her two missing cars—one was found in a facility near LAX, the other missing.

With no further leads from LA, Carnegie took the flight back to Sacramento to oversee the search through the information Perry had spent the previous night researching. Perry couldn't have known too much about the Horsemen or his plan. The demons who'd attacked him hadn't said anything, but there were plenty of others who could fill in the gaps if he looked in the right places.

Carnegie made several calls to his contacts at various safe houses on the phone, advising them to stay vigilant for any sign of Perry.

Carnegie writhed his hands over the phone between calls, furious at the gap exposed in his plan. There were few descriptors better suited for Carnegie than industrious, but this era, this technology, was beyond him and most of the other Watchers. As much as they'd attempted to keep up on humanity's progress, he had never expected he would have to leave hell to personally oversee the final stages.

He began shouting orders and calling for updates the moment he stepped back into the cyberteam bunker at headquarters. "We're compiling the most likely locations Perry could be headed to based on his search results, but there could literally be hundreds. There are three or four more likely than others but—"

"You've had three hours!" Carnegie barked through Lamont. "I want every location from that search accounted for and I want teams there as soon as physically possible. Where is the current list?" An officer extended an open file folder. Carnegie snatched it and flipped over several sheets. Maps held pins with the possible locations.

"I want full teams ready to deploy to every site in New York, Philadelphia, San Jose and Los Angeles at a moment's notice," he ordered. "Focus your resources there to find the car."

"Every site? Sir, there's no way—"

"Then prioritize them. Find that car. Now."

We came to the address that Carmine gave us a little before 10:00 that night. He'd fed us dinner before leaving when he correctly guessed we didn't have much money. Even in Stevie's movie suit I'm sure I looked as haggard as I felt. I hadn't slept much since the night before the Orange Forest Motel, and the little shuteye I'd managed in the time between had been pervaded by the nightmare.

There was never a day when I didn't think about the girls or those last few moment with them, but their memory—my failings—hadn't haunted me so prominently in years. I was hoping all this business of heaven and immortality would have set my mind at ease, but even with the stresses of a pending apocalypse in this world, my girls in the next were always at the forefront of my worries.

Addie maintained considerably more focus. Not to mention energy, which I attributed partly to the advantage of Cora Avery's young, fit body, but mainly to her determination. Or impatience, depending on your outlook. Her eyes still wandered and widened in awe at many of the things she encountered in the city as we drove, but no distraction would deter her from the reason she was here.

She proved this when I asked again if she wanted to get some rest before we investigated Ode to Joy. Carmine had offered to let us stay the night at his house, but Addie politely refused, explaining we had little time and must investigate the bar at once. She took the same position once we arrived downtown.

I parked the car in a lot across the street from the bar. The bar's designated lot was full, but there didn't look to be much activity inside the building itself. The main level was a tavern with several billiard tables visible through the windows blinking with old neon beer signs. It was relatively empty, as would be expected on a Tuesday. According to Carmine, the tavern was only there to cover Ode to Joy in the lower level.

We had only been parked for a few seconds before Addie ducked down past the dash, barely allowing herself view over it. I prepared to do the same but she told me to act natural.

"Do you see that woman walking out from the staircase on the alley side of the building?" she asked me in a needless whisper. I did.

"Demon?" I asked.

"Yes." The staircase she'd come from led underground. It was marked only by a rusted sign drilled into the wall reading something too small to make out in the darkness.

"That's it then?" I asked. She nodded, taking a wider sweep of the area for anything else worthy of note. "It can't be too big if it's just the basement level of that tavern. I have my doubts this is really the lair Carmine made it out to be." Addie didn't say anything, turning her attention back to the staircase.

She gradually leaned up and opened the glove box for the gun she'd left there. "Let's go," she said, checking it and putting it behind her back under her coat.

"Just like that? You don't want to scope it out a little more first?"

"How would we do that? The bar is clearly hidden by intent. We would not find anything walking around up here."

"Well we can't just walk in."

"How else do you propose we gain entrance?"

"Gaining entrance is not the point of all this, Addie. Did you forget what Carmine said? This is a bar full of possessor demons. You think they'll just let an angel walk in? What if they try to kill you first thing? What if they're all in the pocket of the Horsemen the same as the last ones?"

"Like I told Carmine, it's a risk we have to take. And Earth isn't disputed ground in a turf war between angels and demons, Jon," she told me with a sigh of annoyance that a teenage girl would use toward her father. "Not yet, anyway."

"Says the angel who was being hunted by demons in Los Angeles."

"What would you have us do? Why did we come if not to go inside?"

"We came to get information. We can do that by picking up the next demon to wander out and stumble home drunk. We'll catch one in the alley or the parking lot and put the screws to him."

"And you think any random demon we pick up will have the answers we're looking for?" she asked.

"You don't?"

"I think that if this place really is some kind of sanctuary for possessor demons, it has to have been organized by someone. It has to be monitored by someone. Someone who will know more than some drunk nobody. We need to find a leader."

"So you say jump into the lion's den and hope for the best."

"I say there is someone of significance in there and we need to talk to *that* person. This is the only lead we have and we don't have time to wait around. Are you coming or not?" I stared her down for a moment, fighting the urge to argue further, knowing her determination.

Instead I unfastened my seatbelt and reached under her coat. She froze uncomfortably until she realized I was pulling the gun from her pants and stuffing it into my own. "What are you doing?" she asked.

"Reaching for the cheese in the mousetrap, apparently," I replied, opening the door. "Let me scope it out before anyone gets a whiff of your angelic scent. Hopefully I can get in on my own and get what we need."

"Absolutely not. What if there is trouble? You wouldn't stand a chance."

"Gee, thanks. But if there is trouble, having one or two of us to take on a whole bar won't make much of a difference. If anything the trouble would come from an angel walking in. You're staying." I knew she wouldn't want to be told like that, but I wanted to make sure she wouldn't try to sneak after me. She prepared to snarl something in response but folded her arms and turned away.

"Be careful, Jon." I expected an admonition or a curse, at least a sour tone of voice, but as irritated as she was, she said it earnestly.

I was back at the car in four minutes, dabbing the back of my head where blood ran free.

"What happened?" Addie asked in a rush as I took a seat beside her. She grazed a hand through my hair to find the origin of the wound.

"It's nothing," I said, pushing her hand away. I grabbed a roll of paper towels in the back to stop the blood from reaching my white collar, too late. "Not getting in that way."

"What happened?" she repeated.

"I got halfway through telling a bouncer who looked like Schwarzenegger in his prime that I knew what the bar was. I've been hit plenty, but I'd never been actually thrown before."

"Were you followed?" From the way I rubbed my lower back I expected her to ask if I was hurt elsewhere, but I guessed she didn't much care.

"Why would—"

"Because you told them you knew what this place was. Whether they believed you or not, they obviously go to great lengths to keep it a secret." I wasn't so sure if they allowed an 80-year-old to blog about it, but I kept that to myself. She was right. If these boys were in league with the ones in LA, surely they were on high alert for us. I hadn't heard anyone follow me up the stairs or across the street, but I took a moment scanning the darkened parking lot for any sign of trouble.

"So how are we going to get inside now?" Addie asked.

"We're not. Plan B—you ID the next demon to come out then we sweat him for info on the Horsemen or someone who would have it."

"We've been through that—"

"Just like we've been through trying to walk in to a fucking demon bar. Getting killed gets us no closer to stopping the Horsemen." Addie was silent, but I could feel her glare on me.

We waited for several uncomfortable minutes, eyes on the alley to the bar entrance. Addie spent the time fiddling with a messenger bag Carmine had given us. He'd loaded it with some food, a first aid kit that looked far too old to be of use, and a copy of the bible. Addie removed it as soon as we were out of sight. She'd put her book from the Kohler apartment in its place.

Eventually an older woman turned the corner to the stairs while a young man emerged from them. Addie said neither were possessed. About ten minutes passed without any movement before she startled me with a sudden jerk of her head. She was staring out her passenger window.

"What?" I asked in a needless whisper. She pointed with her index finger against the glass.

"That man at the crosswalk. He's a demon." I squinted through the dark and leaned closer, noticing the silhouette of a man tossing something into a trash bin then waiting to cross the street.

"He's walking away from the bar," I observed. "Did he come out from the back side of the alley?"

"I don't know, but if you want someone to interrogate, there he is." I silently grunted and looked for a dark place I could lead him once I put the gun to his back. There weren't many cars passing and no one else on the street. I put the gun in my suit pocket and nodded.

"Okay. You stay here but keep an eye on me. If he takes off or leads me too far before I catch up to him, bring the car around and back me up."

"Hurry or you're going to lose him," she said, watching as the man started across the street. I opened the driver door and began the pursuit, striding at a brisk pace to catch up without drawing attention. There was another series of alleys along the west side of the street. I could probably herd him into one if I caught up at the right time.

I realized I wasn't exactly sure what I wanted to ask him after making it a block from the car. I probably should have had Addie there. She could tell me whether he was lying or not if nothing else.

Considering waving her to catch up and help, I glanced back to the car.

It was empty.

Wheeling around, I caught Addie marching across the street to the bar just short of a jog. I took off in a run, clutching the gun in my pocket. How stupid can you possibly be, I cursed at myself. She would have insisted on coming with me if the guy she saw was really a demon. I wasn't sure if she did it to get her own crack at Schwarzenegger or just to spite me for giving her orders. Either way she was about to walk into a shit storm.

When I tore around the corner of the tavern she had already disappeared into the alley down the stairs. I pulled the gun free as soon as I cleared the tavern windows, ready to swing it down the stairs and shout for the bouncer to leave her be.

I came to the stairs and ground to a halt, but instead of pointing the gun I hid it. The bouncer stood to the side, holding the door open for Addie. They both looked up the stairs when they heard me.

Fight or flight moment.

If I rushed down for her I'd probably get us both killed. If I pretended I didn't know her and let her go in I'd probably never see her again. I could tell from Addie's expression she wanted me to do the latter. As much as I didn't want to, I knew I had to.

Unfortunately it was too late for me to walk away.

"The *fuck* did I tell you before?!" Schwarzenegger shouted, rushing up the stairs for me. I tried backing away with a defensive gesture of my hands. I apologized, trying to act drunk.

He didn't buy it.

This time he threw me down the stairs. The back of my head hit concrete again.

Addie had disappeared past the closing door by the time I landed. The gun slid from my pocket, but I was too stunned to use it anyway. "Now I got the long shift puttin' your ass in the fuckin' ground," the bouncer shouted, kicking my side. "Stupid motha..."

He was talking more to himself than me while he kicked me quiet.

"I'll leave," I tried to say while the wind came back to me. "I'll—"

"You 'bout to be fuckin' paste," he snapped, delivering another pillar to my gut to shut me up. "Ima get dark on this one, I don't giva shit what big man says." He had pulled out a knife when the door came open and another man emerged.

"Hold," he said. "The lady speaks for this man." The bouncer turned back, his scowl biting.

"Bull*shit*. This look like it got feathers to you?"

"She speaks for him, nonetheless."

"So *you* gonna tell big man you cleared a live one in his house?"

"This one is important."

"How the fuck you know that, man?"

"That is her word." The man grasping my leg was quiet at this, still scowling. "Why else would she claim him?" Another moment passed before the bouncer sheathed his knife.

"If big man sends us packin' I'm findin' your ass in the fire," he snapped, pointing at the other bouncer before pulling me to my feet and pushing me at him. "Ain't gonna be no new body for you, Ima make sure a that." The second man said nothing, unhurriedly bringing me into the parlor room and passing me on to Addie.

I nearly collapsed from the dizzying haze of the low red light on the walls, but Addie kept me on my feet. Her expression was half horrified, asking me what I was thinking with her eyes.

"A moment, please," she asked the second bouncer while he closed the outer door.

"Only one, milady. It is from curiosity that we allow you entrance, but he is not permitted in here. To take him past this room—"

"You were correct before. He is important. Surely an exception could be made." The bouncer took in a large breath then told us to remain where we were. He walked the rest of the way down the stairs and lifted a radio from his pocket to carry on a private conservation.

Addie kept her attention on me, taking off her scarf to dab the fresh blood from the back of my head and my mouth. "Are you an idiot?" she whispered, irate. "You had your chance. I was in. You could have ruined our only shot."

"What did you expect me to do?" I managed, spitting blood on the carpet.

"I expected you to wait patiently in the car," she snapped. "Sound familiar?"

"Christ, Addie. What is this, third grade?"

"No, Jon, it's a demon lair. And unless you feel like further decreasing our chances of survival, please refrain from the stupid heroics and let me handle this." I scoffed, debating which caustic remark I'd like to offer in return, but kept quiet when the bouncer returned.

"Very well, the owner will see you both. Please follow me." He opened the bottom door leading into the club. Addie and I exchanged glances and did as we were bid.

Depraved. Violent. Sadistic. These were the words I guessed would come to mind as I stepped into Ode to Joy. Instead it was another word on the other end of the spectrum.

Tranquil.

The bar was nothing like I imagined. I half expected it to reek of sulfur, but instead I was met with the crisp scent of lime and rosemary wafting from the kitchen on a cool jet of the air conditioner.

The British mannered (but not accented) bouncer led Addie and me at a brisk pace. We glanced into rooms we passed in the hallway leading to the main bar space. Everything looked new. Clean and well furnished, at least. Most of the décor was out of an Elizabethan period piece movie.

One room held a row of burgundy leather chairs masked by thick wisps of smoke flowing from the cigars of three women. None of their attire really matched the room design, but they were plenty relaxed.

Another group sat around a poker table in the next room.

I'd expected the entire bar to be lit in the same heavy red as the parlor room, shadows draping the corners. Instead everything was well lit in calming blue and purple glows from glass banks on the ceiling. A subdued purple and green emanated from the waterfall behind the bar in moving contrails.

Candles covered in paper lanterns served as centerpieces, hovering just inches over the jet black tables. Most of them were occupied with patrons and drinks. You'd have thought it was Saturday night from all the activity. Few of them looked like murderers or deviants at first glance, but I remembered none of the bodies matched the person inside.

The moment we walked in all eyes turned to us. A hush befell the entire bar other than a few stunned whispers. I'm sure this was the last place they expected to see an angel. From the bouncers' conversation it sounded like this was a definite first.

"You needn't worry, no harm will come to you here," the bouncer said, having glanced back at us. He was talking to me. I didn't realize I was so tense until I saw Addie. She was far from relaxed, but I couldn't believe how poised she looked. Despite the bouncer's assurances, every pair of eyes on us was hostile. I was uncomfortable enough without being an angel.

The hush of the bar emphasized the strangest element of all. There was no ambient techno, jazz or hip-hop. A symphonic movement reverberated across the room. I'm no classicalist, but I'm fairly sure it was Pachelbel's Canon or something in that neighborhood. At least the bar's name finally made sense. Sort of.

If there truly was a den of iniquity hidden somewhere under the curving, pastel décor and symphonic sophistication of the place, I don't know where they hid it. Don't get me wrong—as urbane and refined as it was, it was unnerving to be there. Beyond the glares directed our way, there was something... threatening radiating from the walls. I'd have felt it even if I didn't know what the place really was.

Still, it was probably the classiest bar I'd ever stood in.

I tried to keep up with the bouncer as he led us into another hallway marked with matching watercolor paintings of dead white men. Philosophers or composers or something. Addie had to keep pulling me on. I didn't think the first bouncer broke any of my ribs, but I was bruised up and down.

At the end of the hallway, our guide turned into another open room and stood beside the doorway. He motioned with his arm for us to continue inside. The symphonic soundtrack didn't extend into this room, but I heard the soft lullaby of a piano nearby.

Unlike the main bar, this room was almost empty. A few tables rested against the walls with chairs stacked upside down over them. Probably an event or overflow room. At the far end was a dais with a full grand piano on top. A man sat with his back to us at the bench, softly playing another classical piece I should have known the name of.

Addie looked uncertain and turned for the bouncer, but he gave her a nod to proceed. Apparently this was the guy we were looking for. She led me on across the gray tiles covering the empty room. I felt significantly less threatened here than in the bar, but I still wished I had the gun.

The man continued playing after we reached the dais, rhythmically swaying his entire upper body to and fro in slow but grandiose movements. Addie and I looked to each other, waiting another few measures before she summoned her voice.

"Pardon," she said just loud enough to be heard. The pianist continued on but spoke after a few measures.

"Do you recognize this piece?" he asked. His accent confirmed my suspicions of his ethnicity from the little I'd seen of his face from the side. Thick Japanese. I guessed Addie's past was the source of her dour expression upon hearing his voice. Still, she answered him calmly.

"Claire de Lune. Debussy."

"Yes," the man replied, still playing. "Which means you died sometime after 1890, but before you did, you were educated."

"Only some," Addie returned.

"And modest," the man returned. "How befitting." The man continued playing, finishing the piece despite Addie asking if he could pause to talk to us. I could tell I wouldn't find this guy agreeable.

Finishing the final chord nearly a minute later, he lifted his hands from the keys and feet from the pedals. He unhurriedly slid around the smooth wooden bench. His eyes were closed. Addie's jaw clenched when she saw his face. He was Japanese alright, probably around 50 years old. A man of small stature, adorned with circle framed glasses and sparse but well maintained chin whiskers.

Before opening his eyes, he reached into his pocket and pulled out a diminutive remote. A single stroke and the orchestra from the bar found its way into this room as well. He set the remote on the edge of the piano, using his opposite hand to trace the tempo of the music with a small but steady dance of his finger through the air.

He smiled once he got a look at Addie. It looked out of place. He said nothing for a moment, taking her in. Never so much as glanced at me. "I encounter my fair share of unexpected guests, but I have never been graced with one such as yourself."

"This is your establishment, then?" Addie asked. He bowed his head, eyes closed once more.

"I maintain it, yes," he answered. "A reprieve for the Lost souls, one might say."

"May I ask your name?" Addie continued.

"Hitoshi Ito," he returned. Addie remained composed in her reply.

"May I have your real name?" The man's eyes remained shut but his smile crept back up.

"I prefer Ito. This is not my body, after all. The least I can do to atone to its true owner is to show him that small measure of respect." I raised an eyebrow. Hardly a demonic sentiment. He opened his eyes again, finally sliding them to me. "But yours are the names of greater interest this night. May I have them?"

"I'm Adelaide Martin. This is my partner, Jon Perry." Ito nodded. I winced at her giving up our real names so easily, but she didn't have a choice. Ito would know if she wasn't honest about anything, and our names wouldn't matter if he was supposed to be looking for an angel and human. He had us.

"I have never known angels to take up a cause with a living soul. Intriguing. Are you injured, Mr. Perry?"

"Your security is exceedingly tight in here," I offered, wiping another dot of blood from my lip. Ito's smile persisted while he snapped over the British bouncer and called for a towel and a glass of ice water.

"Ode to Joy is a very exclusive club, I'm afraid," he stated. "There are several measures in place to ensure it remains that way, the least of which being Mr. Jacobs and Mr. Wellington at the front door."

"A necessary evil," I conceded, though Addie's expression told me she didn't appreciate my sarcasm.

"No evil is necessary in my eyes," Ito returned. "That's why I'm here in this place. But I'm more curious why you are in this place. What is it I can do for you?"

Addie said nothing for a moment, apparently deciding how much to tell him right off the bat.

"Have you not heard of us, Ito?" Addie asked. I breathed a sigh of relief that Addie knew what she was doing. Anything short of 'no' would mean he was in on this somehow.

"Should I have?"

"You didn't answer the question," she returned gently. Ito turned to one side, drumming his fingers along piano keys without playing them.

"I do not recognize those names, but rumors have reached these walls of an angel causing trouble further south. I would not presume to accuse you of being troublesome, Miss Martin, but your very presence here is aberration enough for me to make an educated guess."

"Causing trouble for whom?" Addie asked.

"You have a talent for turning questions back on the questioner, Miss Martin. But I'm afraid I can't answer that one."

"Why not?" Ito took in a long breath and rose from the bench. He took hold of his remote and made his way for the steps of the dais, hands still in motion to the rhythm of the symphony in the air.

"In the spirit of our exchange so far, allow me to answer that with another question. Where did you hear of this place?"

"Would you do harm to the person who told us if we gave you his name?" Addie asked.

"Possibly, so I suppose you had better not tell me if you do not wish him harm. We go to great lengths to keep this place secret. Any patron who speaks of Ode's existence or location to anyone but another patron is never allowed back in."

"How would you..." I trailed off. "Oh, never mind."

"We ask all patrons if they've slipped any details before we allow them entrance," Ito answered anyway. He called demons patrons, I guessed. "Allow me to rephrase my question. What did your contact tell you of this place?"

"Essentially what you've told us," Addie answered. "That it is a sanctuary for possessor demons."

"The Lost, is the nomenclature used here," Ito corrected immediately, swinging around with a semi-stern expression. "The connotations from your word are not accurate."

"How so?" I asked. "You seem perfectly content labeling Addie an angel, but you know as well as I do she's still just human."

"My point exactly. There are no true angels or demons, so if Miss Martin prefers alternate terminology I am happy to ascribe. But I'm sure you'll agree that angel is less deprecating than demon."

"I buy that."

"No you don't. You believe we should call a spade a spade, that we have been judged and should accept the shame that comes with it. But I assure you, Mr. Perry, the afterlife is not so black and white as your church would have you believe." I thought about telling him I didn't go to church and just because he could see through a white lie didn't mean he knew what I was thinking, but that would hardly compel him to help us. Instead I bit my tongue.

"I'm sorry if I offended you," I offered. "In the cursory sense, anyway—I guess you can tell that I don't really give a shit if I offended you or not." Okay, so I didn't really bite my tongue, but I tried. Addie swallowed hard and shook her head in disbelief. She attempted to get us back on track.

"But this is a sanctuary for the Lost," she said.

"'Sanctuary' may be a bit much, but yes. A small respite for those who manage to escape the darkness for a fleeting moment in eternity."

"How do so many of you know about it?" I asked.

"'So many' is not that many, Mr. Perry, but when a Lost soul reenters this world, he or she sometimes seeks out other Lost, many of which know of the club. We see 75 to 100 regulars every week who live here in the city, others come from afar to see if we've earned our reputation."

"What reputation is that?" I asked.

"Welcoming," Ito answered with a smile. "The Lost are afforded little warmth in the afterlife, at least in the spiritual sense. One of my goals is to provide what little pleasure I can to victims of the Injustice."

"You don't think you deserve to be in hell," I said, arms crossed. Ito had made his way down the steps to our level by then. He walked closer, eyeing me from head to toe.

"If you knew it as I do, Mr. Perry, you would think the same. No creature of God, designed by God, existing in a narrative controlled by God, deserves to be forsaken by God. Not like that. That is the Injustice."

"I guess that means all of the bodysnatchers to whom you're serving martinis and cigars in the next room, including rapists and murderers, get the same sympathy, then."

"Jon, that is enough," Addie exclaimed, taking hold of my

shoulder. "That is not why we are here, and you now know from both sides that he is right to call the afterlife unjust." Ito held my gaze for another long moment before closing his eyes and resuming his musical walk past us.

"It's perfectly alright, Miss Martin," he conceded. "One cannot expect one who has not seen the afterlife to see it as we do. It sounds as though you've shared a great deal with him already, but allow me to share one point relating to the purpose of this establishment."

The piece moved into a crescendo, and Ito became the most animated we'd seen him yet, moving his arms as if conducting the entire symphony. "Judgment, Mr. Perry, is final. For whatever reason, God cares only for actions in life, not those in the afterlife, even for those clever enough to find their way back to this realm.

"Any action I take now, any repentance I strive for is meaningless. I will never see heaven. As Miss Martin will never see hell, no matter what evil she could inflict in her form here.

"There are some who believe otherwise, that enough good done through whispering or possession could someday earn God's forgiveness, but I've never heard of such a thing. Others are vengeful at the permanence of their damnation and take their vengeance by corrupting good in this world."

"So what do you do?" I asked.

"Both," he answered loudly, caught up in the climax of the piece. "Whoever enters here first agrees that they will bring no evil in with them. They will be civilized, honorable, and upright in the eyes of God. Any who would harm others or spread evil are not welcome here.

"That is my defiance. This club, our being here in it, is an act of disobedience. I know we will never see heaven, but I will live as a good man anyway. Not for God, but for me. For all those who have been shown the ultimate Injustice because of a twisted sense of morality no one in this realm or any other understands. That spirit lives on with this place whether I am in it or not, and I will always protect that!"

Ito shouted the last bit, at the height of the piece just before it faded to nothing. He was sweating some after the physical exertion of conducting his symphony, and dropped his arms before sitting back on the edge of the dais. He opened his eyes, shifting them between Addie and me.

"Knowing that, you should know why I won't tell you who you were causing trouble for in Los Angeles," he said, recovering his breath.

"I'm sorry, Ito, but I'm not sure that I do," Addie returned.

"There is something in motion out there, Miss Martin. Something I am sure you and Mr. Perry would be eager to stop. If that is your intention, then I wish you well in it. But that is all I can offer you."

"I'm not sure you understand exactly what is happening, Ito," Addie said. "We could be facing the end of this world. You'll have no club left to reside in."

"If what is now in motion succeeds, the Lost would no longer have need for this club. But I will not help those who would see that become a reality, just as I will not help you. Schemes like these have come and gone since people have been living and dying. None of them ever bore fruit.

"This place will endure because we do not involve ourselves in wars between possessors and plots against God. There are many sides to be taken in this, as in all things, and taking one will provoke the wrath of another that could end this place. I, and any of my patrons while they wish to remain welcome here, will remain neutral, as we always have."

Addie and I were silent. I could tell from the look on her face she had any number of other points ready to debate on why Ito should help us, but there was a finality in his last words that preluded them. We both knew this man had given us all the information about the Horsemen he was going to.

That's what prompted my question.

"We understand that you can't help us," I started, "but I wonder if you know someone else who would. It sounds like you know of other groups apart from yours with information." Ito shrugged.

"They come and go, most don't have the initiative or leadership to stay organized for long. I do know of a few information brokers, so to speak, but some would argue that my giving you their names would be tantamount to giving you the information you seek myself."

"Would you argue that?" Ito kept his eyes on me a moment longer before skipping ahead to a new piece with his remote. He stood up, putting his hands behind his back.

"No, I would not," he said. "Because few to none of them are any more likely to help you than I am. In fact, most wouldn't extend you the courtesy I have; most would kill your body, Miss Martin, just for being what you are. I wouldn't be surprised if most are aligned with this latest scheme."

"So you'll give us a name," I said. Ito stepped back up the dais and took a seat at the piano again, lightly playing an accompaniment to the piece from the speakers.

"One," he answered. "And only one that you could have heard from any number of other Lost. But one willing to trade just about anything for a price.

"As I'm sure you know, Miss Martin, some of us are better at whispering than others. I'm decent—this is my third consecutive body, after all. But there's one so adept at it, it's said she hasn't spent a moment in darkness in thousands of years. That she keeps new bodies waiting in the wings for her to enter at will.

"But as I warned, this is not a person I would advise you go see. You likely wouldn't see anything else in this world afterwards. Do you still want to know the name?"

"Please," Addie confirmed. Ito lifted his hand from the keys and turned his head back.

"Alex," was the name. After a long pause, my brow furrowed.

"That's it?" I asked.

"That should be all you need," he returned.

"Well how do we reach her?" Addie asked.

"I'm not sure. She moves almost constantly and doesn't keep in regular contact with any of her fellow Lost. The last I heard she was somewhere in the Mediterranean."

"So you're giving us a generic first name and a last known location that can be seen from space," I said. "You call that helping us?"

"I call that bending over backwards for you," Ito returned. "I've let you into my club, spoken with you personally, and offered you a lead when I should have let Mr. Jacobs bury you to err on the side of safety. I don't know the whereabouts of Alex, but if you were able to find this place, I'm sure you're both resourceful enough to find her."

I was set to disagree but Addie reached out for my forearm and took hold, shaking her head. I think she sensed we had pushed our host as far as he was willing to go.

"Thank you, Ito," she said eventually. "We do appreciate the assistance, and your hospitality."

"And my hospitality will continue to be yours. Please, have a drink and a meal before you leave, on the house. It's not every day we have the privilege of serving an angel. Stay as long as you like this evening." He kept playing but turned back on us, his head swaying. "But once you leave, I'm afraid you won't be permitted back inside. This is a club for the Lost."

Addie nodded in response. I turned to leave but she remained in place, listening to him play. From our angle we could tell he played with closed eyes, the same as he conducted. "Do you always play with your eyes closed?" she asked.

"The sound," was his melodic reply. "Who needs sight when you can hear this?" Addie nodded in silent concurrence.

"I wonder if I could ask one more thing of you," she asked, surprising me. "Could you play your ninth for me?" Ito stopped playing, turning to her with a blank expression. He reached into his pocket and stopped the recording over the speakers.

"I'd be delighted," he answered, to which Addie took a seat on the dais, listening as he began.

nine

She told me we'd just spoken with Ludwig van Beethoven after we got our drinks. When I asked her how she was sure she looked at me like I was an imbecile. I reminded her I hadn't studied music in the humanities, but she said it wasn't what he played so much as the way he played. Drinking in the sound, eyes closed. Something a formerly deaf man would relish, I guess.

"The bar's name is something of a clue as well, don't you think?" she asked as she took a sip of water. My sarcasm was rubbing off on her. I'd ordered something staunch but already forgotten what. Something with tequila.

"Was he that much of a prick before he died?"

"He's one of the most important men who ever lived," she retorted scornfully. Her mood was no friendlier than mine.

"Guess God doesn't figure importance into final judgment," I returned, chewing on an ice cube. We sat along the far corner of the main bar, as apart from the crowd as we could get. About half of them at least pretended not to be staring at us, but brooding resentment emanated from them all.

Ito had promised there wouldn't be any trouble. No 'patron' would risk breaking his rules and losing club privileges for a scuff with an angel, he assured us on our way out. If that was the case I wasn't sure why Mr. Wellington remained within a short dash of us at any moment.

"You think he's wrong to be bitter?" she countered.

"I think grand-theft-body is wrong. At least Ludwig had a full life before hell. The people he's possessed won't even get that." Two men closest to us at the bar turned my way, having heard me. Their expressions might have lowered my body temperature a few degrees had I given a shit. Still, for Addie's sake, I piped down.

She was on edge beside me, sitting straight with both hands cupped around her glass. She stared in silence at the condensation running over her fingers. I wasn't sure if she was more irked by Ito's lack of cooperation or my newfound lack of motivation.

I downed my drink and flagged the barman for another, earning a frustrated huff from my partner. Passive aggressiveness didn't much affect me. "I think we're at the point where one of these may do *you* some good too," I said, leaning on my fist propped up by the bar.

"What point is that? The end? You think we should give up?"

"If you have a lead other than one of the most generic names on the planet and a body of water, feel free to share."

"We have not even researched her yet, why would you give up so easily?"

"Yeah, maybe they have a computer lab with free Wi-Fi in here so I can Google Alex of the Mediterranean. I'm sure she's on Wikipedia." The references went over her head but not the sarcasm.

"What about Carmine?" she asked, retaining her cool. "If he has heard of this place perhaps he knows something about this woman." My drink came, which I immediately turned my attention to.

"Sure, I bet he could paint us her address if we pray for it." When she was silent for a long moment I turned. She stared at me with something between hatred and betrayal in her eyes.

"Why are you being this way?" she asked at last. "Did you bring me this far to abandon me now?"

"I'm not abandoning—"

"Then why are you talking like this?" Her voice shook some, letting me know how upset she was. I set down my glass mid-sip.

"Because I'm an asshole. I'm sorry." Addie let out another sigh and looked back to her water.

"Instead of apologizing for it, maybe you could try not being one. And don't say something sarcastic. It makes you sound pathetic."

I felt my shoulders sink a little. It was her delivery that cut you to size, not the words. She looked as uncomfortable as I'd seen her. Besieged. I'd assumed it was just the location, being surrounded by so many hostile eyes. Which it probably was to some degree. Then I looked past how pissed I was for driving all this way and getting my teeth kicked in just to come up empty handed. I thought about her.

She'd come a lot farther than a drive from Los Angeles.

Remembering what this meant to her, I realized I really had been an asshole. Ignoring her in the car. Nearly getting myself killed at the club door. Picking a fight with the guy who could have killed us as easily as he helped us. Telling her... Oh, Jesus.

"I'm sorry, Addie." She looked at me. "That bit about grand-theft-body. You know I didn't mean..."

"You think that is why I'm upset?"

"No, but..." I shut up. Words didn't matter to her. But I knew what did. Taking a long breath, I pushed my drink away still mostly full. "Let's get out of here. Place makes my skin crawl." She blinked.

"Where will we go?"

"I heard an idea that sounded pretty good," I offered with a shrug. "Maybe Carmine has Wi-Fi too." She didn't smile, but I think she wanted to, and somehow I felt taller for a moment.

We spent another few minutes at the bar waiting for some food to go (we weren't in a position to turn down a free meal, prepared by demons or not). Just before it came Addie tugged my sleeve under the bar. I saw the need for discretion when I found her eyes. I leaned in closer.

"The man on the other side of the bar has been staring at me since we sat down," she whispered. "The coat with the fur collar. Don't be obvious when you look." I followed her advice, staring at the colored waterfall behind the bar. When our food arrived in a bag I made a show of taking in the entire room.

I spotted him fast. Hunched over the bar with a tall drink beside two other guys. Ratty hair and practically gaunt but well dressed. His eyes darted around while he carried on a conversation, but they never strayed from Addie for long.

I grabbed the food and pushed my stool back, showing the man the back of my head while I spoke. "Half the bar's been staring at you," I reminded her. "It'll be fine." She didn't respond other than to follow me up. I grabbed a beer bottle for the road before we left, just eager for something to swing now that I'd been disarmed.

Mr. Wellington trailed us in our long walk through the bar. The hostility followed us until we were back at the front door, bristling the hair on my neck. I asked Mr. Wellington for my gun, which he had on his person. He surrendered it with a placid smile once we were outside. Mr. Jacobs stared me down hard on the stairs. I thought about saying something but thought better of it.

We got around the corner before I heard footsteps behind us on the stairs. We made it down the block past the tavern and a few clumps of people stumbling back to their cars before Addie glanced back. She tried not to make it obvious but it had to have been.

"How many?" I asked while we began crossing the street.

"Four or five demons. I can't tell if they're following us." I wished I'd parked the car under a streetlight.

"Pretend to drop something once we get to the parking lot and take another look." She did and reported the same observation, still unsure if they were following us or headed to their own cars. I gave her the gun in case.

My heart beat fast while we walked into the darkness of the lot, but the bulk of the footsteps continued on past us. I was ready to release the breath I'd been holding until I heard the scuff of a shoe directly behind us. Addie turned immediately, raising the gun.

I matched her move with the beer bottle tight in hand. There was only one. It was hard to make him out in the darkness but it was the man who'd been staring at her from across the bar. He stopped abruptly but slowly raised his hands. He was smiling.

"What do you want?" Addie asked, scanning behind him for any confederates or witnesses. I saw none but checked behind us as well. His smile widened. It was off-putting, anything but sincere.

"You don't need a gun, angel," he said. Addie kept it high.

"Don't call me that. Answer my question." He chuckled under his breath, glancing at me, then back to her.

"I don't want anybody seeing me," he began, lowering his arms, "with you. Like this. Follow me."

"Why would we do that?" I asked as he turned to continue into the parking lot toward another alley.

"Because I know who you're looking for," he returned just loud enough to be heard. Addie held the gun on him even as he slipped past a row of cars. She made a large sweep of the environment, still looking around for a trap.

"Was he telling the truth?" I asked.

"Yes."

His name was Anton Breshkovsky. He was even shiftier looking under the orange pulse of an alley light. His frame looked malnourished, probably from drugs. Despite his overcoat and Italian shoes, he was dirty. Hair product and spray cologne couldn't conceal the fact he hadn't taken a shower in a considerable length of time.

Addie and I took our time catching up to him, checking extensively for any other demons in the vicinity. Anton had stopped midway down an alley beside a backdoor to another bar, directly under a low light. It was obviously a risk, but a risk we couldn't afford to pass.

"What do you want?" was the first thing I asked. He was smoking a cigarette.

"To help you," he said with his toothy smile. He told us his name and that he was a "professional whisperer," that this was his third body. "Just like Beethoven."

"What do you want?" I repeated, unimpressed. He maintained his smile as he looked me up and down, unable to hide his annoyance. He kept his eyes on Addie for the duration of the conversation, despite her holding the gun on him.

"You are looking for someone, yes?" he asked.

"How would you know that?" she returned.

"Ode to Joy is a good place to hear things. When I heard an angel was there I rushed over. I've never talked to an angel before."

"Then let's talk about what sort of things you've heard," she said. "Were you listening to our conversation with Ito?"

"The big man doesn't like people listening in on his business. No one hears him say something unless he wants to be heard."

"Then how—"

"An angel wouldn't show up to this shithole unless she wanted something."

"How do you know what I want?" she asked.

"I told you. I hear things."

"What kind of things?"

"About you? That you made trouble for the wrong people. And now those people are looking for you. But instead of running you seem to be looking for them."

"And you know where we could find them?" Addie pressed. Anton released another silent chuckle, shaking his head.

"I know where some are, but that is a place you could never go, angel." He looked at me. "You, maybe. But I think you'd have a change of heart if you did."

"The Horsemen are here in this world, now," Addie said before I could respond. "Do you know where they are?" Anton smiled and shook his head, leaning against a concrete wall.

"You think I'm talking about Horsemen?" Both Addie and I were silent for a moment. He took a long puff from his cigarette and exhaled above his head.

"Then who *are* you talking about?" I asked eventually. Anton didn't acknowledge I'd even spoken. He flicked his cigarette butt away and thrust off the wall. Still smiling, he put his hands in his pockets and took a step closer. The way his eyes gradually passed over Addie brought me closer to tugging her away and smashing him with the bottle I still held.

"I've always wanted to talk to an angel," Anton repeated at last. "I've always wanted to fuck one too."

"Hey Anton," I said immediately after. "Ask me how happy it would make me to smash your skull into that wall right now. I want you to know if I'm telling the truth."

"This conversation isn't about what would make you happy, it's about what would make me happy. Happy enough to tell you what you want to know."

"How about I just put that gun to your kneecaps," I snarled. "Would that get you talking?"

"No, it wouldn't." I grabbed the gun from Addie's hands and marched to Anton. I shoved him against the wall by the neck and pushed the barrel against his temple. Hard.

"Let's find out." I felt my grip tightening when he just laughed.

"I was tortured by Bolsheviks for treason and then executed, friend," Anton said. "Pain does not frighten me. And if you kill me, I will tell the Watchers exactly where you are." Addie stepped closer, lowering herself to meet his gaze.

"Who are the Watchers?" she asked. "Are they demons?" Anton just laughed, muffled under the pressure of my grip.

"You know how to find out," he answered. I pushed the pistol harder.

"Last chance," I said. "Tell us what we want to know."

"Go ahead, tough man. Kill me. But I don't see a line of other Lost behind me wanting to give you information."

"We'll grab the next one to come out of the bar and see if he's as brave as this one is," I said to Addie. Like we should have done in the first place, I thought.

"The 'next one' isn't going to know where to find the messenger," Anton said. I prepared to grill him further but Addie put her hand on my arm. Her eyes told me to let her handle it. I backed off but kept the gun straight at his forehead. Anton leaned against the wall while he caught his breath.

"Watchers," she repeated just to read his expression. "Do you know what's going on? Why Horsemen and demons are hunting us?" Anton reached for another cigarette in his pocket and lit it, nodding while he did.

"I know who is after you, why, and where they are. Here in this world and beyond. And I can give you the person who knows everything you want to know." He exhaled a breath of smoke just below her face into her chest. "If you give me what I want."

I reached in past Addie and smashed the butt of the gun against his head. He crashed on the wet alley road, reaching to his head with both hands.

"Jon, that isn't going to help us," Addie exclaimed without shouting.

"I don't care if your truth detector is going off or not, this guy is full of shit," I declared. "Why is he the only one who followed after us? Beethoven said anyone who helped us would never be allowed back in the club. Why would he help us?"

"Because unlike most of Beethoven's neutered clientele who live and die by that club, bowing to its owner's pathetic rules that exist for no reason, I do what I please," Anton stated from the ground. "And he doesn't have to know." Addie shook her head in disgust.

"And it would please you just to violate an angel." Anton shrugged.

"An angel with that body, yes," he returned. I was ready to put one through his knee and leave him to rot when Addie pushed the gun down. Reluctantly, I took my finger from the trigger.

"Let's get the hell out of here."

"I am going with him," she said.

I didn't say anything at first, nearly dropping the gun in shock.

"Are you fucking kidding me?" I managed eventually.

"No, I am not. He has what we came here for."

"So might every other piece of shit in that bar!"

"They don't," Anton said, still patiently sitting on the road.

"Shut the fuck up!" I burst. "Addie, he's—"

"He's telling the truth. He's the only one here who knows."

"I don't care! I'm not going to let you..." I trailed off, seeing she was serious.

"What else can we do?" she asked softly.

"What's to stop him from killing you? From kidnapping you and taking you to the Horsemen?"

"I only want her for the night," Anton assured with nonchalance that made my teeth grit. "A few hours. If that. This is the door to my... hotel. You can sit at the door and wait if you like, mister hero. You'll get her back fine. Limping, but fine."

I made it halfway down to hit him again before Addie caught my arm and pushed me back. "What happened to the reverence for Cora's body?" I snapped, grasping for straws. Addie stared at me hard, layers of pain in her expression but oddly calm.

"You aren't making this any easier for me," she said, her voice even. I didn't know what to say. As incredibly, purely wrong as just standing there felt, that's what I did. I stood there while Anton picked himself up, brushed off his fur collared coat, resumed his smile and beckoned Addie to follow him inside the alley door.

I stood silent while he disappeared inside with her.

Carnegie was asleep when the call came in. It was the first time he'd been asleep since taking Lamont's body. Unfortunately the body was an old one, and needed rest eventually. Carnegie hated sleeping. He hadn't come here to let incompetents conduct things at what may have been the most critical moment of the plan while he lay sleeping.

He'd drifted off in an office chair in his makeshift command room, but was roused around midnight by a subordinate. "Sir, we just made the car in San Jose. A citizen called it in." Carnegie came awake immediately, reaching for his jacket behind him.

"Did you get a name from the caller?" he asked. The officer looked puzzled.

"No, sir, just an anonymous tip."

"How exactly did the person identify himself, word for word?"

"Uh..." The officer quickly flipped through paperwork in his hand to a page that traced the call in.

"'...Just a loyal citizen,'" he read. "That's all we got before he hung up sir, but we have the number traced. We can pull up his—"

"Never mind that, we have what we need," Carnegie said as he started out of the room. He raised his voice to the control center outside, shouting the address as he read it. "I want all West Coast units deployed to that address to back up the units already there. Coordinate with the SJPD to have them ready. I want personal transport for myself on the runway in 15 minutes."

Self-loathing was a familiar concept for me, but the proceeding hour and 40 minutes saw a level of such personal enmity that I could barely keep my food down. I nibbled on some of the pork and potato dish we'd ordered from the bar but didn't have the appetite for it.

At first I considered doing as Anton sarcastically advised—waiting by the door in the alley—but I couldn't bring myself to stay that close. I went back to the car for a while but my anger filled the small cab and forced me in the open.

I walked around nearly half an hour, never straying too far from the alley. My eyes were always on the building into which Addie disappeared. I wished I had coffee but settled for the Coke Carmine had packed for us in the messenger bag, slung over my shoulder. Eventually I took a seat on the curb across the street from the parking lot and Anton's alley.

The minutes drug torturously. I spent most of them with my head in my hands, desperate to avoid the image of Anton on top of her. I'd pull my hair, bite my tongue or stand and let a shout fly into the dark to force my mind blank. After an hour I just stared at the door, as desperate to see her walk out as I was dreading it.

What could I possibly say to her when I saw her? I still couldn't believe she'd agreed to it. As strong as she was, as uncompromising... I told myself she must have believed it was the only way. Whatever Anton knew was real. I couldn't appreciate that like she could.

I felt the pork coming back up and leaned over the curb. Any excuse I made was revoltingly pathetic. I knew this was all that mattered to Addie. She would go to any length to stop whatever plot was at work, but... This wasn't what she should have had to come back for. Even if she learned exactly what we needed to know, even if we stopped the Horsemen and saved the world, this would never be justifiable in some grand plan where everything ultimately turns out alright.

My head tilted skyward into the mix of clouds and stars with what I'm sure was a venomous expression.

Did you really send a lonely girl to deal with all this by forcing her to whore herself to someone you sent to hell? Is that your idea of sacrifice? Did she not already go through enough hell in her life?

"Fucking prick," I murmured, folding my arms over my knees. I said it again, louder, as if he was looking straight at me, to show him I wasn't afraid. As much as I hated God I knew it was a waste of time. I could never take my vengeance out on him. I focused my malice on Anton.

More than once I considered storming the building, painting the wall with his brains and getting her out of there. I'd killed before. Promised myself I would never do it again until I eventually killed myself, but I couldn't guarantee Anton Breshkovsky would walk away if I ever saw him again.

I tried to sell myself on the line that Addie would be fine. She could take care of herself. She was plenty resourceful. If he tried anything over the line she'd...

I didn't buy that for a second. Even if she walked out that door without a scratch on Cora's body, Addie would have to carry her wounded spirit forever. And what for? Why should it matter to her if Armageddon came? What difference would it have made in her life?

I wondered what thanks she would she get for all this. Would golden trumpets ring from clouds when she returned? Would God give her some special place in an eternal palace? No, she'd end up on her own in some abstract collection of terrible new memories to ponder for eternity, as bored and lonely as she'd been before.

What a fucking crock. God, heaven, hell, all of it.

I heard laughter and glanced across the street at the tavern. It was empty and closed out but a group of men stood around the alleyway to Ode to Joy, smoking. It was far but I thought I recognized a few of them from the bar. The "Lost." As random and unjust as final judgment turned out to be, most of them were probably no better than Anton. Murders. Rapists. Worse.

No sooner than I thought of the dirt bag I found myself waiting on, I saw him.

There were footsteps to my left. He walked out from the darkened corner of the parking lot, headed across the street back to the bar. He didn't notice me as I stood, already lighting up another cigarette while he headed toward the group outside the bar.

He hadn't come down the alley, I would have seen him. There must have been a front door on the other side of the building that led directly to the street. I scanned the lot for any sign of Addie. He was alone.

I kicked over the last of my Coke as I hurried to my feet, grabbing the gun in my pocket. I started after him in a hurried stride, then a jog. My blood boiled. I wasn't sure what I'd do when I caught up to him.

I was close to shouting his name before I heard a familiar creak from behind me. The door from the alley. I turned back, racing across the parking lot until I came to the orange lit alleyway. I slid to a halt. It was empty, but the door was open. No sign of Addie.

I called her name, starting forward at full stride. There was no response. Heart pounding, I approached the door with the gun pointed. I planned to swing in front of the entrance and clear it for anyone inside, but ended up running straight to it.

I dropped the gun when I came to the entryway. The air rushed from my lungs as my heart dropped. Ironically, the first thing I remember doing after seeing her is taking Jesus' name in vain. She had made it to the door but collapsed before moving through it, laying on her knees in a broken mess.

She'd tried to clean herself up before she dressed, it appeared, but it hadn't helped much. Fluids remained caked on her clothes, skin, hair. Her jacket and most of her pants were still in one piece, but her shirt was only useful as a rag to clot the blood crusted on her arms and chest. It ran free from a gash on her forehead and from her mouth.

Her eyes were vacant when they found mine. I rushed to her after I recovered my breath, kneeling but unsure where to touch her. She wasn't wearing anything under her jacket so I could see the bruises along her midsection and the cut down her sternum.

Nothing looked severe enough on the surface to threaten her life, but I wouldn't have been surprised if she had a broken rib or some other internal injury.

"Addie... Addie..." I don't think I said anything intelligent when I first grabbed hold of her by the shoulders. I wasn't sure if she'd want me to touch her but she leaned into me, laying her head against my shoulder. I asked her where she was hurt. She said he cut her with handcuffs but she could walk.

When I tried to help her up it was apparent she couldn't. She didn't have her shoes. She was disoriented. Drugged, from the look in her eyes. "Hold on, Addie," I told her, picking her up under her legs and her back. The blood stained my suit while I carried her back to the car. I placed her in the back seat like I'm sure she did to me the first night we met.

"I'll be fine," she said a few times while I cleaned her wounds with what water we had in the car and paper towels. None of the cuts appeared life threatening and I pressure checked her for anything broken. I was most worried about whatever he'd drugged her with, but she seemed coherent enough that it wasn't likely an overdose.

"Jon," she said, fresh blood dripping from her lip. "He... he didn't tell me anything."

My heartbreak withdrew like the first wave of a storm, sucked back into the next, larger swell. A swell of anger. I glanced over my shoulder across the street. The same group remained outside near Ode to Joy's entrance. I handed Addie the water and paper towels, then took off my shirt and jacket.

"Here, you put these on, okay? You stay right here, I'll be back after you change."

"Jon... Where are you going?" she managed, trying to sit up. I tucked her legs in over the seat, avoiding the bruises as best I could, then shut the door.

"You stay here and change, I'll be back in a minute," I told her, my voice shaking. I'd picked up the gun before leaving the alley but I went to the trunk, taking out a wrench from the tire change kit. Hands filled, I marched across the street in my undershirt, indomitable rage driving each step.

Anton was with the group, still puffing away on his cigarette. Another of the demons noticed me first, leading the others to turn as I made it to the tavern's corner. Most saw the gun and the wrench and immediately backed away from the stairs. Anton was among the last. His eyes widened in alarm when he saw the look on my face and the gun coming up on him.

When he bolted for the stairs, pushing his way past his buddies, I took off after him full bore. A few in the group asked if I was crazy but none of them tried to stop me. Anton was nearly down the stairs when I tore around the corner, shouting for him to stop. Mr. Jacobs held the door open for him and wheeled around when he heard my voice.

He opened his mouth to say something the same moment he reached into his coat for his gun, but I stopped him with a bullet through his chest. He slammed against the wall and slid down, cursing something incomprehensible. He wouldn't get back up.

Mr. Wellington wasn't in the parlor room, only Anton, racing down the stairs. I let off two shots. The first missed him but the second caught his upper thigh. He tumbled down several steps, screaming as he went. I raced behind him with my bludgeon tight in hand, ready to bring it down to his forehead.

I was caught in something primal. Years of anger I couldn't take out on anyone was about to be unleashed on this man. I wouldn't have asked him a thing if I hadn't been stopped by three men with semi-automatics bursting from the door to the club.

I was too deep into the parlor room to go back and there was nowhere to hide. They could have blown me away, but no shots came. Only orders to drop my weapons, turn around and march back the way I'd come. I ignored them and reached down for Anton.

"I'm taking him with me," I announced, pulling him up by his scalp and pressing the gun to his temple for the second time. The men disagreed, ordering me to release him, but still held their fire. I made it a few steps up before I heard shouting behind me. Then my name.

"Jon, stop!" Addie's voice sailed through the air. "This gains us nothing! You—" She was silenced by someone and I immediately dropped Anton, dashing for the door. I leapt over Mr. Jacobs' corpse with the gun high. Two of the demons still atop the stairs held Addie. She had to have chased after me after hearing the gunshots.

Only one of them had a gun, probably Mr. Jacobs', but one held a knife to Addie and shouted for me to drop my weapon. I did the same to him, moments from pulling the trigger. The gunmen in the parlor caught up and I was surrounded. Still no one fired.

"What's this racket?" a familiar voice echoed from the parlor. I waited a moment, looking back through the door as Mr. Wellington and Hitoshi Ito emerged on the staircase. Ito paused when he saw me with the gun and Mr. Jacobs' corpse below me. His eyes were ablaze.

"You dare?" he breathed. "You *dare*?!" He pushed past Mr. Wellington and marched up the remaining stairs until he was but a foot from my face. "I invite you into my house and let you leave peacefully, and you return to break my code with blood?!"

"No code is going to save that man from me, Ito," I shouted, pointing with my head to Anton. Ito looked back, watching Anton grasp for the railing to pull himself up. "That motherfucker is mine. He made a deal and he broke it, torturing and raping my friend along the way."

Ito's eyes flared and softened in one motion, his fury subsiding as the truth hit him. "Where is Miss Martin?" he asked. I advised him to look down my gun barrel. He stepped outside and saw the men holding her. Again he flared, ordering Mr. Wellington up immediately. "Help her at once," he said, to which the bodyguard slung his weapon over his shoulder and rushed up to take Addie from the demons.

They released her hesitantly but without a fight, observing the other three guards behind Ito still clutching their weapons. "I'm sorry, Mr. Ito," the demon who held the knife said. "We thought—"

"Silence!" Ito shouted, moving so Mr. Wellington could rush by with Addie, her arm slung over his shoulder.

"Wait, where are you taking her?" I said, moving the gun back into the parlor past to Mr. Wellington.

"She needs medical attention, does she not?" Ito said.

"Yes, but, just wait! I'm not letting her out of my sight again!" I shouted. Ito let out a sharp breath but told Mr. Wellington to halt. He did at the base of the stairs, holding Addie in place.

"Jon, please," she begged, still clearly disoriented. I tried to calm down for her sake and lowered my gun. I stared at Ito hard.

"Your patron Anton Breshkovsky agreed to tell us about a group called the Watchers and give us a contact he called the messenger in exchange for a night with Addie. Instead he told us nothing and did *that* to her." I pointed her way with the hand that held the wrench.

Ito said nothing at first, his anger simmering as he took in her bruised and bloodied form. His eyes slid to Anton, now shaking with fear. "May I have your club?" Ito asked, still staring at Anton. I handed it over. Ito walked down the stairs, towered over Anton for a long moment, then struck him across the cheek. Anton squealed and spat out a tooth.

Ito placed the bar against Anton's chin. "Don't make that sound again," he ordered, to which Anton tried to stifle his tears. "You have broken the code of my house. You will never set foot here again in this body or any other. Do you understand?" Anton nodded vigorously. "Now, you will honor your agreement with Miss Martin, or I will send you back to darkness myself."

Anton swallowed hard, turning for Addie. "The Watchers. They're the ones you're after and the ones after you. They're demons—a group of Lost in hell trying to escape. Forever, without possession. They want to break down the entire afterlife, undo the very word of God."

"How?" I asked. "What does this have to do with the Horsemen?"

"You keep talking about the Horsemen, I don't know a damn thing about them. It's the Watchers who want you dead."

"We found the Horsemen in LA, they're the ones out there right now. What do they have to do with these Watchers? What is their plan?"

"I don't know," Anton said. "But the Watchers are always trying to escape hell. To destroy it. They have some plan, I don't know if it involves Horsemen or not. All I know is you and the angel are too close to whatever they're planning and they're coming for you."

"What about this messenger?" I growled. Anton hesitated, glancing at Ito. Ito let out a sharp breath and nodded.

"A woman," Anton said. "With a name I'm sure you'll recognize. Sylvia Plath. She is one of many messengers the Watchers use." Hearing this in the presence of Ludwig van Beethoven made her identity less impressive, but only barely. I almost asked him how Plath or anyone could be sending messages to hell but remembered Carmine. Angels and demons could feel the truth in art even from the beyond. Either way, it was a question for Plath.

"Where do I find her?"

"She is a patron here. You can find her in this city. Mr. Ito will know where she lives."

"And she'll know what the Watchers are up to?" I asked.

"She is Loyal," Anton said. "She will know."

"And Loyal all work for the Watchers?" I pressed. Anton said yes. "Are you one of them?" This time he shook his head no. "Then how do you know any of this?"

"I told you. Ode to Joy is a good place to hear things." I looked to Addie. She looked half awake, slipping in and out of consciousness. I wasn't sure how much she heard, but she must have felt my eyes on her because she told me it was true. I looked at Ito.

"You knew all this." I stated it to Ito. "You know more. What they're really up to."

"Yes to the first, no to the second," Ito returned. "I know of the Loyal. They are not welcome here."

"What about Plath?" I asked.

"I ask patrons if they will follow my code inside my walls. That is all we ask them. She was not Loyal when we first asked."

"So this shithead knew and you didn't." Ito was far from amused. "Her address."

"If I give it to you," Ito answered slowly, "you are not to harm her. Loyal or not, there will be no bloodshed on my hands."

"Unless it comes down to self-defense," I offered back. He glared but nodded.

"Plath can be found at the Dominic Building under the name Young, 1397 S. 8th Street. I'm not sure of her apartment number." I looked to Addie, her head hanging. I rushed down to her despite Ito's men holding their guns on me. I tried to take her from Mr. Wellington but Ito called out. "Going with you after the Loyal will do nothing to improve Miss Martin's health. I will see to her."

"I don't care if you're telling the truth or not—I don't trust any of you," I told him.

"I will take responsibility for this man's actions though they were not mine, Jon Perry, because I care for the wellbeing of this woman," Ito said. "I offer more than I should to keep the balance of this house. Would you reject my help?"

"And you'll let us just walk back out of here after you patch her up? After I've killed one of your bouncers?"

"Issues we will settle once you return," he replied. "But this scum should not have returned here and drawn my men into conflict with you. Punishment will be on his head."

I looked to Addie, pushing a lock of her hair back to see her eyes. She was fading in and out but she nodded. "He is telling the truth," she managed. "But... you cannot go alone. It is... too dangerous." I swallowed hard and looked up to Mr. Wellington, stoic as usual.

"Take care of her," I ordered more threateningly than I'm sure he appreciated. I turned then, moving up the stairs until even with Ito. "I don't suppose your generosity would see fit to give me one of those semi-automatics."

"You will take no tools of destruction from this house that are not your own," he answered. I nodded, but reached out for the wrench.

"I'll take that back then." He handed it to me. I took a quick breath and searched for what I wanted to say. "I... For what it's worth, I think God made the wrong call about you." When Ito said nothing, I turned to leave. He stopped me before I got to the door.

"Do you believe you are going to heaven, Mr. Perry?" he asked suddenly.

"I probably have about the same odds of getting there as you," I returned.

"Well, who knows for certain. God, I suppose. But if I were him, I would not know what to do with you." I stared at him for a moment, then back to Addie, now all but limp in Mr. Wellington's arms. I took off up the stairs.

ten

It was just after one in the morning when I pulled around the block to the Dominic Building. I found myself shaking when I parked and shut off the engine. At first I assumed it was the cold. I was only dressed in a white undershirt from the waist up. The smell of blood from the jacket and rags in the back seat brought out the truth.

I cried in a loud burst for about thirty seconds, hammered the wheel with the butt of my fist. It might have been the first time in five years I'd been that worked up about anything other than the girls. I couldn't believe I left her alone... With Anton or Ito.

I pulled myself together and looked in the rear view mirror. My face was red, covered in sweat and spatters of blood. Some was mine, some Addie's, some Mr. Jacob's, maybe. I wiped it away the best I could and stepped out of the car. I had the gun in my pants pocket but left the wrench on the floorboard. I'd look suspicious enough without it.

Thankfully there weren't many people out in the wee hours of a Wednesday morning. The cloud cover had increased during the drive here. The street was well lit thanks to the rows of small businesses intermixed with apartment buildings.

On the way over I'd wondered how I planned to talk to Sylvia Plath short of kicking down her door. Relegating that to plan B, I decided I'd trying buzzing up and telling her the truth. Hitoshi Ito sent me. I'd have to dodge just about any other question, but hopefully his name would carry enough weight for her to open the door.

I was sure it wouldn't be that easy. Surely a Loyal demon would be more on guard, but there was always plan B.

The ever-cautious investigator in me from a few weeks ago would have balked at that attitude, but I was in something of a rampage after recent events.

The Dominic Building turned out to be a boarding house, not apartments, which worked to my advantage. The only Young was listed on the third floor. Maggie Young. Something about that sounded familiar, but I couldn't place it.

I woke the landlord with a few buzzes at the front door and told her I had to speak with Young right away, that it was an emergency. Still half asleep or stupid, she didn't ask questions. She told me to wait inside while she tried to wake Young.

Turned out she wasn't home. The landlord said she regularly came back late in the night. I wondered if she'd been at Ode to Joy in the first place, but assumed Ito would have known if that were the case. I asked the landlord for Young's cell phone but she replied Young didn't carry one.

She offered to let me wait for Young inside but I declined. I couldn't have her asking questions—I wasn't sure if she was Loyal too. I doubted it from her lethargic manner, but if Young was important enough to know so much about the Watchers, she was likely under protection. I preferred to wait in the car where I could see people coming.

I waited for two hours.

Carnegie had heard of this place before, obviously.

He heard everything of consequence that took place in this realm. The "club" on the West Coast held special significance though. To his knowledge, this was the only organized gathering place for the Lost. Others had come and gone, but never to this scale. Hundreds of possessors had passed through the doors of Ode to Joy at one point or another.

It saddened him to destroy it.

But that wouldn't stop him, of course. Nothing could be left to chance now that they were this close. No loose ends left to unravel a plan of this magnitude. There had never been a plan that would so affect the world—existence—before, and there never would again.

"They don't understand that," he told a Loyal agent in the back of the SUV while they waited. "That's why I have to send them back. I'm doing this for them."

"Yes, sir," the agent returned, looking out the window as the FBI perimeter around the club widened with reinforcements from the SJPD. Carnegie wanted to ensure the Loyal remained that way. Nothing tested loyalty like forcing Lost back to darkness. As he listened to the muffled gunfire, he wondered if the justification wasn't for himself.

Nearly ten minutes passed before the all clear was given. Carnegie checked his watch—3:53a.m. Pacific—then stepped out of the SUV. A unit formed ahead and behind him. Two of them Loyal, two of them Famine and Pestilence. A few Lost had been killed in the street when they saw the feds coming, but most of the violence was contained inside the club.

Carnegie winced and covered his nose as he walked down the steps to the parlor room, slippery with blood. He was accustomed to sensations exponentially more appalling, but they hadn't driven out his humanity yet. Emotion welled in his throat at the sight of so many innocent dead.

He steeled himself as he made his way through the bar. It was necessary, he assured himself. He knew no sane Lost would resist interrogation and risk losing a body worked for so hard, but he needed to know everything they knew immediately. Living federal agents couldn't ask the right questions in interrogation rooms. Only in darkness could the other Watchers probe for exactly what they needed to know.

He'd spared one, of course. The club manager was as renowned an information broker as he was a musician. Carnegie wanted to handle him personally. He was the only survivor, sitting on his knees in a back room by a piano. Cuffed, bloodied, surrounded by corpses who'd gone down protecting him.

Carnegie locked eyes with Ito the moment he stepped into the room. He ordered everyone out but the Horsemen and a few Loyal among his guard formation.

"Herr Beethoven," Carnegie said, lowering his handkerchief from his nose and stuffing it into his pocket.

"And you are?" Ito returned through his heavy breathing.

"My name is Andrew Carnegie."

"Ah, yes. A clever possession, Mr. Carnegie."

"A necessary one." Ito nodded, looking over to Mr. Wellington's body.

"I'm sure you'd characterize your being here like this similarly."

"Yes, unfortunately," Carnegie said. "I need to know what help you've given them."

"Why don't you kill Hitoshi here and be done with it, then?" Ito suggested.

"I wanted to ask you myself."

"I'm sure you did." Ito continued looking to the side, silent. Carnegie found himself frustrated at once.

"What you've done here is commendable, sir, but hardly sustainable. Hardly a solution."

"A solution for what? God?"

"Yes," Carnegie affirmed.

"He is called God for a reason. Like all those before you, you are wasting your time."

"This is not some pagan ritual to summon a non-existent anti-Christ. We are weeks—days—away from correcting the Injustice."

"How?"

"You will know soon enough, and you will thank me for all this."

"You don't trust me?"

"That depends on your next answer. Where are the angel and the man?"

"Not here."

"But you know where they are. You sent them away."

"Yes."

"Where?"

"Whether this house stands or not, I remain neutral."

"Where?"

"I will not tell you." Carnegie felt Lamont's face tighten into a snarl uncontrollably.

"I offer you salvation where he offers you damnation, and you would aid his chosen in stopping us?"

"I would kindly stay clear of whatever it is you and your friends are up to," Ito returned. "Broken though the afterlife may be, no being capable of creating it—of creating sentience—would leave a loophole minds such as ours could exploit."

Carnegie's expression was more wounded than angry. "I'm not sure that I've ever heard more cynical words," he said, reaching for one of the Loyal's guns. "I'd have thought you were more of a humanist."

"You're doing this because you believe in humanity?"

"Yes!" Carnegie replied, desperate to be believed. "I dedicated my life to humanity! I advanced industry, put nations on the road to progress. I was the second richest man alive and gave almost everything to build libraries, schools, universities. To create pensions and tend to the sick. All I wanted was to leave this world better than how I found it."

"It sounds as though I should recognize your name the same as you recognize mine," Ito said. "You were a great man."

"And this is how I am rewarded? An eternity of suffering because I had the audacity to spend my Sunday mornings working for a better world instead of praying for one inside a church? I did not accomplish all that I did to curry favor with a gatekeeper to paradise. I did it because it was right."

Carnegie found himself breathing hard, sweating. He forced himself to calm down, taking slow breaths. "That is the difference between you and I, sir. I work for a better world while you merely wish for one."

"And you do it because it is right," Ito finished. "Is that what you tell yourself when you pull that trigger?" Carnegie was stoic. He pointed the gun at Ito's head, then his knee. "I'll have the truth one way or the other." Ito smiled.

"It will have to be the other," he responded. "You and I have both been in darkness, Mr. Carnegie. No pain in this world will frighten us." Carnegie held the gun on him for a lingering moment then let it sag.

"After all you have been through, you harbor faith for him but not us?"

"I harbor no faith, anymore."

"We are all we have. If we do not try, what are we?"

"Doomed. Either way." Carnegie shook his head, honestly disappointed.

"You may very well be, sir." Carnegie shot Ito through the head. He would never have said anything. The other Watchers would find the truth soon enough. "Concoct a story about all this and send men to gather our primary messenger. I want her at my side when the message comes in. Sweep every inch of this city in the meantime. Find them."

I would have fallen asleep were it not for the rapping on the window. I came awake with a start, spotting a little boy beside the car. Probably no more than 10 years old, all by himself. He wore only a t-shirt despite the cold. When he caught my eye through the window I felt the grip of déjà vu. I had seen the kid somewhere before.

Before I could get out to ask if he was lost and get a closer look at him, he took off across the street. I watched him go, but as he turned the corner, my heart resumed its pounding pace from earlier in the night. A woman was there. She too was alone and it was so dark I could only tell that she was a woman, but when she turned to make her way up the steps for the boarding house I knew.

I considered bolting for her, but I restrained myself and slowly exited the car after she was safely inside the building. I couldn't risk spooking her or she could take off. Or worse, signal any Loyal friends. I slung the messenger bag over my shoulder. Old as it was, I figured I might want the first aid kit handy.

I made my way across the street and buzzed the landlord again. She was in a far worse mood the second time I interrupted her sleep, but I lied that I just got tired of waiting outside and I wanted to stay in the foyer if it was no trouble. She obviously wasn't possessed since she took the line and shuffled back to bed without question.

I made for the stairs once she was gone, working my way up to the third floor at an enterprising pace. The halls were dark. No one was awake on the first or second floor, but I heard footsteps on the third. I hurried my pace, taking two steps at a time. If I caught Plath in the hallway I wouldn't have to worry about forcing my way into her room at gunpoint.

I should have known better than to take two stairs at once in the dark—I stumbled up the last one with a loud smack of my toe against the wood. I barely stopped myself from tripping. When I heard the footsteps stop I turned to observe Plath down the hall. She was in front of her door, staring at me.

Instead of looking away and dusting myself off, I found myself staring back. I don't think she recognized my face, but she must have known who I was. What I was there for. I could see it in her eyes.

I took off in a sprint the moment she turned, fumbling her keys for the door to unlock it. By the time I made it to the door she was inside, secured behind a deadbolt. I considered kicking at the door until I smashed through (it didn't look too heavy) but I heard footsteps on metal from behind the door.

Recalling a fire escape on the side of the building, I dashed for the stairs. I saw her on the ground through a window on my way to the first floor. Again we locked eyes. She took off into a hard run while I regretted Plath had found a body younger than my own to possess.

I tore into the night from the building's front door just in time to catch Plath darting around a corner to the next street. I continued after her, calling both of her names in hopes she would respond to one. I tried yelling that Ito had sent me and I just wanted to talk. She didn't slow, zipping into an alley from the main street. The messenger bag bounced against my back as I ran.

She turned out to be less fit than I'd anticipated. After another block I closed the gap to thirty feet. I could see the glow of a cell phone in her hand. Calling for help.

Aware I was gaining, Plath skid to a halt along another residential street and turned with her arm up. She let off a few rounds from her gun before I could duck behind a stoop. The second one came pretty close. I had my own weapon but killing her would do me no good.

I continued after her when she took off, but she ducked inside a gas station mini-mart at the end of the street. I could see her pulling her gun on the attendant and ordering him to lock the door, which he did. She scanned through the glass for me but I'd taken cover behind a car.

Whatever I was going to do, I knew it had to be at once. I would probably only have a few minutes before her protectors arrived, whoever they were. Worse, Plath could escape even inside the building if she killed her host. She could always come back later if she was as good a whisperer as she probably was.

In a low roadie run, I made my way to the back of the station behind rows of parked cars. I found the back door immediately but it was locked. Thankfully there was a window in the door. I winced at the sound while I smashed it and forced the door open. She'd know I was coming.

She let me know by shouting for me to stay put in the back, that she had the attendee at gunpoint. "I just want to talk," I returned from a back room. "I don't want to hurt you, Ms. Plath."

"You're with the angel. You're trying to stop us."

"You people are the ones after me. I just want to know what's going on."

"My friends are coming. Lots of them. If you leave now you'll have a few minutes to escape." I looked across the back room and saw light coming in from another side. A second entryway into the quickmart.

"I'm not leaving until you tell me who's after me and why. Who are the Watchers? Why are the Horsemen here?" There was no response until the sound of sirens echoed in from outside.

"This is your last chance. Leave before it's too late."

"If I don't make it out of here, neither do you," I barked more angrily than I meant to. The moment my mouth closed I tiptoed to the opposite entrance and peeked around the corner. Sure enough, she had the gun at the entrance from which she'd last heard my voice.

Taking a long breath, I spun around the corner behind a rack of magazines and into an aisle. I crept behind her while she sent another warning to the back room. By the time she suspected I was gone, I was behind her, rising from a slushy machine to press my gun against her back. "Don't move," I ordered. She did, half from shock.

I hit her with my elbow, dropping her to the floor. I kicked her gun away when she landed. The attendant had been cowering in the corner but bolted for the back immediately. "Get up," I told her. "You're coming with me."

"Do you not hear the sirens?" she asked. "Those are Loyal. Or worse. You are taking me nowhere."

"Lady, I have been through too much shit tonight to be polite about this. Now haul your ass up right—"

"Both of you get the hell out of my store!" The attendant reemerged from the back with a shotgun, aimed straight at me. I froze.

"That's what I'm trying to do, pal," I said. "Just—"

"Drop your gun!" he yelled. "Now!" I let out a sharp breath but slowly lowered myself to the ground, setting the gun beside me.

"Keep your gun on her, she's the dangerous one," I said. He didn't respond, looking out the front windows as police cars peeled into the parking lot, forming a perimeter. My heart sank as I looked back. There were five cars and a van already in the street, more red and blue lights on the way.

"Finally, cops when you need them," the attendant said. "Neither one of you move or—Hey!" Plath kicked me in the chest and slid away into the nearest aisle toward with her gun. I leapt after her to keep it away from her. She sent a savage knee into my chest but I overpowered her and took hold of the gun.

We were both about to say something but the sound of glass breaking followed by something heavy hitting the ground cut us off. When I turned I saw a pool of blood advancing over the linoleum. Plath wiped a spurt of blood from her nose and caught sight of the dead attendant through the shelf.

"I tried to tell you," she said. I told her to shut up and knocked over a few boxes of donuts in the shelf between me and the door to get a view outside. Police were everywhere.

"Are they all Loyal?" I asked.

"They might as well be. They're here to protect me."

"Maybe the attendant just got an alarm off."

"So they sent the entire precinct to deal with a gas station hold up?" she asked scornfully. I peered back out, noticing several SUVs and dark cars behind the police. Those weren't cops. I thought about moving Plath toward the back to see if we'd been surrounded yet but a voice appeared on a loud speaker.

"Jon Perry," it said. "This is Deputy Director Christopher Lamont of the FBI. You are surrounded. Release your hostage and come out with your hands up and you will be taken into custody without incident."

"Is he Loyal?" I asked Plath, checking her gun to see how many rounds it had left. She sat silent beside me. "Is he a Horseman?"

"Maybe you can ask him when he takes you into custody," she answered.

"I thought I wasn't making it out of here alive."

"You aren't." I stared at her until Lamont's voice sounded again.

"Jon Perry, I say again. Release your hostage and come out with your hands up. You are completely surrounded."

"So I can end up like the innocent guy you just sniped through a window?" I shouted at the top of my lungs. "No thanks."

"This is your last chance. You have one minute to respond." I swallowed hard, my heart racing as I thought.

"Do they know about Ode to Joy?" I asked Plath.

"You think you would know about it but they would not?" she asked.

Addie.

I stretched my hand out to Plath.

"Give me your phone," I said. She didn't move. "Don't make me take it." She grunted and told me it was on the counter where she'd left it before I attacked her. "Then get up and go get it. And if you bolt for the door, I'll put one in your foot and pull you back." She sneered but rose, obeying.

For a moment I wondered if they would kill her to make sure she didn't give me any information, but I figured they would need her alive the same as I did if she was indeed their link to the Watchers. Sure enough, she made it back to me unharmed.

"Is Lamont in charge?" I asked.

"It sounds that way, doesn't it?"

"He's the one you called?"

"I have no idea who he is."

"Then call whoever your contact is with them." She didn't budge. I thought about threatening her but instead selected her recently dialed contacts. I pressed the last number and put the phone to my ear. There were a few rings before someone picked up. I heard the phone shuffled for a moment before it found the right person.

"Your time is running out, Perry," came Lamont's voice. "Don't test me."

"Who are you really?" I asked. "What's your real name?"

"My name is inconsequential. Yours, however, is the one at the top of the FBI most wanted list. There is nowhere you could go now, no one who would take you in. It's over."

"I might still have some degenerate friends as reprehensible as me," I said. "I'm in the media after all."

"You are surrounded. There will be no escape."

"Maybe not, but in case you haven't noticed, I've got your messenger and a cell phone. And unless you want me to text everything I know to the LA Times and every other major paper in the country, I suggest you take a less threatening tone."

"If you knew anything you'd have sent it already," Lamont stated coldly. "And who would believe you?"

"If you weren't worried, you wouldn't have half of San Jose's police department and the FBI trying to kill me."

"Clever of you to avoid telling me what you know so I can't discern if you're lying or not, which obviously means you know nothing."

"Which obviously means you're some piece-of-shit body-snatcher who crawled out of hell for a vacation. Listen, Lamont. If you ever want to get another message from your Watcher buddies through Sylvia here again, you're going to—"

"You are in no position to give me orders. Not if you care anything for the person inhabiting Cora Avery in there with you." He thought

Addie was with me. "That's right, Perry. Do you really want more blood on your hands? Is your wife and daughter's not enough?" I tasted blood in my mouth from how hard I gritted my teeth.

"Listen, you sack of sh—"

"Threaten Plath all you like, I can pick up a phone to another messenger in a second. Killing her will inconvenience me at worst. If you and the angel want to remain in this world through this night, you'll let Plath go and surrender yourselves. Now."

I looked at Plath, letting the phone sag a little. I searched her eyes for the truth, then said, "Give us a few minutes to think it over. I don't think you'll want to kill us just yet after what Sylvia's told me." I hung up and dialed another number I had memorized while waiting in the car for Plath.

"I've told you nothing," she snapped.

"Yeah, but he doesn't know that."

"He will once he kills you and the Watchers mine your memories in hell."

"Suppose I go to heaven," I said, waiting while the phone rang. She looked at me like it was out of the question. I waited through triple the rings of a normal phone before I decided no one was going to answer at Ode to Joy. Probably not a good sign, but the Loyal couldn't have been there yet if Lamont thought Addie was with me.

Realizing I had no real bargaining chip unless I could get a hold of Ito, I knew I'd probably be dead in a few minutes. At least Addie would still be safe. She could keep up the investigation on her own. Maybe she'd find someone actually worth a damn to help her or—

I jumped in shock as an explosion rocked the entire building. Wheeling around to look through the front windows, I saw a fireball rising from one of the SUVs, torn to a mangled heap. The police and Feds all turned from their cover toward something approaching down the street. Shouts and gunfire peppered the air and chaos engulfed the night.

I shuddered as an unmarked armored truck blasted through a line of police cars, racing past the perimeter into the parking lot. Another two cars followed it. When one of them fired a rocket propelled grenade from the window at a police car I was sufficiently confused.

Another truck appeared from the opposite side of the street, barreling behind the gas station. I heard the skid of rubber from the brakes behind the building. "Move it, Perry! We've got to go now!" The voice was muffled from outside but hoarse from the shout.

I didn't recognize the voice but decided the Loyal wouldn't destroy half of their own forces just to trap me. Seizing Plath's hand, I yanked her to her feet and pulled her to the back. Gunfire poured into the gas station our direction. I kept my head low and shouted for her to do the same.

A man in a Kevlar vest and holding an M4 waited in the back, panting hard. I'd never seen him before. "Let's go!" he shouted, turning in a run for the door. "Keep your heads down!"

When we made it outside I could hear the snap and whizz of bullets passing dangerously close. A few police cars had made it around back but three additional men with heavy weapons laid down enough covering fire to hold them at bay. I ran for the armored truck after the man with the M4.

We got halfway there when Plath slowed down. When I turned she was knelt over, her free hand grasping a pistol dropped by a downed Fed. She got off two rounds before the big man leading me put her down. One tore into my side. In and out, but it put me on the ground. Someone picked me up and hauled me the rest of the way to the truck. We left Plath dead on the pavement.

The truck from the front appeared on the street beside us, laying down a heavy stream of fire. I remember relief as they slung me into the truck, then panic as they pulled a bag over my head and pushed me down. I passed out afterward, probably from blood loss.

eleven

For a while I thought I was asleep, dreaming. Then I realized how much pain I was in. Something cold moved inside me, clawing. The touch of Pestilence on my mind, I flared and tried to push up from the narrow space where I lay.

It was bright when I opened my eyes. I caught a glimpse of two men at my bloody side, one administering a needle into my arm. When I recoiled, pressure came down on my shoulders, holding me in place. Large hands. I trailed them back to the face leaning over me, blocking the light.

"Take it easy," his voice said, reverberating through the small space. I realized I was in the back of a vehicle, moving. "Do you want that slug out of your gut or not?"

"Where..." I managed as my eye lids became heavy.

"We can't exactly make a pit stop at the hospital," the man said. "Just relax. You'll be okay, amigo."

I don't remember much after that. Flashes of lights from the van, sudden bumps, a wider room, and a whole lotta numbness.

"Daddy, do you think Tucker and Kolby are in heaven?" I looked at her after zipping her bag back up. She'd torn into it for her tennis shoes, leaving a pile of her clothes on the floor for me to cram back in.

"Who's that, baby?" I asked, lifting her onto the bench and grabbing her feet so I could tie her shoes.

"*Daddy*—Tucker and Kolby!" Oh yeah. The fish.

"I'm sure they're fine, baby."

"No, daddy—we just left them."

"I'm sure somebody will find them and take care of them."

"But what if they don't? What if they die?"

"Trust me, baby girl, they won't die."

"But they will someday." She'd taken off her tiara and placed it in her lap, rubbing on the shiny center jewel with her thumb.

"Yeah, someday. But there's nothing you can do about that. You have to think about the now, not the later."

"But they'll go to heaven when they die." It wasn't a question this time. She stated it. "They're good fishies." I finished with her laces and waited for her to look at me like she always did when I fell silent. I thought about promising to buy her new fish after we moved. No, I knew that wouldn't help. But I knew what would.

"When we get to the new house, I know someone who's gonna be swimming like a fish. Know why?" Pita's face lit up like I'd just let her loose in a Toys R Us.

"Because we have a *pool!*" she shouted, already back on her feet in the chair.

"Better show me that fish face to get ready," I said, leaning in to touch my nose against hers. She puffed her lips out and flapped her hands against her cheeks. I kissed her and tickled her. She let out a characteristic shriek heard throughout the airport lobby.

"Jonathan, I told you not to wind her up," Gabby called from the hallway. Her face was moist, having gone to the bathroom to splash it with water. We were all exhausted from the midnight exodus from Miami and the flight. Pita was immune to fatigue, of course, powered by birthday excitement.

I made a show of stifling my giggle with Pita, to which she covered her mouth with her hands. Even now, her belly laugh never ceased to make me smile. Gabby took her from me and set her down, smoothing out the ruffles of Pita's pink dress and repositioning her tiara.

"You're getting glitter all over your hair," Gabby said. It was more a tired observation than an admonition.

"Daddy says I can go swimming as soon as we get to the new house, mommy," Pita declared. "When is the car coming?"

"We're just waiting for the nice men to get it for us," Gabby said. "When we get home it will be really late and daddy will have to get the pool ready. You may need to wait until tomorrow." Pita deflated like a balloon.

"But, mo-om! It's my birthday!" I could see Gabby preparing for another speech about why we had to leave so suddenly on her birthday, but I cut her short with a hand on Pita's shoulder.

"I bet if you asked really nice your mom would let us have a birthday treat before lunch," I said. "Like, I don't know, maybe an ice cream." Pita's smile rocketed back into position. She jumped and twirled like a professional figure skater. Gabby glared at me. She hated that I always got to be the good cop. She let it slide this time, allowing the tip of a smile from the corner of her mouth.

"Only because it's your birthday," she conceded. I asked Pita what flavor she wanted (bubble-burst berry swirl—I told her she'd probably have to settle for strawberry) then left the main terminal. The Feds responsible for moving us didn't want me wandering about, but they'd overheard the commotion and agreed to let me walk to the food court.

Aware this was all just a dream, I savored the last echoes of Pita's laugh as I left the terminal. That would be the last time I'd hear it. This was the point where I always tried to force myself awake, but again the memory played out to its terrible completion.

"Jon?" For a moment I thought it was Gabby calling me, but when I recognized the voice, my eyes burst open. I jolted up in a sweat. The bed was in a small room, tucked under the only window. Light shone onto Addie, sitting beside me on a stool. She looked as surprised as me, but motioned with a hand on my chest for me to calm down.

"Relax, you are safe," she told me. I prepared to say something back but winced at the pain in my side. "Just relax. You don't want to tear a stitch." Recalling the flashes of images from the van and another room, I lifted the sheet over me and pulled up the end of a white shirt.

Bandages covered by middle. Where I'd been shot.

Utterly confused, I turned my attention back to Addie. She wore a few bandages herself, but she looked unharmed. She wore no makeup. Cora's golden hair was collected behind her in a loose ponytail.

"Addie. Are you alright?" She nodded, somewhat taken aback. I don't think she expected that to be my question.

"We both are," she confirmed. "You had me scared, though. You lost a great deal of blood. They gave you some, but you'll be weak for a while."

"Who's 'they'?" I asked, looking around the room. It was empty other than my bed and a sink in the opposite corner. Addie took a deep breath and leaned back in her seat.

"Friends," she said. "I believe so, anyway. They saved us, after all." My mind raced back to the gas station and the shoot off between the Loyal Feds and the mystery assailants. Curious as I was about how they'd known to come for me, I asked what happened to her.

"You convinced Ito to help us?" I asked.

"Ito convinced me," a familiar voice stated from the door. When I looked up, the doorway was filled with the imposing figure of the man from the van. The man who led Plath and me from the gas station.

He was tall. And wide. His biceps, though hidden under a baggy black jacket, looked larger than my thighs. A thick beard covered his face though his head was kept cleanly shaven. If I had to guess I'd say he was pushing 40. Lines were etched into the black skin along his face. I wouldn't say he looked hostile, but I certainly wouldn't characterize him as friendly.

He wore no discernible emblem or gear, but I clearly remembered the M4 in his hand from the first time I met him. I was tense. He could see it and folded his arms, leaning against the doorframe.

"Did my guys take care of you, Mr. Perry?" he asked.

"Seeing as I'm still alive, I guess so," I answered cautiously. "But if you're asking how I feel, not too great."

"Blood loss will do that do you."

"So will waking up after surgery in a non-hospital." Addie was already sighing with impatience.

"You know my favorite thing about being a good samaritan?" the man asked. "How grateful everybody is for my help." The ensuing silence couldn't have been much more uncomfortable, but Addie broke it.

"This is Eduardo Valdez, Jon," she said. "He's an angel." I raised an eyebrow and glanced at her before returning my gaze to Eduardo. He was stone faced but gave me a little nod.

"Nice to meet you," he said blankly.

"Uh... you too," I managed. "So... you know Addie?"

"I do now. But I knew Ito long before that. He's why you're both still in this world." I turned back to Addie.

"What happened?" I asked. She took a long breath and sat forward, her hands between her legs.

"After you left, Ito took care of me. Cleaned me up, bandaged me and such. I was out for some of it, but after about an hour we heard gunfire upstairs. I didn't know what was going on, but Mr. Wellington rushed into my room and picked me up. He hid me in a space under Ito's piano room and told me to stay quiet no matter what happened. Help would come, he said.

"Men burst into the bar and fought their way to Ito. They said they were police—some were, some were demons. They killed everyone except Ito, then another man came in. Said his name was Carnegie. Andrew Carnegie. He'd possessed someone high up in your FBI."

First Ludwig van Beethoven, now Andrew Carnegie? I couldn't wait to find out which dead celebrity we'd rub shoulders with next.

"They talked for a few minutes," she continued. "Carnegie knew Ito had helped us. He wanted to know where we were. Ito wouldn't tell him so Carnegie killed him." Addie paused for a moment, forcing down whatever emotion had arisen.

"Carnegie sent men after Plath. I knew you'd be caught so I tried to sneak out, but then there was more gunfire. The Loyal and the men with them were cleared out by Eduardo and his men. They came for me and told me they were on their way to you. Then they drove us out here. I've been waiting for you to wake up for almost a day."

I wasn't sure what to say at first, but looked around again. "And where is here?"

"One of a few stations we keep up," Valdez said.

"Does this station have a location?"

"Even if you hadn't been out on drugs, I would have blindfolded you on the way. I helped you. That doesn't mean I trust you."

"And who are you, exactly, Ed?" I asked, my hostility returned. "I'm grateful for the rescue but who's this mystery 'we' I keep hearing about?"

"Guardian," he returned. He thrust off the doorframe and ambled into the room. "I'm sure you've heard from Adelaide that for some people, heaven isn't all it's cracked up to be. I'm no hero—far from it—but I've never been one to sit back when I see injustice rampant in front of my face. That's all heaven was to me—a front row seat to all the shit that goes down in the world I left behind."

"So you jacked a body and came back to be an angelic vigilante?" I asked with more skepticism than I should have allowed.

"I made use of a body that would have died without my help," he returned. "It happens more often than you'd think. People get killed because they don't have the quick thinking or gumption to haul ass in a life-threatening situation.

"Take Jerome Pallance here. Drove his car into a lake and just sat panicking while the cab filled with water. He would have been gone in less than a minute if I hadn't shown up in his head and taken over. I waited for the cab to fill, opened the door, and calmly swam to shore."

"And now you fight demons?"

"I stand against injustice," said Valdez. "Like I've been doing for seventy years in three bodies before this, one being the body I was born with. I was a teenager in the Mexican Revolution. My family was dead but I traveled with Zapata himself, learning, fighting.

"After I came back the first time, I helped destabilize other oppressive governments. Non-violently when I could, but I found violence was quicker and usually more effective. I was more Malcolm X than Martin Luther King.

"These days I've gathered something of a following—there are nearly a hundred angels in Guardian who think like I do and help me. We've got resources and relationships in governments, businesses, and pockets of influence across the globe. Most of our energy goes into lobbying to affect policy, but a handful of us take a more direct approach."

I suddenly felt extremely uncomfortable and let Addie know it with an unguarded glance. This guy didn't sound too angelic. More like a radical leftist with a gun.

"Then what brought you to San Jose?" I asked.

"I told you. Ito. He gave me a call as this Carnegie guy was busting down his door, told me he had an angel who needed help. When you've been back as an angel or a demon long enough, you get to know the other players. The other good whisperers who keep coming back. Beethoven was one of them.

"I'd been monitoring his little club for years. Demons come and go just like us—it's a fact of nature, so I never made them much of a priority. Guardian's concerns were always on bigger things. Ending apartheid. Stopping genocide in Bosnia and the Congo. Revolutions in Latin America and the Middle East.

"Still, when I heard demons had hijacked the police—the FBI, as it turned out—I activated some men watching Ode to Joy and flew over personally. I wanted to know what was going on. And I'm hoping you two can tell me."

I looked at Addie. "I told him about the Horsemen and how we met," she said. "I was hoping you'd have something to add after talking to Plath." I drooped back into a prone position on the bed, shaking my head.

"By the time I got to her the FBI director—probably Carnegie—had surrounded me. I didn't get a word out of her." The room was silent. Addie sulked in disappointment while Valdez let out a huff and folded his arms again. "Does this mean you're throwing us out?" I asked him.

Valdez clearly didn't like me much. I didn't blame him, of course. He walked to Addie's side with hands in his pockets.

"We're not in the business of revealing our operation to non-angels or taking in strays, but you're welcome to stay until you've recovered. We'll be following up on this Ode to Joy business over the next few days to find out whatever we can. I'll share whatever we find out. If there's anything else you know that might be of help, I'll expect you to share it as well."

"Maybe we can go over everything when my side doesn't feel like it's going to split in half, Mr. Guardian," I said, regretting trying to turn to the side. "I don't suppose you could spare any pain killers?"

"I'll have our doctor bring something more. Take the rest of the day and night to rest. You should be able to walk soon." With that, he turned and dipped his head to Addie then strode out of the room. I stared at her for a moment in the silence, not sure what to ask.

"Are you okay?" was the question I settled with. "I mean…"

"Yes." She looked away for a moment, probably trying to force out the memories from that night. I regretting bringing it up. "I'm sorry. About everything. I should never have let—"

"It was my choice," she insisted. "I am just glad we are both still here." I nodded, shifting my stare up at the ceiling.

"Me too." I wondered if Addie thought I was lying.

Addie had "heard" rumors of Guardian in heaven, but she thought it was just one man, not a coordinated organization the world over. When we wandered their compound the next morning, my arm sorely slung over her for support as I hobbled along, both of us were shocked at how elaborate the setup was.

Of the dozens of men and women under Valdez, only about half were angels, according to Addie. Valdez and his immediate cohort had recruited retired soldiers, spies and mercenaries around the world. They thought Guardian was a secret police-illuminati hybrid, not a network of angelic avengers.

Valdez's penchant for speaking in absolutes made Addie wary that Guardian wasn't a group to be trusted. It sounded as though they had conducted some unsavory affairs and taken their fair share of innocent bodies in positions of influence "for the greater good." It rang dangerously close to justifications one might expect to hear from a Watcher.

Valdez didn't much care what we thought. He stressed that the militant component of Guardian was only a small fraction of the overall organization. The few field agents at his command usually traveled with him. Most were currently in the base with us, he claimed.

He was serious about this Watcher business. I wasn't sure if Addie had convinced him of the threat or if he had encountered something like this before, but he had dropped everything to focus Guardian's full attention on breaking the demonic plot. If nothing else it gave Addie and me some resources to work with.

Even so, I maintained a pretty polarized view of Valdez and his troupe. He hadn't divulged much about their activities or their methods, but from what little he gave us I could tell this was a ruthless bunch. Everyone here carried a "by any means necessary" attitude.

I knew where that led.

Their outpost was an abandoned manufacturing facility of some kind deep in a desert, probably Nevada from what Addie remembered of the drive. She'd been blindfolded but she had a loose sense of how long they'd driven. I couldn't exactly pull up Google Maps and zoom to our location, given our Chinese access to the internet. Half of it was blocked.

Addie and I spent a few days resting. She didn't like the idea of sitting while Carnegie and the Horsemen remained at large, especially after hearing Carnegie tell Ito they could be days away from whatever they were planning. Still, there wasn't much we could do.

We had no viable leads. The Horsemen weren't moving that Addie or Valdez could sense. Guardian's investigation of the FBI takeover had yielded nothing so far. Valdez told us they had tracked a few regulars at Ode to Joy that they were sweating for information, but none had come in so far.

I expected Addie to contract cabin fever after the first day. She was restless and impatient as ever, but restrained and compliant in a manner I hadn't seen before. I think she knew we were both lucky to be alive. For now there was nothing we could do but wait.

She rarely left my side for more than a few minutes at a time. She took care of me. Helping me get around, bringing me food and anything I needed. I still wasn't sure if she liked me in the least, but I got the sense she trusted me.

Probably due to our new company, more than anything. Addie trusted Valdez more than I did, probably because she could tell he was telling the truth when he spoke, but she didn't know if we could count on them in a clinch.

"I'll just have to keep trusting you," she told me on the third night as we ate. "I can. Can't I." She stated it.

"I don't have the best track record for keeping you safe so far," I reminded her, more than a little caught off-guard.

"You're still here with me, aren't you?" I wasn't sure what to say and glanced around the room while I cut a piece of chicken.

"Technically you're here with me," I offered. "This is my room." She smiled and nodded, continuing on with her food.

The scars already forming on her arms and legs kept me from smiling.

We made a sad discovery the next morning. Valdez brought us a daily update of the investigation from Guardian's end (which he seemed perfectly content otherwise excluding us from). He informed us Deputy Director Lamont had survived the gas station firefight, meaning Carnegie was still out there.

Valdez was confident, as was I, that Carnegie would have the Feds backtrack my activity between popping up at Ode to Joy and my last sighting in Los Angeles, looking for clues about Guardian. Valdez assumed Carnegie probably hadn't known about the angelic organization or he'd have taken precautions against it.

Now, with Beethoven back in hell, the Watchers knew everything Beethoven knew about Guardian (which wasn't much, according to Valdez). What Carnegie couldn't know was that Addie and I weren't part of it, leading it, even. He'd have to mobilize against the entire group now, so hopefully that would take some of the pressure off Addie and me.

The sad discovery came when I considered the people we'd interacted with, directly or not, between LA and San Jose. My first thought was Stevie Walker. They'd have found her car with Cora's blood in the back seat. She was still out of the country, but at best, Carnegie would be waiting for her when she came back. At worst she was already dead.

I felt the guiltiest I had in a long time for having brought her into this through no fault of her own, but then we thought about Carmine. I had originally assured Addie there was no way he could be traced to us, but if Carnegie had Stevie's computer, he could have my search history.

We checked Carmine's blog on a secure terminal Carnegie couldn't trace. At first we breathed a sigh of relief to see a blog posted just that morning. Then we read it.

To whom it may concern:

I will no longer be passing messages to anyone, Guardian or otherwise, because I am dead.

Carmine Romano

Addie cried. She didn't understand how Carnegie could have possibly found him. IP addresses and encrypted connections left her confused every time I tried to explain.

I knew others would end up dead before this was over. Seeing blood on my hands wasn't a new experience for me, but I'd never seen it like this. Because I was sloppy.

I almost caught myself saying a silent prayer for Carmine, that he would be taken care of. Almost.

Addie curled up in her chair after dinner. She was reading through Carmine's blog on a laptop. If there was anything that could be of use to us, Carnegie would have taken it down by then, but she just wanted to read his work. I continued researching my more farfetched thoughts about the Horsemen and reported goings-on in the world of the occult. I uncovered about as much as she did.

A knock at the door signaled Valdez. He stepped inside without invitation, thinking it was his compound to go where he liked, I'm sure. "How are you feeling, Mr. Perry?" he asked. I gently patted my side, still heavily bandaged for padding's sake.

"Awesome," I returned with my least favorite word. "Anything on your end?"

"I came to see if there was anything new on yours," he responded.

"I might be able to research more if I had access to more than a third of the internet."

"We'll handle the research. I'm hoping the two of you have remembered something that could help. Anything. Any other names you heard in Ode to Joy. Any other details on the Horsemen while you were tracking them. Any–"

"We've walked you through everything," I answered, leaning on the computer table they'd set up for me. "If you want my help, why don't you include me on your intelligence gathering."

"I've got people on that."

"Do you have people looking for the other messengers? I gave you a list of occult writers like Romano." Valdez prepared to say no so I pressed him. "Do you have people canvasing San Jose for the other Ode regulars who missed the bloodbath? Do you have angels posted in Washington DC watching for other demon senators or high ups?"

I leaned forward, counting off ideas on my fingers. "Do you have people looking for Carmine's body? Are you looking for any of his art that could have survived at the Vatican for messages? Do you have people trailing Stevie Walker so you can intercept Carnegie's men when he comes for her?"

"Mr. Perry, we–"

"Do you have people tearing through every last detail of Maggie Young's life? Have you found out what messages she was sending and how? Have you–"

"Mr. Perry, my men are on it. All of it." His voice was deep enough to be felt through vibrations when he raised it. "I appreciate your fervor, but you can rest assured we're exhausting every possible lead.

"Please understand that as well networked as I am, I only have so many assets to mobilize at once. Many were killed saving your life and Adelaide's. San Jose and the surrounding area is their territory now. I've sent in people to watch their movements, but I can't get anyone close to Carnegie.

"My men tell me your priest's house on the hill is still there, untouched. That means Carnegie is baiting us to come for it. That also means there isn't anything in there dangerous to Carnegie, so Romano is a dead end.

"As for Plath, that entire boarding house burned down the night she died. We couldn't find anything at all published under Maggie Young's name. If she was getting messages from hell she was probably writing them in that room and taking them to some other Loyal at Ode to Joy to pass on to Carnegie or whoever else. Plath is a dead end. We're looking for other messengers but—"

"Wait," Addie said, straightening in her chair. Valdez and I both turned to her, waiting while her eyes darted back and forth, suddenly wide open. "Did you save the bag, Jon?" she asked. She saw I was confused. "The one Carmine gave us. Did you bring it here?"

"I was wearing it at the gas station, but..." I turned to Valdez.

"You had it on when we found you. It should be in the infirmary. I had my men hose it down, it was covered in blood."

"Did you take out the contents first?" Addie pressed.

"I'm sure they did, but why..."

Addie cut him off by dashing past both of us for the door. Valdez and I exchanged confused glances before hurrying after her. Well, as fast as we could hurry as I limped along.

When we came to the room where they'd stitched me up, we saw Addie rummaging through a box someone had given her. The messenger bag, clean, lay on the ground beside her.

"What are you looking for?" I asked. Her face was taut with worry for another moment, but I watched her shoulders drop as relief coursed through her. She rose with the novel she'd been reading. I'd forgotten it was even in there.

"What Conquers All, by Margret Young," she read from the cover.

"You have a book by Carnegie's messenger?" Valdez asked. "How?"

"We found it in the Kohlers' apartment—the couple we think the Horsemen are hiding."

"You think this Young is the same one as Carnegie's?" I asked.

"You think the Kohlers having a book by a writer named Margret

Young is a coincidence?" she countered. "Whatever Carnegie and the Watchers are up to, the Kohlers and the Horsemen are at the center of it."

"Who is the publisher? Why couldn't we find it in our search?" Valdez asked.

"It's independently published, and maybe Carnegie took it off the market." Valdez wasn't so sure.

"We should check to make sure there isn't another Margret Young out there."

"Then check," Addie said. Valdez let out a sharp huff and called for a nearby man in the hallway. I could see Addie was convinced. I wasn't.

"Addie, if this is Plath," I began, "why would she have published a book of messages from the Watchers? Why give one-time marching orders permanence like that? And how would she put them into narrative form? It's a novel, isn't it?"

"Who said she was recording marching orders?" she returned, riled. "What if Plath wasn't getting messages from the Watchers? What if she was sending messages to them?"   ·

"I thought you said this book was fiction."

"What fiction—what art of any kind—doesn't contain a message that tells some truth? Anyone watching or whispering to her would be able to see that."

"So what's the moral of the story?" I asked, folding my arms. "What's it even about?"

"One of the main characters is an angel," she said, as if offering further proof. Her face reddened before she continued. "He meets a living woman and falls in love. The story is about them finding a way to be together."

I raised an eyebrow. "What would that have to do with Carnegie? Is there some sub-plot or something hidden behind the main story?" Addie faltered for a moment, flipping the book open to a spot a little past halfway through where she'd left her bookmark.

"I don't think so, but... I'm not finished yet." Fighting past my disbelief, made easier by the look of restored hope on my partner's face, I took a breath and turned for the door.

"Then I guess you've got some reading to do."

twelve

I found Valdez alone on a balcony of the third floor in the building he'd repurposed as a garage. Vehicles and armaments on the first floor, storage and armaments on the second, armaments and armaments on the third. He was just standing there, overlooking the sunset, so I ambled onto the deck.

"If bullets were strawberries, we'd be drinking a pretty tall smoothie right about now," I said. Valdez turned with his usual stoic expression. He held binoculars in one hand, a glass of something on the rocks in the other.

"It's only what we need," he stated.

"I literally tripped over a crate of grenades on the stairs."

"We need a lot."

"You've got, what, maybe 30 guys here? Double or triple that worldwide? You could overpower a small government with this arsenal."

"Exactly." I released a silent chuckle from the back of my throat and leaned against the railing.

"Is this the part where you tell me about the evils of cultural imperialism and the military industrial complex?" He didn't say anything. "Yeah, you'd probably be wasting your time. I'm sure you've known too many cynics."

"Yes, but you aren't one of them." I couldn't help but smile.

"And here I thought angels were good judges of character."

"You may speak like a cynic, Mr. Perry, but if you acted like one you wouldn't be here."

"How do you figure that?"

"A true cynic wouldn't have risked all that you have to help your friend in the living quarters."

"Maybe I just don't have anything to lose." Valdez took a drink and looked out at the sunset.

"Maybe." For whatever reason, I don't think he believed me, but he didn't care to argue the point. "How's she doing?"

"She's hasn't come out of her room since last night except to spend a few minutes in the cafeteria or bathroom. For as book smart as that girl is, I'm surprised she isn't a faster reader. I walked by her room and snuck a peek—she's still got a quarter of the book to go."

"Still no message?"

"I'm still not sure she's going to find one. We're not even sure that book came from our Maggie Young. If it did and there is some hidden message, she probably wrote it to be just that to the casual eye. Hidden."

Valdez had suggested Addie let his people take a look as well, but she was adamant about finishing first herself. He didn't put up a fight. There was no reason anyone else would have more luck than she would. She was probably more apt to uncover any literary allusions anyway.

He fell silent, lifting his binoculars to the horizon. I wondered if I could be that... calm, if I ended up living a few lifetimes more than I should. I'd seen Valdez as violent and passionate as they came, but he was hardly some fundamentalist grunt. Everything about him was astute. Mature in a way only the very oldest ever become.

"Keeping watch of the perimeter?" I asked eventually, realizing I had nowhere else to be and no one else to talk to with Addie walled up in her room.

"Bird watching," was his answer. I assumed he was messing with me, but he followed up with the observation of a dense owl population in the area.

"I wouldn't have pegged you for a guy with a hobby." He shrugged.

"I like watching the predators work. Nature is simple. Fair. Maybe because there's no sentience. Just instinct."

"That sounds a little atypical of a leftist malcontent."

"Discovering that the God you worshiped is just another mad tyrant shifts your worldview to a larger stage," he observed, a frigid cold hanging from his words.

"I take it you feel a little ripped off by the afterlife too, then."

"Men of valor and courage who I fought and died with—better men than me—were barred from paradise. God's judgment is a sick joke at best."

"You're the second angel I've met to tell me that, more or less. Addie wasn't even a Christian when she died. Went out cursing his name."

"I'm sure she died a good person, nonetheless. I only wonder what befell all the other good people."

"Ludwig seemed like a good guy. An uptight asshole, but a good guy. Is that why you never went after him?"

"I had no interest hunting demon possessors before this," Valdez said, lowering his binoculars. "I weep for the souls demons displace in their own bodies, but I cannot say I would not seize on a chance to escape permanent torture, even if only for a moment."

Valdez turned and kicked open a cooler behind him. He poured himself another glass of what turned out to be juice. He didn't offer me some. "And Beethoven was—is—a good man. One of the more honorable possessors I have encountered. I would never aid him in robbing the innocent of their bodies, but his intentions were as noble as someone in his position could be."

I didn't say anything, but Valdez sensed my brooding disagreement. "He saved your life, did he not? He saved Adelaide."

"I... I'm not pissed at him so much as I am at... the situation."

"What happened to you, Mr. Perry?" The question caught me off-guard. I folded my arms and looked to the horizon, blankly.

"I'm the guy God judged right," I told him. "But he should have just taken it out on me. Not my wife and my five-year-old."

"That is not justice," Valdez confirmed. "I am sorry."

"I'll decline your sympathy until I'm in hell where I could use it."

"You don't know that you'll—"

"I know."

"The beyond is not something you can predict. Ask your friend." I ignored him. I knew. I let my mind drift to the place it always did in moments of quiet.

"You know what's worse than losing them?" I asked. "Worse than fire and brimstone and all that bullshit waiting for me? That I'll never see them again. I'll never know... that they're alright." I smiled and looked away, making sure he didn't see the water on my face.

"You may never be able to join them, but you can rest knowing they are safe."

"How would you know?" Again my words came out sharper than I meant them to.

"I don't. But I could find out if you'd like." I wasn't sure what to say at first, thinking I'd heard him wrong.

"How? Do you have a messenger like Carmine? Would that even work?"

"No. Only you could find someone you know in heaven."

"Then how would you—"

"I can let you see it. Enough that you could find them. To know that they are there." I felt my heart speed up.

"You're telling me angels can give people sight into heaven?"

"I'm not sure that we're supposed to, but I've done it for plenty before you and I haven't been struck down yet. It's not difficult, you'd just need to clear your mind."

I didn't say anything back, didn't move. His brow furrowed when I started to shake. "So Addie could do it too," I said.

"I'm surprised you haven't heard this from her already. You two seem very close. Did you not tell her of your family?" My heart skipped a beat. When I turned for the doorway inside Valdez called after me, asking what was wrong.

I cracked the glass in the door when I threw it into the wall of Addie's bedroom. She yelped in surprise and dropped the book on the bed where she sat.

"What are you—"

"*You lied to me*," I blasted. "After all that bullshit about trust. You fucking *kept them from me!*" She stood but nearly fell back under the onslaught of my volume and presence—I marched within a few inches of her face.

She shuffled back against the mattress. I watched her expression shift from confused to defensive to guilty in one breath. She knew what I was talking about.

When she took a moment to collect her thoughts I wheeled around with my hands in the air. I shouted an expletive. Some part of me had hoped this was just a misunderstanding. That she hadn't known she had this power. But I saw her eyes. She knew.

"Jon..."

"Why?!" My voice betrayed me as the explosive anger gave way to anguished distress. "How? How could you sit there with the only thing I want and hold it over my head?" My voice cracked. She could hear the pain, see it. Tears welled in her eyes.

"You can't understand what it means to—"

"*Understand?!* This is my family, Addie! My baby. Do you have even the faintest idea how it feels to lose something like that? To hold your own flesh and blood in your hands after it's been burned and broken? To be haunted by that every day wondering... what..."

I gritted my teeth, my anger renewed by the sensation of liquid running down my cheeks. Addie tried to take a step toward me, reaching with a nervous hand. I tore away before she could get close, disgusted at the thought of her touch.

"No," I answered for her. "You don't have the tiniest idea what that's like."

"You say that like I could have brought them back," she said "I—"

"You could have shown me they were alright! You knew it was possible and you lied to my face, because of what? Some bullshit philosophy? Because it *felt* wrong?"

"No!" she managed, fighting just to remain on her feet as I tore into her. "Because... because I didn't want to see you hurt."

"What's that supposed to mean?" Addie wanted to look away but couldn't. My gaze wouldn't let her. She grasped her left elbow with her right hand.

"I didn't want to be the one responsible for showing you something that could destroy you if... if you didn't find what you were looking for." It took me a moment to realize what she was implying. A rush of fury exploded from my gut. It drove me forward.

I stopped just before I could raise my hand, but she flinched nonetheless, aware of what I was about to do. I had never seen her that afraid. She turned and sat on the bed, unable to hold back her tears.

I forced myself to breathe for a moment. Nothing good would come from putting my anger in the driver's seat. I'd been down that road before. I turned for the damaged door after a moment. Valdez was there with three men behind him in the hallway, all carrying guns. He stood tense but said nothing, aware of what was happening.

"They were innocent," I said at last. I put my eyes back on Addie. I'd never even considered what she implied in her answer.

"I know," Addie returned gently. "I'm sure your family is in heaven. I'm not saying they shouldn't be. I'm just saying there were innocents who died in my arms as well, and they aren't there. I... I couldn't risk breaking your heart like that."

"I guess you'd be up shit creek if your guide through the 21st century blew his head off in a fit of depression, wouldn't you?"

"How dare you?" she returned, balling her fists. "This has nothing to do with me, I was trying to protect you from—"

"This has *everything* to do with you! You could have shown me the truth either way, and you didn't. You lied to me. Why should I believe a thing you say now?"

"Because I still don't want to see you hurt," she insisted, voice rattling. "Look in my eyes, Jon. You know I'm not lying about that." I did what I was told but eventually shook my head.

"I can't tell the truth from a lie as easily as you can," I returned. I turned my back on her and faced Valdez while she sank.

"Show me," I said. Valdez let out a quick breath and glanced Addie's way.

"There's something to what she's saying, you know."

"That might have sounded more convincing before you told me you've done this for loads of poor sacks like me without blinking an eye," I rebuffed. "Do it." He nodded and gave a quick motion of his head to signal his men down. They relaxed their muzzles and filed out of the hallway.

"Come with me, then," he said, turning. I made it to the door before I heard her.

"No."

"Addie, I'm doing this, so—"

"I'll do it." I stopped and looked back. She was standing, an intent look in her watery eyes.

"I thought you didn't want the responsibility."

"I don't. But it's mine now." I said nothing. "Please, Jon." I remember wanting to walk out without a word. But I also remember that as the moment when I realized Adelaide Martin was probably the only person in the world who cared about me. My anger couldn't overcome that.

I reached for the door and closed it, leaving Valdez outside. I walked back to her slowly, uncertain. I saw the gratefulness in her eyes that I had stayed.

"So how does this work?" I asked. She wiped the tears from her eyes with the butts of her hands. She came closer until there was no space between us. She opened her arms as if to put them around me but faltered and drew them close between us.

She gently lay her head against my shoulder. I felt her fold into me and stiffened uncertainly. "Grab onto me. Feel me against you." I almost drew back until she continued. "You need to remember the feeling. Keep thinking about it. It will help keep you grounded."

"What should I expect?" I asked, putting my arms around her back.

"Emotion. More than you've ever felt. There will be so much it will hurt, so concentrate on what you can feel with your body."

"How will I know what to look for?"

"You'll know," she promised. "They're all you know in that place. You'll find them at once."

"Can I...?" She raised her head, her eyes finding mine.

"No. You'll only be able to feel them. To know they are there."

"And they'll feel me?"

"I'm... not sure. I have never done this before. But I think you'll know if they do." I nodded, suddenly more nervous than I could remember being since I lost them.

She told me to calm down as best I could. We waited for a few minutes while I just concentrated on breathing and spreading my fingers against the fabric of her shirt as she directed. Then all at once, she dug her head deeper into my chest and I couldn't feel anything.

I felt everything. More than everything. I felt in a way I had never realized I could feel, but I couldn't even comprehend what the feeling was.

All I know is that I was feeling a lot. Sensations like images and sounds with infinite dimensions surrounded me. I saw myself outside myself like a man at the edge of the universe looking in at the entire thing.

For a moment I wondered if this was how God saw things, but I realized I couldn't really see anything. It was all just beautiful noise. Fog soft at the touch. I recognized certain feelings in it before I realized they weren't my own.

Soon a few feelings became hundreds, then millions, then what might have been infinity. I screamed a silent scream at the intensity of it all. I would have been lost had I not remembered what the angel in my grasp told me. I couldn't discern that I even had fingers, but somehow I felt the touch of her shirt through them.

I'm still not sure if I took in all those emotions, all those memories, over the course of a split second or a lifetime, but somewhere in that span I realized none of those memories were the ones I was looking for. I had view into a cosmos of memory, but the two stars that should have shined brightest didn't.

They didn't shine at all.

It was at that point I felt my own emotion enter back into my perception. It was panic at first, then rage, then something else entirely. The intensity of it threatened to scatter what self-awareness I retained beyond my ability to retrieve.

I think I might have... not died, but... ended, in that moment, if not for a sharp sensation I recognized appearing in my chest, I felt it again. I recognized my eyelids blinking, and when they blinked, I could see and feel with my eyes and skin once more.

Time as I understood it resumed. All the emotions dissipated in an instant. Except mine. And I'll never forget them, because I once believed I could never experience pain worse than that day five years ago.

I was wrong.

My hands had not only grabbed hold of Addie's shirt, but her skin, digging in to the point where she screamed. She fought to push away from me, yelling my name. Valdez was in the room, rushing to pry me from her. When his hand came down on my arms I jerked and wheeled back, releasing Addie. She fell in a heap before Valdez could catch her.

I don't remember much of what followed clearly. The war between anger and grief pulled me out of my body. I had energy. Enough to pull down the building, it felt like, and I had to get it out. I yelled and thrashed, tipping over Addie's bed and ripping out drawers from a nearby desk.

Valdez ordered a few of his men into the room to restrain me. One of them seized my neck while another collected my arms behind me. I think I'd have passed out had Addie not shouted for them to stop and release me. She begged to Valdez that this wouldn't help. I'm not sure if it was she or my shift from rage to sorrow that persuaded him.

I was crying when they released me. Well, more dry heaving than actual weeping. I felt dizzy, like my brain would pop out of my skull. When I rushed from the room like a drunkard they didn't stop me. I wandered down halls shaking my head and saying things in alternating whispers and shouts.

Darkness had almost fallen when I stumbled outside into the dirt yard between buildings. The cold air rushed into my lungs. I used it to let a scream fly into the night that burned at my throat. My energy spent, I collapsed to my knees one at a time. Vomit felt a second away but never came.

I cried hysterically for a few minutes. Snot, spit and tears moistened my face, red as blood by the time I finally looked up. Addie was there when I did. She knelt in front of me. I think she'd been there for a while but she hadn't touched me, hadn't said anything. I'm sure she looked crushed, but I was too preoccupied with my own emotion to notice hers.

Around the time I'd emptied myself out, she summoned her voice. "I am so sorry, Jon," she managed. I remember shaking my head and sliding to sit on my backside, so off balance I worried I'd fall over.

"Why?" I asked out loud. "Why... why would... What if they've possessed bodies? What if they're back?" Addie saw me filling with desperate hope and put a hand on my arm.

"I... do not think they are possessing anyone, Jon," she said. "For your wife, it would certainly be possible, but... for your daughter, it would not. She would be too young to whisper. I have never known any soul who died below a certain age to possess a body." Her words stabbed.

"How is this right?"

"It isn't," she said. "It isn't."

"I'd kill him," I said. My voice was almost blank with emotion at that point. "I'd kill him if I could." She didn't say anything to that. I looked around. Everyone in the complex was staring at me through doors or windows. Valdez stood with a few of his men at the door I'd rushed from.

I heard Addie slide closer to me but she paused when I lifted and trudged for Valdez. He stared at me with what might have passed for pity from anyone else.

"And demons can show hell?" I asked. "Like you can heaven?"

"Jon," came Addie's voice from behind me.

"Can they?" I pressed. Valdez nodded. "There aren't any here, are there?"

"No."

"Then you have to take me to one."

"I can't do that."

"Why not?"

"I'm trying to keep you safe. Taking you to the people looking to kill you is a terrible way to do that."

"I'm not asking you to drive me back to San Jose. I just need to find one."

"To what end, Mr. Perry?" he asked, taking a step closer. "There's nothing you can do about this. I'm truly sorry, but you'll only bring yourself more pain if you go looking for it."

"I'm going," I told him. Exasperated, Valdez shifted his weight and folded his arms.

"You're here because you're wound up in this Watcher business. If you go out demon hunting you'll place yourself outside it, and I don't have the resources to take on a demonic conspiracy while sorting through your personal baggage."

"Fine," I returned. "Give me my gun and bag and I'll be on my way."

"Jon, please," Addie pleaded, again at my side. "This will accomplish nothing. You wouldn't even know what you're looking for. Have you come this far to give up now? We can't do this without their help."

"Do what?" I recoiled. "Save the world? By looking for a secret code in a love story? This is over. Whatever Carnegie and the Horsemen are doing, they'll win. And I don't give two shits if they do. Who wants to save a world this fucked up?"

Addie looked at me with wounded eyes. She didn't know what to say. "I'm leaving. You can do what you want, Addie."

"You're not going anywhere," said Valdez. I turned to him with a glower.

"What do you care, big hero?" I snapped. "What does it matter to you?"

"You're the most wanted man in the world," he reminded me. "You have no money, no transportation, no friends, no nothing. How long do you think you'd last before Carnegie found you?" I repeated my question. "Because you know about Guardian, and I'm not about to let Carnegie and these Watchers learn anything more from you than they already do."

"So you're holding us prisoner," I returned.

"For the moment, yes, if you want to look at it that way." My glare deepened.

"What are you going to do if I walk out that door?" I asked. "Shoot me? Then Carnegie will know everything I know." Valdez turned and unstrapped a sidearm from one of his men. He pumped a round into the chamber.

"I can shoot you and not kill you," he said. I thought about calling his bluff or rushing him. I'm sure Addie saw me tensing because she moved between us.

"Will you two stop?" she almost shouted. "Have either of you stopped to consider that you're both right?" Valdez narrowed his eyes and asked what she was talking about. "Jon is right—we probably can't find whatever message is in the book on our own. We need another of Carnegie's messengers to tell us."

"If you know where to find one I'm all ears," Valdez said.

"You knew about Ode to Joy, surely you know of other places demons congregate. One of them is bound to have Loyal present who can tell us where to find another messenger."

"Ode to Joy was one of a kind," Valdez reminded us. "The first time I've ever heard of this Loyal network was when you told me about it. Guardian doesn't exist to hunt demons. We make it a point to track a few of the more prominent whisperers but—"

"Alex," Addie said. "Do you know about her?" I'd all but forgotten about the first vague lead Ito had given us. My surprise came at Valdez's answer.

"How do you know about Alex?" he asked. Addie's eyes widened with new hope.

"Ito gave us her name. He said she would give us information about the Watchers if we found her." Valdez scoffed, shaking his head.

"I very much doubt that. She wouldn't even talk to either of you, much less give you information like that for nothing."

"Then you know her?" Addie pressed.

"Alex is *the* whisperer. She died millennia ago and I'd bet she's spent something like three minutes in hell. She makes a point of tracking down other talented whisperers throughout the years. She likes to fraternize. To brag."

"So you've met her?" I asked.

"Unfortunately. It cost me my last body."

"Do you know where she is?" Addie asked.

"She's always moving," Valdez began, "but I might know where to start looking. If you know what you're looking for, it isn't too difficult to find her." He shook his head and handed back the sidearm, apparently convinced I wouldn't be a problem. "But there is no way she is part of this Loyal network of servants. Alex doesn't bend the knee to anyone."

"Ito told us she could help," Addie insisted. "She must know something."

"It's possible," Valdez responded. "But I'm more concerned about what she'd want in return for her help."

"Surely with all its resources Guardian has something she—"

"There's no suitcase of money that would satisfy Alex. She's a junkie, but her addiction is for something we can't just hand over."

"What?"

"Time," Valdez answered. There was a silence after that, but Valdez broke it with a sharp exhale. "But seeing as that's something we're running out of as well, I suppose it's worth a try. Just be warned. Even with me, I can't promise either of you will walk out of her lair alive. Or unscarred." Addie nodded silently, turning to me for my thoughts. I didn't offer any. I just swallowed hard and walked back into the building.

thirteen

Carnegie walked out from the interrogation room frazzled, his breath laborious. Damn Lamont and his old body. Carnegie had never struck anyone before, much less a woman, but he couldn't leave anything to chance.

The men he'd posted on the other side of the viewing glass asked if he was alright, offering him a handkerchief for the blood on his shirt. He batted it away and took his cell phone from the man he'd left it with, then ordered everyone out. They weren't Loyal, but even so he didn't want them to hear the desperate tone in his voice.

"Do they have it?" he asked into the phone, still breathing hard.

"No," was the calm answer. "They left their copy at the apartment with everything else." Carnegie's face tightened in fury. He nearly threw the phone into the brick wall but forced himself to gain control. With a deep breath, he leaned his arm and head against the glass looking into the interrogation room.

"You left the blueprint of our entire plan behind for anyone to find." Carnegie stated it as if inconceivable.

"We had to move them at once. The order was to let them bring nothing. Your order." Carnegie sighed, mashing the phone in his grip.

"To think what you four could accomplish if you could do anything more than follow orders," he observed to himself. "Jon Perry's fingerprints were all over the apartment. He and his apparent army of angels have the book. And the secret."

"But not the Kohlers."

"For your sake, you had better hope it remains that way."

"When you find the angels, send us."

"The four of you will remain where you are. I need War in the Oval Office to give me a longer leash. Famine and Pestilence are out causing trouble in hopes of luring the angels into the open. You will stay in place."

"You've already won. Whatever they know they're too late to stop us." Carnegie hung up and set the phone on the table. He glanced through the glass at Stevie Walker, handcuffed to a chair, bleeding and crying. She hadn't spoken at first, demanding her lawyer. Carnegie didn't have time for that.

His Loyal had advised he kill her since she could only cause problems if she filed a complaint against Lamont. Carnegie would have if he knew for a fact she'd end up in hell, but as things stood he said no. She was innocent, after all. After a few more days it wouldn't matter anyway.

Addie made sure I didn't off myself. I insisted on being alone, but she stayed close. When she wasn't she coordinated with Valdez to station men at my door. No one was ever more than a three second dash from me.

We only had a few hours to sleep before they took us out to an airstrip. A helicopter was waiting to ferry us to Reno where we boarded a private jet. Looked like it belonged to a tech company from the logo. I wasn't paying very close attention.

I'm not really sure why I didn't try. To kill myself. It was like losing both of them all over again, but worse. My one solace over the last five years had been the ardent belief the girls were in a better place. Where they were safe. At rest.

Addie tried getting me to eat repeatedly on the plane, but I refused to touch anything. I wouldn't have been able to keep it down. I felt sick in a way I'd never felt before. Like Pestilence had reached into my soul and corroded it like the flesh on my leg.

"Jon, you have to eat or you can't take your medicine," she implored at one point, out of her seat to kneel beside me with a package of nuts and crackers. I'd torn a few stiches in my rampage at the complex. They patched me up before we left but it hurt like a bitch. I was exhausted, and she could see it. "Will you at least try to get some sleep? You won't have strength for this if—"

"Just let me be, Addie," I managed. I stared out the window blankly. I couldn't bring myself to face her. Part of me was still angry with her for keeping the truth from me. The other part knew that her nagging, her caring, was probably all that kept me from rushing to hell. She had a talent for keeping my mind on something immediate every moment.

Guessing she had pushed me as far as I would go, and that I was still angry, she fell silent. She left the food on the arm of my chair and returned to her seat on the other side of the cabin. I was too proud or ashamed to look at her for a long time, but after an hour or so I glanced her way.

She was curled in her seat with Plath's book. She'd made more progress than I thought. She could probably have it finished by the end of the flight, left uninterrupted. Valdez came and went between the pilot's cabin. He had arranged for Guardian assets to be in place for us when we landed.

"I'm sorry," I said after staring at her for several minutes. Addie looked up from her book. It was dark in the cabin but I could see her surprise. "For hurting you. While you showed me." She swallowed hard and set the book in her lap.

"It's alright," was all she said at first. We looked at each other for the first time all night. "I'm sorry too. You were right. It was your choice to look, not mine. I shouldn't have lied to you." I nodded but didn't say anything. I didn't feel like talking, I just knew I had to say something.

I looked back out the window into the darkness past the wing. I'm not sure if she kept reading or not.

We landed in Philadelphia early in the morning. Somewhere around 2a.m. I think. Rain came down in a fine mist as we walked across the tarmac to an SUV waiting for us. I almost slipped on the concrete but Addie grabbed my arm and got me to the car.

My situational awareness was almost non-existent. It was all I could do to focus on what we were doing. That this demon could show me something. I didn't know what. Even if she showed me what I was looking for it would only make things worse, but... I had to see them.

At least maybe this way I could be with them again, I thought.

No, I was kidding myself. It was called hell for a reason. I cried again in the car. I let Addie close this time. She put an arm around my neck. My head was against her while we drove. Valdez looked back from time to time, always ready to say something but never doing so.

It hadn't taken him long to find Alex. "She hides in plain sight," he'd told us on the plane. "She just moves through locations and bodies fast enough to keep under the radar." She hadn't been in the Mediterranean for months. In that gulf she'd been to Moscow, Orlando and now Philadelphia as a ballerina, an Olympic swimmer and the divorcé of a real estate mogul.

"My guess is she's here for this fashion show benefit for the Museum of Art," Valdez told us once I'd settled down. "Her life is a tour of prestigious events, a who's-who of noteworthy people."

"How did you track her to her new body?" Addie asked. "If she moves through bodies she could appear anywhere."

"Alex doesn't work like that. She sees things she wants and she takes them, host bodies included. There's always a pattern with clear links to the places she goes. She surrounds herself with beautiful things. It's the only way to hide how ugly her soul is."

"What do you know about her?"

"Only what she's told me and the rumors I've heard from other whisperers. They say she was a peasant in some ancient kingdom with the body of a princess, and she used it well enough to become a real princess. A queen. She didn't go back that far when she came to me on my last body. Just told me all the people she's been since.

"She won't say it quite so boldly, but she fancies herself some sort of goddess—immune from the afterlife unlike the rest of us. She looks at everyone else, living or not, like lesser beings, but she can't brag about it to the living so she looks for other possessors every so often to massage her ego."

Valdez turned from his seat in the front and looked back at us with serious eyes. "This woman lives for manipulation. She plays with hearts and minds like toys, takes a body, then discards it when she's bored with it. Sometimes it only takes a few hours. She has a way of breaking you down to putty she can mold. No matter what she tells you, never forget what she is."

"It sounds like you know more about her than rumors," Addie observed.

"It doesn't take long for her to... penetrate you." Addie didn't press the issue.

"What do you think she'll want in return for information?" she asked.

"I have no idea."

"What did she want from you?" Valdez's face remained stagnant. "You said she killed your last host," Addie pressed. "Why?" Valdez turned back toward the front.

"I killed my last host," he murmured. "After a few days with her... I would have done anything she asked. And I did." Addie's expression turned incredulous, part disgusted, part terrified.

"What would that gain her?"

"What's the point of being a god if no one worships you?" he asked.

We pulled into a parking garage in downtown Philadelphia a few minutes later. Valdez guessed that Alex was at or headed to a VIP reception at the Philadelphia Museum of Art that some fashion show would be raising money for the following night.

His plan, if you could call it that, was to stand outside around the red carpet and wait for her to see us. "She'll notice me," Valdez assured. "No matter what body I'm in she'll recognize the soul inside."

"And she'll, what, invite you in for revelry off the street?" was my question.

"She'll do something. That I guarantee. When you've been around as long as she has there are few things that provoke your curiosity. My being here out of nowhere like this will do the trick, especially when she sees another angel with Adelaide's looks beside me."

"How do you know she won't just kill us?" I grilled. "It doesn't sound like you last parted on the best of terms."

"She'll probably try, and succeed, but she'll want to talk first." He looked to his men in the front. "You two hang back. I don't want her spotting you and thinking I've got snipers posted on the roof. If she thinks I'm here in force she'll also think I'm out for revenge. I don't want to spook her out of her curiosity."

He turned back to me. "You'll stay here with them."

"The hell I will."

"You'll do us no good, especially in your state." He saw me ready to refute and before I knew it he was in my face, glowering. "This is my show. My ass on the line. You follow my orders or you go into a cage. Understood?"

I thought about appealing to Addie, but knew which side she'd be on. She knew I was a mess. Whatever usefulness I'd been to her crusade before, it was over now. I considered the possibility that at this point she was only tolerating me out of pity.

I sank into the seat and looked away, silent. Valdez grabbed a gun and stuffed it into a holster along the inside of his jacket. He stepped out of the car, waiting for Addie. I felt her hand on my forearm. "Try to get some rest," she said.

"Just be careful," I returned. She gave me a single nod and exited after Valdez. I watched them disappear around a corner to the street. I almost told Valdez not to let anything happen to her.

I never quite drifted to sleep in 40-some minutes I waited, but my eyes were heavy. I came awake when I saw him standing in the middle of the garage, alone.

A little boy in an orange shirt.

At first I thought my eyes were playing tricks on me. It couldn't be the same kid who tapped on the window that night in San Jose. It even looked like the kid who'd petted Doggy that morning at the Orange Forest Hotel.

I almost said something to the others in the car when he pointed. At first I thought he was pointing at me, but it was just ahead of the car. By the time I turned to look it was too late.

I didn't realize they were gunshots until after the shower of miniscule glass shards bounced off my skin. I felt something warm spatter onto my face. For a moment I thought I'd been shot, but the hollowed out mess that had been the driver's head told me otherwise. He went down first, immediately followed by his partner in the passenger seat.

The shots came through the windshield. I ducked instinctively, knowing I would die if I ran or made a move for the wheel. But I didn't die. No additional shots came. The only sound other than the body of the driver slowly sliding into his seat was the sound of footsteps outside the car. High heels, from the sound of it.

My heart dropped when the back door opposite from me opened. Three women stared me down. Two stood at a distance with guns in hand, the other was right at the door. All three of them were gorgeous, covered in skin tight cocktail dresses and fur coats against the wintery night.

The one closest stepped in and took a seat beside me, closing the door behind her. She swept a lock of flowing brunette hair behind her ear and brushed a few fragments of glass on the seat away from her. If I hadn't been so terrified I'm sure I'd have paid more attention to either the ample cleavage or slender legs on display.

She stared with an eyebrow raised, looking me over as would a scientist analyzing something in a petri dish. "Who are you?" she asked, barely tilting her head. I think I was in a state of shock, but that didn't stop me from being an ass.

"You just killed two people and sat down in my car," I told her. "Who the hell are *you*?" Her head tilted further but she allowed an amused smile.

"Alex," she said almost teasingly. She pointed out the window without looking away. "The sharpshooters out there are Meghan and Lisa."

"I've never seen a sharpshooter who looks like she could be on the cover of Maxim," I commented, still in the fetal position against the door. Alex smiled.

"You should watch more movies. Now I've told you my name, what's yours?"

"Perry," I said.

"And what are you doing palling around with Eduardo and his thugs, Perry?" My hand slipped from the seat. She told me to relax and take a deep breath, smiling knowingly like the popular girl talking to the nerd.

"We were looking for you," I returned.

"Obviously. Why?" I thought about asking her if she was going to kill me too, but I found a more poignant question.

"Is Valdez still alive?"

"As far as I know."

"Then why aren't you asking him this?"

"Because you're the important one."

"How do you figure that?"

"Because you're the only non-angel in his little posse, and because he left you here under guard away from the front line, such as it is. So what do you want, Perry?" I swallowed hard, aware our only shot had landed squarely on my shoulders.

"We need your help," I said. "We need to know about the Watchers." She narrowed her eyes then slowly shook her head.

"You're lying," she told me. I wasn't sure what to say.

"If you are who you say you are, you know I'm not." Again she gave me a peculiar face and leaned back.

"Hmm," she murmured. "Eduardo and his gang may need my help, but I asked what *you* want." As scared and shocked as I was, the dominant emotion hanging over me hadn't changed. I loosened, my face placid as I stared into space.

"I want you to show me hell," I told her. Her eyes were fixed on me. There couldn't have been an errant thought in her mind that wasn't focused squarely about what I'd just said.

"I have heard men and women, angels and demons, tell me many things, Perry," she stated gradually, "but I have never heard that before." She studied my reaction, what little there was. Right before I could ask if she'd do it, she leaned back, coming out of her intensity.

"Not here," she said, opening the wristlet in her lap. She took out a pen and wrote something on a notepad. "I'm very attached to this body at the moment, I don't want any of Eduardo's goons dinging it." She tore out the note and flicked it my way. "Swing by later. We'll work something out."

She opened her door and stepped out, tucking the folds of her fur coat tighter around her slender frame. "Come alone. Just the three of you. If I see anyone else none of you will ever see me again."

Alex flashed me another smile that didn't belong on the face of the girl she'd taken. It was too disarming—I could practically feel the danger emanating from her. She took a moment to absorb me as well, her curiosity apparent. Satisfied, she gave herself a nod.

"And tell Eduardo not to pull up so close next time. He might as well have rolled in here with a convoy of tanks. Ta." With that she closed the door and walked off with Meghan and Lisa, the sound of their heels clicking over the concrete fading.

Valdez and Addie returned to find me sitting at a bus stop a few blocks from the parking garage. I knew it would only be a matter of time before someone noticed the shot up windshield and blood. The FBI's most wanted man couldn't be there when cops showed up. Plus I wasn't partial to sitting in a car with two corpses.

I took one of their radios before I left and told Valdez to get back. He was already on his way, having known something was wrong when he couldn't reach his men. I wandered to the bus stop bench to sit while I waited, raising the collar of my jacket and burying my head in my hands. I didn't have the energy to cry.

Addie rushed to my side when she saw the blood. I promised her it wasn't mine. Valdez skipped me entirely, hurrying into the parking garage despite my warning him it would do no good. He returned after a few moments, despondent and empty handed. Addie asked if they should take the guns and whatever else remained in the SUV that could link to Guardian. Apparently he had men on the way to dispose of the car.

He grilled me about my guest immediately, upset that I hadn't answered him on the radio while they ran back. I told him everything minus my answer to Alex's last question. Thankfully neither of them asked if there was anything else I left out. I wouldn't have told them even if they did know I was lying.

Valdez stared at the address Alex had written for a minute, then told me to get up. "We're walking," he said. He believed Alex's threat to disappear if we showed up with anyone more than ourselves. "She's intrigued. Even if she doesn't know about these Watchers, she's got to know there's a hunt on for you and Addie."

"She didn't know my face in the car," I offered.

"Yes she did," Valdez assured me. "Your face is plastered everywhere right now, Mr. Most Wanted. But as intrigued as she is, she'll still vanish without a trace just to spite me if we don't play her game by her rules."

We walked for nearly half an hour. From the way Valdez's eyes shifted, Addie and I could guess Alex was watching us somehow. Valdez gave Guardian the address as we started walking, but he dropped his radio into the trash halfway there. Apparently he wanted Alex to know we weren't going to try anything.

Her lair, as Valdez described it, turned out to be the penthouse of the Hyatt. The husband of her latest victim had procured it for her during her stay for the Museum benefit. I kept my face down in the lobby to ensure no security cameras or observant guests caught sight of me. I washed the lingering blood spackles from my face in the lavatory before we made our way to the elevators.

From the way Valdez talked about Alex, I expected the place to be laden with security. We walked into the elevator without being stopped. When the doors closed, Addie commented that she hadn't seen any possessors in the lobby.

She saw two when the elevator doors opened on the top floor. Meghan and Lisa. They waited on either side of the door, still in their dresses, like they'd been expecting us. They didn't frisk us. Didn't ask if we were carrying weapons. Didn't say a word. They just unlocked the penthouse and led us inside.

The lights weren't ominously low. No pentagrams, candles or goat's bones decorated the room. It was untouched. As illustrious as you'd expect from the penthouse of a 40-story hotel. A fountain and miniature crystal chandelier took residence in the foyer. Massive paneled windows surrounded the wide living room, providing a captivating view of the cityscape.

Valdez and Addie remained on guard, tense and jerky in their movements. I'm sure Valdez knew what we were getting into. Addie suspected of course, ever the skeptic. If anyone saw things for what they were and not what they appeared, it was her.

My mind was every bit the storm of confusion and anxiety it had been since Alex left me in the car. I wasn't thinking about treachery, that we might never step out of that room again. I wasn't thinking about the Watchers, the Loyal or the Horsemen. I wasn't thinking about Guardian, the fate of the world, even Addie.

There were two people on my mind, and the hope—the terror—of seeing them again.

She appeared from the master bedroom to our left. She'd changed from her tight black dress to a loose purple one. Another beautiful woman followed behind her, zipping the dress up in back while Alex took a sip from something on the rocks.

She paused when she saw us, that tantalizing smile returning while her eyes swept over our trio. She didn't say anything for a moment, lapping an ice cube from the glass with her tongue and sucking on it.

"Eduardo," she began, her voice tickled. "You found me."

"I never lost you," he returned, still as stone.

"That would almost be romantic coming from anyone but you," she said, shuffling the ice cube from one side of her mouth to the other. "What was it you said before you left? 'I'd crawl up Satan's ass if—"

"—if it meant getting away from you for eternity. And I meant it. Why don't we skip through the bullshit. I'm not here because I want to fuck or kill you."

"How disappointing," she returned, walking to a chair overlooking the view in the center of the room. She spun it halfway toward us and sat, draping a leg over her knee. "You're above either at this point, are you, Eduardo? What an angel you have become. I'm sure God would be so proud, if he gave a shit."

Valdez stayed on point. "We're here because—"

"I know why you're here," she interrupted brusquely. "We'll get to that. Right now we're talking about us."

"There's nothing to talk about."

"You mean you don't have anything to say to me after all this time? After how it ended? You haven't been rehearsing some speech in your head every time you think of me to prepare yourself for this moment?" I watched Valdez bristle. I wasn't sure if he was more annoyed at having to play her game to get what he wanted or having to talk about whatever happened between them in front of Addie and me.

"You want to talk about us, Alex?" he asked, more emotion in his voice than I'd heard since meeting him. "Then listen carefully. I don't love you. I don't hate you. You're—"

"That isn't what you said before—"

"You're nothing to me. You're a natural disaster. A plague. An inanimate force I can't do anything about. And now you're a means to an end. That's all."

"You wound me, Eduardo," she said, tilting her head and shaking it. "What about all your promises? That I'd be yours forever. I'd have anything I wanted so long as you had the power to—"

"I also promised to spend eternity hunting down every innocent girl you violate, then skin them with a flensing knife to make sure you get the hell you deserve. I let that go too."

"Yes, and by the end you promised that you'd hide in the devil's ass to make sure you never crossed paths with me again," she said. "But here you are."

"You know I'm here for information," he told her. "Is this what you want in exchange? To work me up enough to kill you?"

"Are you getting worked up?" she asked softly.

"No." Even I knew he was lying. "Just tell me what you want, Alex."

"I want to hear the truth," she said. Valdez swallowed hard. His fists were shaking.

"The truth is I don't care enough to come after you." Alex waited, still smiling.

"But?"

"But nothing. I told you—I'm not here for you, I'm here for what you know."

"If you want to know anything, you'll give me what I want."

Valdez was silent. Alex was relishing in this.

"That's right, Eddy. Stand there with your chest puffed out and tell me you never think about me. Tell me your high and mighty concerns of stopping Armageddon are on a plane I could never understand in my gutter of self-satisfaction. Tell me I'm so beneath you now that I'm not worthy of remembrance."

She glanced at Addie. "Your angel and I know the truth. That's more than enough for me." She took another sip of her drink, then chewed her ice cube. "But I'm still going to make you say it." Valdez took a long breath. I couldn't see his eyes, but I'm sure if I had I'd have found hatred I'd never forget.

"There isn't a day that goes by when I don't fantasize about driving stakes in your eyes and burning you alive." His words seethed. That was all she'd been waiting for. I could tell from the look on her face, practically aroused.

Alex finished whatever she was drinking and set the glass on a table beside her. "You did fall harder than most of the others," she said coyly. "Don't worry, I won't make you tell me how hard. But you should know I think about you too."

She looked at him, her eyes penetrating the same as they'd done to me. "Your last words weren't the only ones I still have memorized, Eduardo. I could never forget those nights. Your touch in the dark. The way you pressed me, bent me. The—"

"Don't," he snapped, his voice heavy. "Don't pretend like you ever gave a shit. You may know me but I know you, demon. It's all just a joke to you—everything. You're no better than God." She didn't like that. Her smile faded and she looked away.

"You really are above me now, Eduardo. And you can stay there. As much as I've enjoyed making the mighty Guardian leader squirm, I didn't open my door because of you." To my surprise, she looked at Addie.

"I know what these two want," she said, pointing at Valdez and me. "But I'm curious about you. You aren't part of Eduardo's little halo club—you're the one everyone's looking for. Perry is only wrapped up in this because of you, isn't he?" Addie couldn't hide her surprise, but she steeled herself.

"How would you—"

"Why else would he be? He's alive. This entire resistance they're all so worried about has been spearheaded by you from the beginning, hasn't it? Who are you?"

"No one," Addie answered after a moment. "Just a restless soul."

"Just someone who cares, is that it?" Alex was decidedly less cordial to Addie than she had been to either Valdez or myself. "You think you can stop all this with a suicidal journalist and a failed utilitarian terrorist?"

"Then you know about the Watchers," Addie said. Alex scoffed, folding her hands in her lap.

"More like the Squabblers," she returned. "It took them a thousand years or more to find what they were looking for because they all hate each other so much."

"Who are they, then?" Valdez asked. "What is it they've found?"

"Why would I tell you?" Alex asked, having abandoned her playful attitude with Valdez.

"I still have that flensing knife," he said. I turned to see if Meghan and Lisa would respond but they stayed in place behind us. Alex only laughed.

"First, you're high and mighty now, remember? You wouldn't butcher this sweet girl's body on the off chance I would talk. Second, I wouldn't talk. You know it. Third, in the time it would take for Meghan or Lisa to kill you, for you to find a new body, for you to get back in touch with Guardian—which by the way, even for you is a stupid fucking name—and for you to find a new knife, the Watchers will have enacted their plan ten times over. So don't threaten me. Your odds of walking out of here are bad enough as it is."

"You'll help us because you have to," Addie said. Alex raised an eyebrow, irritated.

"What did I just say about threatening me?"

"It's not a threat," Addie returned. "It's fact. By your own admission, if the Watchers succeed in whatever they're up to, this world will end. Probably more than this world. It will be hard to continue whispering your way into new bodies if there are none left alive."

Alex opened her mouth to say something but paused, narrowing her eyes.

"And you're going to save the world, little angel?"

"I'm not sure if I can yet," Addie answered. "I need to know the problem before I can think of a solution." Alex's scowl was deep. I guessed she wasn't used to anyone having leverage over her. I can't imagine she enjoyed it. Still, she rose from the chair and walked to the window with her back to us.

"There were seven of them in the old days," she said flatly. "There are probably many more by now—I haven't been back in a very long time. Pompous assholes spanning back to the days of stone thrones. They're the particularly bitter ones. The ones who hate God and the Injustice the most.

"One day they started 'talking' and dedicated their existence to overthrowing God. To murdering him and taking control of everything. They're an eclectic bunch, the Watchers. Some are mad dogs who deserve to be in hell. Others are righteous men on a quest for justice. But all of them are desperate for revenge.

"I might have been one of them myself, but when I was still kicking around down there it was a boys-only club. People carry the same prejudices they have in life with them into death, after all. I became Loyal instead."

Alex chuckled dryly. "Probably the only time anyone has ever called me that. I was one of the first. They saw my talent for whispering and decided they could use me in the mortal world. It wasn't long until they realized I was anything but Loyal. At that point I still wanted into heaven. Thought I could buy my way in if I spilled information about the Watchers to angel possessors and so on.

"By the time the Watchers figured out I hadn't been helping them in years I lost interest in heaven. I already had it at my fingertips. They were on the hunt for me for centuries, but even between bodies, I was never in hell long enough for them to do anything.

"Then one day, not too long ago, in fact, they just stopped looking for me. As far as I could tell, anyway. Even in the seconds I was in hell to whisper into the next body, they completely ignored me.

"At first I assumed they realized the futility of trying to catch me, then I heard rumblings from their latest Loyal that they were finally on to something. A way to take power. A way to kill God."

When it became apparent her pause was in fact the end of her story, Addie spoke. "How?" she asked, captivated. "What did they find?" Alex turned, her arms folded below her ample cleavage.

"I don't know," she said. I looked to Addie to see if she was telling the truth. From Addie's expression, I guessed she was. The penthouse was quiet for a long moment, no one sure what to say.

"So why aren't you out there trying to find out what they're up to for yourself?" Valdez asked at last. "Why aren't you trying to stop them? You must have realized before now that your perfect afterlife would be over if they succeed."

"They aren't telling the Loyal anything more than I've told you," she said. "At least not the ones I've talked to. If the Watchers are going to bring down the heavens, I can't stop them any more than they can stop me from staying out of hell. Especially not with the... help they've enlisted."

"The Horsemen," Addie said. "They're what brought me here in the first place. Do you know what they're doing? How would demons have brokered a deal with constructs?"

"Have you ever seen constructs in heaven?" Alex asked. Addie shook her head no. "Well there are none in hell either. Where do you think they live? The Horsemen are always spread throughout humanity, waiting for the end times. The Watchers approached them in possessed bodies and convinced them they were in the right."

"How do you know that?" Addie asked.

"They wouldn't be working with the Watchers otherwise," she said with a roll of her eyes that made Addie feel like a dolt, I'm sure. "At the end of the day, constructs are just dolls with what appears to be sentience. I'm not surprised that they were lodged loose from God. Either way, they're immune to my charms, so whatever they're doing out there is beyond my power to stop."

When I turned to Addie I saw conflict in her eyes. Apparently making her decision, she reached behind her to turn around her bag and pull out Plath's book.

"We think an important message was sent to the Watchers through this book," Addie said as she lowered the cover for Alex to see. "It was written by one of their messengers in San Jose." I saw the spark of curiosity ignite in Alex's eyes. She walked to Addie and put her hand on the book. Addie maintained her hold distrustfully.

"Do you want my help or not?" Alex asked. Addie swallowed hard but released the book. I knew it was special to her beyond whatever code it carried—that was her only real possession since she'd been here.

"That is the only known copy," Addie informed her as she walked back for her chair.

"I've never been much for reading," Alex said, sitting down, "but I'll see what I can see." She flipped to the publication date to see it was almost 40 years old. "Though I doubt it's a current message. Is there anything else you haven't told me?"

"We think the Horsemen are protecting two or more people

named the Kohlers," Addie said. She told Alex about our search in Los Angeles. Then she told her about Carnegie.

"That must be a new one," Alex said of the possessed FBI Deputy Director. "Certainly not from my time." I was surprised she hadn't heard of Andrew Carnegie. My guess is she lived a very selective life, ignoring all that didn't interest her.

Once Addie finished and assured Alex that was everything we knew, the demon took a long breath and rose with the book under her arm. "Very well. I'll take it from here, little angel. You may go." Addie looked confused.

"I don't think you understand," she said. "We only have days left before the Watchers achieve whatever they've put in motion. We don't have any time to waste."

"Then I will not waste any," Alex said. "Goodbye."

"Wait, how will you contact us with information?" Addie pressed. "How will—"

"Little angel, you're lucky to be walking out of here alive," Alex stated. "Your part in this is done. If there is a secret in this book, I'll find it. Maybe I can even use it before the Watchers and kill God myself. If there isn't, I guess we're all fucked. Either way, I'm giving you a few more days in that wonderful body, so I suggest you make the most of them and leave while you still can."

Addie prepared to protest but I precluded her.

"What about me?" I asked, finding my voice. Alex smiled.

"I haven't forgotten about you, Perry," she said. "I was going to have you stay behind after class so we could have some private time." Addie figured out what we were talking about at once and reached for my arm.

"Jon, no," she said. I quickly pulled away and took a step closer to Alex.

"Show me," I said. Alex set the book on a table.

"What would you offer me in return?" she asked.

"What do you want?" Alex tilted her head.

"That you could give me, Jonathan Perez?" she asked. "Nothing. Except…"

"What?" I asked.

"Well, there is one thing you could do for me," she said. "It sounds as though all the Watchers but Carnegie are still in hell. If I show hell to you, would you let me show you to hell?"

"What does that mean?"

"I want them to know I have you," she said. "That I am on to them. That I know what you know. If nothing else it will… give them pause."

"What do I have to do?" Alex sauntered around me.

"Endure more pain than any living soul ever has," she said as casually as one could say such a thing. "It would only last a moment, but you'll have to be exposed for them to see you. So they know you're with me. It will not be pleasant."

"Jon, please, you don't know what you're—"

"Neither do you, sweet thing," Alex snapped, stepping up to Addie. "You have never felt the burn of hell. Do not speak as though you have. And this is not your choice."

"I'll do it," I said mechanically. Again Addie shot forward but Valdez seized her and gave her a look that silenced her. Had she spoken again I'm sure Alex would have ensured it would never happen again.

I couldn't imagine any pain worse than what I'd already felt. Than what I felt at that moment. And if Gabby and Pita were there in the middle of it, I had to know what they were enduring. I turned to Alex.

"Do it." Her smile was dark in a way I hadn't seen before, and I was afraid. More of what I would find than what I was sure to feel.

She took hold of my hand and led me to the chair. After she sat me down, she climbed on top of me with her legs outside mine. She leaned her head close to mine. Her scent would have thrown me off balance had I not been so terrified.

I caught a glimpse of Addie waiting beside Valdez before Alex moved in. She looked as pained as I'd ever seen her, like she might rush forward at any moment to throw this succubus off me. Still, she remained in place. After all we'd been through, I knew she understood I wanted this.

Alex whispered for me to close my eyes. I breathed her in for nearly a minute as she instructed, then I felt her lips on mine. I knew something was wrong when they felt cold. And then there was heat.

It wasn't a gradual realization that I was out of my body like with Addie. One moment I was in the chair, the next my mind was astray and on fire. The heat didn't come from hellfire or brimstone, it was the pure, raw hatred.

Hatred was all I could perceive. So much that it strained my sanity after seconds, if that's what they were. The only thing this place had in common with heaven was the absence of time in any comprehensible form.

It was the exact inverse of heaven. The abstract structure of infinite emotions was the same, but if heaven was a placid sea, hell was a roiling ocean. There was no peace here. Every identity, every soul, was caught in a perpetual hurricane made up from their own resentment. Pain stemmed not from devils with pitchforks, but rather the sickening memories of each other's lives.

Hearing that on earth wouldn't have garnered sympathy from me, but being here, if only on the fringe, I suddenly knew why Carnegie and the others wanted revenge as much as they wanted out.

I might have been crushed under the pressure of the enmity radiating from everywhere, everything, had I not clung so tight to my purpose. Remembering Addie's advice, I concentrated on the memory of the girls. It was difficult to imagine my affection for them amid so much hatred, but I tried.

Then I felt something slash across my soul. Alex. I could feel her. All the billions of souls across the landscape without form 'turned.' They saw me. A living soul among them. If I thought they were frenzied before, I hadn't seen anything yet.

I'll never be able to tell anyone what it feels like to have one's soul torn at by billions of hateful dead. I would never want to try. All I knew was the Watchers were at the forefront. As infuriated as they were at my presence, they were more furious with Alex. They couldn't touch her though, only me.

Just as I was sure that every unit of abstract measurement which encompassed my very identity would be ripped to shreds and leave me as nothing, I felt the cold grip of fingers along my back, grasping me. They pulled me up and out, and I was safe.

I was on the floor of the penthouse when my eyes opened. I felt blood on my face and my gut. I'd torn the stitches again, but the pain was literally soothing compared to what I'd just experienced.

I was tangled in a ball with Alex, wrapped over me like a knot on the carpet. She was bleeding as well, having cut her forehead on the corner of a wall we'd slammed into. Her fingers dug into me like mine had dug into Addie's after viewing heaven.

Addie was on top of us. She fought to pry Alex from me despite Valdez shouting at her to stop. He stood in the center of the room with his gun drawn, in a standoff with Meghan and Lisa. We might have all been dead in another few seconds had Alex not raised her voice.

Not to speak, but to laugh.

She came off me slowly, ignoring Addie as she worked her way between us. Before she lifted up, she smiled and kissed me again. "Thank you," she said as if I'd just brought her to climax. "That was perfect."

Addie shoved Alex against the wall with force that brought Meghan and Lisa's guns to her. Alex raised her hand for them to wait, still enjoying herself too much to care about Addie's temper.

My eyes were open but I wasn't sure where I was for a moment. I couldn't concentrate on anything. I didn't realize I was in Addie's arms until a few minutes passed, my thoughts coming back to me while the noise of all the hateful shouts faded.

"Are you alright?" Addie asked for the tenth time before I finally responded. I nodded, sitting up slowly. I gradually pushed her hands from my arms so I could just sit there on my own. It was silent but for Alex's blissful chuckles.

Eventually Alex turned to me, wiping her messy hair back. "Well?" she asked. "Did you find what you were looking for?" I looked at her, then at Addie.

"No," I managed, just audible. "They aren't in hell either."

fourteen

We were airborne in Guardian's jet within the hour. Valdez was agitated, to say the least, but he was the type to focus all the harder on business at hand to channel his frustration. He really was an idealist— probably more so than Addie. He lived for this.

Having clearly accomplished all we were going to in Philadelphia, he ordered the jet to Washington DC. His initial inclination was to head for New York, where the bulk of Guardian's holdings and resources were located. There was no centralized base, of course, but Valdez told us most of their members were spread throughout the city in banks, legal firms, talent agencies, city hall and the UN.

Not to mention a warehouse full of guns and men who knew how to use them.

The report that the Director of the FBI was also possessed changed his mind.

If Carnegie was in the body of the West Coast Deputy Director, it stood to reason whoever was in the body of Director Wells was another Watcher or someone even higher up. Either way, it was our best new lead. The FBI had clearly been commandeered by the Watchers. The last thing they would expect is us staking them out in their backyard.

That's what Valdez assured us, anyway. It was less than reassuring to Addie, who for once advised caution. Her suggestion was to regroup and consolidate Guardian's strength as opposed to rushing headlong at the Watchers before we learned anything more about Wells.

She was shaken up. I think it was just the rush of the 21st century finally catching up to her, feeling out of her element on a frightening scale. She'd been something of a spy before her death, but the scale of all this—Guardian, the FBI, the Watcher/Horsemen conspiracy, real-time global communications—I could tell she was exhausted trying to keep up. And she didn't like being left in the dust.

Part of her exhaustion came from worrying about me, I'm sure. I'd been a mess—I mean a total fucking disaster—over the past day. I was practically catatonic after we left Alex's penthouse. Still, Addie was there, helping me with everything from seatbelts to making sure I didn't rush into the street in the path of an 18-wheeler.

I'd have expected the Addie from our first few days together to kick me to the curb, but we'd been through a lot since then. We'd known each other for less than a week, but after all this... She probably looked at me like an old gimp dog she didn't have the heart to put down.

Alex let us go without a fight. She kept the book, much to Addie's displeasure, but we weren't in a position to argue. Turned out she had six other "disciples" in the penthouse in addition to Meghan and Lisa. Probably more. Valdez told us we were lucky to still be alive.

He wanted to put as much distance between us and Alex as he could. Whatever she said, he was convinced she'd have us killed if she got the chance. Addie disagreed, pointing out it would do Alex no good to take us out of the equation when we could only help her stop the Watchers.

"She doesn't see them as a real threat," Valdez told Addie once we were in the air. "Like she doesn't see us as a real answer to a threat. She'd kill me just to remind me of my place. And she'd kill you because she doesn't like you." Addie bristled.

"Why not?" She knew it was a pointless question but asked it out of reflex.

"You're everything she's not. Beauty to her hideousness." Addie left out a muted huff.

"I'd thank you but I know it wasn't a compliment," she responded. She turned to me, having talked enough about Alex. She'd sat directly beside me this time, patching up my gut herself after tearing the stiches with Alex. She didn't ask if I was alright. What a pointless question that would have been. But she sat there waiting until I came out of my shock. I didn't until much later, but I was finally coherent enough to formulate the question.

"Where are they?" It sounded like a whisper with my head in my hands, but Addie heard it. I turned and looked at her. My face was red but the expression blank. I'd never been so... stunned.

She didn't say anything at first, glancing at Valdez as if he had something to offer. "I'm not sure what to tell you," she said. "I suppose it's possible you, well, missed them. Probably in heaven of course—"

"You said that was impossible," I told her, my volume escalating. "That there was no way I could miss them. Hell was no different than heaven. I felt all of them. Gabby and Pita weren't there."

"I wonder if, because of what Alex did to you while you were adrift, you weren't able to—"

"No!" I didn't mean to shout but I did. "I'm telling you, they *weren't there*." Addie shrunk back, again unsure what she could offer me. My mind raced. "There has to be something else. Some purgatory, or something."

"There isn't," Valdez stated from where he stood behind another chair.

"How would you know?" I blasted. "How would any of you know? How do you know there aren't millions of heavens and hells of different degrees? What if—"

"There is heaven, and there is hell," Valdez stated as deadpan as before. "We can see across the veil to the other. There is nothing else."

"Then you tell me," I continued, ripping off my seatbelt and rising from the chair. The burn from my stomach wound kept me hunched. "Tell me where my wife and daughter are!" Valdez was halfway to telling me to sit and calm down, but Addie interjected, putting a hand on my arm.

"Jon," she said as gently as she could, "this may sound foolish, but... are you certain that they actually died?" I wheeled on her, ready to unleash more of my exasperation, but I held my tongue. As much as I wanted to blame someone, it couldn't be her.

I sat, running my hands through my hair and staring at the floor. "I held Pita's charred body in my hands," I managed. "I buried them both in the cemetery where Gabby's family has been laid to rest for generations. They're gone."

Addie nodded, as sure as I was. We sat in silence until I thought of something else. "The Watchers," I said, acid dripping from the words. "Could they have...?"

"There is nowhere else for souls to go once they have been judged," Addie said. "The Watchers could not have taken them elsewhere."

"There's here," I remembered. "How do you know they haven't possessed bodies?"

"I already told you, Jon," she said. "Gabby might be able to, but Pita could not."

"What if the Watchers forced them into bodies somehow, what if—"

"Listen to her, Perry," Valdez said. "It's imposs—" I jerked up, pointing at him.

"Don't tell me it's impossible!" I shouted. "You don't know shit about impossible. An hour ago you didn't know the Horsemen had always been in this world with you. For all you know, God could be here living in some body too." He didn't say anything, his temper under far better management than mine.

I leaned back, shaking my head. "All I know is, they weren't in heaven or hell. They have to be somewhere..." The three of us were silent for nearly a minute before Addie spoke.

"Perhaps if you told us how..." She stopped herself from finishing. I looked at her. I knew what her question would have been as well as she knew I wouldn't answer it. There was no conversation after that. I sat alone with my thoughts. My memories.

I walked into Addie's bedroom just before dawn. I stood at the door for a moment, still unsure if I wanted to walk through. I did after she saw me. She wasn't asleep either. She'd been gently tapping a finger to the touch-lamp beside her bed, staring blankly as the light flickered on and off.

She had changed into the sweats Valdez's men gave us when we arrived at the hotel. It was a few blocks from the Guardian "outpost" in DC—an angelic congresswoman's house with a basement full of money and guns. Valdez left us there under guard while he met with Guardian personnel the world over via satellite video feed. He hadn't issued a full report about his activities over the last few days.

Addie leaned up from where she laid when she saw me, surprised but not startled. Like she'd been waiting. She left the light at its lowest setting. Neither of us said anything for a moment, but whatever urge pulled me across the hall to her coaxed me on now that I was there.

"I met Gabby on assignment in Houston," I said. "She was a public relations coordinator, an intern, with Senator Downey's re-election campaign. I was investigating the scandal with her boss and the cartel that was greasing him. She intercepted me every time I tried to get an interview. I had a reputation for being a bully with questions, especially to politicians."

I allowed a smile, drifting through my favorite memory. "She always wore a high working ponytail and these brand new power suits she'd just bought out of college. She was ready to change the world from her little campaign cubicle.

"I knew right away she was probably the only one on staff with a conscience, so I started following her around. We spent so much time together that our love-hate relationship turned into something more. I told myself I was just using her until I got the information I needed, but I wasn't kidding anybody.

"I never ran the story when she told me the truth about Downey. She'd done some investigating of her own and found out everything. It would have put me on the map, but she was more important. I didn't want her name dragged through the mud.

"Instead we worked together to hit the story from the other side, exposing the cartel. The Downey story came out on its own without implicating her. It was more her story than mine, but to keep her name out of it mine was the one that the Pulitzer recognized.

"We moved to New York when I got the offer from the *Times*. Gabby and I got married right away. She worked for another campaign for a while before she got pregnant with Pita. I should have just gone local and stayed with her, but I had a taste for the big-time. I wanted more.

"I went after another drug ring case. A kingpin in Miami named Quito. I worked my way in with the Feds on the case. They recognized my name and figured they could count on me to tell the story their way once they made the bust.

"Turned out the bust wouldn't come easy. Quito was a regular Al Capone. Played it cold and dirty. Even his competition worked for him one way or another, mainly because they were scared.

"We built the case and cases around it for nearly four years. I missed Pita's birth, but eventually Gabby brought her down to live with me in Miami. She knew I was getting in too deep, but she said my heart was in the right place. She knew me well enough to know better, that I needed it for my ego, but she never told me so.

"Every time we had Quito nailed to the wall he slithered away somehow. His network was too big, changed too often, to get a hold of. We tried cutting off his suppliers and forcing him to buy from an undercover Fed source, but he always saw us coming. When we did get something he'd plant evidence on fall guys in other outfits. Then he'd start killing Fed families to send warnings.

"It got to the point where we decided we'd take him any way we could. Quito had a fragile alliance with a new batch of dopers from

Cuba, but they only took orders because he paid so well. They operated with their balls instead of their head. We figured we could use that.

"Me and a few other guys stole a load from Quito and mixed it in with the new guys' stuff before it got to a buyer. Then we rigged a bomb to hit a birthday party for some son of the new dopers. It was Quito's MO. And my idea." I paused to give the clump of emotion in my throat time to escape.

"I was watching while it happened. I didn't know there would be families there. Little kids. But it... it was the only window we'd have with all of them together. We told ourselves they were all scum or soon to be scum. We called it an eye for an eye for the Fed families. We went through with it.

"Sure enough, we let the leash off the mad dog and Quito got mauled. It made him sloppy and gave us the excuse to make arrests on leadership we couldn't have touched before. We finally got him, but Quito's network was bigger than one man. He'd have known it was us that sparked everything. Anyone with a family, Fed or otherwise, got the hell out of there.

"I was no different. I told Gabby what we'd done after the fact. I knew she would have stopped me otherwise. She was furious. She said I made her sick. I don't think she understood the risk I'd put her in until that moment. She threatened to leave with Pita, but I told her the Feds were the only way we could get out.

"We took off the night Quito was arrested. It was Pita's sixth birthday. We left everything. They were going to relocate us with a new identity somewhere in the Midwest. The story was we'd been killed in the cartel reprisals. They were going to notify Gabby's parents in California the next day, but..."

Tears were flowing freely by then. I felt weak on my feet.

"You can sit, Jon," Addie said from the bed in her smallest voice. I didn't.

"We were waiting for a car to pick us up from the airport. Pita was decorating her tiara. She was confused why we made her leave all her friends, her school, her toys. But it was her birthday. She was still happy as ever.

"Gabby was devastated. Afraid. But she'd forgiven me. It was my fault, but when the moment came, she knew I picked her and Pita over the career, the life. She said we'd be okay. As long as we had each other..."

I leaned against the door and slid onto my backside before I fell over. My voice cracked.

"I went to get Pita ice cream. I was almost back when the bomb went off. At first I was sure it was Quito, that he'd found us somehow. I found out later that Quito was already dead by then. He was shanked in a holding cell his first night. Because he snored.

"Maybe you know the rest from Cora's memories. It was the Stomach Bombing. Hardline fundamentalist Fayez al-Mihdhar had been waiting for UN Ambassador Desmond Ford to arrive outside the airport. Ford was on the way to deliver a commencement speech at the University of Chicago.

"Apparently something about Ford was an affront to God, but that was nothing three pounds of C4 strapped along al-Mihdhar's chest couldn't fix. Ford touched down about five minutes after we did, so when al-Mihdhar saw men in suits in the lobby, he figured they were for Ford. All he got were three Feds and the woman and child they were protecting."

I shook my head, staring into space. "The Feds tried to tell me we were just in the wrong place at the wrong time, but I knew that wasn't true. God wanted us there. On Pita's birthday. Just like he wanted me to be far enough away that I would live. That I would have to watch my wife and my baby girl be incinerated. Like I watched wives and little children burn that day in Miami."

I looked at Addie. She stared at me from the bed, unmoving. I ran a hand under my eyes to wipe them dry. "After the funeral I went back to work. I had nothing else to do other than kill myself. As much as I wanted to, I knew Gabby would hate me for it.

"I squeezed into new cases more as a mercenary than a journalist. I came under investigation by the Feds for planting evidence. They were right, but it got covered up from the inside. The Feds couldn't risk a conviction—it would have led to an investigation of how we handled Quito and overturned everything.

"They forced me out of their investigations the same as the paper forced me out of writing. I got blacklisted fast, nobody wanted me. I roamed for a while but ended up in LA since it was close to where I buried Gabby and Pita. I worked freelance writing jobs but the only thing I was any good at was investigating.

"I opened my P.I. shop but it never panned out. As much as I knew Gabby would hate me giving up, I hated myself more. I was going to blow my head off the night you saved Cora, then I got pulled into all this." I gave her a hollow smile. "I guess you saved me, too. What a waste."

Silence hung between us for a moment. I had said everything I could, but still I felt empty. Addie took a long breath, thinking everything over, and eventually swung her legs from the bed. She walked to my side and sat against the wall.

"For whatever it's worth," she started, "I don't believe you are a bad man. You may have done something terrible, but I hear the truth in your words when you say you wish you could take it back. God should have forgiven you."

I looked away, smiling darkly. "You want to know what the funny part is? For years I told people I didn't believe in God anymore. But I did. More than ever. I just laughed when people said he works in mysterious ways. I know exactly how he works. I know his perverted sense of justice.

"There isn't a day that passes when I don't regret what I let happen that afternoon in Miami. And there isn't a day that passes when I don't hate God with everything I have for blaming Gabby and Pita for my mistake."

I looked at Addie. "Have you thought that maybe we're the bad guys in this?" She looked confused.

"What do you mean?"

"The Watchers," I told her. "Should we really be trying to stop them? Do you think they're wrong to want some semblance of justice in the afterlife?"

"We wouldn't be any better off with them at the helm of the universe," Addie said.

"You think we'd be worse off?" I challenged. She looked uncomfortable for a moment. I didn't want to press her, but I continued speaking my mind. "There's nothing I've wanted more in these five years than revenge on God. You have as much reason to want it as I do. Why should either of us bother protecting him?"

Addie's eyes gradually glazed over, staring at nothing while she sifted deep inside.

"I'm not sure that we're doing the right thing," she offered. "I haven't been since I first took control of Cora. I don't know if Carnegie would make for a more just God than the one we have or not. But I know that as much as I want revenge, that isn't why I came here. I can't let that become the reason I am here."

"Why not?"

"Because if we replace God out of vengeance, where would that leave us? With another vengeful God?"

I wasn't sure what to say. I didn't know if she was right or wrong, if her argument was valid or not. But I knew her heart was in the right place. That was all I had to go off anymore.

I sat up a little straighter, taking a long breath. "Well the day you find a way to overpower God with love, you let me know," I said. She was silent for a moment, but allowed a subdued smile before long. It was the closest I'd come to levity in a long time.

I might have sat there with her until the sun rose had she not lifted herself up a few moments later, her eyes wide.

"That's it," she said, a burst of energy coursing through the words. "I know what Plath was telling the Watchers."

fifteen

"Love," Addie told us once Valdez and I were seated in her bedroom. "That is the weapon the Watchers are planning to use against God."

I watched Valdez for his reaction. He turned to me for mine. He had rushed back to the hotel the moment word reached him of Addie's epiphany. I'm sure he wasn't expecting this to be her realization, but he kept a controlled visage.

Valdez was tired. The lines over his brow looked deeper. His hair was oily and he didn't smell particularly good. He hadn't slept any more than Addie or me, busy mobilizing Guardian resources and searching for information across the globe.

I was still somewhat... unsettled, after what I'd told Addie only half an hour before, but less so than I expected. In a way it was the best I'd felt in years, even after the madness of the past night. I hadn't told her the truth for its therapeutic value, but I had to admit that my state of mind was peaceful in a way I'd all but forgotten.

I didn't think much about it, too surprised by what she'd said.

"I assume there's an explanation to follow," Valdez managed after she gave us a moment to let her words sink in. Addie was the only one standing, excitement visibly bristling in her movements. She'd been this way since her revelation.

"I don't know how I didn't see it before," she continued. "At first I was looking for some sort of hidden code in *What Conquers All*. I spent hours working out allegories and metaphors from the characters. Somehow I never thought the message would be the plot itself."

She saw both Valdez and I frustrated and realized she was rambling ahead of herself. Forcing herself to sit on the edge of the bed, she put her hands in her lap and started again.

"Plath's novel was a love story," she reminded us, her excitement reined in. "*What Conquers All*. At first I took the title for sentimentalism completely at odds with the author, but now I can't think of a more appropriate title. I didn't finish the book before we gave it to Alex, but I was less than a chapter away from the end. Even so, I think I know what message she was sending to the Watchers.

"There are two main characters. A woman and a man. The man is an angel. That was why it caught my eye in the first place. The story begins with him. He had married several beautiful women throughout his life, but none were ever beautiful inside. When he died he found that he never truly found love.

"With sight beyond eyes in heaven, he observes a woman among the mortal world that he knows to be beautiful in the manner he always hoped to find. She isn't without sin or malice, but he had never known someone to care as deeply as she does. For the first time he falls in love, albeit from afar.

"One day the woman is caught in a building during a violent earthquake. The angel senses her fear, knowing that she is about to die. So he takes the body of another man beside her also about to die. In the moments before they would have been crushed, the angel grabs hold of her.

"A miracle happens. While the collapse should kill them both, they survive. The woman knows it was a miracle and believes the angel when he tells her who he is. Over time she comes to love him as well, but jealous demons beset the couple, attempting to drive them apart. Even God sends angels to retrieve the man, knowing their love cannot be.

"At various points in the book, the angel again uses power to protect the woman from any harm—anything that would separate them. By the book's end they are both elderly in their bodies. The angel fears God's anger, that they'll be sent to hell, but the woman believes they will both be together in heaven."

Addie paused, studying both Valdez and I. "That is as far as I got. I do not know if they ended up together or not in the final pages." Valdez raised an eyebrow as if waiting for more.

"You believe there is truth to this?" he asked.

"I believe that this angel was able to wield some sort of power to protect the woman. Because he loved her."

"That is impossible," Valdez rejected immediately. "This world is structured. Divine magic, or whatever you're describing, is not a part of that structure."

"And yet constructs are free from the structure," Addie challenged. "What about the Horsemen? What about the son of God?"

"Constructs are not angels or demons," Valdez continued. "You know the rules, Adelaide. They are not written, but they are known. You may inhabit another body in this world, but you are still constrained to live inside that body as would its owner. If we were capable of miracles simply because of love, we would know."

"Do you really know that?" Addie pressed. "Most in heaven feel nothing of what occurs in this world after they leave it. Perhaps we can't tell when this happens."

"Impossible is a strong word for a dead guy living in a new body," I offered to Valdez. "A dead guy with the power to show people another plane of existence and tell truth from lies." I'm not sure he cared for my opinion on the matter. He kept his focus on Addie.

"Love," he repeated. "You're saying that is all it takes to perform a miracle? I have loved. Where have my miracles been?"

"The angel in the book couldn't perform them at will," Addie clarified. "But when the woman was in danger, when he knew she would fall to harm if he didn't protect her, something happened. The rules changed, if only for a moment, if only around those two."

"The rules can't change when they are God's rules," Valdez reminded her. "If they did, he would not be God."

"That's what the Watchers are out to prove," Addie said. "I think love is the one transcendent force that allows the rules to be bent. For God so loved the world that he gave his—"

"Don't quote that drivel to me," Valdez snapped. "None of us here believe in God's love."

"Then believe in your own," Addie pressed. "The Horsemen are out there protecting a secret. I think this is it." Valdez looked unconvinced, releasing a frustrated huff and folding his arms.

"Well what good would this secret be to the Watchers? Suppose they have a way to perform a fleeting miracle. How does that bring down the kingdom of God?"

"You have already said it, Valdez," Addie implored. "They know of a way to bend the rules. Bending them as the angel did, to save a loved one, doesn't affect anything beyond the couple. The world will continue on according to the structure God built for it."

"But suppose the Watchers bend a rule that results in a consequence. One that changes the structure. If they outright break a rule—if they disprove the word of God—what would that mean for this world? For all three worlds?"

I could see Valdez was uncomfortable with this line of thought. He'd known the Watchers were up to something, but I don't think he ever really took them as any more of a threat than Alex did. He shook his head, still skeptical.

"What rule could be broken by an angel or demon in love?" he asked. Addie leaned back a little, her shoulders finally sulking.

"I am not sure," she confessed. There was silence for a moment, while Addie thought of hypotheticals to prove her theory and Valdez thought of hypotheticals to disprove it. I ended up with the first idea.

"You said you didn't know if the angel and the women ended up in heaven," I thought aloud.

"That's right," Addie confirmed.

"Could you tell from reading this if they were real people? If they were more than just fictional characters to convey a message?"

"I can only see the piece as a whole in determining truth from fiction. I believe the book's theme is true, I am not sure about the details of the plot or characters. What difference would it make?"

"Suppose they're still out there," I offered. "This angel and woman. Would the Watchers have use for them? Enough to put them under the protection of the Horsemen?"

"The Kohlers," Addie said. "And they are the ones who had the book in the first place."

"So the Watchers are holding your mystery couple hostage?" Valdez asked. "Why?"

"Final judgment," I said. "Addie said it's just that—final. Once you end up in heaven or hell that's where you stay. But here you have an angel who bent the rules one too many times. The book said God was after him. Is it possible he could end up in hell after all? What would that do to the rules?"

"He wouldn't be sent to hell," Valdez affirmed. "Even if this is true, there is no evil at work in this story. The angel will return to heaven, likely with his lover, if she is truly this saint in the making. And why would the Watchers be protecting them before death? Even if they believed the angel would be sent to hell to contradict final judgment, why wouldn't they just kill him and have it done with?"

I didn't have an answer so I shrugged, leaning back in my chair. Addie remained confident. "There must be something else at work here," she asserted. "Either way, we need to find the Horsemen. Whatever they are guarding, the Kohlers or something else, they will have the key to all this."

Valdez's expression finally signaled agreement, if only on that one statement. "I've ordered the lion's share of my resources, men and otherwise, to DC and the other major FBI headquarters around the nation. They'll be watching closely for demons or the Horsemen. We'll snag one eventually, but in the meantime we'll be watching Director Wells like a hawk."

"What about Carnegie?" I asked.

"He flew in to New York late last night around the time we arrived in Philadelphia. My guess is he's trying to bait us. Lure us to him since he knows we'll be watching him. My men will be doing just that, but I want our focus here."

Valdez rose from his chair and stretched. "As for you two, I think it's time we sent you off to safer locations away from all this. You've done more than necessary already." I leaned farther back, bracing myself.

"Necessary?" Addie asked, also rising. "We appreciate your help, Valdez, but there is no way in this world or any other we are leaving now. This is our business."

"There is nothing left for you to accomplish," Valdez said. "My men will uncover the Horsemen and move in to find whatever they are hiding. I will alert you both to everything we learn as soon as I can. Your being here now is only a liability. Especially Perry. If the Watchers get ahold of him they will know everything he knows about Guardian."

"You peg me for a squealer?" I asked blankly.

"I think that if they kill you and you end up in hell, they—"

"No one is going to be killed and no one is going to hell," Addie exclaimed from beside my chair. "Jon and I are among your best sources of intelligence. You'd be a fool to ship us off to some bunker if new information comes to light. You will need us."

"I'm not going to have you out investigating or leading a raid, Adelaide," Valdez returned. "The Loyal will be looking for you. If they spot you it could blow our entire operation."

"Then keep us hidden close by."

"I can't guarantee your—"

"Of course you can't. But if you can't protect us here, where you've concentrated the crux of your force, you certainly can't protect us in some remote complex." Valdez shifted his gaze to me.

"You think this is a good idea?" he asked.

"If she stays, so do I." Valdez stared me down for a moment then released another huff.

"I'm going to oversee our reconnaissance on Wells," he told us. "You two will not leave this hotel unless authorized by me and escorted by my men. I'll bring you to our mobile command room for briefings as we have them. Do you understand?"

Addie nodded yes, but didn't look too happy about it. Valdez left us alone, posting two men down the hall. Apparently the hotel was owned by Guardian. We were the only ones there so at least we had some breathing room in the building.

Addie was looking at me when I turned, her eyes uncertain despite her confidence before.

"Do you really think Plath figured out a loophole to the word of God on her own?" I asked.

"It's more likely she was simply told. They only called her a messenger, not an oracle or anything." We were silent afterward. Neither of us had anything to do but wait.

Valdez brought us to the congresswoman's house that night. Apparently Guardian spotted over twenty demons milling about FBI headquarters throughout the day, including Wells himself. The trouble was getting one alone and obtaining the right information. If Guardian started abducting Loyal, suspicion would build when they were missed by Wells.

The focus was finding an address for where the Kohlers were being held. Guardian had a few sources in the FBI itself but none close enough to the Director to be of immediate use. They identified a series of addresses under investigation thanks to a mole, but it would take Guardian time to investigate so many leads thoroughly.

Even with their "full force" mustered, there were only a dozen men in DC. Valdez didn't want the Loyal noticing a sudden influx in angels nearby, so he kept his celestial forces distributed evenly across the country. Most of those under Valdez's command were living men and women under the impression that Guardian was a splinter black ops program organized by private donors. Which was true enough.

We met Congresswomen Sheila Danes, or at least the person in control of Danes' body, Charlize Mirabeau. Addie didn't like her much after hearing that Charlize took Danes' body for its tactical value as a member of the House armed services committee. It was a reminder that Guardian and Valdez were far from altruistic. Most of the angels who called themselves Guardian had taken their hosts through the same manipulation utilized by demons. All for the greater good, of course.

Danes was likely to be under close scrutiny from the Loyal now that they were aware of Guardian. They couldn't know she was a part, especially since Guardian didn't have any visible structure other than Valdez and a few men in the field, but they only had to see her on TV to know she was an angel. Valdez kept traffic to and from her house to a minimum, disguising himself and his team as dinner guests, foreign dignitaries, influential campaign contributors or cleaning staff.

Addie and I were the latter.

He dressed us up in coveralls, hats and glasses to make sure no one could get a good look at us. Apparently we were shifting "base" to another location on the other side of the capitol in the morning. It wouldn't be safe to stay in one spot too long. Thankfully moving would just be a matter of packing up computers and a little other equipment. Guardian was nothing if not mobile.

Addie and I attended a daily intelligence briefing focused on Wells and Carnegie. The Watchers had leaked information about Guardian to the media in hopes of drawing some component of the network out. It hadn't worked yet, but Valdez worried something would give soon.

We listened in on the plan to bug Wells' office and car in the coming days, worried that we might not have days remaining if what Carnegie said to Ito was true. Valdez had been right. We didn't really have any part to play going forward. Like it or not, we'd handed everything off to Guardian. It was probably for the best, despite

Addie's reservations.

She tried to shoehorn herself into Valdez's plan for a while but abandoned the fruitless effort when she was approached by the congresswoman's son. He was just six years old, an only child. I think Addie felt sorry for him—his mother had been stolen from him and he'd probably never even realize it. It wasn't hard to imagine the lack of attention he received since the possession.

Addie read to him in the living room upstairs. Some junior chapter book like the kind I used to read for Pita. I was too far away to hear her, but I watched from a distance. Eventually she caught me looking her way. She kept reading while I turned in a hurry for the next room. Valdez stood in my way. He looked to have been standing there a while as well, leaning against the railway to the stairs with folded arms.

"If she's right," he said, "this could be dangerous for her."

"What do you mean?" I spoke in an unnecessary whisper, as if Addie could somehow hear us from the adjacent room.

"Suppose she's right, Perry. Suppose love has the power to transcend the creator of the universe and all his omnipotence. Suppose it could indeed incur his wrath along with a second judgment. I'm not saying it's likely, but is it something you want her to risk for you?"

"I still don't follow."

"Please, Perry. I've seen the way you look at her." I tried to keep from looking off balance but probably did a shitty job of it.

"It's hard not to look at Cora Avery's body," I said, folding my arms as well. "That's what got me into this mess." His look was intended to remind me he could tell when I was lying.

"I suppose that doesn't matter. It's the way she looks at you that would be the problem."

"She keeps me around out of pity more than anything," I said. "She's got a big heart. That doesn't mean she's in love."

"Is that why she spent the day at your bedside in the Nevada complex waiting for you to wake up? Praying to a God she despises for you to be alright? Is that why she sits next to you everywhere you go? Is that why—"

"Why don't you stick to toppling capitalism and leave the psychoanalysis to somebody who knows what the fuck they're talking about." I'm not sure why I got angry about it, but he backed off, giving me a defensive gesture and disappearing back down the stairs.

I just stood there with my back to the wall separating Addie and me.

Two days passed and Guardian moved no closer to the Horsemen. Nothing came from the bugs in the FBI headquarters and they still hadn't managed to bug Wells' house or car. For all of Guardian's resources, it turned out the FBI was still a fairly tough shell to crack.

Valdez moved Addie and me to a location across town—a lobbyist's townhouse. Infinitely nicer than the hotel. Valdez still wanted us hidden somewhere in another country, but Addie refused to leave.

I didn't much care for just sitting there twiddling my thumbs, but she was walking up the wall. She must have called Valdez and Congresswoman Banes' house every other hour asking for an update. They basically ignored her by the second day, but eventually we heard that Wells had flown to Texas. Several Guardian agents followed him.

Valdez remained in DC since Carnegie was apparently inbound for the capitol. He was certain the Watchers were attempting to lure us out with all the movement. It was likely they thought Guardian was much bigger than it was. With the exception of a few weapons caches scattered across the nation, it was only a network of information and influence.

I worried that Carnegie had picked up on the subterfuge and was mobilizing another taskforce for us. Every time I glanced out the window I half expected the National Guard to be there. Still, things remained quiet.

I spent most of the time wondering where Gabby and Pita were. I couldn't imagine Gabby possessing a body if it meant leaving Pita behind, but I knew to an absolute certainty they weren't in either heaven or hell. At least not the versions Addie and Alex showed me.

As relieved as I was at the revelation they weren't in hell, the notion of them being lost in some void—some desolate, lonely purgatory—terrified me plenty. Perhaps some souls didn't live on. Maybe the ones that didn't deserve either heaven or hell just ceased to be after death. The notion fueled my rage for the Almighty, but I knew somewhere deep down they were still out there somewhere.

I woke on the third morning, our first in the townhouse, to Addie shaking me. She stood beside my bed in a trench coat and beanie. It must have barely been dawn. The room was mostly dark.

"Come on," she whispered. "We're leaving." I rubbed the sleep from my eyes in a hurry.

"What's wrong?" I asked, pushing aside the bedspread.

"We're wasting time, that's what's wrong," she said, throwing a shirt at me.

"So what do you want to do?" I asked, somewhat annoyed. "Run away from home? Where would we go? We have nothing."

"We can always come back, but we're doing no good sitting here. It's been nearly a week since Carnegie told Ito they were days away from their endgame. I'm through sitting here waiting on Valdez to get lucky. We don't have time for spy games with Carnegie and the FBI."

"Then what do you want us to do?" She heard the skepticism in my voice and gave me the look I'd been accustomed to in our first days together.

"You can do whatever you like," she declared, rising full length. "I am going out there."

"For what? Are you going to go door to door checking for Death and his buddies?"

"We may only have hours left, Jon. Minutes. If there was ever a time to act, it's now. I'm going into the open. To... I don't know, shake things up. They're looking for me. If Carnegie and his Loyal or the Horsemen come after me, Valdez will have his target."

"Fishing never works out too well for the bait, especially when the bait's not attached to a line. You think Guardian will take on the FBI in broad daylight in the open?"

"Anything is better than just sitting here!" she exclaimed in a sharp whisper. "What part of days or minutes are you not understanding, Jon? We have to *do* something. Now." I stared at her hard through the minimal light before shaking my head with a long huff.

"So, what, you're gonna climb out the window?" She took a look outside, suddenly less confident. It was the second story and the roof was coated in snow.

"I was hoping you would go first," she said. I rolled my eyes and threw the covers from my legs. I hid my smile while pulling the shirt over my head. She must have known anyway since she was smiling when I looked at her again.

"I suppose you want me to chloroform the guards too," I said.

"Do you have any?" she asked. I paused but knew she was kidding when her smile remained.

"Let's just sneak out the back before they wake up, okay?" She nodded and waited patiently (for her, at least) while I went into the bathroom to wash my face and brush my teeth. Even turned around, I could see her blushing as red as her scarf when I came back to the bed to change into my jeans.

My charming Sheila from the '40s.

My condition for walking into the maw with Addie was that we stop to get coffee first. The lack of Starbucks on every corner reminded me why I preferred the West Coast. We ended up stopping in a diner that had just opened. I had enough money from Guardian's take-out allowance to get us each a cup. And breakfast burritos.

It was cold. Nearly four inches of powder had fallen that night, still untouched across the streets and lawns. A few flakes fell as we walked, shimmering as the rising sun pierced pockets of the heavy cloud cover now and again. It couldn't have been much quieter.

Addie wasn't eating. I figured she didn't like it at first, then I saw her expression. I'd never seen anyone so mesmerized. It was like taking Pita to the movies for the first time. "You've never seen snow before, have you?" I asked. She shook her head slowly.

"It's... so..." She smiled and looked at me. "It's more beautiful than heaven." I raised an eyebrow and sipped at my coffee.

"That's depressing." She ignored me, content in her rapture.

"For all the snow this city has seen and will see, there has never been a snowfall quite like this one. And there never will be again. That is what makes real beauty."

"What's really depressing is that angels get bored of heaven." She shrugged.

"Only this one, apparently," she said. "Heaven is nice, of course, but it's so... constant." Lonely. That's what she meant, but I didn't press her.

"'Constant' probably sounds pretty good to most people," I offered. "You don't have to worry about 'constant'."

"Unless it's constantly something you don't want," she returned.

"You're telling me you'd rather do this over and over again for eternity? Pay bills? Get old? Most people are worried about surviving from day to day, and the rest spend life chained to a cubicle. Some life."

"You don't have to live that way. Here you can make a choice. There is only one way to live in the beyond."

"Nobody really has a choice here either, you know. You're born into something, and that's where you stay. The product of your environment. You should know that better than anyone, Miss

Arranged Marriage."

"You say that like there is no happiness to be found anywhere."

"You think there is?" She looked at me like I was crazy. "Nobody above the age of 18 is happy, Addie. They think they are for a moment or two, then they realize whatever they have isn't enough. Then they realize whatever they have will get taken away. Then it does. Everyone is afraid. Or in pain. Or lonely. All the time."

"I wasn't."

"You told me you died alone and miserable."

"I did. And I would give anything to live that life again. Even with all the pain, there was so much happiness. Years in the bush on horseback. The time, short as it was, with the children. Teaching them to ride. Singing and playing with them.

"But even when I lost them, even when I was given to a man like property, even when my father ignored me all those years... Even when I was tortured and killed by those I hated, I lived the life I wanted to live. I was a part of something bigger than myself. I was happy.

"I want to *live* happiness, Jon, I don't just want to remember it in an abstract fishbowl. I want to *do* something with my life—all of it. I didn't feel alive again until the moment I took Cora Avery's body. It's the first time since my death that I've been... happy."

We walked in silence for a moment, eyes on our boots as we trudged through the snow. I couldn't wrap my brain around it. Happy? How could she say that after the nightmare she'd been through since returning? I'd seen up close what possessing Cora had done to her. I'd listened to her cry that night after realizing the world had left her behind. I'd felt the numbing horror and shame after Anton.

She knew that's what I was thinking and answered the question I hadn't asked. "I don't regret anything I've ever done. That's the only thing I really have to show for the life I've lived, this part of it included."

"Then you're one in a million, Adelaide Martin," I told her. "In a billion."

"You regret getting involved in all this?" she asked.

"My life is one giant regret. Living it the way I did killed the only two things I ever cared about. The only good thing I ever contributed to the world."

"Gabby and Pita never would have been a part of your life at all had you not lived the way you did. As you are."

"They'd have been better off that way."

"Pita would have been better off not existing?" Addie pressed.

"Maybe," I murmured, slowing down. "I don't even know where she is now. If she's alright or not..."

Addie was silent this time, but I felt her draw closer. She might have grasped for my hand had it not been occupied with my coffee. I felt her eyes on me even though she looked ahead.

"I've never told anyone the truth, you know," I said, still looking down. "Not even Gabby's parents." I laughed even as I felt a tear freeze to my cheek. "You're my only confession."

"Have you ever told God?" she asked. I stopped, prompting her to do the same.

"What do you mean? He's the only other one who knows the whole truth."

"Have you ever told him you're sorry?" I felt my grip tighten around the styrofoam cup.

"Why would I waste my time? What possible good would that do now?" Addie shrugged.

"What harm would it do?" she countered. I felt like snapping at her but she cut me off. "Beat him at his own game, Jon. Don't do it for him. Do it because you want to. Because Gabby and Pita would want you to."

I looked around. We had made our way to 22nd Street. The Washington Memorial rose into the heavy clouds further to the south. "I'm not sure I can be sincere anymore," I said.

"Your pain is sincere, isn't it?"

She was waiting for me to do it right there and then. I swallowed hard. There was a bench coated in snow behind her. I walked to it and sat. I set the coffee down and let out a long breath. It rose in a visible column into the morning cold. I folded my hands and dipped my head.

I did it silently. It took about five minutes, I think. At first I'd assumed I would just cut to the chase and be done with it in twenty seconds, but the more I thought about what I was doing, the more I was caught in something I couldn't escape. Aside from a drunken insult or threat, it was the first time I'd said anything to God in years.

It was like pouring my soul out to Addie all over again, especially with her at my side. She was there when I opened my eyes, looking at me. She pulled off her gloves and wiped tears from my face with her fingers, offering a sad smile.

"Think he'll forgive me?" I asked, my voice shaking despite the sarcasm.

"Who cares," she said casually. "You didn't do it for him. You did it for you." I nodded and took a long breath, putting my hands on my knees.

"You know, other than a dog, I think you're the only person in five years who's given a shit about me," I said. Again she shrugged.

"You are a good man, Jonathan," she said. "That isn't hard to see." I gave a silent chuckle.

"Jonathan. No one's ever called me that but my mom and Gabby," I said more to myself than her. She immediately looked down.

"I'm sorry. I didn't mean to..." I looked at her. Part of me wanted to put an arm around her and say thank you, but I knew I couldn't. Not after my last conversation with Valdez.

Instead I stood up, grabbing my cup.

"I'm gonna need to find an Irish coffee after that," I said. I pointed to the gift shop across the street with the flashing espresso sign. "Come on."

"I'll wait here," she said, fiddling with the ends of her scarf. "I'd just like to look at the snow for a while." I figured it would be even more awkward if I just walked off so I grabbed her by the scarf and gently pulled her up. She grinned and caved in, trailing me across the street.

Addie and I were the only ones in the gift shop. It was about 8:30 by then but the snow had kept many off the streets, certainly anyone who'd be visiting a gift shop. Addie glanced at the rows of novelties, curiously inspecting miniature replicas of the monuments she'd observed over the past few days. I ventured to the far side of the shop to inspect the espresso machine.

I ordered a double latte (it turned out Addie had snuck nearly a hundred bucks from our Guardian houseguests before waking me) and a muffin for Addie. She hadn't eaten any of her burrito. I put my hands in my pockets and took a long breath, zoning out amid the howl of the espresso machine.

As unnerved as I was about everything, a unique sense of tranquility had found its way over me. The calm before the storm, maybe. Along with it came an unmistakable sensation that the endgame to all this—the Watchers' divine conspiracy, my time with Addie, the world as I knew it—was upon me. I'd felt the unrelenting squeeze of fate before. This was it.

In that moment, everything that had transpired over the past weeks, from meeting Addie to the revelations about the girls, felt somehow interrelated. The detective in me knew there was some common thread woven around Addie, Valdez, Alex, Carnegie, the Horsemen, even Gabby and Pita. It was right there in front of me, but I had yet to pull it loose and unravel its mystery.

Once again God was herding me to an end. Maybe this time it would be mine. I wasn't sure. Only that my world was about to reach a boiling point again.

"$3.25, thanks," the barista called after setting my drink on the counter. I pulled Addie's money from my jacket, brought out of my trance. I paid, but the moment before I reached for the cup I saw him.

The boy in the orange shirt.

He stood outside in the snow, staring at me. One of his fingers curved along the glass, writing something in the frost. I was so startled I nearly yipped. He was just a little boy, but seeing him there, again... It was one of the more disturbing things I'd ever seen.

I stood silent for a moment, unable to move while our eyes remained locked. When he pulled his finger from the glass I looked at the letters he spelled. *Hurry.* Then he ran. Bolted from the sidewalk around the corner.

"Addie!" I shouted, tearing out the door after him. I shot through the snow around the corner to an empty parking lot. He was fast, already on the other side. He paused a moment to catch my eye, then disappeared behind another building. I chased him around it to another street, losing ground despite his size.

I heard Addie behind me shouting my name over the snow. I knew I'd have to stop soon from the pain in my gut or risk tearing my stitches again. I kept on at full bore down the length of another street anyway, determined not to lose him.

I think I'd run nearly nine blocks by the time I did lose him. My last view was him ducking into a corner grocery store. I followed in after him but there was no sign—no place for him to hide unless he'd gone into the back. I asked the manager and the one customer if they'd seen a little boy in a t-shirt. Both looked at me as if I were crazy.

Addie caught up to me panting in the bread aisle. I was exhausted and my side was on fire. Nearly as out of breath, she asked me what I was doing.

"The kid," I managed between breaths. "Did you see him?"

"What kid?"

"The little black haired kid in the orange shirt. I've seen him before. In Philly. And San Jose. Back at Beeks Place before I ever met you. He was there when Alex showed up in the parking garage. He—"

"Jon, calm down," Addie implored. I was stuttering over myself, probably not making any sense. "You're saying there's a little boy that you've seen all across the country? How could—"

"It was him!" I exclaimed, again irritating the customer trying to buy a gallon of milk down the aisle. "I'm telling you, it was him. That kid has been following me."

"You're just telling me this now?" Addie pressed. "Why did you not mention this before we went to Alex?"

"I wasn't exactly in the best state of mind that night," I snapped, trying not to sound defensive. "I meant to tell you, I honestly just forgot. I almost thought it was déjà vu or something until now, but... it was him. He's real."

"You think he has something to do with the Watchers or Alex?"

"Why else would he keep popping up wherever we go?" I asked.

"How old is he?"

"Dunno. Ten maybe."

"He could not be a possessor from either side, then. That is too young."

"Well there's no way he's normal. Living, I mean."

"How do you know?"

"I... I can just tell. There's something in his eyes." Addie looked at me as skeptically as when I looked at her in our first meeting, but she heard the truth behind what I was saying.

"Well he can't be Carnegie's," Addie stated. "If the Watchers knew where we were they wouldn't be sending a little boy after us. It's got to be something else."

"Hurry," I said, to which Addie tilted her head. "He wrote that on the glass of the gift shop just now. Hurry. Nothing else."

"Hurry?" I watched Addie muse but come up empty. "You're sure he was talking to you?"

"To us," I confirmed. "He had to have been. He was looking right at me."

"Did he escape?"

"I lost him in here. But they said they never saw him." I leaned up, still breathing hard with blood pumping. "I was pretty far back though. Maybe he went around the corner instead of in here. Either way he's gone."

"I don't think so," Addie said. "He clearly wanted you to see him. To bring you here. He must still be around or..." I could tell from the abrupt way she trailed off that she'd seen something. I turned to look for the boy, but there was only another grown man walking in.

Addie took hold of my wrist and pulled me behind a rack of drinks and canned goods. I knew something was wrong from the way she squeezed. She didn't say anything for a moment, just pointed at the man who'd walked in. He was tall. He wore a heavy coat and a grey beanie. Walking on the other side of the store, he grabbed a frozen dinner, a bag of potatoes and a few other items from the shelves.

Addie pulled me deeper into the back of the store before she risked a whisper. "Death. That is him." My heart sank.

"*Him?*" I studied the man closer, ready to bolt for the front door or the back room if he came our way. Instead he grabbed his few items and made his way for the counter, patiently waiting to be rung up behind the other customer. "What do we do?" Addie didn't respond, standing as still as the shelf we hid behind.

"Follow him," she said at last. She looked at me as if for approval. I swallowed hard but nodded wordlessly. It felt like suicide, but we'd just been handed a miracle. Trap or not, I wasn't about to let it pass us by. We waited for a few minutes while the Horseman checked out and returned to the exit. If he had noticed us he didn't let on.

We crept to the window cautiously, making sure Carnegie wasn't outside in force. Not seeing police cars or snipers in windows, we inched our way outside. Death had entered a car parked up the street. I acted fast, memorizing the license plate number before it disappeared.

Addie acted faster, hustling me toward a taxi making its way up the street. She told me to signal it while she waited with her back turned, protecting her from Death's rear view mirror. We climbed into the cab before it even came to a complete stop, giving the driver the classic order to "follow that car."

Addie tried to make up some lame excuse for why we were trailing the car, but I told her not to worry—the cabbie would drive either way. She slouched in the back seat just in case we came close enough for Death to turn and get a look at her. He'd see an angel before he recognized her face.

The cab ride was short—two minutes across fewer blocks than I had run. We were in a residential segment just outside the District of Columbia. When Death pulled to a stop on the street we directed the cabbie to do the same after circling the block and parking out of sight. I jumped out, throwing him twice the fare. Addie rushed to a corner and peered around.

Death unhurriedly pulled the paper bag of groceries from the car and walked to an apartment building. Making his way up a stoop, he keyed a dial pad and someone buzzed him in. I found Addie's eyes.

"Look familiar?" I asked.

"The Kohlers must be inside," she returned, excitement coursing through her whisper. "What are the odds that in the entire country we could just run into Death again?"

"We didn't run into anything," I reminded her. "Valdez may have gotten lucky picking cities where the Feds are based, but that kid brought us to Death. We were supposed to find him."

"It's almost too obvious to be a trap," Addie mused, staring across the street. "Who would have sent the boy? Alex? One of Ito's men? Why not just contact us?"

"Alex and Ito didn't know we existed the first time I saw that kid. He's got to be something else." I gritted my teeth in frustration that Addie hadn't gotten a glimpse of him to tell me what he was.

I joined her in gazing at the apartment. "Well we're here now, and we know Death is in there. Should we call Valdez?"

"With what? You don't have a phone, do you?"

"No, but I could go find one. There has to be a..." I trailed off when Death appeared again. Less than two minutes had passed since he entered the building, but, empty handed, he returned to the car and pulled back onto the snowy road, disappearing down the block.

Addie turned to me with "now's our chance" written in her eyes. I wasn't persuaded.

"If this isn't the world's biggest setup I don't know what is. If we go in there we're dead. We probably wouldn't get across the street. What if there are more demons watching the place? More Horsemen? They could be anywhere."

Addie looked back at the apartment building, fixing her gaze. Eventually she shook her head. "No. It was just Death in there with them. They're alone."

"How can you be sure?"

"Because we're here." She turned her attention to me, her eyes focused like I'd never seen. "We were brought here for a reason, Jon. This is it. Our chance. Likely our last chance. We have to trust that."

"No offense, Addie, but I don't know that I feel comfortable trusting a gut feeling when it comes to going up against the Horsemen of the Apocalypse. Who would possibly have wanted us to find this place? God? Why would he suddenly help us now? You've never even seen the kid. Why would you trust him?"

"Because I have faith that we should." That was the last thing I was expecting. I'd never heard her use that word. She read my surprise clearly. "I don't know who is helping us or why. Maybe it is God. He may have lost my trust and my love, but I still believe he can move us. All I know now is that something—someone—is moving us."

"Like pawns," I interjected. "How inspiring."

"Am I wrong? Tell me, Jon. You are the last person who would believe in random chance." I stared at her hard, unconvinced by her argument, but possibly by her passion. She believed what she was saying. "We were meant to do this, Jon. Today. Now. You and I."

I sighed, my breath escaping in a jet of steam through the air. "Let's do it then, oh ye faithful." She allowed a little smile. I regretted not bringing sunglasses to hide our eyes, but we pulled up our hoods and hid Addie's hair best we could. Steeling ourselves, we walked across the street.

"Suppose we get in alive," I said as we walked. "Suppose the Kohlers are actually in there. What makes you think they're going to open the door for us? They weren't exactly cordial in the Colonial Building, and if they're the couple from your book they'll see through any bullshit we slip them."

Addie didn't respond right away, lost in thought. She glanced at me, then looked away in a hurry. She was actually blushing.

"I have an idea."

"What?" She blushed brighter.

"You'll need to trust me."

sixteen

The winter saved us at the door. The buttons on the dial pad were still frosted over from the night. Only three had been touched since the morning. One in particular was clearest, so we hoped it was the one Death had buzzed.

We didn't push it. There would probably be no answer if we did, and it was possible anything we said would be heard for the lie it was. Instead we waited for someone to open the door. I sweated bullets just standing there, expecting Death to pull back up from some other errand any moment.

He didn't though. No Horseman or demon spotted us, and if they did, they let us pass. A man came to the door for a walk with his dog after about ten minutes. I pretended to be fiddling with the buzzer while Addie asked if he could hold the door for us. I'm sure it was Cora's face more than Addie's words that convinced him.

Our best guess from the dial pad was apartment 207. We took the stairs, both looking for any sign of Loyal in the vicinity. The halls were empty. 207 was at the corner of the second floor. The building was old but a step up from the Colonial.

When we came to the door Addie took a long breath. I still didn't know what she was planning, but I let her go ahead with it. I put my hand on her shoulder. She didn't look at me but I could tell she was still blushing.

Raising a hand, she knocked on the door. Not anticipating an answer, Addie spoke. "Is this the residence of Mr. and Mrs. Kohler?" Still no sound. "My name is Adelaide Martin. I read your copy of *What Conquers All*. I was hoping to talk to you about it." Nothing. "Please. I am an angel. I need your help."

I felt like I'd been punched in the gut when she fell silent. She'd given away everything. If Loyal were in there we were dead. I felt like whirling her around by the shoulders and asking if she was insane, but I held firm. It would do no good now.

I wasn't sure what possible plan she could have in revealing everything, but I'll be damned if it didn't get results. After another moment both Addie and I straightened at the echo of a creak in the floor. Someone moved toward the door. Addie stared into the peep hole, her expression as sincere as her words.

"You have our book?" a woman's voice asked from behind the door. My heart skipped a beat.

"I'm afraid we lost it," Addie replied. "But I read it. I'm hoping you can tell me about love. I need to know."

A long pause.

"You are the angel looking for us," the woman said. "The one they warned us about."

"Yes," Addie returned. "Will you help me?"

That was the longest pause yet. Then we heard the sound of a deadbolt unlocking and the door opening. An elderly woman stood behind it, looking at us uncertainly but without fear.

"Am I not what you were expecting?" she asked Addie. I looked at my partner and the shocked expression on her face.

"You're a demon," Addie observed aloud. The woman nodded, then stepped aside.

"Yes. Come in."

Addie and I exchanged a look when she disappeared from view, but we did as instructed and followed her inside. I shut the door behind us then observed the room. It was even smaller than their last apartment, furnished with less.

The woman stood at the end of a short hallway and beckoned us closer. A living room was at the end, occupied by an elderly man rising from a recliner chair. He looked far more on edge than the woman, but still calm.

"You trust them?" he asked the woman. Obviously he knew who we were as well. The woman nodded, raising a hand to the man.

"The prune is my husband, Jim. I'm Elizabeth. Jim, this is Adelaide Martin and Jon Perry."

"What do they want?" Jim asked his wife.

"Jim, please," she scoffed with a chuckle, then turned to us. "Would you care for tea?" Addie and I exchanged another glance.

"I think we're alright," Addie said.

"Well I've got a pot on, I'll fetch some anyway. Please sit. Jim won't bite. He probably doesn't have any teeth left anyway." The husband grunted and returned to his chair. When Elizabeth left for the adjacent kitchen, Addie led me to the sofa against the wall.

"Thank you for your hospitality," Addie managed to Jim. He didn't say anything, looking away. We sat in silence until Elizabeth returned with a little platter and three cups.

"I hope you'll try some. Jim refuses so I never have anyone to enjoy it with." Addie and I both let her pour us a cup. She sat across from us in another chair. She took a long sip, relaxing. Addie cleared her throat in the silence.

"Raspberry?" Addie asked. Elizabeth beamed.

"That's right," she confirmed, again taking a sip. Addie set her cup in her lap, looking to enjoy the warmth in her hands.

"Can I ask you something?" she began. Elizabeth nodded.

"What is your real name? The one you've taken from Jim, I mean."

"Oh, it's Kohler," she answered. "We didn't need to change it until recently."

"I'm sorry," Addie offered. "I'm still not exactly sure what is going on."

"Yes you do," Elizabeth said with a smile. "You read Young's book." Interesting. Either she was toying with us or she wasn't aware Plath wrote the book. The latter could mean Addie and I knew more of what was going on than the Kohlers, I thought.

"It's true, then?" Addie asked. "Love has the power to circumvent divine law?"

"You said you read it. You know it's true." Elizabeth looked at me for a lingering moment, taking me in. "He is the one." Elizabeth chuckled when Addie blushed and nodded. "I wasn't asking, dear. I can see it plain as day." She set her tea on the table between us and reached for Jim's hand. He took it but didn't look any happier about the decision his wife had made.

"And you're worried that he won't return with you," Elizabeth said.

"Yes," Addie said. "You believe... I could change that?"

"Yes," Elizabeth said.

"How?"

"I have no idea, dear."

"Then how are the two of you..." Addie trailed off, not sure what she was asking. Elizabeth must have seen from my expression that this was the first time Addie had admitted her feelings for me. When she spoke next it was to me.

"I am a demon, Mr. Perry. My husband is not. I assume you've read Young's book as well?" I told her that Addie relayed the story to me. "I see. You should read it yourself someday, it's masterfully written." She took another sip of tea.

"Jim and I met much as the angel and the woman in the book did," she continued. "I was lost in hell. The only reprieve from my agony was focusing on the spirit of a man among the living. He came through so strong to me, and the more I thought about him, the more in love I fell.

"Until one day I escaped into the body of a young girl. Mary. She was drowning, you see. Couldn't swim. I could, so I offered help. She took it, and I sought out the man I'd fallen in love with from afar."

Elizabeth smiled coyly at her husband. "I didn't tell him the truth at first. I didn't think he'd believe me. Then one day he was hurt. Fell off a roof he was laying. The doctors told me there was no way he'd survive, but in his final moments I brought him back somehow. I wasn't sure how, but I knew I'd done it.

"It wasn't long after that we were approached by the Horsemen. They told us they'd felt my act to save Jim. They showed me *What Conquers All* and told us there was a way we could be together forever."

"Why?" Addie asked. "Did they come to you, I mean."

"They have never said," Elizabeth answered. "We've always assumed it was pity of some sort. When I first saw them I thought they were there to kill me for what I'd done, for breaking the rules. Instead they offered us protection. They told us that God would be vengeful toward a demon's love, that he would send forces against me.

"Jim and I lived a lifetime together, and I never believed they were right until recently. You weren't what I was expecting, Ms. Martin."

"So it's just been the Horsemen taking care of you all this time," Addie said, careful how she framed the question.

"They've only been helping us about in our old age, but yes," Elizabeth replied. "They were more protective as time went on, keeping us indoors all the time. It suits us fine, though. Jim and I have done about everything we wanted to already. We're just waiting now."

"For what?" Addie asked.

"For heaven." When Addie wasn't sure what to ask next, I spoke.

"I don't mean to put this indelicately, but... how?" I asked. "How can love reverse your final judgment?"

"Love can do anything, Mr. Perry," Elizabeth returned. "I... experienced its power when I saved Jim that day all those years ago. It was only for a moment, but I knew in that moment there was nothing in this world or any other that I couldn't do with that power brought to bear. Once these bodies give out, I'll take us both to heaven, whether God wants us there or not."

"Not to sound crass," I told them, "but what are you waiting for? Why not ask Death to expedite the process if you are both ready?"

"It should be natural," Elizabeth affirmed. "The Horsemen agreed. They promised they wouldn't let anything happen to us in the meantime." She paused, tilting her head as she observed Addie. "Did God send you to stop us somehow, Ms. Martin?"

"No," Addie answered. "I came of my own will."

"But you didn't learn of love's power until you found the book in our apartment. Why were you looking for us before?"

"I saw the Horsemen acting on your behalf from heaven," Addie answered. "I thought something was wrong." She left it at that.

"But then you met Mr. Perry." Addie nodded. "Well don't worry, dear. When the time comes you'll be able to take him back with you."

"How?" she asked. "I'm not sure that I'll know what to do." I raised an eyebrow. She was making this pretty convincing. Or she meant it.

"You will. You'll be faced with losing him, but in that last moment of desperation it will just happen. I promise."

Addie took a long breath and looked Elizabeth hard in the eyes. "Elizabeth, I hate to pose negativity to your optimism, but I wonder if you've considered the implications of what you're planning." Elizabeth didn't seem to understand, still smiling but tilting her head.

"What I mean is, if you succeed in bypassing God's judgment, will that not do the impossible and prove God wrong? Have you thought about what it would mean to undo the word of God?" Elizabeth's warm smile dissipated slowly.

"You believe I'm wrong?" she asked.

"No, not in the least. But I am wondering if you've considered the impact your action could have on existence itself."

"You don't really think Elizabeth's entry to heaven would undo the world," Jim said, his voice laced with antagonism.

"In my search for you, I uncovered a group of demons called the

Watchers who believe exactly that," Addie said. "They believe that your action will effectively kill God and allow them to take hold of the universe in his place."

"That's... No, how could that be possible?" Elizabeth asked. "I've already broken the rules here by saving Jim. Why would this be any different?"

"It's been suggested that a temporary shift in the mortal realm is a precedent already set by God himself. But to overrule his authority in final judgment..."

"This is rubbish," Jim barked from his seat. "They came to stop us, Liz. All this has just been a ruse. Call for Death. Get them out of here."

"You don't have anything to fear from us," Addie assured them as Elizabeth looked visibly shaken. "We couldn't stop you if we wanted to, Elizabeth. No one can. The choice to enter heaven is yours alone. I'm only asking that you think about the implications of that choice."

"You're asking her to stay in hell for eternity because of some theory!" Jim shouted at us, straining his frail voice.

"It may not have to be that way," I offered, seeing Addie off balance. "Elizabeth is capable of possession. Maybe you are too, Jim. What if the two of you—"

"What, steal bodies until the end of time?" Jim recoiled. "What sort of monsters to you think we are?" Both Addie and I tried to rephrase but he cut us off. "Even if our going to heaven did cause the end of the world, I would rather have the world end than live in one where an innocent, good soul like my wife is condemned for eternity. She should never have been sent there at all! I've never known a more beautiful, decent human being in my life!"

"Jim, please," Elizabeth said.

"No! I haven't lived a lifetime with you to come to the end now and be told we're in the wrong! It's God who is in the wrong! And if our love is what finally proves he's in the wrong then so be it! I won't let—"

He stopped at the sound of a buzzer from the door. All four of us turned to face it. My heart dropped while I watched Addie deflate.

"Let's see what the Horsemen have to say about your theory," Jim snapped, rising to buzz in Death or whichever of them were outside. I rose instinctively, blocking his way.

"We have to get them out of here," I told Addie. Jim laughed and raised his gnarled fists. He punched me across the jaw. Harder than I figured he'd have the strength for.

"I'd like to see you try you little—" I shoved him back into his chair.

"Jon, no!" Addie told me, rising as well. "Don't hurt them."

"We can't stay here, Addie," I implored. "We've got to get them out."

"And do what? Force Elizabeth to return to hell? We have to talk to her."

"Well you've got about two minutes before Death figures out something is wrong and comes barging in here. I'm guessing you'll need more than that to talk to Mrs. Kohler. So I suggest we take her to Valdez and continue our discussion at one of his places." I saw the pain in Addie's eyes as she considered our options, but eventually she turned to Elizabeth.

"I'm truly, sorry, Elizabeth, Jim," she began, "but we need to take you away from here. The Horsemen are not the allies you've been led to believe. They are working with the Watchers in the plot to overthrow God."

"What?" Elizabeth gasped. "Impossible! They've always been—"

"Maybe we can continue this on the way out," I said, reaching to pull Elizabeth out of her chair. Jim pounced on me instantly. I told him I didn't want to hurt him but I had to pop him in the stomach to settle him down. He kept thrashing so I yelled for Addie to get Elizabeth. She resisted at first, but Addie promised we didn't want to hurt them.

We grabbed a pair of coats for the Kohlers and herded them out of the apartment. I felt something heavy in one of the pockets and found a gun. When I asked Jim if there were any more in the apartment he wouldn't respond.

We tried to be as gentle as possible pushing them down the hall. Elizabeth pleaded for us to use an elevator if we insisted on taking them captive, but I told Addie we couldn't risk it. Death was probably already barging in the front.

I saw an emergency exit and went for it. I ended up carrying Jim down most of the stairs. We didn't have time for a slow descent. The door on the ground level was coated in warnings about setting sirens off if opened. I turned to make sure the Kohlers' coats were tightly secured.

"Alright, we're gonna have to move fast the second this door opens, Addie. If they fall, we pick them up. We'll make for the first car we see and commandeer it." Addie looked nearly as worried as Elizabeth.

"What if—"

"Then we roll with it. There are probably more on the way already, the panic button has already been hit by now. This is just going to make it official. Whatever happens, keep these two alive." The look on Addie's face signified her realization we were about to step into a warzone no matter how many Death just sent a warning to.

"Are you ready?" I asked. Jim cursed and kicked but I ignored him and pushed him out the door first. The alarm made Elizabeth cry out, piercing the quiet morning. "Move!" I shouted, jerking Jim after me.

There were no Feds, gangbangers or stray Horsemen on the street, but there weren't any moving cars either. I rushed down the sidewalk as fast as Jim could go, silently praying for a car. We made it to the end of the block before I saw something.

A man had come outside to investigate the alarm. There were keys in his hand and a truck in his driveway, so we bee lined for him. He was probably just headed to work. I felt guilty as I raised the gun but we didn't have time to negotiate.

He surrendered the keys without a fight but was already on his way inside to call 911 by the time we got the doors open.

"Jon!" Addie screamed from the passenger side as she helped Elizabeth into the back seat. I turned and saw Death bursting out of the apartment building. He was already running at us full bore. We had twenty seconds, maybe.

Heart racing, I flipped the gun in my hand and smacked Jim across the back of the head. I didn't have time to drive and subdue him at once. Heaving him into the back seat beside his hysterical wife, I jumped into the car and locked the doors.

"Hurry!" Addie yelled as she watched Death close the gap between us. The engine sputtered a few times. Old Ford piece of shit, probably hadn't been serviced in years. The moment the engine turned over I revved hard and put us into gear.

We swung out of the driveway in reverse, throwing snow from the sliding tires. In my panic I'd gunned it too fast and lost traction. It gave Death the seconds he needed. He leapt at the front door just as we got moving. His elbow sailed through the glass, scattering it over me as he reached in.

Addie saved me, driving her leg into his chest before his bare hand made it to my face. He staggered back but held firm on the door. Elizabeth kept me from reaching for the gun by grabbing my collar and reefing on it, shouting for me to stop. Addie restrained her but Death was back in the cab.

This time I hit him with a round through the shoulder. He grunted and dropped to the street, rolling through the snow behind us. Elizabeth cried. When I looked through the rear view mirror I was shocked to watch him raise the gun to his head and pull the trigger. He dropped in a mess of blood.

"Why did he do that?" I shouted to Addie. She turned to see what she'd missed. Her face lit up with panic but before she could say anything the car in the next intersection sped up and slammed into the back of the truck, spinning us around.

"It's Death!" she shouted.

"He can take another body that quickly?!" I asked more from reflex as I shifted gear and got us moving again. I got my answer when I looked back to see an additional three cars waiting at the stoplight of the perpendicular street blast through a red after us. If the Horsemen knew where I was I wondered why they didn't just take my body, but I remained in control.

Addie seized the gun from my lap, checked ammo and pumped a round into the chamber. I expected her to exude confidence when she looked at me, but she was searching for it in me.

"Unless we shake all four of them in the next few minutes, Guardian is our only shot," I told her, racing into downtown DC. Addie turned as if to fire out the window but thought better of it. We didn't have the ammo and it wouldn't deter our pursuers any.

"Wait, we lost one," she said as we passed under a skywalk bridge. I would have looked through the mirror to see which one we'd shaken had I not seen the man dropping from the bridge at the last minute. He landed squarely in the back of the bed with a lurch that shocked all of us.

Before I knew what was happening the back window shattered and a man reached in. I jerked the wheel to throw the attacker off balance. He recovered by pushing his way off of Jim. The old man groaned at the touch.

Addie screamed for Elizabeth to move away. She took care of the Horseman with a single shot to his head, throwing him into the bed against the tailgate. I made a quick glance back to see Addie and Elizabeth lifting Jim up. The flesh on his neck was already receding, rotting and putrid. I remembered the smell all too well.

Pestilence found his new body in the driver of a city garbage truck just ahead of us. It jerked from the opposite lane and plowed for our truck head on. I swerved to miss it just in time but another of the Horsemen caught up and rammed us hard enough to send us spinning over the snow.

The passenger side of the truck slammed into a street pole. Addie's head violently struck the window, cracking the glass. I shouted her name when she slumped over. She was stunned but looked to still be conscious. Elizabeth wailed in the back, trying to wrap her husband's rotting neck with his handkerchief.

I couldn't get the truck back into gear. The engine just sputtered. Any of the Horsemen could have driven their vehicles into us and finished it, but they screeched to halt and came after us on foot. Even now they wanted to protect the Kohlers.

I grabbed the gun from the floorboards and raised it through the broken window, still trying to get the truck into gear. I unloaded what was left of the clip, taking two of them down. They found new bodies from the adjacent fast food joint instantaneously.

I thought about making a run for it with Addie, hoping they'd let us go if we left the Kohlers. I didn't have to when all four of them were mowed down in a shower of bullets. Three black SUVs raced up the street, automatic weapons extended out the windows. They stopped beside us, letting a few men out while the others focused their fire on the Horsemen's new bodies exiting the restaurant.

"Aim for the legs," one man shouted as he exited the SUV. "Keep them from taking new bodies!" It was Valdez, running for us in full tactical gear. He opened the door and extended his hand. "What the *fuck* do you think you're doing?" he shouted. I pointed to the back seat.

"Meet the Kohlers," I said, taking his hand and stepping out. He saw the elderly couple, eyes going wide. Thinking quickly, he handed me his side arm and told me to load the Kohlers into the SUV. "Your chase went out over the police radio. We found you first because we were out looking for you, but your buddy Carnegie is going to be on us in less than a minute."

I delegated the Kohlers to two of Valdez's men and reached in for Addie myself. Blood dripped from the cut on her forehead. I tried picking her up but she told me she could walk. I put her arm around me and hustled her to the closest SUV.

We turned in surprise at the sound of the throng suddenly screaming from the restaurant. Everyone inside and everyone on the street was charging at us, maddened looks on their faces. "It's War,"

Addie managed. "He's driving them to violence."

Valdez relayed his order to wound only but the six or seven men wielding guns didn't have much time to make that distinction as dozens of attackers sailed at us headlong. Guardian held the Horsemen and War's incensed army back at the expense of many lives, but Carnegie arrived ahead of schedule. Three police cars skid to a halt around the restaurant, followed by two unmarked cars and an FBI armored truck.

I recognized Lamont when I saw him. He stared me down hatefully from one of the rear cars, raising a radio to his mouth. A helicopter soared overhead and commenced firing on all of us. Guardian pulled out the rocket launchers I'd seen in San Jose and forced them back but reinforcements continued to arrive.

By the time we'd loaded the Kohlers into one of the SUVs only Valdez and two of his men remained. Valdez smacked the hood of our vehicle and shouted, "Airport!" as loud as he could.

"What about you?" I shouted, holding the door open.

"We'll drive off in different directions! Just get them out of here. Guardian will find you wherever you end up. Look for—" A shot pierced his Kevlar vest and dropped him to a knee. I shouted for the driver to wait but he took off as the occupants of another building descended on the other two vehicles. One of them had to be Death, and I knew that would be the last time I saw Valdez.

Ours was the only SUV that got away, and Carnegie was on us the moment we started moving. A column of police cars trailed us, painting the snow banks in reds and blues as we passed. Our only support was in the sky. Addie and I jolted in our seats as the FBI helicopter crashed into the side of a building, brought down by another black chopper with a gatling gun mounted from the window.

All at once a shower of bullets peppered our SUV, shattering windows and popping tires. Our driver went down in the first barrage. Addie was still fuzzy but she saved us, grabbing hold of the wheel from the front and sliding past the corpse to assume control. "Carnegie is trying to kill the Kohlers!" she shouted while she turned down another street to escape the spray of bullets.

I turned back for Elizabeth when I noticed she'd stopped crying. "Shit," I said, rushing to her side. "She's been hit."

"Can you help her?" Addie asked.

"Just keep your eyes on the road!" I shouted as she swerved hard. "It went in and out but she's bleeding hard." I tried to push Jim back. He was weak from Pestilence's touch but continued trying to pull her away from me.

"Jon!" Addie screamed from the front. I turned and saw a blockade set up for us at the end of the street. The windshield shattered as gunfire hit us head on. Addie ducked but I felt what was possibly the last of our tires blow out. We weren't getting to the airport.

I left Elizabeth with the last of Valdez's men and rushed to the front. "There!" I shouted, grabbing the wheel. I turned us into a parking structure to the right. We couldn't escape but we wouldn't have lasted more than a few seconds on the open street. Carnegie didn't let up, following us into the building.

Addie took us up to the fifth floor in hopes the Guardian helicopter was still out there to support us. She turned too sharply on what remained of our tires in the final turn. We slid into a parked van, coming to a standstill.

Carnegie's car and two more pulled up behind us but we kept them back with what weapons we had left. I figured we could lay down enough suppressing fire for Addie to get the Kohlers to the roof. When I looked back for her she was gone.

As were the Kohlers.

Peering through the open side door across from us, I saw Jim carrying Elizabeth away toward the roof. Addie chased after them. Unfortunately there was no black helicopter to be seen, only two FBI birds circling the building. "God dammit!" I shouted, grabbing the heaviest gun I could find and bolting for the door.

I tried to grab our last man but he stayed firmly in place, emptying his magazine for my cover fire. I ran as hard as I could for the roof. The whiz of bullets passed close. I caught up to Addie just as she grabbed hold of Jim, tugging him back toward the cover of a parked car.

"They're going to kill you both!" she shouted as she pulled. When Jim fell to a knee, Elizabeth grunted and looked up, her last vestige of strength brought to bear. She looked me dead in the eyes, a righteous fury emanating forth.

There was a momentary hush over the chaos in the air, then the world shattered. Addie and I were thrown off our feet as a storm of energy erupted around Elizabeth. "Leave us *alone!*" she bellowed louder than was possible.

I remember tumbling over concrete like I'd been caught in the shock wave of a bomb. My ears rang and my skin burned when I regained my sight. I pushed my way up from the snowy roof we'd been cast onto. Addie lay beside me, pushed against the wall of the roof. We'd likely have been blown off had it not caught us.

Addie was staring past me, eyes wide. I turned and saw it. The singularity. A bubble of demonic power covering half of the roof. It had no color but it looked hot, like a contained sphere of boiling air. It distorted everything inside, but I could see two bodies at the center.

"It's Elizabeth," Addie said. "She's... protecting Jim." We rose slowly, staring at the orb of energy in wonder. Something about it was terrifying, but it was the most incredible thing I'd ever seen.

The gunfire had stopped. At first I wondered if Elizabeth had done something, then I realized there was no one left for Carnegie to shoot at. The Watcher himself walked around the orb after a few moments, trailed by four men. He took a brief look at the orb, pressing his hand up against it. He flinched in pain, examining the burn on his skin.

His men circled the sphere, weapons raised. No one knew what to do, and Carnegie remained silent. Eventually he looked our way, his scowl returned. He marched through the snow for us, the Horsemen behind him.

He stopped a few feet in front of us. He didn't say anything for a moment. His expression was more intrigued than angry despite trying to project the latter.

"Who are you?" he asked. Neither of us said anything for

a moment.

"Does it matter?" Addie said eventually. "Everything is up to Elizabeth now." Carnegie breathed hard.

"What did you say to her?" he asked.

"Probably not enough," she returned. Carnegie shook his head, unable to find words for a moment. He glanced at the orb, then back to us.

"Do you have any idea why I'm doing this?" he asked, pitiable desperation in his words. "Why this has to happen?" Addie looked ready to say something but chose not to. She was right. It didn't matter now.

"Because God's a prick," I offered, leaning back against the wall. "The trouble is, so are you." Carnegie stared at me.

"Better the devil you know. Is that it?" I shrugged.

"It's all fucked up either way. I gave up on it a long time ago."

"That's what makes you the bad guy and me the good guy, Perry," he told me.

"Thinking that way is what would make you as shitty a God as the one we have now." Carnegie didn't react for a moment. He took a deep breath a wiped his nose with a gloved hand.

"Maybe you're right." He looked at Addie, then me.

Then he shot me.

I slid back against the wall, grasping at the hole in my gut. Addie cried out and dropped beside me, pulling off her coat to put pressure on the wound. Carnegie dropped his gun and turned back for the Kohlers.

"Make sure they don't cause any more problems. It'll be over soon." As he walked away the Horsemen closed in on us.

"Lift me up," I told Addie with what strength I had.

"Jon, I want to tell you something," she said.

"Lift me up first," I said again, louder. She swallowed hard and did was I asked. All four of them were reaching out for us. I barely had the strength to stand, but somehow I had enough to grab Addie and jump. "You can do it, Addie."

She screamed as we tumbled over the side of the wall, plummeting through the air. We painfully bounced off the building in the fall, but I held onto her. The five stories seemed like 50 as we dropped.

I dreaded the crush of impact every second, but when it came, I didn't feel pain. On the contrary, I felt something I hadn't experienced in a long time. It was warm. Circulating through every inch of my body. Even as I lay dying, I don't know that I'd ever felt so safe.

It passed after a moment, the winter's cold again besetting me. I lay on the road in the snow. Some of it was red with my blood, but other than the gunshot, I was fine. Addie lay on top of me, tightly clutching me. She was staring at me, eyes wide and tears streaming from them.

"Thanks," I managed. "We... should probably go." Overcoming her shock and whatever other emotion was swelling inside her, she looked around at the people surrounding us. Some were cops, some civilians. Addie grabbed hold of a stunned officer's gun straight from his hand and pointed it in an arc while she backed up with me around her shoulder.

The crazy thing is none of them stopped us as she dragged me to the nearest car. They were all too busy staring at the sphere of energy atop the parking structure. It had widened considerably, encompassing most of the roof. I stared at it the same as everyone else while Addie tucked me into the passenger seat and drove us off.

seventeen

Addie brought the car to a stop when she realized I wasn't going to make it all the way to a hospital. No cops or Feds pursued us. Not even the Horsemen. I guessed there was no way either of us could really prove a threat to Carnegie again.

She pulled over in the back of an empty parking lot. "Keep putting pressure on it, Jon," she instructed. She ran outside the car to the passenger door and opened it, kneeling in front of me. She was crying. "Let me see."

She pulled my increasingly limp arms away and lifted my shirt. She fought her tears as best she could and pressed her hands over the wound. She closed her eyes. I watched her desperately concentrating. I knew what she was trying to do.

"I don't think it works like that, Addie."

"Shut up. Don't talk, save your strength." She kept pressing her hands around the wound. I let her try, but after a few long moments her touch softened and she sank to her knees on the edge of the car.

She opened her eyes and fought for words through her emotions. "Why won't it work?" she asked. I managed a silent chuckle.

"I guess bleeding out isn't as imminent a threat as falling off a roof." She stared at me through her tears then leaned in to wrap herself over my chest. Her thumb grazed the hair above my ear.

"I'm so sorry," she cried.

"For what? For bringing me into all this? I could have left you anytime, Addie. I didn't. You don't have to apologize." She lifted her head to show me her eyes. I saw what she was really apologizing for.

"When did you know?" she asked.

"You told Elizabeth in front of me," I reminded her.

"But you knew before that." I shrugged.

"You're an honest person, Addie. It's never been tough to read you." She stared at me, searching for something.

"I never would have said anything, Jon. I know you still love your wife."

"You don't have to apologize for that either. Dumb as you are to love a guy like me, you—"

"Don't talk like that," she practically snapped. "Like you are a bad person. So you've made mistakes. You've suffered for them. But still after all you've been through you are the best man I've ever known."

"Were all your drover friends cowgirls?" She shook her head, allowing a tiny smile. It didn't stop her tears. I looked out the window past her. I could see the tip of the sphere on the rooftop. It was still growing, pulling the clouds toward it. "What's going to happen?"

Addie swallowed her emotion as best she could, turning to look out the windshield as well. "Elizabeth will have to make her choice," she said. "She won't last much longer with her wound, and Pestilence's touch will kill Jim soon after. Carnegie will wait them out."

She looked passive for the first time. "Maybe it will be alright. Maybe this is what needs to happen." I sighed.

"I was talking about me," I said. "What's it like? Dying?" She turned back, tears renewed.

"I don't know," she said. "It happened so fast to me. I was just... gone." She stared at me hard then pulled in again. She cried while the world got darker. For me at least. Then, right before I felt sensation slip away, I felt the warmth from before. It spread from the wound throughout all of me. It felt like all the pain I'd ever known was erased.

I stopped her.

I gave her a gentle push. Back to reality. I wasn't even sure if she knew what she was doing, but I shook my head. "Leave me be, Addie. I've been waiting for this for a long time. I... I don't know how to live without pain. I need it."

She wasn't sure what to say. As much as she wanted me to be alright, she knew I wasn't hers to save. She let go of me, as pained as she'd been before she knew she had the power to heal me. The wound hadn't quite closed, but the bleeding had stopped. She'd probably saved me already, at least for the time being.

After a moment Addie leaned back, forcing the emotion from her head and wiping away her tears. She turned and looked at Elizabeth's power again. "I'm going back," she said.

"What? Why?"

"Maybe I can try talking to her one last time."

"No. What are you talking about?" I asked. "She probably can't even hear you through all that. If she's even still conscious. And do you think Carnegie will just let you waltz back in to have a conversation with her?" She took a long breath and smiled.

"It's worth a try," she said. "This is it, Jon. It's the reason I came." I tried to get up but I was still too banged up.

"Addie, no," I called. She pushed me all the way inside and closed the door.

"You can't go with me, Jon," she said. "You've taken me as far as you can. If by some miracle I get through to her, I want you to live." I felt the cuffs around my wrist. She'd locked me to the door.

"Addie!" She smiled.

"Thank you, Jon. Maybe we'll see each other again someday." I kept calling her name but she turned and made her way back down the street along with the rush of people headed to investigate the sphere. I lost her in the crowd.

I would probably live now that the blood had stopped flowing, but I remained exhausted. It was the second time I'd been shot in basically the same place within a week. It's not pleasant, even with an angel's magical touch to help.

I just sat there for a while. If I called out to anyone for help they'd recognize me as the FBI's most wanted and call the cops. That wouldn't get me any closer to Addie. I considered letting her go, accepting that it was probably all about to end anyway.

I looked around for a way to free myself. I could have blasted my way free of the chain with the gun Addie left, but then I realized there was probably a key somewhere. It was a squad car after all. I was rifling through the dash box when I saw him.

The little boy.

He stood on the edge of the parking lot by the rushing crowd, staring into the car at me. Still in his orange t-shirt. It was like no one even noticed him standing there. I couldn't take it anymore. "Who the hell are you?" I shouted, though he could never have heard me from inside the cab.

I wasn't going to give him the chance to run away this time. Abandoning my search for the key, I reached for the gun, kicked open the door, and fired a round through the chain. When I painfully rose from the car he was gone. I spotted him running for the alley between the buildings. He looked back at me then hurried on.

I gave chase as fast as I could, at no more than a hobbled jog. I felt the blood begin flowing from my gut again but pressed on. I wasn't stopping for anything. I went into the alley, looking for anyplace he could have been hiding. "Where are you?" I shouted. I made it down the length of the alley, checking through windows and trying the one locked door, but my energy was gone. I leaned against the brick wall and tried to catch my breath.

I felt something, then. Another sensation filtered through my body, encompassing every cell. The noise of the world seemed to drain away as the air grew still. The little breeze whipping through the alley died. The shadows grew longer. I knew I wasn't alone. Straightening myself, I turned around.

He was standing in the middle of the alley behind me.

"Who are you?" I asked. He didn't reply. "Why have you been following me?"

"I've been helping you," he said at last. "Who do you think kept the Horsemen from taking your body?" His voice was small, reserved. It should have sounded innocent. It was anything but.

"Why?" I asked.

"Because I don't want the Watchers to win either," he said.

"What do you want?" He just stood there in silence for another moment. The light seemed to flee from him. I had never thought the stare of a little boy could be so menacing. It grew more so when he approached. He came within a few feet of me.

"I want what you want," he said.

"How do you know what I want?"

"It's what everyone wants. It's what everyone deserves. To live without fear. Without pain. To live the way you want to live. Always."

"Who are you?"

"The Watchers are right about God, though. You and Addie are right about him too. The world isn't fair. Not the way he made it. You should fix it."

"How?"

"I could help you. The Watchers won't fix it. They'll just destroy it. But Addie is right about you. You are a good person. You could fix it."

"I don't get it. How?"

"I'll show you how. I can give you the power to save Elizabeth and Jim. And Addie. She's going to die if you don't help her."

I almost asked him who he was again, but I didn't have to. I knew full well who he was. But I was still curious what he was.

"Are you a construct?" I asked. He nodded. "Do you know where Gabby and Pita are?" Somehow I knew he'd know the names.

"Yes."

"Can you take me to them? Can you make it so they're alright?"

"Not without you. You have to save them, not me." I stared at him, as fearful as I'd ever been. "There isn't much time. If you don't act now, it will all be over. I can't help you if the Watchers win."

"Why me?" I asked. "You've been following me since before all this even started."

"Why not you?" he asked. "You know everything that is wrong with the world. You know what to do to make it better."

I knew to an absolute certainty that the boy was evil. That what he was offering was dead wrong. But somehow I knew he wasn't lying. He did have the power to help me, to let me find Gabby and Pita, to change the world.

As wrong as I knew this was, I wasn't sure what right or wrong meant anymore. All I knew was the world was broken, about to be broken further, and this was probably the one way to do anything about it.

"What do you want me to do?" I asked.

"Believe," he returned. "Just believe in what you think is right. I trust you. I'll do the rest." It was hard to argue with that.

I nodded.

He reached out and touched me. I'm not sure what I was expecting. The rush of dark power or a numbing cold, maybe. Instead I was greeted with the same blissful warmth from Addie's love. My wound was gone. I felt as fit, healthy and energized as I ever had. I remembered what Elizabeth told us in her apartment.

There was nothing I couldn't do.

I blinked and we were on the roof. There was no magical energy from a teleportation, we were just there. The boy was at my side. No one noticed us at first. Not until I started walking toward the Kohlers. Carnegie and his Loyal had been pushed back into the garage from the size of Elizabeth's sphere.

The Horsemen were the first to recognize us. All four of them tensed as if to charge but froze when they caught sight of the boy. They remained where they stood. Carnegie saw us as we walked into Elizabeth's power, unscathed. I couldn't even feel it. Carnegie shouted at the Horsemen to attack us but still they stood by. Carnegie was terrified, I saw it on his face.

Addie appeared from a staircase. She saw me as well, raising both hands to her mouth in shock. She slowly slumped to her knees, unable to form words. The Horsemen saw her and moved in but the boy raised his hand and made a fist. Their host bodies vaporized like dust, and this time I knew they wouldn't be coming back in new ones.

The boy and I continued on despite Carnegie's threats and Addie's pleas. We came to the Kohlers quickly. I hadn't been able to see them clearly when the sphere first appeared, but I could now. Jim was on his knees, nestling his wife's head in his lap. She lay in a pool of her own blood, as pale as the snow around her.

She was as terrified as any of the demons who looked upon me. I saw she only had moments left and turned to the boy. "I can't keep them alive forever," I said.

"You can if you want," the boy corrected.

"But I shouldn't. It shouldn't have to be that way."

"You can make it any way you think it should be."

"But only in this world," I said. "I can't feel heaven or hell."

"You don't need heaven or hell. You can make new places in this world. You can make new bodies for all the people who have died. You can all live here, happy. Forever."

"What about God?"

"What about him? If you cease to believe in him, he won't have any power over you. He should be thanking you. He made you to have desires. Why should you live rejecting them? Should you reject what you are in the hope he'll deem you worthy enough to get into some listless, abstract paradise? Who is he to judge you for doing what he made you with the capacity to do?"

"I can't do it either," I told him. "I can't decide what is right and wrong. That would be no better than what we have now."

"Then decide it is right to let everyone else decide what is right for themselves. Be your own gods. Deny the pompous judgment of one."

I stared at him for a moment. His tone was as serious as his words were true. I could feel it the same as Addie or Valdez mined through truth and fiction. If I wanted to I could recreate the world. Add new planets with new bodies for everyone in heaven and hell. Keep them alive forever. Cut out the creator from the world he created.

But...

"Where are Gabby and Pita?" I asked him. The boy took a step back, caught off-guard.

"Take God's power from him, and you can reclaim them," he told me.

"From where? I know that you know. Why won't you tell me?"

"It doesn't matter," he said, his voice becoming louder, deeper. "They were taken from you. You can bring them back. That is what matters." He put his little hand in mine and appealed to me with urgent eyes. "You have to hurry, Perry. There isn't much time. All you have to do is believe in what is right."

Believe in what is right.

I stared at Elizabeth and Jim. I saw through them, past the wrinkled and bloodied flesh to their souls. Even then I saw how in love they were. Its power may have burned anyone else but it was completely pure. The superficial pain remained, but in a few moments it would be replaced by the joy in knowing they were together. That they would always be together.

My gaze swept back to Addie. She stood at the edge of the sphere, pressed against it to the point of burning herself. She was crying. Confused. Courageous as ever. I don't know if I'd ever known anyone who genuinely cared as much as her, anyone with a will so strong.

Possibly Carnegie, I thought. I saw his fury, his desperation as he stood smoldering from the blockade, waiting to see if all his efforts would be wasted. His desperation had driven him to the extreme, but I saw him for what he was. A man doing all a man can ever do—trying to make the world better.

In the end they were all the same. They'd all made mistakes, sure, but all of them had lived the best they could. Made an impact in the life of another. Carnegie and Elizabeth were no more demons than Addie and Valdez were angels. They were all still just... human.

That's when I stopped thinking like a man caught in a divine conspiracy and started thinking like an investigator. I came back to the one lesson I'd learned through my career.

It always comes down to one thing.

One missing piece.

One errant detail.

One stray thread that weaves everything else together.

I finally knew what it was.

And I solved my case.

When I turned back to the boy I saw a look of panic rising in his eyes. "You have to save them, Perry," he implored. "Do it now!" I didn't respond. Didn't move. I just kept staring at him, aware of what I was looking at. I wasn't terrified anymore. I knew I didn't have to be.

The boy ripped his hand from mine. The cement at his feet buckled and scattered like buckshot from a gun as he recoiled. "*Do it!*" he screamed, his voice a deafening eruption. He threw his gaze to the Kohlers, quaking with panic and rage.

His anger morphed to grief and anguish after a moment. He knew what I knew and dropped his arms in defeat. "How many fathers have to lose their wives and daughters, Perry?" he asked in a sob. "How much pain will you endure before someone says enough?"

I didn't have an answer for him.

But I think that was the point.

He read it in me and knew he'd lost. His face twisted with anger but I turned away to watch the Kohlers in their last moments. Elizabeth's eyes were placid as they fell to me, just for a moment, before they closed. I felt her slip away the same as everyone felt it. I felt Addie's horror and Carnegie's elation, but none of it lasted long.

The boy shuddered with such rage, released such a howl of contempt, that his little body couldn't contain it. His frame expanded into a mutated mountain of gore and black sludge before it detonated and consumed the roof. As sickening as it felt sliding over my skin, through my soul, it didn't hurt me directly. The warmth left me. The force of the explosion smashed the building to dust.

I fell, my body cast into a pile of metal and stone. I broke and ripped, bled and convulsed.

Then I died.

eighteen

I hated airports.

Other than my brief stint in the Guardian private jet, I hadn't gone near a plane since losing the girls. After the trial and my inglorious exodus from the peak of journalism, I had driven to LA from the East Coast. It wasn't an easy trip. I remember crying every time I passed an airport sign on the freeway.

But there I was, inside an airport.

And not just any airport.

I stood smack in the middle of the Chicago O'Hare terminal. I actually felt my mouth slip open as I took in the rows of chairs at the boarding gates. The greasy aroma of fast food from down the corridor. The ramp way that led to the lobby, where I'd been thrown off my feet from the force of the explosion.

I could never forget that place, but even so, it took me a moment to realize where I was. I was... confused, to say the least. I had died. I knew that. And yet, there I stood, in my own body, at Chicago O'Hare. It felt like my body, anyway. I checked myself over, rubbing my stomach for any sign of wounds. I examined my clothes for any blood stains, my skin for any protruding bones.

I was fine.

I figured it for some sort of dream, a final flash of memory before death, but a woman accidentally bumped into me walking for the bathroom. She begged my pardon and continued on. It felt so real that I nearly told her it was no trouble.

There were plenty of other travelers moving through the corridors to various gates. Some waited in the long rows of chairs, others sat at the food court enjoying a quick bite or beverage, others still boarded their planes and disappeared from sight. None of them seemed in a particular rush.

I just stood there for a time, trying to figure out what had happened. I moved out of the way eventually, walking from the middle of a hallway to one of the window banks. It was night. That was all I noticed until I came close to the window, looking for lights outside on the airstrip.

Then I noticed the lack of the airstrip.

I pressed my hands on the glass, staring out with childlike wonder at a sea of stars and nothing else. There was no tarmac, no planes, no tower, no ground. Only infinity. Endless, glittering stars against black. I turned to see if anyone else noticed. An elderly woman sat in a chair beside me.

"Where are we?" I asked her. She turned to me contently as if I were a child.

"The airport," was her response. She rose after a moment, hearing a call over a loudspeaker that her flight was boarding. I thought about following her but ended up staring back out the window. I stood alone for another few minutes before I felt someone else at my side.

He was a younger man. Chinese, I think. Fairly average build. Nothing particularly notable about him, other than the fact he was the only other person staring out at the stars.

"Is this real?" I asked him. He kept his gaze out the window but gently smiled with deep satisfaction too mature for his face.

"Oh yes," he affirmed. "This is one of my favorite spots. Right on the edge of the Iblis Nebula. That's what they'll call it when they discover it, anyway. For all the vast beauty in the universe, there is no other view quite like this one. Where the blues in the gas clouds nearly overtake the black. It's almost more a sky than space."

I immediately knew this wasn't just another traveler casually on his way to a plane. There wasn't any aura or mystical vibe off him, it was just the tone of his voice. Commanding and gentle all at once.

"Who are you?" I asked. He chuckled and looked at me.

"Promise me you won't deck me if I tell you."

"Why would I do that?"

"When you run an airline," he began, "there are always going to be passengers who don't much enjoy the ride. Unfortunately some of them blame the pilot for the turbulence. And you've had a pretty bumpy ride, haven't you, Jon?"

When I took a defensive step back, he only laughed again.

"Don't worry, Jon. You may not be my biggest fan, but I'm still a fan of yours. Come on. I'll buy you a cup of coffee. Settle your nerves some." He turned and made his way from the gate to a coffee machine standing near one of the flight reader boards.

He told me to hurry up, then handed me a paper cup filled with black coffee when I arrived behind him. The way I liked it.

"You're... God," I said, capturing the impossibility of it with my tone. He raised an eyebrow, stirring sweetener into his drink.

"Would that really surprise you after the things you've seen over the past week or so?" he asked. I stared at him for a moment, taking in the young Chinese face.

"You're telling me I'm at the pearly gates?" I asked after a moment. "*These* are the pearly gates?"

"Wouldn't that be something?" he returned, taking a sip of his coffee. "Bit of a culture shock for everybody expecting clouds and St. Peter with a tally book. No, this is someplace between your imagination and mine. A pathway to worlds. You're seeing it now as you understand it."

"The people are real then," I said, turning to look over the crowd filtering by to their gate. "Souls."

"Yes. They're on their way." I looked back at him.

"To heaven and hell?" He smiled.

"You know better than that, don't you, Jon?"

"Is that why I'm here?" I asked. "Because I figured out some riddle?"

"I know you're feeling a bit testy, Jon, but let's see if we can't have a civil discussion. That's why you're here. I thought you'd like to talk."

"Where were you before?" I asked, part of me remembering my ire over the past few years, part of me terrified at what I was saying to... God. "Where were you that day five years ago? I had some things I would have said to you then."

"Oh you've certainly had some choice words for me over the years, I know," he said, "but for all the things you've wanted to say *to* me, you haven't wanted to talk *with* me in a long time."

"So now that I saved the world I've earned a rare chat with God, is that it?"

"Not in the least. Everyone gets to talk with me eventually, Jon. You haven't hit 'eventually' yet, but like I said, you ended up a little ahead of the curve thanks to recent events. So here you are."

I stared at him for another long moment, letting the silence hang other than the periodic overhead speaker announcement and the constant shuffle of footsteps. "So what do you want to talk about?" I asked at last.

"You," he said. "I want to talk about what you want to talk about. You've been looking for answers for a long time, Jon. You found most of them on your own, but there are a few more I can give you now that you're here."

He smiled and waited, giving me the floor. For all my questions I realized I didn't have the faintest idea where to start. He must have known it from his smile.

"Why don't we take a seat," he said, extending a hand toward a nearby row of chairs near an empty gate. I walked to the closest one and sat. He took the one beside me. I stared at him in continued bewilderment, still sinking under the realization that I was looking God in the eyes.

"Okay, first... Why a Chinese kid?" I asked. God raised an eyebrow.

"Why is that surprising?" he asked. "At this moment in time, the most common face you'd encounter on the planet is a Han Chinese male, age 25." He chuckled and took another sip of coffee. "Would you be more comfortable if I were elderly with a long white beard?"

"I'd be more comfortable if we weren't in the one place I hate more than any other," I told him. "Why here? Are you trying to provoke me to something?"

"I'm trying to help you, Jon. You've spent five years barred in a prison of the past. How long will you stay there? You can remember the pain from this place, or you can remember the happiness."

I stared at him, about to tell him what I'd told Addie about happiness, but I stopped short. I remembered the last time I was truly happy. "It was here," I said out loud. "Just before." I stared into space, tears forming in my eyes.

"Where are they?" I asked. "Tell me where." God set down his cup on the adjacent chair and folded his arms.

"It will help if we start with where they aren't," he said. "When did you figure it out?"

"Don't you already know that?"

"Yes. But let's talk about it. You have questions about it, don't you?"

"Okay. I think I knew it since seeing heaven and hell. I just didn't put two and two together until the end. It wasn't right. There were too many good people in hell and too much wrong with heaven."

"Go on."

"There isn't any real difference between Addie and Carnegie. They are what their lives have made them, sure, but in the end they're still just people who believe in something. There was no inherent good or evil to them. There are no real angels and demons. There is no heaven and hell."

"And?"

"And... Gabby and Pita were the key. They had to be somewhere. They weren't in heaven or hell. Addie and Valdez both said there was no purgatory, there was no alternate heaven or hell. It all just... made sense."

"And that's why you let Elizabeth and James pass away," God said.

"I figured if there was no heaven or hell, if there were no angels or demons, they couldn't possibly overrule any judgment you laid down."

"Seeing as I'm still here, I suppose you were right," God stated.

"Then what are those places?" I asked. "Why are all those people trapped there? All of them think they're in heaven or hell."

"No one is trapped, Jon. They just aren't ready, yet."

"For what?"

"To find their way back to me."

"What does that mean?" God paused and glanced past me to one of the boarding gates. He pointed over to it.

"You see those people? They're on their way to what you thought was heaven. They lived good lives. Genuinely cared about leaving a worthwhile legacy, about helping others. But they aren't ready to let go yet."

"To let go of what?"

"Oh, any number of things. Love. Family. Regrets. Unfulfilled dreams. Some of them died like your friend Addie. Resentful. Unwilling to give up control." He shifted position in his seat, crossing his legs and placing his hands in his lap.

"But most are just afraid. There is no fear like the fear of the unknown. It's difficult to let go of life if it's all you've ever known. If the ambitions of your time on earth are all you ever lived for."

"So there is a purgatory," I said.

"I call it the Waiting. Where those who aren't ready to let go can reconcile things."

"I'd say the Waiting was a slightly different experience for Carnegie than it was for Addie."

"The Waiting is different for everyone who ends up there. Most of the time it is what a soul expects it to be. Most people know what they deserve after the life they lived. Those who don't are sometimes in for quite the shock, like Carnegie. His Waiting wasn't as terrible as you might imagine, but it is what he needs to achieve his theophany."

"Theophany?"

"That's what everyone in the Waiting is waiting for, Jon. A revelation."

"So the Waiting is a giant time out for people to... what, realize the error of their ways? How? All the people I've met who've been waiting haven't changed. They still believe what they believed in life. They still live to do what they think is important."

"That's why they're still waiting." I must have worn a frustrated expression but God just smiled. "A theophany can happen quickly or slowly, Jon. There are some who have been waiting for millennia; some wait for moments. But it strikes everyone eventually."

"I don't get it. What strikes them?"

"The knowledge that I love them," he answered simply. "People discover it in different ways. Some of them come to the realization as they have time to look back over their life, to pull out of the detail and observe the larger picture I have painted.

"Some, like the ones you have met, need a more direct approach. That's why they can see back to the world they left, even reenter it. One way or another, they all come to see the truth. The only thing holding them back is themselves. Once they're ready to let go of the lives they lived, to make peace with their actions, and accept my love, they are welcomed into my arms."

"So there is a heaven," I said mostly to myself. "Addie and Carnegie couldn't see it, but..." I stopped and turned to God. A tear fell down my cheek. "Then Gabby and Pita..." He smiled.

"With me," he said. "As they always have been." I swallowed hard, trying not to cry.

"They didn't... they didn't need to wait?"

"Children very rarely have need of the Waiting, and it's a very different experience for them. Gabrielle waited for a moment, but you should know she was ready, Jon." I nodded, unable to hold back my tears.

I put my head in my hands and wept for a few minutes, release like I'd never known sweeping over me. God put a hand on my shoulder when I began to calm. "I know you've suffered, Jon. You've passed through what hell there is. You haven't quite reached your theophany yet, but you're well on your way."

I leaned up, wiping the water off my face as best I could. "Can I... see them? Can you show me?"

"My kingdom cannot be so easily shown as the Waiting, I'm afraid," he said. "They're with me now, Jon. You'll see them again someday." I nodded.

"So you took them just because of me?" I asked. "You denied Pita a life of her own for me? What about her? How is that fair?"

"The answer to that question isn't one I can simply tell you, Jon. Not until you're ready. What I can tell you is that fairness doesn't enter into that part of life. You of all people know that. Life is a permanent thing. The part of it you spend on earth is incredibly important, but its length is irrelevant next to eternity. One day you'll understand that. Until then, it's a matter of faith."

I wasn't sure what to say. As unjust as life had played out for so many, suddenly I had view into justice I'd long believed didn't exist.

"There isn't a hell, then," I said, realizing the implications of what I'd heard about the Waiting. God shook his head.

"Not an eternal one, anyway. Life and the Waiting can be rough on those who have made mistakes, but eventually everyone finds their way back to me. If they didn't, the afterlife would truly be broken, wouldn't it?"

"Something must be broken somewhere for the constructs to have gone wild like that," I said. "How did the Watchers convince the Horsemen to join them if they're just programmable dolls? They made a choice to betray you."

"They did," God confirmed. "So obviously they are not as robotic as Addie and the Watchers believed."

"So what will you do with them?"

"I will leave them be, of course. They still have a function to perform. They will perform it one way or another before the end."

"What about Satan?" I asked. "What function does he have to perform?"

"You know the answer to that better than most, Jon. He's there to test. Prod. Tempt. More cross paths with him than you'd think. He believes he's in the right the same as any man with a belief. But one day even he will return to me."

"Is that the way it should be? Some men believe evil things. Some men deserve hell."

"Do they?" God returned. "What is evil, Jon? A thing you're born with? A carefully defined path one can take through life? A predisposition to hurt?"

"Why don't you tell me?" I grilled, growing frustrated. Still God kept his smile.

"I love philosophers and theologists. They barely scratch the surface and yet completely overthink things. All of them are wrong and all of them are right, but I really liked the essence of Kierkegaard's thinking—life is about a leap of faith. Devoting yourself completely to an ideal, good or evil. That's what gives your existence on earth meaning."

"You're saying it's okay to be evil in life?"

"I'm saying that in your eyes, good and evil are imperfect perspectives at best. There is good and evil in everything. You can only do what you believe is right."

"That's all it's about then?" I asked. "Living right? What about the church? What about Christianity? Why found a religion if any religion, if any belief, works?"

"Everyone is eventually faced with the reality that I am here, Jon.

That I created the world, that I sent my Son to die for them, that I will forgive them for all their wrongs and love them the same. Whether they face that truth in life or the afterlife is of little consequence to me, and you'd be surprised how many Christians end up in the Waiting.

"Religion really doesn't matter much to me. There is no right or wrong way to worship me, for those who do. All the rules the denominations of my church have made are rules *they* made, not me. I'm more interested in where your heart is, and what you do as a result. Good is in right-action. What you do every day, what you believe, is what makes you a good man or not. Everything else gets rectified in the Waiting. Some people live their entire lives without ever hearing about me. Obviously I'm not going to hold that against them, so that becomes the path to their theophany."

"What's the point then?" I asked. "If everyone ultimately ends up back to you, realizing the same thing, is there even such a thing as choice? I'm not vouching for hell, but what's the point of choice if it can only result in one outcome? Don't you need hell for existence to mean anything?"

"Ah yes, the meaning of life. That's what makes sentient life unique throughout all the universe. The search for purpose. You're thinking about the ends without looking at the means, Jon. The reason I started this whole thing was to take a journey, not to arrive at a destination.

"It doesn't matter that there is only one place to arrive at because you have to find that place. That's the purpose of your existence as a whole. You're forced to live under uncertainty, not knowing where you might end up, if anywhere. You still have to make choices that lead you to back to me."

"I still don't see how the first part of life matters, then," I pressed. "If Adolf Hitler is destined to end up in the same place as Mother Teresa, what does it matter how they live?"

"You're still thinking about meaning only as it pertains to your time on earth. Your task there is simply to believe something and act on it. That gives you the context to reach a theophany. Some people reach it in life, others in the Waiting. But that journey to understand the life you lived is what matters."

I looked away, shaking my head. "I don't know that I can accept that. How can all the needless, wanton pain be the only way to justify this?"

"We could sit here talking philosophy and ontological arguments around the problem of evil for days or years, but the bottom line is that I love you," God said. "I know it looks backwards from your end—getting cancer or losing a loved one to murder is hardly an expression of love. But it's the reality you forge for yourself given those circumstances, the choices you come to, that give meaning.

"Only in a world where you can lose everything do the wins mean anything. Suffering—learning from it—is what paves the way to your personal theophany. There's a path through all the pain and hurt for each and every one of you that eventually leads back to me. I lay it at your feet, but you have to walk it."

"I guess I'm just struggling with the notion that thousands of kids are born and die with AIDS in the name of your mysterious master plan," I said. "What possible reason could there be for that?" God took a deep breath and nodded, glancing at a row of kids walking by for their gate.

"I'm characterized as a bit, shall we say, heavy-handed, in the Old Testament," he started. "Still, it's sort of like what I told Job. I created the universe, bud. Where were you when that was going on? I know that doesn't taste good going down, but I'm the only one who needs to see the complete picture.

"The grand scheme of things, if you will, is, well, too grand to explain to you with words or anything else your mind can deal with as it is now. Until you find your way back to me, you'll only be able to see the smallest fraction of the whole."

"Take it on faith," I paraphrased for him. "You realize that's one of the big reasons people cease having faith in you, right?"

"I do. But that is faith, Jon. Believing what you know to be impossible. Believing that there can be good in evil. That I shine light from even the darkest places. Because if you're looking for it, you'll find it. Even you."

"If faith is something people have to come to on their own, why are you handing it to me now?" I asked. "Why do I get a special chat with you?"

"I'm not handing you anything, Jon. Knowing I exist or the truth about the afterlife isn't faith—that's just knowledge. You knew that letting the Kohlers find their way to me wasn't going to trigger doomsday, but that wasn't why you let it happen. Faith is trust in something beyond logic and reason. You let the Kohlers go because you had faith that everything was somehow going to be alright. You didn't know why, you just did. You know the truth now, but that doesn't mean you have faith in it or in me."

"Is that why you picked me for all this? To help me find my faith?"

"You never lost faith, Jon. You may have given up on me, on yourself, but never your fellow man. Addie was right about you. Past the abrasive shell you've encased yourself in, you never lost the heart of a good man. You just needed a little push to use that heart again."

"It wasn't just coincidence that Addie and me met, was it?" I asked.

"You were exactly what each other needed," God confirmed.

"Where is she? Will she be alright?"

"You know the answer to that." I stared at him.

"You mean to tell me she's still waiting after all this?"

"For now," God confirmed. "She isn't quite ready yet."

"Let me see her. I can help her."

"Addie must find her own way, Jon." I thought for a moment.

"She loves me," I said.

"I know."

"So what happened to love trumping the rules?"

God leaned further back in his chair with a knowing smile. He took a deep breath then pointed down one of the corridors. I followed his finger to a reader board displaying flight times and locations. One person stood there, looking up at the humming screen.

I didn't recognize her. Short brown hair, small but stocky frame. She wore old-fashioned jeans with a tan button down shirt, possibly military issue. She was the only one I'd seen so far who looked lost.

I knew it was her.

I stood up, but before I could get too far God called out. "It wasn't *her* love that brought her here, you know," he said. I looked back but hurried on, jogging down the hall to her.

She heard me coming and turned. She froze, and I came to a halt about ten feet away.

A hand came up to her mouth and tears to her eyes. "Jon?" she said. I let out a chuckle in spite of myself, taking her in.

"You have freckles," I said. She swallowed hard then rushed at me, hugging me while she cried. I held her for a few minutes, but eventually she pulled herself together, allowing a smile when she saw mine.

"I bet you're missing Cora right about now," she said, wiping her tears. I helped her and shook my head.

"No. I'm glad I got to see the real you." She laughed silently, working to control her breathing. She shook her head, her expression incredulous.

"I suppose we were wrong about God, weren't we?" I looked at her uncertainly but she smiled. "I just came from the beach where I lost the children. I... talked to Him. He told me the truth." She looked down, her smile softening. "He had to, He said. I would never find my way back to Him if I was looking for you, wondering where you went."

I nodded, not sure what to say. "Do you... know where you're going?" I asked. She shrugged, glancing back at the board detailing the flight schedules.

"I think I just figured it out," she said. "I don't have much time, though. Will you walk with me?" I nodded and followed her back down the corridor to the gates. We didn't say anything for a long moment, both surprisingly speechless. "I'm glad Gabby and Pita are alright," she offered eventually.

"Thanks. Me too. Guess I'll only have to worry about you now." She looked at me.

"Why?"

"I'm worried you're still waiting for something," I said. "The Horsemen are still out there, and the Watchers. They'll try something like this again I'm sure. They'll never be able to win, of course, but they'll keep hurting people along the way."

"And you think that will keep me in the Waiting," she said.

"I don't want to see you become like Valdez. Going back to fix things body after body. You can never fix things back there, Addie. They're supposed to be broken."

"I know that now," she said as we came to her gate. She stopped in front of it, watching as a line of people rose from their chairs to file into a line. "It isn't easy letting go, but I think I can." She studied my eyes, searching. "Did God tell you I wasn't ready yet?"

I wasn't sure what to say. I'm sure she could still tell if I was lying. "I probably wasn't," she acknowledged. "But that was before I knew you were alright." She smiled. "You're the only thing I would have waited for, Jon."

I grabbed Addie and hugged her. "Thanks for saving me, Adelaide. I never thought I'd love anybody again when I first met you. Now look at me." She tightened her hug on me.

We stood there as long as we could before the voice on the intercom sounded a final call for passengers. She broke away from me slowly and turned to make her way for the boarding gate. "Are you scared?" I asked her.

"Yes. I think. But not of letting go."

"I'll see you soon, Addie." I found myself crying the same as her while she walked away, but all tears shed were of joy. I knew her waiting was done. Somehow she'd found what she was looking for from all this.

She looked back one last time as she entered the ramp way to the plane that wasn't there, giving me a little wave. I returned it, and then I was alone.

It only occurred to me after Addie disappeared that she was the last person in the airport other than myself. And the Han Chinese man over at the window bank where I'd first seen him, of course. He stood with hands in his pockets, staring out at the Iblis Nebula.

I sauntered over to Him and stood at his side. "Thank you," I said without looking at Him.

"Love is a powerful thing, Jon," He said with a broad smile. "It's the only thing that carries over between life, the Waiting and my kingdom. She'll carry it with her forever." I was silent for a moment before looking around.

"I've never known an airport to close," I said. "I hope you were saving a flight for me."

"I called you a cab, actually," He said. "You arrived a bit early for your flight." When He turned from the window my brow furrowed in confusion. Then I turned, and the airport was gone. And so was God. There was just an open star field, stretching on for eternity.

"What do you mean?" I asked, standing on ground that wasn't there.

"I mean I'm not done with you yet, Jon. Think of what Gabby would say." His voiced echoed away that time as if He had just left me in some remote corner of the universe. Then the beautiful blues of the nebula seemed to brighten around one star. It grew larger, expanded, and familiar warmth settled in over me.

Again I cried while I watched the light take shape. The shape of Gabby. Light radiated from her as she slid before me. A smile touched the corner of her lips. She leaned in and gently kissed me. It felt like her. I tried to kiss her back, to hold her, but she leaned her head away with her smile wider.

"There is good left undone in you, Jonathan," she said. "Go do it."

Then there was only light, and the uncomfortable sensation of an IV drip.

epilogue

"Connor and Manuel—we don't make crosses at church for you to have sword fights with them," I shouted across the lawn. "Stick them back in the grass or I'll stick you back in the classroom for the rest of the summer." Or I'll stick them up your asses, is what I wanted to yell at them. Noisy little bastards made me glad I never had a boy.

"Sorry Mr. Perez," both boys chimed mechanically as they drove their miniature crosses back into the yard where they belonged. I shook my head and scanned for any last wayward kids scampering around the yard. Most of them took off to find their parents in the church commons as soon as I dismissed class.

I waited until Connor and Manuel's parents showed up to get them out of my hair, then turned for Macey, still on the swing. "Mace, c'mere and help me clean up, okay?"

"Okay but watch me first!" she shouted back. Ever the daredevil, she swung herself as high as her little frame would allow, then launched herself off the swing into the grass. She landed on her legs but quickly tumbled off of them in a roll that left a grass stain on her white flower dress.

"Did you see?" she asked, rising even as her head spun from

dizziness.

"Mace, your grandma would kill me if she caught you doing that," I said, picking her up and handing her a bucket of the ribbons and assorted crafts we'd used to decorate the crosses. I tried to rub off the grass stain as best I could with a rag I dipped in the church fountain. "You're the one she's gonna kill for this, though."

Macey just giggled from ticklishness as I rubbed the rag on her tummy.

We wandered inside with the arts and crafts stuff then locked up and made our way to the car. I wouldn't have been able to keep up with Macey even if I could still run. I'd broken about every bone in my legs in the fall. The doctors told me it was a miracle I hadn't been paralyzed or killed. I walked with a gimp these days, pushing my way around on a cane.

I tried talking to a few of the congregation on the way out but Macey hurried me along, excited to get home for lunch. I reminded her we had a pit stop to make first. She would have groaned from impatience any other day, but she knew this was special and minded her manners.

We pulled up to St. Mary's a few minutes later and got out of the car. Mass had just ended but I stayed in the parking lot. I didn't feel like the judgmental stares of my old congregation at the moment.

Macey and I leaned against the hood of the car while we waited. She had a habit of mimicking me, as Emilia reminded me when I let a four letter word slip. "Why do gramma and papa go to this church too?" Macey asked.

"Gramma and papa are Catholic, remember? They've been going to this church for most of their lives. They come to our church sometimes too because you and I go there."

"Why don't we all just go to one church?" she pressed, still trying to wipe away some of her grass stain.

"I like our church better," I said. "There are less rules."

"Why does this church have more rules?"

"Because it's been around for a lot longer, for one thing. And some people like all the rules when they worship God."

"You like rules," she reminded me. "I have to brush my teeth three times a day even if I *didn't* eat before."

She was sharp for an eight-year-old.

"Yeah I like rules plenty. I like rules like saying your prayers before dinner and going to church every Sunday. But God doesn't care as much about following church rules as He does about you doing the right thing. That's what matters most, right?"

She nodded. "Mmmhmm. Don't worry, dad, I don't like very many rules either," she declared, folding her arms like me.

"Believe me, I know," I said, grabbing her and pushing her against my side. She giggled.

It was still strange to hear her call me that. She'd been my daughter for over a year now, but most of the time she'd just called me Jon. Dad had only kicked in over the last few weeks after her first parent's day at the new school.

I met Macey at church three years back, two after I'd woken up in the hospital in DC. The pastor at New Community had wrangled me into teaching Sunday School with another member of the congregation. I was one of the few who knew the bible well enough to do it. One nice thing about being raised Catholic.

Macey was in my first batch of students, only five years old when I met her. I think I took a liking to her since she was the same age Pita had been. She attended every church function we put on. Vacation bible camp, Christmas pageant, weekend daycare. Sometimes she just sat on the swings behind the church by herself.

She used to be very quiet, but I got her talking to the other kids and brought her out of her shell a bit. I figured she was just shy until I saw the bruise one day. Turned out she stayed away from home whenever she could because her father came and went, beating up the family as he did.

The first time Macey told me about it I called the cops. The mom had disappeared and the dad wound up in jail. Macey was slated to settle into foster care until I stepped forward. I'd known her for two years by then. I was about the only adult she trusted, figured it was the right thing.

It took me a while to sort through the adoption process because of my past legal issues, but I'd never been convicted of anything so it all went through. Despite my being the FBI's most wanted at one point, the world had all but forgotten about me. Guardian had found a way to cover for me and clear my name in the wake of the "bio-weapon" attack in Washington DC. I was grateful to Valdez, but I never saw him again. I knew he was out there, though. That boy had a lot of waiting left to do.

I never would have imagined my being a dad again, but it turned out to be quite the blessing. Macey and I got along famously. I gave her the childhood she deserved, she made me feel vital in a way I never had before. She thought I was the most important person in the world, after all—I was a staff writer for the Chula Vista Daily. Oh boy.

I didn't bring in much of a paycheck, but it was nice to stay in one place and have a steady one flowing in. I still had Pita's college fund intact for Macey someday too, so that was a load off. I wrote a blog with decent readership worldwide in my spare time. About faith. I didn't give the game away (no one would have believed me anyway) but I shared my theories. Even linked to Carmine's blog once or twice.

Macey spotted Luiz and Emilia making their way down the church steps first, leaning up to wave. Gabby's parents were only too happy at my sudden revitalization. Their daughter and grandchild had been gone for a decade now, but even after I finally told them truth about Miami, they still called me family.

They were the first people I came to after I was released from the hospital in DC. I moved out to Chula Vista to stay with them and be close to Gabby and Pita. I even lived with them for the first year. These days Macey and I lived down the street in an apartment but I was saving for a little house.

"There's my girl!" Emilia called as she entered the parking lot. Macey ran at her for a hug while I walked over to Luiz. "Oh! What have you done to your dress, you little hooligan?" Macey apologized while Luiz and I laughed.

The four of us walked to the graveyard behind the church. Macey had been to see Gabby and Pita before, but she knew this was a special day. Ten years they'd been gone. They let me go ahead alone first. I lay down flowers for Gabby and a new tiara for Pita.

"Your sister likes action figures and baseball instead of princesses," I told Pita as I leaned back up. "Makes birthdays easier but I still like going into the girl section to get your crowns every once in a while." I swallowed hard and took a deep breath. I remembered how painful it had been in the first few years and thought about how much had changed.

I took a few more minutes by myself then waved the others over. Emilia, Luiz and I told Macey a few stories about Gabby and Pita, most of which she'd probably heard before, but I didn't cry. Not even when Emilia told Gabby how proud of me she'd be.

I added a third grave to lie beside the other two. The body had been lost to time long ago, but I wanted some sort of marker left behind. I made out the epitaph to read:

Adelaide Martin

1918 – 1944

An Angel Among Us

I thought about her almost as much as Gabby and Pita. I'd only known her for a little over a week, but she was the most important person I'd ever known. When Emilia and Luiz asked about her I just told them she was the person who saved me from myself.

I never thought I'd still be alive ten years after losing Gabby and Pita. Not only was I alive, I was happy. I always missed them, but it was something to know they were safe and waiting for me. In the meantime, there was still good left undone.

THE BROKEN AFTERLIFE
The End

about the author

Tyler Tullis is a fiction writer from the Pacific Northwest of the United States, born in Pendleton, Oregon and raised in Selah, Washington.

His breakout science fiction series, *The Sophie Trilogy*, was written and published during his college years at Gonzaga University. His other works include the spy thriller *Everlast* and the western *Hanging Virginia Crowe*. Tyler currently lives in Spokane, Washington.

Learn more at www.tylertullisfiction.com.